# THE LAST DANGEROUS VISIONS

# THE DANGEROUS VISIONS
# COMPLETE COLLECTION

*Dangerous Visions*
*Again, Dangerous Visions*
*The Last Dangerous Visions*

# THE LAST DANGEROUS VISIONS

EDITED BY

## HARLAN ELLISON

BLACK
STONE
PUBLISHING

Published in 2024 by Blackstone Publishing
Cover and book design by Sarah Riedlinger





Printed in the United States of America

ISBN 979-8-212-61378-1
Fiction / Anthologies (multiple authors)

Version 1

Blackstone Publishing
31 Mistletoe Rd.
Ashland, OR 97520

www.BlackstonePublishing.com

To Harlan and Susan Ellison and the many writers who were, are, and will forever remain a part of *Dangerous Visions*.

# CONTENTS

# A BRIEF INTRODUCTION TO
## *THE LAST DANGEROUS VISIONS*

### BY J. MICHAEL STRACZYNSKI

*Dangerous Visions*, the first volume of which was published in 1967, is viewed by critics and literary historians as one of the most important and influential anthologies in the history of speculative fiction. The book was the brainchild of Harlan Ellison, who during his life published over seventeen hundred short stories and won more awards than any other living writer. He gained the attention of television viewers through his scripts for the original versions of *The Outer Limits*, *Star Trek*, and *The Twilight Zone*, and his better-known prose works within the genre include *I Have No Mouth, and I Must Scream*, *Shatterday*, and "'Repent, Harlequin!' Said the Ticktockman."

During the sixties, most SF emphasized technology over character, producing stories that existed in a sanitized bubble safe from the social upheavals of the time. But the mandate of *Dangerous Visions* was to publish cutting-edge stories that spoke to our humanity in all its flaws, faults, and glories. Ellison's willingness to embrace stories of consequence and controversy took the genre to a new level of cultural relevancy, offering newfound creative freedom to such previously established writers as Isaac Asimov, Robert Bloch, Philip K. Dick, and Damon Knight, while giving momentum to the careers of such up-and-comers as Roger Zelazny, Norman Spinrad, Samuel R. Delany, and Carol Emschwiller. *Dangerous Visions* kicked over the tropes of the form, helped birth the New Wave Science Fiction movement, and inspired an entire generation of dreamers to write stories that were more personal and visceral.

The critical and financial success of *Dangerous Visions* led to Ellison's *Again, Dangerous Visions*, published in 1972. The book once again rocked the world of science fiction, presenting thought-provoking and culturally relevant stories by Ursula K. Le Guin, Gene Wolfe, Ray Bradbury, Kate Wilhelm, Kurt Vonnegut, Joanna Russ, Piers Anthony, Gregory Benford, and Dean R. Koontz.

For both volumes, Ellison wrote lengthy introductions to each of the stories that ranged from personal anecdotes to discussions of art, literature, politics, society, and the future. These essays were considered by many to be at least as important as the stories themselves.

The final volume, Ellison's grand finale for the entire series, *The Last Dangerous Visions*, was scheduled to appear in 1974.

It was never completed.

For fifty years.

No explanation was ever publicly given.

As might be expected, speculation raged in the science-fiction community about why *The Last Dangerous Visions* had, for all intents and purposes, disappeared. In a genre known for mysteries beyond human comprehension, it became the biggest real-life unsolved mystery ever encountered by fans and practitioners of the genre. Other than Ellison and a very few close friends, no one knew the *real* reason behind the two most-often-asked questions posed by SF fans at conventions and other gatherings for nearly five decades: *What the hell happened to* The Last Dangerous visions? And: *When will it be published?*

There is finally an answer to both questions.

The answer to question number two is: *Right here, right now.*

The answer to number one is revealed in "Ellison Exegesis," which begins in just a few pages.

What? Did you seriously think you were going to get the answer to the question of the ages this early in the book so you could read it in the bookstore before putting it back on the shelf, or courtesy of a quick peek at the *Look Inside!* feature on Amazon? Fans of the literature of the fantastic know that the answers to the secrets of the universe must be earned. And this isn't an easy five-word answer, like *he lost his typewriter ribbon*. It is the story of a life lived in the pursuit of art while being haunted by a shadow that each year grew more oppressive and destructive before finally being exorcised, at great personal cost.

The first *Rocky* movie came out while I was still in college, and I assiduously avoided any spoilers because I'd heard that the ending was a stunner. I maintained this cone of silence right up to the day I showed up at the Vogue Cinema in Chula Vista, California, when just as I handed over my money and was about to go inside, a kid sitting on the low parking lot wall yelled over, "Rocky loses!"

You wouldn't want me to be that kid, betraying to you, gentle reader, the end of the story before it's even begun, would you?

Of course not.

This is all being done for your benefit.

You're welcome.

With the passing of Harlan Ellison in 2018 and, two years later, that of his wife, Susan, I became the executor of their estate. Anyone who's ever been charged with such a responsibility knows that it's a nightmare of legal and court documents, death certificates, city filings, and lawyer fees sufficient in magnitude to stun a police dog at twenty paces. We also found ourselves going to war with banks that tried to take advantage of their passing and claim ownership over their accounts. Suffice to say, they failed: fast, hard, and irrevocably.

As I write these words, September 6, 2023, those court battles and many others have been won, and the estate has been folded into the Harlan and Susan Ellison Foundation, the centerpiece of which is the home they shared together, Ellison Wonderland: a place of art, beauty, and architectural wonder, it will be preserved as a mecca for academics and others to visit and study the thousands of pages of story drafts and correspondence between Harlan and some of the genre's greatest talents.

One other responsibility also needed to be addressed.

Over the years, Harlan and I discussed at length the frustration he felt over being unable to complete *The Last Dangerous Visions*. It was only toward the latter part of his life that he was finally able to understand, confront, and address the source of the problem elaborated upon in "Ellison Exegesis." With that knowledge came fresh resolve, and he made it clear to Susan and several of his friends, including attorney Christine Valada, that he very much wanted this book to come out.

So, upon becoming executor, in keeping with his wishes, I set most of my own work aside for nearly four years in order to deal with the estate, the legal work, the foundation, and to at long last finish *The Last Dangerous Visions*. (For those curious about how decisions were made concerning what went into this book, what was set aside, and how various writers were selected or solicited, see the afterword at the back of this book.)

While assembling the final roster of stories for *The Last Dangerous Visions*, I realized that many of the topics addressed by the earlier writers are still being pursued today by contemporary writers: misogyny, racism, the role of religion in society, the abuse of science, the universality of scapegoats, and the willingness of those with political or social authority to make us fear the Other in order to advance their own agendas. Anyone who's been paying attention for the last decade can track the retrograde trajectory of our political climate into something regressive and violent, marked by open expressions of sexism, prejudice, and gender intolerance. The lingering relevance of those issues made manifest in these stories makes it clear we still have much to do, and far to go.

As a result of that realization, rather than presenting these tales chronologically, the stories, writers, and themes are interwoven with one another, unified through the amazing artwork of Tim Kirk. Absent the occasional time-stamped data point—an in-story reference to a name, event, or a person of prominence from earlier years, left in for the sake of authenticity—it is almost impossible to tell them apart.

Because our fears are universal, and constant, and often renewed.

But so too are our hopes, our dreams, and the capacity of the human heart for empathy and love and loss.

This publication of *The Last Dangerous Visions* is meant to knit together generations of dreamers in the realization that we are one people, one species, one world, moving with great difficulty toward the dream of a better tomorrow that sometimes seems to be situated on an infinitely receding horizon. We have grown in some ways and fallen behind in others; have allowed ourselves to be divided and set against one another; but despite the efforts of those who most profit from sowing such divisions, we remain united by our hopes for the future and the common coin of our shared humanity.

Harlan was fond of saying that science fiction is the only inherently optimistic literary genre, because it's the only one that presents a tomorrow for the human race. It may not be the *best* of all possible tomorrows, but it's still there; we don't die off and leave it all for the roaches. We persist. We grow. We love and fall and fail and get up and keep moving.

There are still tomorrows waiting for us to decide what to do with them.

So, with a full heart, I commend to you the tomorrows that appear on the following pages.

Good night, Harlan—I hope I got this right.

# ELLISON EXEGESIS

## BY J. MICHAEL STRACZYNSKI

A little of this I have spoken of before.

The rest has been kept secret.

Because that's what a friend does.

But there comes a time, and this is that time, when the curtain must be pulled back, and things that were not previously discussed can and should be.

Because that's *also* what a friend does.

Behind all the mythology concerning Harlan Ellison—the stories and the sightings and the controversies and the *ohmygoddidyouhearabout*—there is much you do not know, or understand, about who he was, to me and to the many others who loved him; why he was the way he was; and what that has to do with why *The Last Dangerous Visions* is finally being published. That silence is about to be broken.

I'll start the ball rolling.

Buckle up.

I was twelve in 1966, a street rat living in the Projects of Newark, New Jersey, which would shortly become ground zero for the Newark

Uprising, one of the biggest social upheavals in American history, in which thousands of African Americans, pushed beyond the limits of human endurance by a racist, nonstop, slow-motion police riot that nightly left dozens of civilians bloodied and beaten in the streets, finally rose up in anger and said, "Enough!"

We were broke, subsisting on food-bank donations, with ketchup in hot water offered as tomato soup, bits of old bread in milk as cereal, and a seemingly endless supply of violence and despair courtesy of my father, the vilest human being I have ever known. I survived only by vowing to become everything he was not.

Some of us become what we are in *spite* of our fathers.

And others become what we are *because* of our fathers.

May 1, 1949. Harlan Jay Ellison, a few weeks shy of his fifteenth birth-day, lives at 89 Harmon Drive in Painesville, Ohio, with his parents, Louis and Serita, both fifty-one. Harlan is constantly in trouble at school for fighting and his negligible attention span. His teachers describe him as a problem child, uncontrollable and undisciplined, prone to sudden and unexpected fits of anger and nervous agitation.

At this moment he is walking into the kitchen, where his mother is making "the Fave," his father's favorite meal: roast beef on white toast with gravy and extra-crisp french fries. Suddenly, Louis cries out from the living room. Harlan runs in to find his father on the floor, breath-ing hard, clutching his chest as the blood stops on the way to his brain. Screaming and crying, Harlan watches his father die.

He never entirely recovers.

My nights in Newark were a blur of beatings and starvation, with my days spent trying to avoid the gangs who worked the streets, capital-izing on the growing chaos for their own enrichment. Everything and everyone in my life said I was a dead-ender. No prospects. No hope. No voice. Because that's what it was to be a street rat.

I'd developed an early interest in science fiction because it took me out of this world to others that were infinitely more interesting: the far-flung universe of Ray Bradbury's silver ships and elegant, golden-eyed Martians; Robert A. Heinlein's lunar revolt; and the lens-wielding Galactic Patrol of E. E. "Doc" Smith. The stories had no bearing on the life I was living in Newark, but I figured that's just what stories *were*: tales of other places that didn't touch the real world at any two contiguous points. The mainstream novels pushed on me at school were not much better. I found no resonance in the wolves of *White Fang*, the whale quest of *Moby Dick*, in *Treasure Island*, *The Swiss Family Robinson*, or *Great Expectations*.

Despite a lack of personal connection to the subject matter, I found myself increasingly drawn to the idea of being a writer. The more I read, the more I fell in love with words and stories, until at last that dream became the single driving force of my young life. But according to my teachers, writers came from proper families and went to the finest schools, got good grades, and wore expensive lounging jackets as they smoked pipes and discussed lofty subjects with other writers of similar backgrounds. If *that* was the profile needed to become a writer, then my dreams were dead on arrival.

Then one afternoon, half-starved, I wandered into a used bookstore, clutching the twenty cents I'd liberated from my father's dresser when he was too dead-drunk asleep to hear me do it. I never considered it stealing because sometimes it was the only way I could get anything to eat, and back then you could buy a kid's burger and a Coke for twenty cents. But more than I wanted food, I needed something to read that would take me far from my life, so I began prowling the narrow bookstore aisles in search of that ineffable *something*.

Stacked in the dime box by the door were three books: *Memos from Purgatory*, *The Deadly Streets*, and *Gentleman Junkie and Other Stories of the Hung-Up Generation*, all by Harlan Ellison. The garish covers reflected a street-level view of a world that included gangs and urban despair and everything else that had come to circumscribe the borders of my life.

I flipped to the back cover of *Gentleman Junkie*, and beneath an author's photo that would've done James Dean proud read this:

Stories of Controversy!

HARLAN ELLISON had his first novel published at the age of twenty-one. A relentless story of juvenile delinquency the *NY Times* noted as "marked by economy and narrative vigor plus a convincing authenticity," the author ran with a teenaged gang in Brooklyn to gain background. Here in 22 short stories ranging from a razor-sharp indictment of anti-Semitism to a terrifying new look at Negro prejudices, this often shocking, never boring writer provides a hornbook of the hung-up generation . . . perceptive and often alarming insights into the hip, the lost, the ones with no way out, with no doors, no windows in their lives. Unable to cope, afraid of love and doomed by their own acts, the people in these stories exist on the thin edge of desperation. Now 27, Ellison has lived in the frenetic, hyped-up world about which he writes.

These were stories and real-world memoirs written *for* street rats *by* a street rat, someone who had come from nothing to achieve the dream of becoming a writer.

I bought two of the books and shoplifted the third.

I'd intended to spread the reading process out over a couple of weeks, but Harlan's writing was electric and intense; once it had you by the throat, it never let go. I read one book per day for three days, then read them again and again over the coming weeks, studying every sentence in an attempt to figure out how each effect had been achieved. The words were like slivers of glass driven into my brain by someone who knew *exactly* what he was doing. *Don't be afraid. This is gonna hurt, but it's good for you.*

In Harlan's words, I found a voice I recognized, a renewed hope for my dreams, an inspiration for my own work, and most improbable of all, a role model.

*Shibboleth. Shib-bo-leth (noun):* Usually defined as "a concept, phrase, or, most often, a single word that distinguishes one people, or one person, from another. Shibboleths have been used through history as a password and a means of self-identification."

I spent the next several weeks prowling used bookstores for Harlan's other works, a search that sometimes led through some of the most dangerous parts of Newark. I'd run from the bus stop past the panhandlers, gang members, and drug dealers who lurked in the doorways of abandoned buildings to the sanctuary of the bookstore, catch my breath, and head for the "Authors by Alphabet" section, searching *E* for Ellison. Slowly, my collection grew, adding *Paingod and Other Delusions, Ellison Wonderland,* and *I Have No Mouth, and I Must Scream.* If I had the money to spend, I'd pay for the book, wait until I could see the bus approaching, then run back the way I came, jumping on just as it pulled away.

If I didn't have the money, the result was the same, except I ran faster.

Ellison's stories were daring and smart and *honest*, written in a voice like liquid mercury, smooth and infinitely volatile, but I found myself returning most often to his introductions. In those deeply personal essays, he talked about the writing life, about *his* life, as if speaking directly to me. He wrote about battles against censorship and stupidity, bureaucracy and racism, railing against a system that rewarded the compliant over the controversial, the predictable over the problematic, and the privileged over everybody else.

Another day, another bookstore. I went to *E* for Ellison and found something I didn't entirely understand. The book had his name on it, but the stories were written by other people. Some of the names on the back cover were familiar, but the rest were unknown. Who the hell was Roger Zelazny? Or Samuel R. Delany? Or J. G. Ballard? Damn it, I'd come looking for a book by Harlan Ellison, not *this* crew!

Worse still, this was a hardcover, and expensive, and way too big to fit under my jacket without being noticed.

I studied the cover image, a surreal graphic of a giant green eye. What the hell was *that* about? I was tempted to put it back on the shelf and forget about it, but the title kept reaching into my brain, promising stories, ideas, and worlds I'd never previously imagined, tales that I wouldn't know I needed to read until I'd read them, because they came with a promise by Ellison himself that these were—

*Dangerous Visions.*

Since I couldn't afford to buy the book, and I'd never get away with trying to steal it, I resorted to digging through trash cans behind liquor stores and supermarkets, collecting discarded soda bottles for the two-cents-apiece refund. (This was my alternate means of making money whenever my father got suspicious about where his spare change was going.) When I finally had the necessary funds, I returned to the store, grabbed the last copy of *Dangerous Visions* off the shelf, and ran proudly to the cashier's desk.

He looked at me. Looked at the book. Looked at me. "How old are you?" he asked.

"Thirteen," I said proudly, having recently hit what I considered the Earth-shattering milestone of having the suffix *-teen* in my age.

"This isn't a kid's book," he said, frowning. "There's a lot of rough language and things your folks probably wouldn't want you reading about."

"Yeah, really don't care."

"Okay, but *I* need to know that *you* know what you're getting into. Have you read anything else by this author?"

I not only listed the titles of every Ellison story in all the books I'd found thus far; I recited parts of the introductions that I had committed to memory as mantra-like passages of inspiration and education.

Halfway through the performance, the clerk laughed and held up his hand. "Okay, you win," he said, and rang up the purchase.

I hurried back to our tiny apartment, the book hidden among my school texts, and shoved it under the couch where I slept nights. I had to be careful because if the book was everything I'd been warned about, it would almost certainly be confiscated by my parents. When at last everyone was asleep, I pulled the book out from beneath the couch, tented the covers of the blanket with my knees to hide what I was doing, switched on a green plastic Boy Scout flashlight, and began reading.

In a lifetime spent in the company of words, there are only a handful of occasions when what I read blew the back of my head off, and reading *Dangerous Visions* for the first time counts as three of them.

Before *Dangerous Visions*, I was a fan. Afterward, I became a fanatic who could not stop talking about the work of this amazing author, whose tales were transforming everything I thought I knew about storytelling on an almost cellular level. Whenever we moved and changed schools, my first coherent sentence upon being introduced to someone was always, "Have you ever read anything by Harlan Ellison?"

If you knew the name, you were cool. If not, not.

Shibboleth.

1967. The Daisy is the first members-only discotheque in Los Angeles. Located at 326 North Rodeo Drive in Beverly Hills, the Daisy is frequented by such celebrities as Warren Beatty, Paul Newman, Sharon Tate, and Frank Sinatra. Much to his astonishment, Harlan Ellison has joined the ranks of these luminaries, courtesy of his frequent appearances on such TV talk shows as *The Today Show, Thames Television, The Merv Griffin Show, The Tomorrow Show with Tom Snyder*, and other programs that proclaimed him the *enfant terrible* of science fiction. He is the darling of the college lecture circuit. Students line up for hours to hear him speak, drawn by his books; his work on such television shows as *The Man from U.N.C.L.E., Star Trek*, and *The Outer Limits*; and his incendiary columns as television critic for the *Los Angeles Free Press*. His short stories are praised by Dorothy Parker, critics heap accolades (and some stinging critiques) on his work and public persona, and in a growing number of literary circles, his name is spoken in the same breath as Philip Roth and Kurt Vonnegut.

Harlan works the Daisy in search of stories, conversations, and a night's companionship. As much as he is famed for his nonstop energy, rapid patter, and a willingness to fight anyone foolish enough to start something unpleasant, he is also known for having a nearly supernatural ability to get someone of the opposite sex horizontal for an extended period of time. Over the course of his life, he would speak of having bedded down over seven hundred women, a number that has passed the test of time and tattletales. This obsessive behavior was considered *macho* by some of his contemporaries; to others, it was a projection of insecurity.

In clinical terms, today it would be described as *hypersexualized.*

But you don't know that part yet, and neither did he.

As Harlan pushes through the crowd of dancers dressed in skintight clothes spotlit by the glitter-pop of the ceiling disco ball, a thin, wiry young man with curly black hair, wearing jeans and a black leather jacket without a shirt, waves to him from the bar. Sal Mineo, considered by Harlan and many critics to be one of the finest actors of his generation, approaches and extends a hand.

"Are you Harlan Ellison?" he asks. "God, this is such an honor. I'm a huge fan."

In the weeks that follow, they become close friends, drawn by their shared experiences of life in the streets. On January 10, 1968, Harlan joins Sal and several of his friends for a celebration.

I'll let Harlan tell it, in words that have never previously seen the light of publication:

*In the darkened living room the smell of grass rises sensuously, and the television set plays on mindlessly. The room is full of people, but only one person watches the set. On the screen a young boy of eighteen is playing a young boy of seventeen. His curly hair hangs over his forehead with a casual forelock. The huge, startlingly liquid eyes and the babyfat lower lip belie the snarling, insipid remarks he is making to his parole officer. The young turk on the tiny screen is Dino, back from Parkinson Reformatory. Dino is Sal Mineo and he is giving a hell of a rough time to Brian Keith and Frank Faylen and Joe De Santis. It is 1957.*

*Sal Mineo sits and laughs at his performance. This person watching this actor laughs, because it isn't the kind of material one would expect to be done by an actor twice nominated for the Academy Award. He chuckles, but it is 1968 in that darkened living room, not 1957. It is January 10th, and it is Sal Mineo's twenty-ninth birthday.*

*He remembers, and the big liquid eyes are sad behind the brightness. But none of the oh so close friends in the room—not one of whom will be around eight years and one month from now— none of them see what's really going on with Sal. Oh, maybe one of them sees, but he's a writer, and everybody knows what assholes they are: always trying to find deep meanings where none exist. All they see is the kid in the T-shirt on the television, holding up a gas station, and it reinforces their subliminal belief in the myth-background of their host; and all they see is the latter-day incarnation of the kid on TV—the twenty-nine-just-now young man with the Sgt. Pepper mustache and the Lash LaRue cowboy hat slouched on the fur-bedecked sofa drinking black coffee with two sugars— laughing at himself.*

As other partiers splinter off or hook up in bedrooms and alcoves, Sal tucks into a corner and opens up to Harlan about the tragedies of his life, stories that echo Harlan's own past. By the time gray daylight filters through the windows, they begin to understand how deep the well of shared experience goes, and how powerful the bond between them is growing.

A few days later, over coffee in an all-night diner, Harlan asks Sal's permission to interview him and tell his story. There is a measure of vested interest in the question, because Harlan knows that in telling Sal's story, he will also be telling a part of his own.

At first Sal demurs, saying it's not that interesting, but Harlan persists, and one year after their first meeting, Sal sits in Harlan's living room, a reel-to-reel tape recorder whirring softly in the corner.

"Tell me everything," Harlan says. "Tell me the core of what brought you here, and why you do what you do, so people can understand who you are."

Shibboleth.


Over the years, more Ellison books are added to my collection: *From the Land of Fear, Love Ain't Nothing But Sex Misspelled, The Beast That Shouted Love at the Heart of the World, Over the Edge*. Whenever I was in doubt about my path to becoming a writer, it was his voice that challenged and inspired me. I reread his books so often that the spines began to give out, forcing me to buy additional copies: one to keep, one to read.

In 1972, the year I graduated high school, *Again, Dangerous Visions* exploded at the heart of the science-fiction genre, once again bringing new and established writers together in a series of stories that challenged the status quo. As the bookseller bagged my purchase, he said that a third volume, *The Last Dangerous Visions*, was going to be announced in '73 and out by '74 at the latest.

As I turned to leave, I noticed a rack filled with critically acclaimed novels by Vonnegut and Roth, Anthony Burgess, Roald Dahl, and Ira Levin, writers who had managed to straddle the line between mainstream and genre. Harlan had done much the same, especially in his early works, but short fiction rarely had the same cultural impact as novels, which received major reviews and were more readily incorporated into libraries and university curricula. It was only through novels that careers of real literary significance were made.

So why was it that a writer as talented as Ellison only seemed to produce short stories?

Summer 1974. Harlan's home in Sherman Oaks, dubbed Ellison Wonderland, contains many remarkable spaces, including a secret room built to hide draft dodgers on their way to Canada during the Vietnam War. But he spends most of his time upstairs in his two-story office, a sanctuary filled with books, photos, awards, music, and memorabilia. A fifteen-by-fifteen-foot opening in the center of the second floor permits a view down into the first-floor poolroom and is encircled by a waist-high, freestanding wooden shelf where Harlan keeps works in progress. At the moment, the shelf is covered almost entirely by the hundred-plus short stories he has purchased for *The Last Dangerous Visions*, a total of nearly seven hundred thousand words that would span three volumes. Just the essays and introductions Harlan planned to write for the book would constitute at least one hundred thousand additional words, equivalent to a novel, making it the biggest sustained single writing project he'd ever tackled. It would be the Mount Everest of his long career.

There was just one slight problem: this was 1974, and the book was supposed to have been published by now. But the raw, typewritten manuscripts are no closer to publication than when first purchased. The manuscripts could have easily been stored out of sight in a box or any of the huge filing cabinets that line the room, but Harlan keeps them on the shelf in plain view in the hope that seeing them every day will inspire him to finish the task. Their presence only adds to his growing sense of depression and futility.

He'd managed to write longer works in the past, but never to his satisfaction. The few short novels that bore his name, including some over-the-top youth gang books, had become lifelong sources of embarrassment. The rockabilly story *Spider Kiss* (1961) was marginally acceptable, but *Doomsman* (1967) had turned out so badly that whenever fans brought copies for him to sign, he would tear up the book and offer to refund whatever they'd paid for it.

Bad as the novels were, he'd at least managed to finish them. But in recent years, it had become increasingly difficult to concentrate on anything book-length. He could summon the energy needed to focus on short stories that could be written in white heat, in one sitting, but for reasons he couldn't understand, his attention span had diminished to the point where even the *idea* of writing a novel, let alone a really *big* novel, was painful to him. So the prospect of tackling something as massive as *The Last Dangerous Visions* was enough to send him into a tailspin of depression. Thus far, he'd only managed to write one of the hundred-plus introductions he had committed to, for Ed Bryant's "War Stories."

*Let's try to write the general intro, he decides. That's the longest one of the bunch. If I can get that one done, the rest will be easy-peasy. Don't think of climbing the mountain. Just keep putting one foot in front of the other until we run out of mountain.*

He slips a fresh sheet of bond paper into the Olympia typewriter on his desk, gathers his thoughts, and begins typing.

*When the Witch of Endor Seduced the Wizard of OZ*
*by Harlan Ellison*

*At the corner of 47th Street and Second Avenue in Manhattan at Dag Hammarskjöld Plaza, there is a wonderful monumental sculpture by Claes Oldenburg. It is called the Giant Mouse. It's eighteen feet high and has a red ear that is nine feet in diameter. It's great fun, and it is great art, as well.*

*Oldenburg cites the piece as an example of how scale-changes affect form. If you look at a tiny photo of the metal sculpture, you see precisely what he means, and you can laugh. But when you stand close beside it, as I did in May of 1974, the joke seems to overpower, and it becomes simply Art without a smile. I like his Mouse better from halfway up the block.*

*As I write this introduction to the final volume of* Dangerous

Visions *stories, it is only four months shy of nine years that the project was begun, October 2, 1965. By the time you read these words, it will have been at least ten years from conception to culmination. I have stood up very close to the Giant Mouse called* Dangerous Visions, *and I must tell you frankly that it will be a joy to wander up the block, sit down on the curb, and look at the monument from a safe distance. Here in the middle of it all, there's a lot of Art, but the smiles are frequently forced. Hard work does that to me.*

*One of my hate mail correspondents recently dropped a spatter of pigeon-flop on me to the effect that he considered* Dangerous Visions' *sequel,* Again, Dangerous Visions, *a great disappointment, filled with stories he didn't understand. Without knowing he was doing so, he pursued this introduction's opening analogy by commenting, "The mountain labored mightily and brought forth a mouse." Heh heh . . .*

*Had he but known I have a quotation from Donald Barthelme over my desk that reads, "The Purpose of fiction is the creation of a small furry object that will break your heart," he might not have played into my word-twisting hands so easily.*

*I've labored for almost ten years, and hallelujah! I've—*

And just that suddenly, midsentence, everything stops.

*Come on, goddamnit,* he thinks. *We can do this.*

But the words stubbornly refuse to manifest, and after a long, anguished while he turns off the light, leaving the unfinished page in the typewriter. *I'll try again tomorrow. Or maybe I'll tackle one of the other introductions.*

More days turn into more weeks, then more months. The phone rings incessantly as the publisher, the fans, and the critics, *especially* the critics, pillory him over the delays, adding stress that only worsens the situation. *What's wrong with you?* they ask. *You promised us we'd have the book. What's the problem?*

But how can he articulate his situation when even *he* doesn't understand it?

*I can't. I don't know why. I just know that I can't. That's all.*

Every morning for the long years that follow, he will walk to his desk, past *The Last Dangerous Visions* stories arrayed on the office shelf, thinking, *Today's the day I'll pick up one of the stories and start climbing back up the mountain.*

But there they remained, until gradually, incrementally, with the cold, hard certainty of a terminal diagnosis, he began to realize that the mountain could not be climbed.

Only the Ed Bryant introduction would ever be completed.

While getting my psychology degree at San Diego State University in 1976, I took the leap of faith required to try and make a living as a writer. The year that followed was desperately hard, but Harlan's words kept me going through the rejections and the poverty consequent to that decision. His essays in *Approaching Oblivion, Deathbird Stories,* and *Shatterday* inspired me to write better, to *be* better, to refuse to settle for the merely adequate, or surrender to the bullying of those eager to see me fail. Had it not been for those words, I would surely have collapsed under the weight of what I was trying to do.

*I owe this man I've never met a debt greater than I can ever repay,* I thought, more than once. *I just hope someday I can tell him that, and find a way to repay him.*

I had no idea where that thought would take me.

January 4, 1976. A box arrives at Ellison Wonderland from editor Terry Carr containing advance copies of the anthology *Universe 6.* The centerpiece of the collection is Harlan's story, "The Wine Has Been Left Open Too Long and the Memory Has Gone Flat," which Harlan has already earmarked for inclusion in his next hardcover collection, *Strange Wine.* He is pumping out short stories at a phenomenal rate, selling them to SF magazines, then gathering them into collections at a rate of nearly one book per year. The shelf of awards beside his desk continues to grow, but each newly won Nebula or Hugo fails to satisfy. He is being forgotten by the mainstream world, and increasingly annoyed at being typecast as a science-fiction writer, or worse, a "sci-fi" writer, or *skiffy*, as he pronounced it. Yes, he wrote SF, but he also wrote fantasy, magic realism, and noir fiction. It's such a point of contention that when the on-screen chyron for a TV chat show described him as a science-fiction writer he walked off the show.

He's determined to claw his way back into the mainstream, but only a novel-length or "literary" work will achieve that, and the river between his desire and his ability to deliver on the former is still too wide, which leaves only the latter possibility. He dreams of someday having one of his stories appear in the annual *Best American Short Stories* anthology . . . but really, what are the odds?

January 13. Harlan and Sal Mineo share breakfast at Ben Frank's Restaurant at 8565 Sunset Boulevard in Hollywood. Writing much later, Harlan describes an exchange that would remain with him for years afterward:

*Just clowning and smiling tough like Bogie, Sal says, "I'm going to be murdered or run over by a truck. It's inevitable, the way I'm living." We both laugh. He's clowning. Neither believes it for a second. Everybody says dumb things like that.*

February 12. Almost exactly one month later. Sal is parking his car in a narrow alley in Hollywood Heights. As he turns, a figure rushes from the shadows, drives a knife into his chest, then escapes into the night. Bleeding out, Sal calls for help. He dies before the ambulance arrives. Time of death: 9:43 p.m.

11:00 p.m. Grief and horror come to Ellison Wonderland. *I tuned in the late news on Channel 2 and saw the films of Sal's sheet-covered body lying in the alley driveway. There he lay, and a lot of markers he had let out would never be called in; I felt mine was one of them.*

Harlan had lost not just a good friend but a soulmate. And when he learns that his ill mother does not have long to live, he spirals into an even deeper depression. Looking for something that will pull him out of the darkness, he finds the box of audiotapes containing his interviews with Sal—stories that had been entrusted to no one else and would die with Sal unless Harlan told them in the book he had pledged to write.

For most of his career, Sal Mineo had been the subject of rumors, gossip, speculation, and innuendo about everything from his spending habits to his sexual orientation; writing this book would set the record straight, allow Harlan to burn through his grief over the loss of his friend, and exorcise his feelings toward the imminent death of his mother. But to tell the story properly meant writing a big book, and he hasn't been able to write one of those in a very long time.

He forces himself to sit behind the typewriter. *I can do this*, he tells himself. *I* have *to do this: for Sal, for my mother, and for myself. So it's going to get done. Period.*

He begins:

*Sal Mineo: The Death of the Dream*
*By Harlan Ellison*

*Sal is lying on his back in the alley, bleeding to death. The wide-bladed knife went in almost dead center over the heart. The killer knew where he wanted to put it; he must have had experience in hand-to-hand; maybe in the 'Nam, maybe in the street somewhere. One punch of steel, and a minute later Sal is staring up at the chill Los Angeles sky as a wash of blood slowly crawls down the inclined alley—fifteen, twenty-five feet toward Alta Lorna Terrace.*

*He's dead and the thousands of people who knew him, who made a special point of calling themselves his friends, who took what he had when he had so much he didn't know enough to hold back a little, who weren't around to give some back when he was down and needed . . . the millions who saw him on movie and television screens . . . the smoothyguts operators who got him into the business deals that went sour even while they copped their commissions and got fat . . . all the agents and the lawyers and the personal managers who clipped him for 10 percent of his life . . . all the smooth, tanned succubi and incubi who murmured warm words into his ears over all the years . . . where are they? Not in the carport alley behind 8563 Holloway Drive in West Hollywood. Not at 9:43 p.m. on Thursday, February 12, 1976, a little less than three hours away from Friday the 13th. They were always around, but not now.*

*All alone, at final moments, the kid from the Bronx who became the very first authentic genuine !teen!age!idol! for Christ sakes, he's lying on the asphalt with his feet aimed west and his head aimed east, his left leg tucked under his body, his right leg straight out, with one arm under his body. All alone, and the last words he ever spoke still ringing in the empty alley, getting softer and softer, the last words anybody ever really says. Help. Help. Help. Getting softer.*

*He's dead and oh God how some of us miss him.*

Then, later:

*I don't know about you, but I loathe books and articles written by ex-maids or second assistant secretaries that cash in on the death of notables. Books on Howard Hughes or Marilyn Monroe or James Dean, written by literary ghouls, make me want to puke. All you have is my word that I'm writing this because I told Sal I would, to square accounts with a buddy, and to blow off all the yellow journalism that's being written about him.*

*This article is written with affection. Which doesn't mean I intend to lie or gloss over Sal's life.*

*Where I get off writing this, about Sal Mineo, with a hot note of bitterness in my voice, is that Sal and I were friends. As I sit writing these words about a friend who is dead only six months, my mother is dying in a hospital in Miami.*

*She is seventy-six years old and they are pulling a Karen Ann Quinlan number on her. Five massive coronaries and numberless crippling strokes have sent her into a coma. Nothing is going to the brain and she is paralyzed. For all but vegetable purposes, my mother is dead, and the fuckers won't pull the plug. I sit here writing about Sal, to keep myself busy, and I wait for the phone calls from my sister who has set up what I pray to God is only temporary residence beside a pay phone outside my mother's room in the Miami Heart Institute.*

*You'll forgive me if the thought of death is very much with me right now.*

He returns to the typewriter the next day energized: the words are coming, and he's standing on solid ground, confident for the first time that he can finish this. He continues writing:

*Somebody dies, and you have to make sense of it all. You have to say, "What does the death of this person mean?" My mother, Sal Mineo, the last person you lost. What does it mean? Why, beyond the grief of losing someone whose singularity will never be seen again, because each of us is a receptacle of qualities that can never be precisely matched, should we give a damn if an old lady in Miami or a faded movie star in Hollywood has died?*

*Because sometimes they go out wearing a bum rap and even eighty-five years after she was tried and acquitted, most people still believe Lizzie Borden took an ax and gave her mother forty whacks, and the massed belief in myth instead of reality is maybe enough to foul up the records. If not in Heaven, or Wherever, then on Earth for sure. And Sal was too good a guy to be remembered the way* Time *piped him overboard.*

*This is my way of giving back. This is me paying off an obligation to Sal, because we were friends. Not nearly as good friends or as constantly-in-touch as we meant to be . . . we were both always running off somewhere on some project or other.*

*Sal Mineo was a genuine original, a man of enormous complexity, with fine dreams and considerable love, who was a helluva lot better man than he was ever permitted to be, who died on the downhill side because of his own weaknesses, his own strengths, and the fact that he was, to his ultimate misery, one of the ones who bought the phony gold brick called Hollywood.*

But as he hits the twenty-first page, the overwhelming depression that he battled for years, which had acquired new power after Sal's passing, takes hold and refuses to let go.

The words stop. The *book* stops.

He sits back in horror, staring at the blank bottom third of page twenty-one. *It can't just end like this*, he thinks. *Not with this book, not this time.*

Harlan would often say, "Writing isn't just what I do; it's what I am. It's what defines me." Writing is his life, his career, his identity, his self, his soul, his *salvation*. But if he couldn't make the words come, if he couldn't *finish*, then who was he? *Why* was he? Yes, he had been blocked before, and yes, *The Last Dangerous Visions* was still sitting on a shelf in his office, but those were just made-up stories. This was *real*—this was about Sal, about his life and their friendship and what it all meant. If he couldn't write about those things, it would be like Sal dying all over again.

*I'm not leaving. I'm staying right here until I get this written.*

The clock ticks. Jazz plays on the massive electrostatic speakers that hang behind him. Hours pass, evening comes, and the words do not appear. Surrendering to the awful truth that the book cannot be finished—*will* not be finished—he descends the long, winding steps to the first-floor poolroom, continues down the hall to the bedroom, and climbs naked beneath the sheets. He wants to sleep. Can't sleep. The depression won't allow it.

*What the hell is* wrong *with me?*

October 8. Six weeks later. Harlan's mother, Serita, dies.

He never entirely recovers.

Though I hadn't yet sold any short stories, by 1980 I had published nearly a hundred articles in various magazines and newspapers, including the *Los Angeles Times.* Deciding that it was time to make the Big Move, I headed to Los Angeles on April 1, 1981, along with fellow writer and my fiancée, Kathryn Drennan. For the first time, I was within the same city limits as Harlan. When I learned that he appeared regularly at Dangerous Visions Bookstore in Sherman Oaks to speak, read, or sign autographs, I lobbied for an introduction through Arthur Byron Cover, who shared ownership of the store with Lydia Marano. Graciously, he complied.

I have never been more nervous than I was the night of the event. Severely lacking in the social graces department, I kept rehearsing all the things I wanted to say until they sounded reasonably spontaneous.

When Kathryn and I arrived—twenty minutes early, of course—there was already a long line of fans stretching out of the bookstore and down the street. Once inside, Arthur introduced us to some of the other writers present for the event, a roster that included Michael Reaves, Len Wein, Marv Wolfman, Mel Gilden, and Steven Barnes. Some were in the "inner circle" of Harlan's friends, while the rest were hangers-on hoping to transition to inner circle.

Me? I didn't know anybody; all my prior work was in journalism, not fiction or scripts; and I was new in town, so I didn't *have* a circle.

I was, at most, a circle jerk.

Ten minutes after the event was scheduled to begin, we heard a commotion from the street as Harlan arrived. In the years that followed, I would come to understand that *Commotion* is just *Harlan* misspelled.

"Of *course* he's late," Arthur said, grinning lopsidedly. "Harlan's *always* late. That's how we know it's him."

Harlan's voice carried up and down the street as he worked the line in performance mode, telling jokes, posing for photos, chastising fans for the slightest infraction, real or imagined, and generally being Bigger Than Life and Twice as Loud. The patter continued as he entered the store, calling out, "Cover! Art! Some asshole parked in my spot out back! Whatsamatterwithyou?! Go kill the sonofabitch!"

Then he was everywhere at once, shaking hands, calling out to people he recognized, and giving everyone in his path well-intentioned shit. The energy surrounding him was palpable, intense, electrifying, and intimidating; he was everything I'd expected, and more. He was a force of nature. A free-floating agent of chaos.

He was Harlan Ellison.

He kept up that level of energy for the next three hours, talking and making jokes, telling stories about going into ridiculously perilous situations confident that if things went badly he could fight his way out, and taking on anyone foolish enough to challenge him, pounding them into the ground with a magnificent stinging retort. Talking as fast as an auctioneer hustling a big payday, he switched topics with lightning speed, then zoomed back to the original point and kept right on going, talking even faster. Three *hours.* Nonstop.

I confided my astonishment to one of the other writers.

"That's just how Harlan is, all the time," he said. "Just this crazy energy. It's like he never stops."

And something began scratching at the back of my head that I couldn't quite pull into the foreground. Like there was something familiar about what I was seeing.

*You've been reading Ellison since you were twelve. Of* course *it feels familiar.*

As the evening drew on and the crowd began to drift out, autographed books in hand, Arthur approached me while Harlan was in the restroom. "Okay, I'm gonna hook you two up," he said. "Don't be offended by anything he says. It's just how he is."

Great. No pressure.

When Harlan emerged, Arthur nudged me forward and put a hand on my shoulder. "Harlan, Joe Straczynski. Joe, Harlan."

"Hey, Sparky," Harlan said, somehow managing to look *at* me and *past* me at the same time, as if gauging whether or not I would be of sufficient interest to hold his attention. "How you doing?"

Instantly, everything I had planned to say flew out the door.

How do you tell someone you've never met that he's been the most important figure in your life, more even than your own father, which frankly wasn't saying much? How do you say, in a sentence, what his work means to you? How do you express your thanks, your respect, and your regard; show gratitude without trying to ingratiate; and pledge fealty to someone who sees you only as an imperfect stranger?

"Hi," I managed.

He waited. *Amuse me.*

"I love your work," I said.

He nodded.

"Everything, all of it, the stories, the introductions, especially the intros, they kept me going through some dark times, and I just want to thank you."

I heard the egg timer behind his eyes go *Ding!* as he held out his hand to shake mine. "Thanks, man. Much appreciated." Then he moved off to engage with people infinitely more interesting.

A moment later he called, "Dupar's!" to the members of the inner circle who had been waiting all night for the invitation. "We're going to Dupar's," he said again, referencing an all-night restaurant down the street in Studio City. "Who's coming?"

The Inner Circle hands shot up. The rest knew better than to wander into the line of fire.

"Let's go!" he said, and almost immediately the place was empty.

"They'll be out until three in the morning," Arthur said as he and

Lydia began clearing up the debris. "Swear to God, the man doesn't sleep. Don't know where he gets the energy."

And as he said it, the two pieces of data that had been searching for each other in my head finally connected. The first was Harlan's nonstop performance, which was less a matter of high-spirited energy than manic behavior: compulsive, extreme, and over the top, constantly searching for the laugh, the shocked reaction, the acknowledgment.

The second piece of data was a documentary I'd seen while getting my psychology degree: a hospital interview with a manic patient during one of his episodes of mania.

The vibe was exactly the same: the loudness, the nonstop patter, the restlessness and inability to sit still for any amount of time, with zero attention span and a need to keep changing subjects, the mood elevated and euphoric and at times nearly hysterical.

*Put the degree away and stop analyzing people*, I thought as Kathryn and I headed out into the night. *Focus on what's important, like completely blowing your chance to impress the one guy you respect most in all the world.*

*Idiot.*

*Besides, if he* was *manic, or manic-depressive, in all this time surely someone would've noticed.* Somebody *would've said* something, right?

The term *Bipolar Disorder* first appears in the third edition of the American Psychiatric Association's *Diagnostic and Statistical Manual of Mental Disorders*, published in 1980. Prior to that, the condition was more popularly known as Manic-Depressive Disorder. The symptoms and telltale signs of the disorder are very specific, both in how they initially present themselves and how they change with time.

Phase one of bipolar disorder often begins in childhood and continues into adult years, as the individual flips from mania—often manifested as high energy, charm, and humor, but also as combativeness, impatience, and agitation—to moments that seem more normal in tone, punctuated by varying periods of depression. The other key symptoms in this first stage include:

1. decreased need for sleep
2. racing thoughts and accelerated speech
3. restlessness and agitation
4. overconfidence
5. impulsive and risky behavior
6. hypersexualization

Phase two of bipolar disorder covers the second half of an affected person's life, as the manic episodes they and others have come to view as normal behavior become increasingly difficult to sustain; attempting to maintain that energy leaves them drained and irritable. It's less that the mania fades than it mutates, as *euphoric* mania gives way to *angry* mania. Similar volume, different frequencies. There are still moments of normality, but they diminish in frequency and duration as depression begins to take center stage. Sometimes the individual will try to keep up appearances by being as loud and energetic as before, but because the route to happy thoughts has been subsumed by depression, the result often manifests itself not through humor or charm but in erratic, irrational, impulsive, or angry ways. This can lead to inappropriate comments or actions made in an attempt to elicit the big reactions they'd received previously without understanding that the "big reaction" now comes from offensiveness rather than humor. As they grow older, their actions become increasingly inappropriate and, eventually, self-destructive.

The key symptoms of this second stage include:

1. feelings of hopelessness, despair, and depression
2. withdrawal from friends and family
3. lack of interest in work or outside activities
4. changes in appetite and sleep (often sleeping too much or staying in bed all day)

5.  problems with memory, concentration, and decision-making
6.  preoccupation with death and thoughts of suicide

I had no interest in being in Harlan's "inner circle," mainly because it seemed like everyone else was constantly fighting to get there. All I wanted was to tell him what his work meant to me, that I owed him a massive debt for the inspiration of his work, and that if there was anything I could do to repay that debt, I was keen to do it. But the opportunity always seemed just out of reach. I attended his lectures and autograph parties, said *hello* when I saw him and *thanks* when he signed my books, and that was the extent of it.

*Except* that whenever I saw him at these events, it became increasingly evident that there was something wrong, and the words *bipolar disorder* kept flashing in the back of my head.

*Leave it alone. You don't know him, and it's none of your business. He's probably already working on it.*

Besides, I had my own career to address. Since everyone around me was writing for animation, I decided to try it when my journalism career went south, and I was soon on staff at *He-Man and the Masters of the Universe*, then *She-Ra: Princess of Power*. By February 1986, I'd transitioned to *The Real Ghostbusters*. Things were going well.

But for Harlan, 1986 was a brutal year.

The preceding December, he'd resigned as creative consultant on the CBS revival of *The Twilight Zone* in protest over censorship. The resultant drop in income was precipitous, made even more difficult by having been unable to write more original scripts for the series. Of the three Ellison stories that aired during the season, only one, "Paladin of the Last Hour," was an original script; the others were adaptations of his stories, penned by Alan Brennert. To explain his decreasing output, he begins telling people he suffers from Chronic Fatigue Syndrome (CFS) even though he had never been formally diagnosed with it. He chooses CFS because it sounds good when he has to bail out of an assignment, carries no larger mental health implications, and nobody around him had any idea what the hell CFS actually was.

Another punch to the gut comes five months later, on May 6, when Mike Hodel, host of the long-running radio talk show *Hour 25*, and one of Harlan's closest friends, dies at the age of forty-seven from a previously undiagnosed cancer. The disease was so aggressive, and had so thoroughly metastasized, that it was only a matter of weeks between diagnosis and death. As one of his last acts, Mike asked Harlan to take over as host of *Hour 25*.

Mike had been a surrogate father figure to Harlan, who was devastated by Mike's death. Losing him so suddenly put Harlan right back in the living room at 89 Harmon Drive as he watched his father die in front of him. That grief was still in evidence during Harlan's appearance at a Writers Guild conference Kathryn and I attended at Lake Arrowhead the weekend of June 6. When he wasn't speaking at panels or being pulled into sidebar meetings, Harlan spent much of that weekend closeted in his room, trying to write and shake off the lingering shadow of Mike's death.

Kathryn and I didn't know many of the other attendees, so we often found ourselves in a trio with Harlan's latest (and last and greatest) love, Susan Toth, who was three months away from becoming Susan Ellison. She was devastatingly funny and bright, and in every way his absolute match. We had come to watch Harlan do his Harlan thing, but ended up bonding with Susan during the hours when Harlan was sequestered, leading to a decades-long friendship.

At the end of the weekend, Harlan returned to Los Angeles and a pitched court battle over something he'd said about another writer while riffing during a published interview. In going for a laugh, he said something he didn't think would cause offense. But offense was the consequence, and the libel suit dragged on for months, as lawyer fees chewed ferociously through his finances.

One day a mutual friend mentioned that things were getting desperate. "Harlan's almost out of money. He's afraid he's going to lose the house."

I couldn't let that happen, so with Kathryn taking point and a pro-motional poster by famed comic artist Frank Miller, we organized a roast for Harlan at the Los Angeles Press Club on July 12, 1986. Among those speaking (or blaspheming) about Harlan that night were Robert Bloch, Robert Silverberg, Ray Bradbury, Stan Lee, and Robin Williams. The receipts from the event would not only save Harlan's house but allow him to eventually prevail in court.

A few days after the roast, Harlan invited us to dinner at his home. This was my first exposure to the architectural miracle that is Ellison Wonderland, which was as offbeat and colorful as Harlan himself. He began the evening as Ellison the Performer, but when he realized we didn't require a performance, and were happy just to chat, that side of his persona stepped down so he could just be himself. I think he appreciated that he didn't have to be That Guy.

Midway through dinner, the phone beside the table rang, and whoever was on the other end of the line passed along something unpleasant allegedly said by someone involved in the lawsuit, and Harlan went from zero to ninety in less than a second. There was no ramping up, no slow growth of annoyance—just a switch that flipped inside his head, and suddenly he was yelling in white-hot rage. Then he hung up, and his mood flipped just as hard toward depression, and just as quickly. Everything was hopeless, and screwed up, and would never get any better. He regretted picking up the phone, saying that people would often call to give him news like this, or rumors, or "he-said-she-said" just to wind him up and watch him spin out.

Maybe it was because we never asked anything of him, never needed a favor or a loan, never wanted anything other than to be of assistance, but gradually Harlan began to invite us more often to hang out or bring in dinner: "the Fave," his father's favorite meal, roast beef on crisp white toast with extra gravy from Dupar's, and fries from McDonald's. Sometimes we'd find Manic Harlan waiting for us when we arrived; other times it was Depressed Harlan, and once in a while just normal Harlan, the modest, charming, funny guy who liked to shoot pool and chat about everything and nothing.

It was during one of the calmer nights that I finally had the chance to fully explain the debt I felt I owed him, and that he should consider me his personal Knight-Errant. If there was a task, a mission, or a call to duty, I would get it done, no hesitation, no questions asked. We were still early in our friendship, so I don't think he entirely believed me, having heard similar promises from others only to be disappointed, but eventually he accepted that I was sincere.

What you have to understand about the preceding sentence is that Harlan was always surrounded by people who loved to say, "Harlan Ellison's *a friend of mine*," in the way of someone who collects charms on a bracelet, as a piece of property to be flashed around so everyone could see it, using his name and reputation to impress others, while pushing him into performance mode at the very moments when what he needed most was support, quietude, rest, and kindness. Some of these were the same people who liked to wind him up just so they could tell stories the next day about what happened next. They were too busy enjoying the fireworks to give much thought or care to what lit the fuse.

Then there were the few of us, the *very* few, who would say, "I am *Harlan's* friend," meaning *we* were there for *him*, not the other way around. Any time, any place, whatever, whenever.

The folks in the latter category, including people like Neil Gaiman and Patton Oswalt, know who they are.

And I hope those in the former category *also* know who they were, and are.

Because we do.

For years Harlan had been putting out collections of new material as fast as the stories could be written and published in magazines. *Paingod* (1965); *I Have No Mouth, and I Must Scream* and *From the Land of Fear* (both 1967); *Love Ain't Nothing But Sex Misspelled* and *Dangerous Visions* (1968); *The Beast That Shouted Love at the Heart of the World* (1969); *Over the Edge* (1970); *Partners in Wonder* (in collaboration with others, 1971); *Again, Dangerous Visions* (1972);

*Approaching Oblivion* (1974); *Deathbird Stories* and *No Doors, No Windows* (1975); *Strange Wine* (1978); *Shatterday* (1980); and *Stalking the Nightmare* (1982).

But there had been no new books, and little new writing to support one, in 1983. Or 1984. Or 1985, 1986, or 1987. With every passing day, he found it more difficult to write anything longer than a few pages. If it couldn't be done in one sitting, it couldn't be done, so the bulk of his stories became incrementally shorter. He had little energy, and when he did manage to summon up some of his prior fire, it tended to come out more in anger than the kind of euphoria he had demonstrated that first night at Dangerous Visions Bookstore.

As the depressive episodes grew in frequency and duration, he became increasingly preoccupied with thoughts of death and dying. One night, as the two of us sat in his upstairs office, he mentioned that he'd been forced to start repackaging old stories under new covers and titles to sell books to pay bills. "I haven't been able to finish a new story in months."

When I asked why, he shrugged and said, "I'm fifty-two years old."

I didn't see the connection. Many writers worked until their eighties and beyond.

"My dad died at fifty-one," he said at last. "I never thought I'd outlive my dad. And here I am at fifty-two, and I'm not dead, and I don't know what to do."

And there it was.

Shibboleth.

The closer he'd gotten to fifty-one, the greater the anxiety had become. He was sure that at any moment he'd fall over dead, just like his father, as he'd *seen* firsthand. The pain of that day, never far from his thoughts, had returned with a vengeance, manifested as renewed trauma, a profound sense of foreboding, and a growing obsession with his own death. The writing suffered because *he* suffered. Living past fifty-one not only failed to ease that sense of foreboding but his sense of imminent death actually *worsened*, augmented by a lack of purpose. He had set a terminus on the horizon for his death, and not dying unmanned him, leaving him directionless and lost.

"And here's the part that fucking kills me," he said. "The month I turned fifty-one is the same month my dad died *and* the same month Mike [Hodel] died, and Mike was forty-seven! So what the hell am *I* doing still walking around?

"For most people, a birthday's a great thing. But when I think of mine, all I think about is death. I think about my dad dying, and I think about Mike dying, and I think about how any day now I'm gonna go down, just like my dad. Some prick says 'happy birthday' to me, all I hear is, who's going next? And it's not right. Mike's the one who should be here right now. I should be the one who's dead. That's what I expected when I hit fifty-one. I kept waiting, like, when's it gonna get here? Instead, it took Mike. He was *forty-seven*, man! God-damnit! And people wanna know why I can't *write*? With all *that*? Seriously?"

I argued that his father dying at fifty-one wasn't a fiery hand writing *mene, mene, tekel* across the sky. Logically, he *knew* that; he'd been telling himself the same thing for years. "But it doesn't help. I can't get past this pain in my gut that tells me I'm gonna die."

Then the room turned quiet for a moment, and as he stared out the glass doors that looked out over the valley, I came to a decision. Having been given permission to delve into the most personal part of his life, I asked—very slowly, very gently, knowing that I was risking our friendship in doing so—if he had ever considered seeking therapy.

"I could be wrong," I said, "but what you're describing, and what I've seen in the time I've known you, sounds a lot like bipolar disorder."

The only thing that stopped him from throwing me down the stairs was the knowledge that I was trying to help. But he refused to even consider the idea. "I'm just tired, that's all," he said. "Besides . . . look, I make my living with my brain, and yeah, sometimes there's not as much of it left as I'd like, and sometimes it gets a little screwy in there, but the last thing I want is to start poking around the machinery because God only knows what'll happen. At least now I can write a *little*. I don't want to risk messing it up and being unable to write *permanently*.

"So I don't want to talk about the therapy thing again, okay?" he said.

I nodded, conceding the point. But I didn't mean it. And I could see that he knew it.

June 20, 1987. I was awakened at 9:00 a.m. by the phone. I knew it was Harlan even before I picked up the line because everyone in our group knew that I spent most nights writing until nearly 3:00 a.m. Harlan was the only person with dispensation to call whenever he liked. Anyone else would have been murdered.

"I need you to do me a favor," he said, his voice agitated.

"Done." As had become our pattern, I agreed to it even before I knew what *it* was. We'd decided that my role in life was on par with the silver-haired hit man in *The Godfather Part II*, the guy in the black jacket, black turtleneck, and black hat who stands silently at Michael Corleone's side through most of the movie. Whenever Michael needed something or some*one* dealt with, he'd nod to the man in the black hat. No discussion, no hesitation, no *youwanna*? It just got done.

Hence: "Done," I said, and waited to be told what I'd just agreed to.

"I've had it with those fuckers at KPFK," Harlan said. He had honored Mike Hodel's last wishes by hosting *Hour 25* for almost two years, only to be worn down by repeated tugs-of-war with the station about content, and power struggles over who was in charge of what. He'd loved Mike and wanted to keep his promise, but there was a point beyond which Harlan could not go in tolerating bureaucratic interference and censorship. That point had been reached the night before, and Harlan told the station manager he was going to quit the show.

"I want you to take over as host of *Hour 25*," he said.

"What about the guys at the station? Don't they get a vote in who takes over?"

"No, fuck 'em," he said. "Mike gave it to me, I own it, I copyrighted the show in the name of my company, now I give it to you. You know the genre, the people, you used to be a reporter, you've done radio. . . you're the best guy for the job."

To be clear, the only thing I hate more than public speaking is appearing on the radio or on television. Worse still, hosting *Hour 25* was an unpaid, volunteer gig. But I was the guy at Michael Corleone's side, so the following Friday night at ten o'clock, a panel lit up at KPFK-FM reading ON THE AIR, and I started talking. I remained with the show for five years before being driven away by the same bureaucratic interference that had sent Harlan screaming out into the night.

With every passing year, we were becoming increasingly linked at the hip.

*Angry Candy*, Harlan's first anthology of new fiction in six years, is published in 1988.

The central theme of the book is an obsession with death.

*Doesn't anyone else see what's going on?* I thought. *He's telling you, right here in black and white, what he's obsessing over. Hello? Is this thing on?*

One of the things that makes bipolar disorder difficult to treat, and hard for friends and family to understand, is its unpredictability. The person can jump between smiling and happy, sullen and angry, and depressed and lost on a daily, sometimes hourly basis. So as his condition worsened, Harlan was increasingly ricocheted between moods—sometimes fine, sometimes not, and the periods of *sometimes not* were getting longer and more intense.

But there were still moments of clarity, when he could pick a fight on the right side of history or extend unimaginable kindness to strangers. The following two stories will tell you everything you need to know about who Harlan Ellison was, *really*.

One of the things Harlan and I bonded over was the fact that we were both hard-core, unapologetic liberals, openly supporting the National Organization for Women (NOW), the American Civil Liberties Union (ACLU), Planned Parenthood, PEN International, and various other Left-leaning organizations. As a lifelong feminist, I'd chosen to have a vasectomy in my early twenties because not nearly enough men who know they don't want children take responsibility for their choices; they remain casual and careless, happy to let the woman deal with the consequences of a mistake. Harlan also had a vasectomy at a relatively young age for similar reasons, reinforcing the fact that while lots of men *say* they're in favor of birth control and protecting women's contraceptive rights, very few are willing to put their vas deferens under the knife to back it up.

Where Harlan and I differed is that while I'd previously spent my fair share of time behind the barricades and at protests, in recent years I only rarely went into the streets. (This includes being present at Occupy Wall Street, when they went into Times Square, and holy crap is *that* another story for another time.) But Harlan was physically engaged as an activist for most of his life. One of his proudest moments was walking in the now-famous Equal Rights March with Martin Luther King at Selma, Alabama, in 1965. As Harlan would say later, "You can't write what I've been writing for fifty years and not have to walk the walk as well as talk the talk."

So when Arizona failed to ratify the Equal Rights Amendment, and NOW called for an economic boycott of the states that had voted against it, Harlan found himself on the horns of a dilemma. He had agreed to be the guest of honor for that year's World Science Fiction Convention in Phoenix. None of the other guests had an issue with attending the convention, but as a strong supporter of NOW and the ERA, Harlan couldn't justify doing anything that would add to the Arizona economy by virtue of his presence.

So he canceled the flight that had been booked out of Arizona to bring him to the convention, canceled the hotel room that would have been paid for by the convention (and all the room-service perks that would go with it), rented a recreational vehicle, and stocked it with enough food for five days. Then he drove the RV from Los Angeles to Arizona, loading up on extra gas just before crossing the state line, and lived entirely out of the vehicle (with the outside temperature averaging 110 degrees) for the duration of the convention in order to avoid spending even a *penny* inside the Arizona border. He also coordinated his actions with NOW in order to focus media attention on Arizona's position and raise funds through the convention for the ongoing battle over the ERA.

The second story is smaller, but perhaps even more to the point.

On Sundays, Harlan liked to drive from his home in Sherman Oaks to the Golden Dragon Restaurant in downtown Los Angeles for a brunch of dim sum and anything else incautious enough to wander past the table. But Harlan, *being* Harlan, didn't like taking the freeway like everyone else. He preferred to zoom down little back alleys and side streets that led through some of the most dangerous parts of Los Angeles. We're talking serious gang turf, drug, and high-crime areas where the only people on the street were those with very specific reasons for being there, and they did *not* appreciate strangers intruding on their space or their places of business.

The brunch crowd this particular morning consisted of Harlan, Susan, me, Kathryn, and a fifth soul whose name I cannot remember with any certitude. The trip down to the Golden Dragon concluded safely, and prodigious amounts of dim sum were consumed. When no more could be eaten without risking Monsieur Creosote–level eruptions, we piled into the car, which now seemed considerably smaller than when we'd arrived, and started back up the same way we'd come down.

There is one stretch of territory, about a mile long, where one simply does not stop, ever, for any reason—where you do not go unless you *really* know what you're getting into *and* you have permission from the local power brokers. We were dead center in that part of town when we drove past an elderly African American woman sitting on the curb. I can see her in memory as clearly as I saw her that day, one hand shielding her face from the hot sun, the other holding on to a shopping cart containing all her earthly possessions. Her eyes were tired; these were eyes that were *always* tired, sanded down by time and loss and confusion.

Harlan hit the brakes, hard.

As some of the street denizens looked up from their delirium, startled by the sound of screeching tires, Harlan glanced in the rearview mirror to where she was sitting.

"Goddamnit," he said, his voice low and surprisingly soft. "She's all alone."

Then he climbed out of the car and started walking back to her.

Everyone on the street followed him with their eyes. *What the fuck?*

I popped my door on the front passenger side and kept it open so I could back him up in case there was trouble.

The trouble watched us but didn't move, curious to see where this was going.

Harlan stooped down in front of her until they were at eye level. He was just far enough that I couldn't hear all of it, only his side since she spoke very little and very softly. But this was the gist of it.

*Are you okay?*

*Are you hurt?*

*Do you need anything?*

As they talked, he reached into his blazer pocket, where he kept his wallet, moving slowly and carefully so no one would see him doing it, and pulled out a clutch of bills without looking to see how much it came to. Then he leaned in as if patting her hand, and quietly slipped her the money.

*Don't let them see this,* he told her. *Don't let them know you have it, or they'll take it away. If they ask what I wanted, tell them I got lost and was asking you for directions.*

He leaned in to meet her eyes. *It'll get better,* he told her. *Swear to God, it'll get better. You just have to hold on. Can you do that? Can you hold on just a little longer?*

She nodded.

*Okay*, he said. *Okay.*

Then as the neighborhood looked on, he walked back to the car, got in, and we continued on our way.

It says much that when I called Kathryn to confirm my memory of the incident, her first words were, "Which time? He was always doing stuff like that. If he saw someone who was lost or hurting, that's where he went. Every time."

This I know above all else: no one other than Harlan, driving down that street, in that part of town, would have seen that woman sitting alone on that curb.

And for *sure* nobody else would have stopped, and gotten out, and talked to her, and done for her as he did.

*That* was my friend. *That* was the man I knew and respected.

*That* was Harlan Ellison.

By 1991, the number of new works by Harlan, and the attention they received, had slowed to a crawl. Whatever cachet he had in the work of mainstream publishing and media had largely faded. Sometimes he felt as if he was looking at himself from far outside, watching as he disappeared into darkness like the dot of a tiny ship against the horizon. *I'm slipping away*, he would say, more than once. And as the days passed, he realized he could either accept that fate or do something about it. Like Robert Redford coming to bat in the last inning of *The Natural*, if he had to go down, he would go down swinging.

So he decided to write something unexpected, something nobody would see coming. It couldn't be a novel—that was still beyond his reach—but a short story that would let him push the envelope of his storytelling ability and prove to the world that he was still relevant, still had something to *say*. He practically barricaded himself in his office, working night and day with what little energy he had, until he was finished. The story represented his best work, and who he really was as a writer, not the "sci-fi guy" so many had decided was all he was.

The end result, "The Man Who Rowed Christopher Columbus Ashore," was selected for inclusion in the 1993 edition of the prestigious mainstream literary collection *Best American Short Stories*. For Harlan, it was the achievement of a lifetime.

And for a little while, the world was significantly more beautiful.

April 10, 1996. I was shooting season three of my series *Babylon 5* when Harlan—who I had hired as our conceptual consultant in order to have access to that twelve-story brain—suffered a heart attack and underwent quadruple bypass surgery at Cedars-Sinai Hospital in Beverly Hills. I went to see him as soon as visitors were allowed, and found him understandably subdued, tired, and pale.

"Well, I'm still alive," he said, sounding almost disappointed.

Three years after recovering from the surgery, his anthology *Slippage* is published by Houghton Mifflin. It is also the *last* collection of original, non-reprint stories from a major publisher that Harlan will see in his lifetime. The theme of the collection is the process by which a man's life begins irrevocably falling apart. Harlan is putting his fears, and his mortal dreads, right out in the public eye, perhaps curious to see if anyone notices.

The public thinks it's a metaphor.

It's 1997. Harlan Ellison is sixty-three, and for reasons he cannot fathom, he is not dead, and he has no idea how to face that terrifying reality.

He is lost.

I spent 2001 through 2003 in Vancouver, Canada, producing *Jeremiah*, a TV series for Showtime; two years that, on reflection, would have been better spent driving metal spikes into my eyes. I kept in contact with Harlan by phone whenever possible, and in those conversations, it was clear that the depression was taking an ever-greater toll on his relationship with Susan. Fights became more frequent, louder, and more cutting. Sometimes she would leave overnight, staying at a hotel until the situation cooled off.

"Half the time I don't even know why I'm arguing with her," Harlan said over the phone. "It's like I'm looking at this *thing* yelling at her, just screaming at the top of his lungs, and I can't stop it."

One night, desperate to pierce the cycle of depression, Susan left a note on his desk before taking off for another overnight hotel stay. "I love you, and whatever you do or don't do is fine with me. If you decide never to write another word again, that would be okay as long as you were happy. What I'm trying to say (and I think you know this too) is that you're not working and you're not *not* working. You're stuck in some gray limbo. You're certainly not enjoying not working. You're not doing any of the things you promised yourself you would do. And you're not doing the one thing you seem to love most: writing . . . you haven't lost the talent, what you've lost is your way . . . it's tough to break this downward spiral, but I think you've got to do it soon."

When I returned to Los Angeles at the conclusion of *Jeremiah*, I spent the first few weeks settling into my new digs—Kathryn and I had decided to go our separate ways, all of it very amicable, no horror stories; we're better friends now than when we were together—then visited Harlan as soon as I was caught up. I found him in the living room, listless, subdued, and distant, with barely enough energy to speak. His eyes were tired, and his voice, once clear and booming, had become low and gravelly. Everything about him radiated exhaustion. It wasn't the heart surgery; he'd rebounded from that before I left for Vancouver. No, this was something else.

The depression that had been gnawing at him for years had finally opened its mouth wide and was devouring him whole. He was sleeping too much, leaving the house only when he couldn't argue his way out of it. After spending decades assailing the vast wasteland that was television, he now spent most of his days sitting up in bed, watching game shows and reality programs, hour after hour.

He had checked out.

As Susan and their assistant, Sharon Buck, prepared dinner, Harlan and I adjourned to his office to talk privately. The typewriter sat untouched on his desk, and the long shelf at the center of the room was still covered by a mountain of unfinished manuscripts. The stories for *The Last Dangerous Visions* had been sitting there for so long that the cover pages had become yellowed and brittle. It reminded me of Miss Havisham's untouched wardrobe in *Great Expectations*, which apparently had more resonance with my life than I'd expected at age twelve.

*Don't worry,* Harlan used to say about the piles of unfinished pages. *I'll get to it eventually.*

But *eventually* had come and gone, and he no longer said such things.

"I keep having the same dream," he said tiredly. "I'm standing in front of the house, in the middle of the street, and I know something's coming around the corner, something terrifying, and it's going to kill me, and I start yelling for help, but nothing comes out. I'm standing there, and nobody can hear me, and nobody shows up to help, and I'm alone with whatever's coming."

"Harlan, you need to see someone," I said, not for the first time, or the fifteenth.

He shrugged. "It's too late."

"No, it's not. Look, you can't say for years that there's not a problem, then when you concede that maybe there *is* a problem, say, 'Well, it's too late.' That's not fair to me, to your other friends, and it's definitely not fair to Susan."

"She'll be okay," he said, waving to encompass the house. "This place is my legacy to her. It's paid for, and there's enough art and collectibles to support her for a lifetime if it comes to that. It's my tombstone."

Then he stopped, smiled faintly, and said, "Well, technically, *this* is my tombstone."

He opened the sliding glass doors, and we went out onto the roof, where a new part of the house was under construction. Bright red, it was accessible through an ornate round clockwork door that, when completed, would be flanked by two sleek, six-foot-tall silver art deco sculptures. It looked like the burial chamber for an Egyptian pharaoh, if Egyptian pharaohs had been fond of art deco and red paint schemes.

"It's my keep," he said. "The last of the house to be built, and the last of me."

"Susan doesn't want the keep, or the house, or the legacy. She wants you. Alive."

He shrugged again and said nothing.

Later, after Harlan had gone to bed, I pulled Susan aside and told her about my conversation with him. "You need to get him to a psychiatrist," I said.

"He won't listen," she said, throwing up her hands in frustration. "When I bring it up, he tells me not to get into it, then shuts down. I can't force him. You know how he is—he doesn't force. Push him left, and he'll go right every time. All I can do is hope he'll snap out of it eventually."

"He won't. He needs therapy, he needs meds, and he needs a proper psychiatrist."

"Not arguing. Totally agree, totally necessary, totally not gonna happen."

Anosognosia, sometimes referred to as "lack of insight," is defined as *a symptom of severe mental illness that impairs the ability of an individual to understand or even perceive their illness. It is the most common reason why patients with schizophrenia or bipolar disorder refuse medication and decline to seek treatment. Affecting roughly 40 percent of bipolar patients, it is often associated with increased danger of stroke and other neurological complications.*

Medical journals also warn that, as bipolar disorder slides further into depression, the person's ability to make appropriate choices recedes at an exponential rate, leading to incidents of inappropriate behavior caused by severely impaired judgment. *Patients become increasingly incapable of understanding the consequences of their behavior.*

Harlan's disorder was affecting his behavior in ways that were self-destructive and often inappropriate. He wasn't *trying* to be inappropriate;

it's just that the parts of his brain that were responsible for discerning the difference between what was and wasn't appropriate were being ripped out and short-circuited. It's difficult to discuss the following incidents, but it's necessary in order to understand what was happening to him, and why, and how it all culminated in The Incident With The Gun.

Incident the First: Since Harlan was spending most of his days in bed, he rarely dressed for company, sometimes wearing only a robe with nothing underneath. One evening, after dinner, several of Harlan's friends and I were heading for the door when he remembered a gift he wanted to give one of the other guests, which was sitting on his desk upstairs. In full view of the attendees, he shucked the robe and raced upstairs to the office.

Upon returning and putting the robe back on, he seemed genuinely confused by the shocked expressions he encountered. He explained, as if it were the most logical thing in the world, that shedding the robe made him more aerodynamic, allowing him to go and return more quickly. He was literally incapable of understanding why his actions might not have been correct.

Incident the Second: Harlan was invited to a party at the home of Haskell "Huck" Barkin, a friend of many decades. At one point during the festivities, thinking it would be amusing, Harlan dropped his pants. When confronted by a furious Huck, Harlan couldn't understand why he and the other guests were upset. Retelling the story later, Harlan was almost in tears at the prospect that he had somehow given offense to his good friend. He genuinely couldn't understand what he had done wrong, or recognize that his ability to monitor his behavior was being eaten away by the illness.

Incident the Third: Impulse spending sprees are as textbook bipolar as the manic episodes that lead to them, and Harlan's growing inability to make good decisions began to decimate his savings. Despite a precipitous drop in income in the years after *Babylon 5*, Harlan kept making high-price impulse purchases of comics, artwork, and collectibles. Susan would tell him, repeatedly, "We don't have the money." But the cash went out anyway, leading to panic when the bills came in, often paid with loans from friends, followed by the same reckless spending and crippled decision-making when the financial dust cleared.

"He can't control himself," Susan said. "I've had to hide the credit cards."

Incident the Fourth: Determined to get Harlan out of the house, eight of us took him and Susan to dinner. Though he was happy to be outside, it didn't take long before he began making inappropriate and sometimes offensive comments. Eager to conjure up the image of his earlier, performative self, he was oblivious to the looks his comments received from the group. We rode it out until the female server returned with the signed check and thanked me for the tip.

"If it's not enough, there's always porn," Harlan said.

The server walked away, nearly in tears.

The conversation that followed afterward constitutes one of only two instances when—to my eternal shame, because I should have known and *did* know better—I lost my temper with Harlan and raised my voice. The other was—

Incident the Fifth: I wasn't there the night it happened. I only heard about it the next day.

It was WorldCon 2006, and Harlan was onstage with Connie Willis in front of a huge audience, doing their "Bad Baby Harlan" routine. As can be seen in a YouTube video of the convention, this involved Connie, who was quite a bit taller than Harlan, wrapping her left arm around his neck in a hammerlock and smushing him against her chest as if trying to breastfeed a cranky, difficult infant, while Harlan did everything in his power to escape. (This is what passes for humor at a science-fiction convention.) Though visibly fatigued and depressed, Harlan did his best to hold up his end of the shtick, trying to struggle free by grabbing anything he could find on the podium: pens, paper, a hammer (I still have no idea what the hell a hammer was doing on the podium) . . . at one point he shoved the entire head of the wind-screened microphone into his mouth, as if mistaking it for the breast he was *supposed* to be paying attention to, while Connie kept strangling him closer. After about two minutes of this, she released him to the applause of the audience. But Harlan was still caught up in the Bad Baby routine, and some part of his misfiring brain decided it would be funny if he finally seemed to make a move on one of the breasts he had been smushed up against.

Unfortunately, and *unforgivably*, the move connected, and contact was made.

Upon hearing the news the next day, I immediately called Harlan. "How could you do something like that?" I yelled. I knew he was ill, that he wasn't making good decisions, that his judgment was impaired, and he was acting irrationally and out of control, and there was a demon in his head that was eating him alive from the inside out, and nothing he did made sense anymore, but *how the hell could he do something like that?*

"I don't know!" he yelled back, disconsolate and near tears. "I don't even remember doing it! All I remember is thinking it'd be funny if I—"

"God*damn*it, Harlan—"

"It's the same way I sometimes lean into Susan, and it just happened—"

"This is the last straw; I'm serious. This isn't just about you anymore; it's affecting other people and it's wrong and it's hurtful and—"

"I didn't mean to—"

"What you intended was wrong in the first place, and what you didn't *mean* to do isn't the point! It got done and it got done to a friend, to *Connie*, for chrissakes, in front of an entire ballroom full of people! You need to *see* someone, you need to get *help*, and you for *sure* need to fucking apologize and go public and tell people what's been happening to you—"

He sobbed and hung up.

Incident the Sixth: Unable to forgive himself for what had happened with Connie, with the bills, with his work, with his *life*, but unwilling to seek treatment, Harlan began to spin out, spiraling from despair to self-rage to depression and back again.

When I wasn't available to visit because of work or travel, Kathryn looked after them as best she could, getting Susan out from under by taking her to Pilates, meals, and shopping expeditions. One afternoon, as she dropped Susan off at the house, they noticed that the back door of Harlan's car was open.

They approached to find Harlan splayed out on the rear seat, in the throes of a deep and wrenching depression. "What are you doing?" Kathryn asked.

Barely able to speak, he said, "I'm waiting to die."

When he didn't die that day, or the next, he decided to accelerate the program.

During the summer of 2010, in the throes of an ever-worsening depression, he announced he would no longer be appearing at conventions, that he was done with writing, and done with life. In an interview with the online magazine *Isthmus*, published September 23, Harlan said, "The truth of what's going on here is that I'm dying. I'm like the Wicked Witch of the West—I'm melting. I began to sense it back in January. An old dog senses when it's his time."

After that he rarely left the house, or his bed. He would lie between the sheets, barely paying attention to the TV at the foot of the bed tuned to a steady parade of game shows and reality television. He didn't want to see anyone or talk to anyone. No appetite. No writing. No hope.

Waiting to die.

Incident the Last: The Incident With The Gun.

In early February 2011, Harlan called me at home. For a change of pace, he waited until I was actually awake. "I need you to do me a solid," he said.

"Done," I said, as was our tradition.

"Don't say yes until you know what it is. Because this is big, and messy, and difficult, and if you say you don't want to do it, I'll understand. Okay?"

"Sure. Shoot."

"I want you to be executor of my estate."

"Done."

"Will you for chrissakes knock it off and listen to me? If I die now—"

"You're not gonna die—"

"Just shut the fuck up, okay? If I die now, obviously Susan inherits everything. But there's the question: What happens to all this if she dies? I mean, she's younger than both of us, so it probably won't be an issue, but just in case something happens—we get hit by a truck or a meteor slams down out of the sky, whatever—I want to make sure this place—the house, the stories, my legacy—gets protected.

"But you gotta understand, being an executor is a thankless job. It's lawyers and bills and paperwork and banks and creditors and death certificates, all the stuff I know you hate as much as I do, which is why we both have people who do most of that crap for us. But all of this would fall directly on your shoulders. I know a lot of people, but you're the only guy I know who will get it done right, who won't get distracted or use it to make their bones somehow because you've already done that. Bottom line: I trust you, and only you, to do this. So, you in?"

"Done."

"Then I can relax," he said, and there was something very final in the way he said it that I should have picked up on, but didn't.

Harlan's will (and a separate will for Susan) was finalized and signed on February 14, 2011. Valentine's Day.

Thirteen days later—Sunday, February 27—Harlan's assistant, Sharon, was working in her office at the back of the house when she heard Susan crying out. She rushed into the hall to find Susan struggling with Harlan.

He had a gun and was planning to kill himself.

Desperate to talk him out of taking his life, they implored him to see a doctor, to get professional help. The conversation went back and forth on a sea of tears. The gun was in his hand. Finally, reluctantly, Harlan put down the gun and agreed to see a doctor.

But he still refused to see a *psychiatrist*. He consented only to see their regular GP at the Toluca Lake Health Center. Still, it was a start, and to avoid losing momentum Sharon made the appointment for the next day.

On Monday, as promised, Harlan met with the doctor. But because he believed he was only there because Susan *wanted* him to be there, not because he actually *needed* to be there, he downplayed the severity of his problem. He acknowledged that he'd been feeling depressed for some time, but asked only for a *referral* to a therapist, which he was already planning to find some excuse to ignore. And eventually the gun would find its way into his hand again.

And he probably would've gotten away with it, but for one crucial mistake.

Harlan was a storyteller. He loved drama. Even in his worst moments, he loved performing, and being stuck at home, he hadn't had an audience in a long time.

So he told the doctor about The Incident With The Gun.

And the doctor nodded and said *um-hmm, really?* and *You don't say?* and made notes and said he was going to arrange for some tests at Glendale Adventist Hospital just down the street, nothing major, just some small things, and could Harlan by any chance go right on over there?

But it was already late in the day, and Harlan didn't want to fight traffic all the way back to Sherman Oaks, so he promised to go by GAH the next day.

The following morning, on the assumption that he was only going in for a few tests and to *maybe* talk about some treatments, Harlan arrived at Glendale Adventist Hospital, checked in at the front desk, and was asked to wait in a room off to the side.

Five minutes later, police and hospital staff took him into custody on a seventy-two-hour psychiatric hold for attempted suicide.

He was allowed one phone call.

In Harlan's shoes, which at that moment were being removed, along with the shoelaces, who would *you* call?

"You gotta get me outta here!" he yelled over the phone. "Joe, I can't stay here. There's crazy people and they took away my belt and they're gonna keep me here for three days but they can decide to keep me longer if they want and I can't do it. If they make me stay, I swear I'll fucking ki—"

Someone standing nearby must've looked in his direction, because he caught himself and lowered his voice. "You're the only one I can trust to get this done. You gotta get me out of here."

I knew that if he stayed there for the full three days, he'd dig in and refuse to cooperate in ways carefully chosen to avoid giving the doctors grounds to extend his stay. In the end, he'd come out the other side even *more* determined to avoid treatment, which would put him right back on the .32 caliber freeway. So I decided to use the situation to leverage Harlan into finally taking real action.

"I'll make a deal with you," I said. "If I can get you out before the seventy-two hours, will you agree to do *exactly* what I tell you to do? No arguments, no yes-buts, and no *let me think about it* because if you were making good decisions, you wouldn't *be* there in the first place."

"Okay, yes, anything. Just get me the fuck outta here."

In the state of California, there are only two ways to get a patient out from under a psychiatric hold—technically known as a code 5150—earlier than the seventy-two-hour minimum: you can either get a court order or have the psychiatrist you were already seeing for whatever caused you to be committed intervene on your behalf. Unfortunately, Harlan didn't *have* a psychiatric doctor because he hadn't fucking *listened* to me for the last ten years, we didn't have grounds for a court order, so I went another way, *and* we were coming into the weekend when everyone would be out of the office.

My first call was to Jaclyn Easton, publisher of the *Babylon 5* script books, who with Jason Davis had begun publishing print-on-demand and small-press volumes of Harlan's prior works. Jaclyn knew every doctor in town, so I asked her to start calling around to find a psychiatrist who might be willing to jump in. While that cooked, I got Susan, Kathryn, and others to ask every high-visibility person we knew in TV and film to call the hospital and tell them know who Harlan was, that he was a Very Important Person, that this was all some kind of hideous mistake, and that they should let him go because the Whole World Was Watching.

The barrage started almost instantly and didn't let up.

We got him out in thirty hours.

This is the voicemail Harlan left me when he got home. And yes, I still have it.

"This is Ellison calling to say thank you again. I suspect this is going to go on for a number of days in which I will just call you and say thank you. You and Jaclyn and Susan and Kathryn got me out of that situation. For thirty hours, a little more than thirty hours, they were among the top five worst thirty hours of my life. I mean really, really, really fucking horrible, and I thought I would just keep calling to say thank you, because shoulder bumps and fist bumps and manly shit like that doesn't quite do the job."

I gave him the night to recover, then showed up at his door early the next day to remind him of his promise, pressing the advantage while the experience was still fresh.

"Whatever you say, I'm on board," he said, with Susan sitting beside him.

"Okay, then here's what we're going to do. I know how you are, how sometimes things that need to get done are forgotten or postponed because, big surprise, something else comes up, or you're running late and have to cancel, or you don't wanna, so we're going to bulletproof this.

"In addition to the doctor Jaclyn called to help get you out of there, I've found a psychiatrist in Orange County who specializes in bipolar disorder. I've booked her for the entire day, so it's physically impossible for you to be late to the appointment. To make sure you don't decide it's too far to drive, I've hired a car to pick her up and bring her here to the house. She will be at your disposal for that entire day, so there's no getting out of this. I want you to tell her *exactly* what's been going on from the first time I said you should see someone until now. *All* of it. Deal?"

And for the first time, he said back to me, "Done."

And he kept that appointment.

And for the first time, he received an actual diagnosis of his problem, confirmed by both the psychiatrist from Orange County, and later, a psychiatrist based in Glendale, that he was suffering from lifelong bipolar disorder that had begun with manic episodes in childhood, morphed over time into manic depression, and had now exploded into a full-blown case of severe clinical depression. They finally made him understand that it wasn't just a matter of feeling tired or depressed; he was suffering from a genuine psychiatric disorder.

When Harlan learned that the disorder could be treated, that with the proper meds he could maybe-possibly-with-luck be brought back to the man he had been previously, he was nearly in tears.

"Let's do it," he said. "I'm in."

It took a while to find the right cocktail of antidepressants, mood stabilizers, and antipsychotics, and the road was often difficult, but gradually the meds began to have the desired effect. He started to feel better. Rather than spending every day in bed, he would walk around the house, tell stories, laugh, and chat on the phone. Friends visited more frequently. He began eating more. And for the first time, he was able to fully open up to me about what he'd been going through since childhood all the way up through his career, the ups and downs, the disappointments and the heartaches, some of which are described in this document.

After years of hiding his condition, he was finally strong enough to open up to the world about what was going on. "Things went from bad to worse," he told *Salon*. "There were several hospitals, things got about as bad as they could possibly get, short of being plowed under with a backhoe. [Then] I drifted into the embrace of the Wizard of Oz, a neuropharmacologist, who figured out I had clinical depression, and they put me on drugs." He seemed actually relieved at being able to say, *I didn't know what was wrong with me, but now I do, and I'm getting better!* It was as though a great weight had been lifted off his shoulders.

Best of all, *he started writing again*, working on stories and essays and graphic novels.

He began to talk about going to conventions again.

He stopped waiting to die.

He even returned to *The Last Dangerous Visions*, which somehow didn't seem to be as unconquerable a mountain as he'd previously believed, telling Susan, Jason Davis, friend and attorney Christine Valada, and others that it was time to finish the goddamned thing. He began pulling out long-expired contracts and contact information, and looking around for new names to add to the roster. He felt hope for the very first time in a long while. *I've got this . . . I've got this.*

But the universe is a mean motherfucker, and the demon in his head wasn't done with him yet. *No escape, Ellison! What was that collection you wrote?* No Doors, No Windows?

*No doors, no windows, no escape!*

The counterattack started on October 4, 2014. Harlan was at a party—he was actually *out of the house and enjoying himself*—when he began to feel, according to Sharon, "a little wobbly." He shrugged it off but left early.

This was almost certainly minor stroke number one.

On October 7, Sharon and Susan returned from shopping to find Harlan on the floor in the foyer. They wanted to call an ambulance, but he refused, insisting he would be fine. They helped him into bed, and Susan made an appointment with their doctor for the ninth.

This was almost certainly not-quite-as-minor stroke number two.

On the morning of the ninth, Harlan couldn't move his right side, but his pride prevented him from being taken out in an ambulance. Instead, he sent Sharon to a medical supply store on Van Nuys Boulevard to buy a wheelchair, which cost precious time but at least allowed them to finally get Harlan into the car. When they arrived at the Toluca Lake Health Center, the doctor immediately diagnosed this as a major stroke emergency and had him hospitalized at Providence Saint Joseph, in Burbank.

As usual, I went to see him as soon as visitors were allowed.

"Hey, Sparky," he said, his voice raspy and low as he lay in the bed, hooked up to an assortment of monitors. "Looks like they got me locked up again after all."

The doctors said he wasn't doing too badly for a stroke of this magnitude. Six months of physical therapy would put him very close to where he had been prestroke.

After being released, Harlan put on a show of making a good-faith effort at the physical therapy, but soon began to balk at the treatments and eventually stopped working out altogether. It was as if some part of him said, *Enough. Seriously. Enough. I'm done.*

*Let's just let this one go, okay?*

And he never got better.

The long, downward slide had begun.

The last time I saw Harlan he was incapable of getting out of bed by himself. A nurse came by several times a week to look after him, but there was only so much she could do. His voice was thin, his face sallow and drawn, his right arm nearly incapable of movement. He'd lost a lot of weight, but his eyes were still Harlan.

Since he couldn't leave his bed, I crawled in beside him, and he and I and Susan chatted about nothing important because there comes a time when all you want to hear are trivial things that won't force you to think about anything else. Then Susan left the room to make dinner, and we talked about some things that *were* important, but there are some conversations, even in a document like this, that are private, and personal, and none of anybody's business.

Then Susan returned, announcing mealtime, and helped Harlan to sit up, preparing him for dinner. This was my cue, so I took it and began to stand.

As I turned, he reached over with the arm that still worked and kissed the back of my hand. He had never done this before.

And we both knew why he was doing it.

"Thank you for being a friend," he said. "Thank you for looking out for me and standing by me when practically everybody else ran. I love you."

"I love you too," I said, and turned and left before he could see the tears.

Harlan Jay Ellison, who had been my friend, mentor, and father figure long before we ever met, the man who could have been spoken of beside Kurt Vonnegut or Philip Roth or Studs Terkel or Gay Talese before the Demon began ripping apart his synapses . . . the enfant terrible who could simultaneously be the gentlest and the most annoying person on the face of the planet, died in his sleep on June 28, 2018, from pulmonary arrest. He was eighty-four.

What no one saw coming, what no one could have *imagined*, was that Susan would pass away of the same cause two years later, on August 3, 2020. She had just turned sixty two months earlier.

The day after her passing, a conversation with Harlan that I had long ago forgotten, because I thought there would never be the need to remember it, returned when I received a call from an attorney reminding me that I was now executor of Harlan's estate. I would inherit none of it but be responsible for all of it. Most executors get to walk away after the bequests, the disposition of property, and the estate sales, but realizing Harlan's wishes to transform his home into a memorial library, and managing his literary legacy, would be a lifetime pro bono obligation.

"You don't have to say yes," the attorney on the other end of the phone said. "You can let this go to someone else, but the odds are they'll just sell everything off and be done with it rather than spend the next twenty years doing the work needed to create and maintain the library and assets. So it's your call: Do you want to take on the job?"

I paused, and considered, and said, "Done."

So why have I told you all this?

Because I want you to know the Harlan Ellison that I knew, not the mythology, the rumors, or the backroom assassinations. The man himself: flawed, brilliant, generous, and maybe a little screwy. Because he was important not just to me but to tens of thousands of fans and untold numbers of writers who drew inspiration and strength from his work. Because people need to know that bipolar disorder and other mental health issues can happen to anyone, and it's crucial to seek out treatment even when the person in question doesn't see the problem, because they are literally *incapable* of seeing the problem.

And finally, I'm writing this because of what Harlan said in his piece on Sal Mineo. Words that could describe his own life as much as they did Sal's:

> *He's dead and the thousands of people who knew him, who made a special point of calling themselves his friends, who took what he had when he had so much he didn't know enough to hold back a little, who weren't around to give some back when he was down and needed . . . the millions who saw him on movie and television screens . . . the smoothyguts operators who got him into the business deals that went sour even while they copped their commissions and got fat . . . all the agents and the lawyers and the personal managers who clipped him for 10 percent of his life . . . all the smooth, tanned succubi and incubi who murmured warm words into his ears over all the years . . . where are they?*

And:

> *I don't know about you, but I loathe books and articles written by ex-maids or second assistant secretaries that cash in on the death of notables. Books on Howard Hughes or Marilyn Monroe or James Dean, written by literary ghouls, make me want to puke. All you have is my word that I'm writing this . . . to square accounts with a buddy, and to blow off all the yellow journalism that's being written about him.*
>
> *This is written with affection. Which doesn't mean I intend to lie or gloss over [his] life.*

And then there's this part, which is as much about Harlan and me as it was about Harlan and Sal:

*Somebody dies, and you have to make sense of it all. You have to say, What does the death of this person mean? My mother, Sal Mineo, the last person you lost. What does it mean? Why, beyond the grief of losing someone whose singularity will never be seen again, because each of us is a receptacle of qualities that can never be precisely matched, should we give a damn if an old lady in Miami or a faded movie star in Hollywood has died?*

*Because sometimes they go out wearing a bum rap and even eighty-five years after she was tried and acquitted, most people still believe Lizzie Borden took an ax and gave her mother forty whacks, and the massed belief in myth instead of reality is maybe enough to foul up the records. If not in Heaven, or Wherever, then on Earth for sure. And Sal was too good a guy to be remembered the way* Time *piped him overboard.*

*This is paying off an obligation to Sal, because we were friends.*

Because we were friends.

Harlan and Sal were friends, and that necessitated truth, understanding, and kindness.

Harlan and I were friends, and the obligation is no less.

What unites the three of us across the years is that we all came from the streets, and when that's your world, nothing is more important than looking after the guy next to you in your gang. You stick together. You don't cut and run. You back each other up. You do what's right.

And what's right is to tell you who Harlan Ellison was, and why he was, and why he mattered. To honor his memory, and our friendship.

But the publication of this book does not mark the end of ensuring that Harlan achieves the place in literature that his work deserves.

It is only the beginning.

Postscript: September 5, 2023.

On behalf of the estate, and as director of the Harlan and Susan Ellison Foundation, a nonprofit corporation, I spend most of my day, every day, looking after Harlan's legacy, literary and otherwise. We are in the midst of repairing and refurbishing Ellison Wonderland in all its marvelous eccentricity as a place for lovers of art and words and the intersection between them; and as a resource for artists, architects, and researchers eager to study the house and the art, as well as Harlan's papers, documents, and correspondences.

I don't drive, so I call an Uber to visit the house. I go as often as I can, usually at night, to sort through papers, letters, and manuscripts. There are still decisions to be made about what clothes should be stored, donated, or kept on-site. Hundreds of collectible T-shirts. Boxes of photographs and clippings. Silk shirts and cotton underwear. His prized Borsalino hat. And why on earth does anyone need *that* many ties?

While I await the Uber, I check my mailbox. Harlan's forwarded mail is there—boilerplate letters from the ACLU, Planned Parenthood, and other organizations asking why the donations have stopped. The key to his home sits on a key chain beside my own. Fifteen minutes later, I unlock the front door of Ellison Wonderland and go upstairs to the office.

After sifting through the stories and artwork created for *The Last Dangerous Visions* one last time to make sure I haven't missed anything, I sit at his desk, behind his typewriter. Nearby shelves hold his Nebula and Hugo awards, his Edgar and Writers Guild awards, and a long row of his books—seventeen hundred short stories, including some of the most vital and important stories in the history of twentieth-century science fiction: *I Have No Mouth, and I Must Scream*; "'Repent, Harlequin!' Said the Ticktockman"; *A Boy and His Dog*; *The Beast That Shouted Love at the Heart of the World*; "The Man Who Rowed Christopher Columbus Ashore"; *All the Lies That Are My Life*; "Paladin of the Lost Hour"; "The Whimper of Whipped Dogs"; *Paingod*; "Shattered Like a Glass Goblin"; "Pretty Maggie Moneyeyes"; "Strange Wine" . . . a stunning body of work whose legacy will endure long after I have gone to dust.

Then, at the far end of the shelf, I spot the title that caught my eye in the dime box in a bookstore in Newark, New Jersey: *Gentleman Junkie and Other Stories of the Hung-Up Generation*. I pick it up, reliving that moment.

Harlan could never have imagined the effect his work would have on a lost and lonely twelve-year-old with dreams bigger than he was.

Nor could I ever have anticipated him.

With that book, and *this* book, the circle is finally closed. But there are more tasks remaining, so the work goes on, because I have promises to keep, a lifetime of debt to repay, and obligations that will end only when I do.

Because I am Harlan Ellison's friend.

Shibboleth.

# ASSIGNMENT NO. 1

## BY STEPHEN ROBINETT

*For as long as there's been a human race, we are all confronted, sooner or later, with the same question: What do we do about Grandpa and Grandma? How do we face the fact that the one person, who for most of our lives was the most necessary, has now become the most difficult, painful, or inconvenient? That question is as timely, as of-the-moment, now as it was when this story was first written, and the answers provided in the following pages may not be strictly a matter of fiction for very much longer.*

Ted Willis
4th Period
Thought Processing
September 13, 2046

Something I Did Last Summer

This isn't very important or anything. I mean it happens every day to old people and nobody thinks much about it. It has to do with my Grandpa

Willis who is an old person. He came to live with us for a little while last summer. The day he came, my parents got into a fight. They don't fight much, but this time they had a big one. I was in the living room with my grandfather and I could hear my parents shouting in the kitchen. I thought it was about sending me away to school.

"But I don't think he wants to," shouted my father and said he needed more time to think everything over.

"He'll like it once he's there," said my mother and told him there was nothing to think over.

Finally my mother said something about a tank farm and I knew they were arguing about Grandpa Willis. That was a big relief. I like this school and didn't want to go away. All my friends are here. Anyway, once I figured out they were arguing about Grandpa Willis and not about me, I looked across the living room at him. All I could see was the back of his wheelchair and the top of his bald head. After dinner my parents parked the wheelchair in front of the big window to get Grandpa Willis out of the way. We live up in the hills and out the window I could see all the glittering lights from Los Angeles and flitters drifting around over the city like bunches of fireflies. I guess Grandpa Willis liked looking at them. According to the doctors, he could still see and hear and understand. The strokes he had just made him so he couldn't move or talk right. I knew how *I* felt about going away. I wondered how Grandpa Willis felt about it, especially about going away to a tank farm.

I walked over to his wheelchair and stood in front of him with my back to the big window. His face looked weird, sort of frowning and angry with his ears sticking out from his bald head. It was like the stroke got him when he was angry and froze him that way. It kind of scared me. At the same time, it looked like the way Grandpa Willis should look. What I mean is all his life Grandpa Willis was angry at somebody—not me, he liked me—but other people. Back in the 1980s he organized the Information Workers of America and was made its president. That meant he fought all the time. The union called him "Iron Will" and he used to tell me people got names like that for fighting for what they believed in and trying to make it real and he was proud he always did that. I spent a lot of time with him before he had the strokes—he was retired from the union—and he talked a lot to me about things like that. So anyway that angry look kind of went with how he was.

"Grandpa," I said. "Mom and Dad want to send you away to a tank farm."

The angry look on his face got even angrier when I said that. He turned sort of red and his lips shook, kind of, and he barked.

"Ooahnaye!"

That scared the socks off me. I jumped back, hit the big window, scared myself again when I hit it, and ran to the kitchen to tell my parents Grandpa Willis was barking or something.

The next day my father finally agreed to take Grandpa Willis to see a tank farm. They picked Golden Tomorrows in Pasadena because my Grandma Willis was already a floater there. I never knew my Grandma Willis. She went into a tank about ten years ago when I was only two. She had some kind of painful disease and decided being a floater in a tank farm was better than living with the disease. That's what my parents said anyway. Once, I asked Grandpa Willis about it, but the question got him so mad he wouldn't talk about it. I thought for a long time he acted that way because of losing a lifelong companion and all that, but I don't think so now. I think what got him so mad was Grandma Willis going into a tank at all.

Anyway, so we went out to Golden Tomorrows. All the way out there I kept looking at my grandfather in the back of the flitter and wondering what he thought. He still looked angry. I felt all right about going because I had never seen a tank farm and that sounded interesting and also because I thought if Grandpa Willis saw it and didn't like it, he would say so somehow and then just live with us. I liked that idea best, him living with us. He always seemed strong to me and I felt good around him.

It was afternoon by the time we got to Golden Tomorrows. I didn't like the look of the place right off. There were wide marble steps going up to the entrance and tall marble columns beside the entrance and nobody at all around, which made it all look like some kind of deserted monument. They had a special ramp for wheelchairs—I guess they get a lot of wheelchairs—and it carried Grandpa Willis and his chair up the marble steps and into the lobby. We had to walk up.

The place was even weirder inside. A big mural of a pasture stretched all around the lobby. They painted it with kinetic paints so the flowers waved and the cow's tail wagged and the weather vane on the roof of the barn moved like there was real wind—but no people. Weird.

A Mr. Slocum met us in the lobby. Mr. Slocum looked about as lifelike as the mural, maybe less. He had a gray tunic and a gray face. He smiled a lot but it looked like it took him a lot of effort to do it. He volunteered to push Grandpa Willis's chair and led us out of the lobby.

We must have walked forever, Mr. Slocum pushing the chair, my parents on either side of it, and me tagging along behind. The place had halls that branched off to more halls that branched off to more halls. They all looked the same, long and deserted. All I could hear in all those halls was our footsteps, which gave me this weird and creepy feeling we were the only things alive anywhere in the building. We kept passing a lot of wide double doors like entrances to old-fashioned ballrooms. Signs above the doors had names on them like "Easy Street" and "The Yellow Brick Road" and "May to December Promenade." Not that anybody behind the doors was doing much promenading. About all they were doing was floating.

We finally got to some doors called "Memory Lane." Mr. Slocum opened them with a wave of his ID card and pushed Grandpa Willis into a somatorium—that's the real name for a tank farm. The place was as big inside as a soccer field! And it did look kind of like a hydroponic farm, except the tanks were different. These were big coffin-size tanks on both sides of a wide aisle—maybe a hundred tanks on each side going back all the way to the far wall so you almost couldn't see the last ones—and a full illumination ceiling like a hydroponic farm, probably to give everything an outdoors look, though it seemed to me it was outdoors on a pretty gloomy day. All the tanks had transparent domes on them and sat on a base with life-support readouts.

Mr. Slocum led us halfway down the aisle and stopped us next to my Grandma Willis's tank. While he told my parents whatever he thought he should tell them—most of it sounded like a sales pitch—I looked in my grandmother's tank.

Like I said, I never knew her, but she looked pretty much like her pictures, peaceful too. Floaters—Mr. Slocum called them recumbents—float face up in this cloudy blue fluid with just their faces showing above the fluid and my grandmother was right there doing that. She looked like an old person in a swimming pool on a Sunday afternoon, her eyes closed and her wrinkled old face out just enough to breathe, except I don't know if she was breathing. I think maybe floaters take in oxygen along *with* the other stuff they need through the fluid. She had a skull-cap thing on her head with a cable connected to it. The cable went down into the blue fluid and disappeared. It was all pretty interesting.

I started to tap on the transparent dome to see if I could get her attention, but my father saw me about to do it and frowned. He asked Mr. Slocum if my grandmother knew we were there, which is what I wanted to know anyway.

Mr. Slocum said recumbents live in a world like a daydream, but because of the skullcap—it gives them a feedback loop through Golden Tomorrows' mainframe computer—a daydream as real as life. It lets them live any dream they want. After all, he said—this sounded like more of the sales pitch—why should people who worked hard all their lives, people who contributed all their lives, be forced to live out their sunset years in any way but the way they wanted?

My mother nodded agreement to that one. My father just glanced at the back of my grandfather's wheelchair, looked funny for a few seconds, and told Mr. Slocum to go on.

Mr. Slocum said just like people can pull themselves out of day-dreams by an effort of will, so recumbents can pull themselves out of their daydreams and make themselves aware of their surroundings, the somatorium, people near the tank, whatever they wanted. Most of them just decided—he made a big deal out of how it was the floaters themselves that did the deciding—to stay in their dream lives since the dream lives were more real to them than reality, which sounded weird to me. He said they deserved the happy life they always wanted—the sales pitch again—they deserved to live out the dreams reality never gave them.

My mother agreed.

My father looked funny again but kept quiet.

At this point Mr. Slocum reached down and touched a plate on the base of my grandmother's tank. The wall behind the tank lit up, showing an outdoors scene on a spring day in the country.

I blinked at the screen several times before I got it. There was this young man under a tree wearing the old-fashioned kind of clothes they wore at the end of the last century and in front of him a checkered tablecloth and on the tablecloth an open picnic basket and next to the basket a bunch of wildflowers. The man was Grandpa Willis with more hair. I was looking at all of it like my grandmother was, a picnic in the country with Grandpa Willis when they were young.

About the time I got it, Grandpa Willis got it. His wheelchair was parked looking right at the screen. He started making his barking noise like he did at me at home, but this time it sounded like "Sly! Snaw-eel!"—it echoed like crazy in the vault—"Sly! Snaw-eel!"

The second time he said it, I figured it out—*It's a lie! It's not real!* I mean I figured out the words, not what Grandpa Willis meant, but I think my father knew. He stopped looking at the screen and wouldn't look at me or at Grandpa Willis.

Mr. Slocum—he didn't understand anything—leaned around the wheelchair, smiled his weak smile at my grandfather, and said, "I can see you like the idea, sir."

Grandpa Willis glared up at Mr. Slocum and turned beet red and barked, "*Huh-oo!*"

I got that one right away. So did my father. He kind of turned white and smiled funny. Then Mr. Slocum shook his head and asked me what

Grandpa Willis said to him. I sort of felt like Mr. Slocum deserved it so I just shrugged and said I didn't know.

When we finally pushed Grandpa Willis back to the flitter and went home, I felt pretty good. I figured one visit to Golden Tomorrows was the end of it and now Grandpa Willis would just keep on living with us. After all, he made it pretty clear how he felt about going into a tank and my parents understood that. I sat in the back of the flitter with Grandpa Willis all the way home and held his big rough hand and felt good.

They came for my grandfather the next morning, two men dressed like Mr. Slocum. This part is kind of upsetting for me but it happened so I'm going to put it in. My father was already at work when the men got to our house. Nobody told me they were coming but I knew right away what they wanted.

So did Grandpa Willis. They started pushing his chair toward the front door and he started barking at them and glaring and spitting. It was the only weapon he had left, spit.

I tried to help him and stop them. I ran over and held on to him and the wheelchair and yelled too and kicked at them and cried. I didn't want to cry but I couldn't help it. My mother came over and pulled me away from my grandpa and apologized to the two men for the way I was acting and that got me even more upset because what did I do to apologize for but love my grandpa and want to keep him but they took him anyway and he barked at me like he did before and said, "*Ooahnaye!*" and I still didn't know what he wanted to tell me and that got me all upset all over again and when the door closed and my mother let go of me I just yelled a lot of things at her and ran off to my room and cried some more. I don't even hardly remember much about that except it felt bad.

I didn't talk much the next few days. I didn't want to. Most of the time I just stayed in my room. My parents argued some more. I could hear them from my room. They finally decided I thought Grandpa Willis was dead and blamed them. I did blame them, but I knew he was alive, floating in that cloudy blue liquid. They decided a trip to Golden Tomorrows would help me understand.

Mr. Slocum met us in the lobby again. My parents told him about my problem. He nodded a lot and kept giving me sympathetic looks like he felt sorry for me because I had a deadly disease. When my parents finished telling him, he tried to pat me on the shoulder. More sympathy. I shrugged off his hand and stared at my shoes and I guess sulked. What I wanted was Grandpa Willis, not sympathy, but I already knew I couldn't have him.

I kept on sulking all the way to the "Memory Lane" vault. They had my grandfather in the tank next to my grandmother. Mr. Slocum put us all between the two tanks and started giving me a simple version of his sales pitch, explaining how the tank worked, its life-support system, and the fantasy feedback link to their computer. He kept talking to me like I was simpleminded, which I'm not.

I just ignored him and looked into Grandpa Willis's tank. His face stuck out of the blue liquid like my grandmother's and he had on a skull-cap like hers with a cable coming out of it. People in tanks are supposed to look peaceful I guess, but Grandpa Willis didn't. He looked angry. What really got me was his eyes were open.

I guess I flinched when I saw Grandpa Willis had his eyes open. Mr. Slocum quit talking to me and peered in the tank. He saw right away what startled me and reached down and touched the plate in the base of the tank. The screen on the wall lit up and I looked at it. It showed a picture of me seen from the side. When I shook my head, the picture shook its head. Then I looked at Grandpa Willis but watched the screen out of the corner of my eye, the picture of me looked straight out from the screen with its eyes looking to the side.

Mr. Slocum patted me on the shoulder again and explained. He said some recumbents took longer to adjust than others. He said my grandfather was that kind, that my grandfather was choosing to stay aware of his surroundings until he felt more comfortable. Adjustment, said Mr. Slocum, rarely lasted over a few days, never more than a week. My grandfather would soon adjust, relax, and begin to live out his golden tomorrows.

Mr. Slocum might have said some other things too. I don't know. Just looking at Grandpa Willis there in the tank with his eyes open and his face angry was getting me all upset again. I guess I was crying again, too, because the picture on the screen was crying, at least until Mr. Slocum touched the plate in the base of the tank and cut it off and started us back toward the front of the building.

I didn't want to leave Grandpa Willis, but I knew I had to, so I just kept looking back at his tank until the big doors closed and he was left in there with all those other floaters. After that I followed my parents and Mr. Slocum through the long, empty halls and kept wondering how come my parents put Grandpa Willis there instead of at home where he wanted to be. I kept seeing Grandpa Willis's angry face and hearing him bark, "*Ooahnaye!*"—which I finally understood—*who am I?* It was like his voice echoed off the walls of the place, louder than our footsteps echoed—*Ooahnaye!*

To my mother I guess Grandpa Willis was just a nuisance, an old man in the way. I know everybody puts old people in tank farms to get them out of the way and it's not important, but what if they don't want to be floaters? I think maybe my father knew what Grandpa Willis wanted and felt guilty about it but did it anyway. He never went to see Grandpa Willis again.

I did though. I went back by myself a lot all summer. I get upset every time I go, but I guess I'll keep going. Mr. Slocum said floaters adjust in a week. Every time I go back to see Grandpa Willis he's still there with his eyes open and he still looks angry. I guess all he's got that's real is that tank and the blue liquid and me coming to see him sometimes. I guess he's still fighting for what he believes in too, like always. I don't know why they did that to him.

When we got back to the lobby, Mr. Slocum asked if we had any questions and he looked at me in particular. I only had one, but I already knew the answer, and I was too upset to say anything and didn't want to anyway.

Mr. Slocum used all his effort again and smiled at me. "I hope this little visit has helped ease your mind about your grandfather, young man. He is alive and well. His golden tomorrows are ahead of him, any life he chooses. You don't ever have to concern yourself with him again."

*Stephen Robinett is thirty-four and lives in Los Angeles. At this moment he has written two published novels,* Stargate *and* The Man Responsible. *He will go on to publish more novels while working as an attorney and a business journalist before passing away on February 16, 2004, at the age of sixty-two.*

# HUNGER

## BY MAX BROOKS

*Max Brooks is one of the few writers able to effortlessly move between writing genre stories and mainstream geopolitical thrillers. His specialty is doing tons of research into real-world technology and political trends, which inevitably puts him five minutes ahead of everyone else. So this cautionary tale of political blackmail and ecoterrorism should be taken very seriously.*

To the President of the United States of America
The White House
Washington, DC

Mister President,

I write to you on a matter of grave urgency, regarding tonight's address to the American people. It has come to our attention that you intend to publicly declare your opposition to our unification with the rebel province across the Taiwan Strait. It has also come to our attention that, in conjunction with tonight's speech, you will order naval and air assets into said straits, as well as taking the unprecedented step of deploying ground forces into the province itself.

It saddens me personally, and alarms the entire world that you have chosen to risk armed confrontation over what is, and has always been, an internal matter. Make no mistake, Mister President, force of arms will not deter our liberation fleet, or our resolve to finally unite our long-divided nation. That is why I warn you, in clear, direct language, that if your forces reach Chinese waters and your speech reaches American ears, you and your people will suffer the horrendous consequences.

But what can we do to you? Isn't that the rhetorical question you will ask your people? Do not be surprised that we've already read the text of your speech. As we both know, there are no more secrets. We know that you intend to boast about your military might, highlighting certain weapon systems such as the B-21 Stealth Bomber, the F-40 Air Dominance Fighter, and the reborn Crusader self-propelled artillery system. We also know that these are just the tip of a very deep and deadly martial iceberg. We know that autoloading rail guns on your Ruben Rivers Main Battle Tanks can easily shred the armor on our VT-7s. We know that the upgraded HELCAP-3 lasers will allow your Constellation-Class frigates to incinerate our aging Stonefish anti-carrier ballistic missiles. We know that your X-37G unmanned spaceplanes carry enough hypersonic missiles to disintegrate every satellite we have on the first day of a conflict. And we also know that your fléchette-firing, autonomous Murder Hornet drones can launch from any platform, and swarm in such sun-blotting numbers that they would massacre our marines on Xialiao Beach.

We know that we could never hope to match you in a conventional, kinetic conflict. In fact, we've known this since the winter of 1991, when the legions of George H. W. Bush utterly atomized the world's fifth-largest army in barely one hundred hours. It wasn't a coincidence that this hyperslaughter was broadcast to the world on twenty-four-hour cable news. You wanted all your potential rivals, including us, to see exactly what would happen if we ever tried to challenge you on some future battlefield. Which is exactly why our post–Desert Storm strategy has been to avoid that battlefield at all costs.

To be sure, we embarked on a rapid, expensive, military modernization program, and we made sure to publicize every step of that program. From artificial island bases to the new Type-005 Aircraft Carriers to the J-22 fighters that streaked over our last "show of strength" parade in Tiananmen Square. And while these investments do have practical applications—guarding trade routes, influencing neighbors, and, of course, reunifying our homeland—when it came to America's war machine, our dragon's teeth were merely weapons of mass distraction. We wanted you to see and fear our "show of strength," the same way you wanted us to see and fear "the highway of death." We wanted you to obsess on a new Desert Storm, plan for it, train for it, and, above all, believe that we were doing the same.

And how ironic. As you continued to prepare for a new Cold War, you completely forgot how you won the old one. In his book, *Give War a Chance*, the late neoconservative P. J. O'Rourke wrote: "While they [the Warsaw Pact] may have had the soldiers and the warheads, the West ultimately achieved victory with Levi 501 jeans, Sony Walkmans, and Paula Abdul videos. Now they're lunch," O'Rourke crowed, "and we're number one on the planet." And his assessment was so accurate that it inspired our strategy to make you, in his words, "taste the ash heap of history."

While you've been consumed with the next generation of attack helicopter or hunter-killer submarine, we've were pioneering alternatives such as cyber warfare, economic warfare, information warfare, and how to synchronize them into a cohesive strategy. And we did it in the light of day. No subterfuge, no *maskirovka*. Two of our finest minds, colonels Liang and Xiangsui, even published our intentions in a document that was readily available on Amazon. "Ten Thousand Methods Combined as One." That was chapter 7 of their book, *Unrestricted Warfare*. If only more Americans had bothered to read it. But there were just so many Netflix shows to binge, so many TikTok videos to make. What did the journalist Thomas L. Friedman once observe about our two peoples? "In China, Bill Gates is Britney Spears. In America, Britney Spears is Britney Spears."

Like the French in the 1930s, you failed to see how easy it was to circumvent your Maginot Line. And like Guderian's panzers, our weapon is right in front you, and has been all along. When P. J. O'Rourke referred to the defeated Soviets as "lunch," he had no idea how prophetic he was, because our not-so-secret weapon is the removal of a resource as simple, primal, and as vital as the air we breathe. If you decide to defend Taiwan, Mister President, we will shock and awe your people with hunger.

Try to control your laughter, and your urge to delete the remainder of this message. It must seem comical that my country, which has often struggled to feed its citizens, could even think of threatening the "land of plenty." Not only is your country so bountiful that morbid obesity has reached epidemic levels; it also holds the unique honor of being the only great power in world history that has never been vulnerable to famine. In fact, even during the darkest days of your civil war, you still grew enough surplus grain to export it to Great Britain. This fact was not lost on our strategic planners, who initially dismissed food blackmail as one of our ten thousand methods.

Until 2013, when your Supreme Court ruled in *Bowman v. Monsanto* that genetically modified seeds were "intellectual property," no different than songs or software. And like songs or software, it was therefore illegal to copy them without permission. Just think about that for a moment, Mister President. Think about what that meant for farmers all over the world.

Since the dawn of the agricultural revolution, those who work the land have been setting aside a portion of their harvest for the next season's planting. Now, according to your Supreme Court, replanting those copies of the original, patented, Monsanto seeds would be the equivalent of intellectual piracy. This meant that every planting season customers would need to purchase these "self-replicating technologies" directly from Monsanto. Imagine what that meant to the financial security of individual farms, as well as the food security of your entire nation?

No one did, however. No one in your Supreme Court, your government, or the public at large (what few actually heard or cared about this story). No one seemed capable of imagining the long-term ramifications. The American Right, as usual, was so greedy and callous that they were more than happy to watch one of their mammoth corporations crush the livelihood of small, family businesses. Meanwhile, the American Left, as usual, was so disorganized and incompetent that it focused all its energy on the potential health risks of genetically modified food. No one realized, in 2013, that this level of agricultural dependency left your country as vulnerable to blackmail as the 1973 OPEC oil embargo. We realized this, however, and so we bided our time for the perfect opportunity to strike.

And that opportunity came in 2016, when Monsanto was sold to the German conglomerate Bayer. We couldn't believe our luck, or your stupidity! Where were your safeguards? Where was the Committee on Foreign Investment in the United States? You originally created this panel of twelve federal agencies for the specific purpose of regulating private transactions that might someday threaten the security of your nation. Where were they? Where was the same congress that, in 2006, voted 62–2 to block a Middle Eastern company from taking control of six major seaports? How could they be so vigilant over critical infrastructure and so utterly daft when it came to their stomachs?

As I've previously stated, we could not believe our good fortune, and from 2016 onward, all we had to do was rely on our culture's most powerful asset: patience. We waited as the organic food craze rose in America and Europe, and riots raged through the rural villages of India. We waited while our policy of banning GMO foods altogether sent shock waves through the boardrooms in Leverkusen. We waited patiently for the right moment to make an attractive offer to Bayer, and when we did, the Germans were more than happy to sell.

Again, we were astonished at your apathy, your head-spinning lack of concern. Yes, Monsanto was sold to a "private" company. But what would it take to convince you that, while American corporations saw themselves as global, Chinese companies were Chinese. Even if our state has the power to force its merchants to kowtow, that power is rarely ever used. Our people still love their country. They still know what it means to serve a higher calling. Monsanto's new corporate mandarins willingly and eagerly embraced their role as loyal patriots on a great crusade.

And that is why they have been doing everything possible to tighten our grip on your heartland. As far back as 2016, genetically modified crops accounted for over half of all US farmland, roughly 170 million acres, with crops including 95 percent of all soybeans and 80 percent of maize. The latter was of particular interest to us, as it was so deeply embedded in your society—animal feed, sweeteners, plastics, and, above all, the holy grail of biofuels. How ironic that, in your attempt to become independent of the Arabs, you made yourselves even more dependent on us.

Not that you noticed, as Monsanto slowly devoured your amber waves of grain. Sometimes we cashed in on customer debts. It had worked so well in India. Sometimes we simply bought out the competition. More than a few times we relied heavily on absurd, almost comical court rulings that genetically modified pollen that found its way into non-Monsanto fields could somehow be classified as copyright infringement. The lunacy. The insipid self-destruction. When it came to suing stubborn family holdings out of existence, the answer turned out to be, to quote Bob Dylan, "Blowin' in the Wind."

Lawsuits, buyouts, bankruptcies. Wheat, barley, rye. But for me, the greatest personal victory was not what grew on the fruited plains but under them. Potatoes, Mister President. Another tragic lost lesson from history. I still cannot believe that one of your most numerous and dynamic ethnic groups, Irish Americans, don't know the true details of what drove their tribe from the Emerald Isle. They might know about the potato famine, but how many know that if their ancestors had only diversified their potato strains, instead of relying on a monocrop of "Irish Lumpers," their sustenance might have escaped the blight? I often wondered if there were any nineteenth-century agronomists or even forward-thinking peasants who tried to sound the alarm. And if there were, did anyone listen?

No one has in America. And why would they? Even if we remove the greed and willful ignorance of your present-day culture, it has never been easy to wrest a living from the soil. I still remember reading your 2018 Center for Disease Control and Prevention's breakdown of suicide rates by profession, and how American farmers came in first. Why shouldn't they be as grateful for one of our high-yielding, drought-pest-disease-resistant miracle seeds, as the Irish of old were grateful for their Lumpers? My grandfather would have been grateful for anything to ward off the famine of 1943, when his little village in Henan was reduced to eating all their animals, then the insects, then another, desperate source of protein. To his dying day, he never ate pork. "Too familiar," he called it.

What a contrast from your family, the frozen-food barons whose fortune allowed you to rise to power. What a lucrative product were those TV dinners. Of course, what your family was really selling was comfort, laziness, and isolation. Gone was the care and community of cooking a family meal, replaced by disposable plates on folding trays in front of a glowing screen. How fitting that your country's slogan used to be "do your part," because your family certainly did their part in planting the seeds of American decline.

And now the harvest is upon you, Mister President, the moment I warned you about at the beginning of this communiqué. If you make your speech tonight, your country will wake up tomorrow to our declaration of a comprehensive, immediate, seed embargo.

And, to turn the mirror on your speeches, "What can you do about it?"

Dip into your reserve seed supply? If only you had one. Since the 1990s, your entire national security network has been trending toward last-minute purchases from the private sector. No more expensive warehouses of supplies. No more inefficient bureaucracy to oversee them. "The era of big government is over," declared President Clinton in his pathetic attempt to capture the fading light of Ronald Reagan. That is why, to this day, your Defense Logistics Agency has had to scramble for eleventh-hour materiel from big box stores. That is why, in the early days of COVID-19, you found yourself with such a lethal dearth of personal protective equipment.

That pandemic should have taught, or retaught, you the lesson of paying back into a federal insurance policy. That is what so many of us were worried about in the 2020s. The Biden administration did try so valiantly to "secure our domestic supply chain." So much so that we anticipated our purchase of Monsanto would galvanize you into creating a Strategic Seed Reserve, the same way the OPEC embargo spawned your Strategic Petroleum Reserve.

But, fortunately for us, subsequent administrations managed to roll back Biden's meager progress. And that regression, coupled with your grocery-store model of choosing fresh, same-day delivery items over preserved products, ensures that your supply chain is far from secure.

You might try purchasing essential foodstuffs from other countries, but which ones? Canada? They are just as dependent on Monsanto seeds and therefore just as vulnerable to blackmail as you. Brazil? That teetering, quasi-autocracy is our most loyal client state. They may not love us, but rest assured, they hate you. The remaining contenders, all European, might have helped, if their once mighty union still existed. But now these squabbling principalities need our trade deals as badly as they need natural gas from our friends in Moscow.

You can try a more direct approach and simply take what you want, in a modern-day version of the Carter Doctrine. If that supposed dove could declare that military force would be used to secure Middle Eastern oil, why not you, an avid hawk, declare the same for midwestern grain? But if you tried, your prize would be only ashes.

As we speak, Monsanto security personnel are preparing to burn every stockpile from Maine to California. All of them were trained at the Erik Prince school of asymmetric warfare in Xinjiang. All of them know what is at stake. One word from us, or at the first sign of trouble, and there won't be enough grains of rice or kernels of corn left to put in a flowerpot.

And we will blame you for it! "American mobs loot and burn Monsanto silos across the country." That will be the story from our American media outlets, with each voice tailored to their specific market. The Left will be told that white supremacist militias are responding to our embargo with "racist, Asian hate," while the Right will hear that the culprits are "anti-corporate ecoterrorists." We even have digital actors, deep fakes, ready to scream into cameras as the flames rise up behind them. These videos were produced months ago, in concert with the second wave of stories about how America "now faces starvation."

And *faces* is the key word, Mister President, because the truth is that none of your people would have to starve. Our Guanbo red teams have literally run millions of simulations over the last ten years, and in all that time, not one American has perished from an empty belly. The main reason being your diversity. I speak, of course, about climate diversity and the staggered nature of your agricultural cycles. Even if our embargo goes into effect tomorrow, there are already plenty of crops in the ground today. When these fields are combined with organic farms, an emergency victory garden program, a trickle of foreign aid, and a nationwide, disciplined rationing program, your populace wouldn't suffer anything more than a prolonged "crash diet."

But that is not what would happen, my arrogant, gluttonous American friend. From Xiyuan's exhaustive war-gaming, we have determined that anywhere between several thousand to several million Americans will die in the ensuing months. Not from hunger but from the fear of hunger. You see, Mister President, while you Americans have always been an isolationist, inward-looking people, the rest of the world has been studying you with rapt attention. From the West Coast riots following Pearl Harbor to the infamous run on toilet paper in the first phase of COVID-19, you have always been prime targets for hysteria. That is why we have determined that the greatest weapon we can unleash against America is sheer blind panic.

Our media outlets will bombard Americans with an onslaught of endless conspiracy theories. We will tell the Left that "the millionaire and billionaire classes" are hoarding precious provisions at the expense of "marginalized communities," while the Right will hear that the "deep state" is giving those provisions away to minorities, illegal immigrants, and other undeserving "takers."

And there is nothing you can do about it. Because you've already done it to yourselves. You have been consistently dividing and dumbing down your own people for selfish, shortsighted gain. From education cuts to deregulated media, you have slowly turned a clearly thinking, iron-spined civilization into a flock of gullible, jittery dullards. "Don't trust anyone over thirty," "Fake news," and my personal favorite, "They're coming for you."

Wasn't that your favorite catchphrase, when you were a much younger, much thinner, cable news personality? How many times did you terrorize your adoring fans with tales of impending doom? How many minds did you melt with exaggerations, wild stories posed as questions, and out-and-out lies to keep them coming back each night? Your parents might have sold sloth and complacency, but you sold fear and hate. And now, as the saying goes, you will reap what you have sewn. Even if you manage to convince a fraction of those citizens still loyal to you, they only make up a fraction of all Americans. Thanks to decades of voter suppression, you now only have direct influence over barely 20 percent of your population.

The rest will descend into chaos—looting stores, pillaging farms, sniping from their homes at anyone they suspect is "coming for them." And they will do it with the highest-grade military firearms. Who do you think saved the National Rifle Association from bankruptcy? We did. Who do you think sells 51.7 percent of semiautomatic guns, conversion kits, and tactical gear to your citizens? We do. And while the profits have enriched many of our citizens over the years, the real reason for pushing so hard to arm you is that we knew, someday, you would turn those arms on each other. If you're lucky, the violence will be contained to the citizenry itself—race against race, mob against mob, neighbor against neighbor. But if you're not, as the war-gamers in Xiyuan predict, you may find yourself with a full-blown insurgency on your hands. If we laughed when you referred to January 6 Capitol rioters as "tourists," we will positively howl when those tourists return with Norinco assault rifles.

Of course, you may recover, at least as a shadow of your former self. But by the time the smoke clears, our flag will be flying over Taipei, and we will be dancing in our streets while you wash the blood from yours.

These are the consequences that I now lay out for you, Mister President, along with two very clear options. Please take ample time to consider them. As I send this, the time in Washington is exactly 1:05 p.m. For this reason, I would encourage you to wait until you've finished your lunch. As we both know, you think more clearly on a full stomach.

*Max Brooks, forty, is a senior fellow at the Modern War Institute at West Point, New York, and the author of* World War Z. *He is also an actor and a military historian, and lives in Santa Monica with his wife, Michelle Kholos. His future is yet to be revealed.*

# INTERMEZZO 1:
# BROKEN, BEAUTIFUL BODY ON BEACH

## BY D. M. ROWLES

It was a beautiful body. Six of them found it early, lying very still, soaking the sand around it. Long, shimmering limbs bent at a dozen sharp angles, not at all touched by the slick, thick ooze that coated all other shoreward-drifting objects. Even the wings—a soggy, trailing mass of blue, lavender, and rosy shades from shoulder to hip—were free of the slime.

The six, nameless and scabrous, ringed the broken, beautiful form and quibbled over rights of possession.

One saw it first.

One reached it first.

One touched it first.

One wanted it first.

One named it first.

One claimed it first.

The six, nameless and scabrous, walked every morning on this filthy strip of sand searching through the cast-up castoffs of the rest of that world.

It was a beautiful body. Six of them found it early, part of its face pressed deeply into the sand. The right cheek, ear, and forehead-to-eye were thin, elongated, and shimmering in the dull light. (No sun would break the slate-gray smoke of atmosphere—at best would lighten to linty soft gray.) Six of them, huddling and hidden in the remnants of no one's clothing, ringed the shattered, shining form and questioned its origin.

One thought it a bird.

One thought it a costly toy.

One thought it a botched experiment.

One thought it a discarded sculpture.

One thought it a disease victim.

One thought it an angel.

The six, nameless and scabrous, existing here outside time and rules, had walked this strip of beach so long they had forgotten why, until they found the lovely, broken thing face down and oil-free, soaking the sand and shimmering in the no-light of a hidden sun.

It was a beautiful body. Six of them stood marveling at it most of the day. The skull was curved and rose-veined and fragile looking. Small scavenger ants roamed over it, some of them traveling the rose veins like highways.

The six, nameless and scabrous and lonely, ringed the wonderful drift creature and began to hate it.

One kicked it.

One spat on it.

One tore out huge handfuls of the wet, fragrant wings.

One threw sand on the right side of its face.

One crushed the long, thin fingers.

One cried.

The six, nameless and scabrous and lost, built a big fire from the oily refuse, and picking up the shimmering thing—how light it was!— tossed it onto the blaze. It burned to ash in seconds, in flames of blue, lavender, and rosy shades and smelled very sweet, very clean.

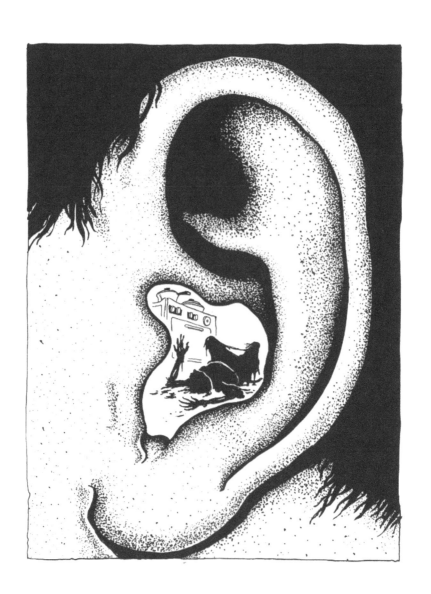

# NONE SO DEAF

## BY RICHARD E. PECK

*Post-traumatic stress disorder hits no two people in the same way. For some, "the world is suddenly too much with us," as Wordsworth wrote. For others, the world must be pushed away, shunned, and silenced. This is a story about what happens in the latter case . . .*

Warren Patterson could hear. He could hear because he was deaf. Thus, his story begins in paradox. It ends no less paradoxically. Between beginning and end, mounted on the wall of his basement listening room, hangs a plaque. It reads: "In the country of the deaf, the one-eared man is ?????"

Patterson composed that enigmatic statement scant weeks after his wife's death, after the onset of his deafness, after the onset of his new hearing, and after discovering his unique talent.

"Compensation," the doctor wrote on the slate he carried. He held it before Patterson's eyes and paused to see whether Warren understood.

He did. They had been telling him that for days now. His hearing was gone—psychosomatic, they told him—but he would develop compensating skills, or senses; that part wasn't clear. Patterson refused the offer of the slate. He had no answer to give. He merely felt foolish, trapped in a silence whose origin he understood but could do nothing to change. He managed a wan smile of agreement.

The doctor shrugged and left the room. There was nothing more to be done, not for someone who refused even to speak, someone who didn't want to help himself.

Patterson didn't. Rachel had died because of his metaphorical deafness. Puttering in his basement workshop, as always, he had tuned out her monologue. Somewhere in the back of his mind he knew she was speaking to him through the open kitchen door above, but he heard nothing of what she said—her complaints, questions, remarks all merged into white noise. Her voice was the background against which Warren regarded his own thoughts. He didn't consciously hear her screams, until they stopped, and silence called attention to itself. He found her then on the kitchen floor, beside the gas range, her black hair gone to wisps of silver ash clinging to the blistered, swollen flesh. She was no longer screaming.

They had brought him here, to this room, to the many useless explanations. He didn't hear them, though he understood perfectly. He would never hear anything again. He had chosen not to listen once before; they said he was still choosing not to hear. He agreed, and shrugged, and dwelt in silence. Dressing to leave the hospital, he accidentally dropped a shoe to the floor and thought of the old joke. Intentionally, he dropped the other shoe. It bounced, noiselessly. He left the hospital and nodded to the receptionist. Her carmine lips moved in slow motion; the cords in her neck stood out in bold relief: she was articulating clearly, loudly, for his benefit. He saw that, though he had no idea what she said. He smiled in response to the impulse behind her effort.

Outside, he began to appreciate the affliction for the first time. Though traffic filled the street, he was spared the raucous, honking din. He began to see noises: the heel of a hand pounding a steering-wheel horn ring; bristles of a broom scratching the damp pavement before a fish market; the livid face of a traffic cop waggling one meaty finger at a stalled car. He stood watching.

A blow at his back hurled him to the sidewalk. He scrambled to his feet and whirled to see a teenager, a boy whose fingers snapped in time to a private melody: the boy wore an earplug, twisted the dial of a transistor radio strap slung from his shoulder, and walked on in blindness.

*Call it compensation*, Patterson thought. Drowned in noise of his own choosing, the boy hadn't seen him. One sense overloaded, another canceled out. Each man has his own fixation. Patterson debated shouting at the boy but recognized a dilemma. Would he hear, inside his mind, whatever sounds his voice might make? He didn't want to know.

He walked home along three miles of ghost-ridden streets.

He carried to the basement what few items he thought necessary to his new life: a cot, clothes, a hot plate, boxes and cartons and cans from the kitchen cupboards, a dictionary (he never knew why), and a can opener. Then he took a maul and hatchet from the workbench and climbed to the attic. Moving downward from attic to first floor, he destroyed the contents of the house, carefully, methodically, one room at a time, reducing to rubble every piece of furniture, every fixture. He smashed mirrors to black and shimmering snowflakes fluttering silently to the floor. He tore to shreds all of Rachel's clothes. His hands felt differences: corduroy ripped with a soft, mushy pout; velvet puckered, gathered, puffed in his hands as if fighting its destruction; cotton pulled into neat strips; silk resisted his strength, and he haggled it to scraps with the hatchet blade. The bed was easy. He imagined the groan of splintering wood but didn't hear it; in a sweating frenzy, he tore at the mattress and scattered cotton batting over the rolling, bouncing springs. His maul bounded off the bathtub as if alive in his hands; half-moons of black winked back at him from the dented, fractured white. Extension cords spat blue sparks at his hatchet blade: once. Then they were dead, and chopped into tinier lengths of deadness. None of the destruction made a sound.

Warren Patterson retired to his basement. Within days, he had divided the dank space into two rooms: a large room for eating and sleeping, a smaller cubicle for listening. He lined the cubicle with light-bulbs, all four walls and ceiling covered with light (he had once read about a room like that), a perfect place for solitary listening. In his listening room, he sat silent for one hour each day, until the heat from the hundreds of bulbs drove him sweating from that cubicle. He heard nothing—as he expected—but considered it his obligation to make the daily test. Each day he came from his lighted cubicle, smiling, washed the sweat from his hands and face, and took a brief walk around his neighborhood.

The pattern of his life reassured him, until the day the pattern was broken.

On the twenty-fifth of May, Rachel's birthday, Warren was unable to listen for his accustomed hour. The room oppressed him strangely. Nervous, disturbed, he left for his walk earlier than usual. He passed the grade school as the children were arriving. He watched their shouts of joy, saw blushes, anger, lassitude, discomfort imprisoned in patent-leather shoes or circled by a tight collar. He saw the crossing guard's officious comments, noticed children, big-eyed, hero-worshipping, heed the warnings. All but one.

A small boy, no more than six or seven, ducked beneath the out-stretched warning arms and dashed into the street, into the traffic, into the side of a moving truck, where he lifted in a silent spiral to float on the morning sunshine for a long moment before falling at Warren's feet like a sack of crushed grapes. His life splattered the sidewalk, blind eyes stared up at Warren, broken jaw flapped and clattered noiselessly.

Patterson backed away from the obscenity at his feet. Others ran to surround the body. Children gathered. A teacher came from the schoolyard. Motorists stopped to swell the gathering crowd. Patterson saw the faces. Faces all around. On some, here and there, the look of pain, discomfort, hints of pity, but, most of all, curiosity. Simple curiosity.

He saw the faces and wheeled to run. He managed two strides before he heard it. Screaming. The boy's screaming, in his mind's ear. And all the pain he'd ever known swelled in that sound: shattered glass, screeching brakes, the wail of animals at slaughter, fingernails on blackboards, prayers and pleas and pain expressed in wordless, keening agony. It all assaulted Patterson and drove him cowering to his knees.

Still he heard. Couldn't hear, but heard: pain and terror mingling in his head. He clapped futile hands over deaf ears, but the sound swelled louder. He had begun to hear again.

The same doctor explained to Patterson, this time on a steno pad, "It was only a reaction to your wife's death. A delayed reaction. Won't happen again."

Warren nodded. That was the best way. So long as they believed the screaming had stopped, they would let him go home. No more cold baths, no more shock therapy, no more sympathetic glances past him at the other doctors in the room. He wrote on the pad: "Yes. Thank you. All gone now."

Writing was difficult. He had to steel himself against flinching, as the screams marked time in his head like a metronome of pain. But he was learning. Expected, rhythmic, regular, the screams were not impossible to withstand. He could not ignore them—he would never again be able to ignore them—but he could function; he could appear to others not to hear the sounds.

"We don't hear anything, do we?" one of the nurses mouthed at him. He shook his head. His mind answered, *No, you don't hear anything, do you?*

Again, they dismissed him, after exacting a promise that he would return whenever he began to feel tired or imagined any sounds out of the ordinary.

He agreed. With a clear conscience, he promised, for the screams he heard—he had already recognized—were not "out of the ordinary." They were a most ordinary phenomenon indeed—the very essence of life itself, whether or not anyone but he attended to them.

At home, Warren Patterson coined a cliché and painted it on an old cedar shingle, which he hung in his listening room: "In the country of the deaf, the one-eared man is ?????"

There were several sources for his slogan, analogues to it, but none of them completed the equation in a way he could accept. What does it mean to be the only one who hears?

The daily hour in his listening room stretched to three, then four. The scream sounded fainter as he grew accustomed to it, till one day he found himself anticipating, waiting for the sound, hoping for it, marking time through silences that echoed louder than the boy's pain did.

He left his house and went collecting sounds, sounds only he could hear. A wino rummaging through the trash gave off a guttural drone. Warren added it to memory and filled a portion of the silence in his mind. From a hospital whose corridors he wandered, till a doctor made him leave, he gathered whimpers, anger, pain of various tones. He knew them all as different: death in childbirth has an anguish, while a heart's simple failure is a flutter less of pain than of bewilderment.

In his mind, a symphony was building, theme announced, then dropped to reappear in concert with a counterstatement. It was not enough. As though in equal ratio, silence swelled as well, but not relief. Each added pain brought surcease from an earlier cry and left him longing, Faustian, to know it all.

"Compensation," they had said. His came in unexpected fashion: He grew able to recall old agonies of which he'd read, or heard, or which he could recollect. His mind ranged time and distance and, each hour of his quest, found new examples of the pain or terror never heard, ignored, or disregarded at its birth. Places named themselves: My Lai, Bataan, and Waterloo, Gethsemane—persons too: Vanzetti, King, and Savonarola, Swift, Iscariot.

When the time had done, and all the names exhausted, all the pains of history compiled, collected, added to, augmented—when for the first time all the hurt and sorrow, all the anguished cries of humankind were really heard as though a single sound, he opened wide his mouth and uttered it.

The onslaught of that scream destroyed the world. Riven, shattered, blackened pieces of the world returned to chaos.

But only—of course—for Warren Patterson.

*Richard E. Peck, thirty-eight, received his AB degree at Carroll College and his PhD at the University of Washington. He will go on to teach at the University of Alabama and Arizona State, and attain the position of Professor Emeritus Field(s) in the American literary studies department of the University of New Mexico while still dedicating his time to writing stories, novels, scripts, poetry, and plays.*

# ED BRYANT'S "WAR STORIES"

## BY HARLAN ELLISON

One of my pet theories about Life is that we all share certain small things in our past, and writing about those easily forgotten, easily remembered similarities causes a frisson of recognition that unites us through the wonder of Art. We all remember a particularly meaningful holiday meal at Grandma's house, during which something happened that sent us skittering across the line from childhood into adolescence. We all remember the first abortive kiss that it took us weeks to work up to with a now vaguely remembered love object. We all remember how we felt when we got our first Social Security card. We all remember the first time we heard Gershwin's *Rhapsody in Blue*. (Bill Venable's house in Pittsburgh, circa 1953, lying half asleep across a bed, fully clothed and whacked-out from having driven nonstop from Cleveland: magical melody unforgettably filtering through the fog.)

And we all share the memory of getting a report card from school on which the "Attitude Toward Observing Rules" box was sullied with the word *poor*. Don't lie to me—you had a rotten attitude toward "the rules," even as did I. Had I not developed that poor attitude toward authority and following the rules almost before I was yanked squalling from my bassinet, I would not have been thrown out of Ohio State University after a year and a half, I would not have been court-martialed three times while serving with the US Army (1957–1959), I would not have wound up on Ronald Reagan's enemies list when he was governor of California . . . and you would not now be reading "War Stories" by Edward Bryant.

One of the unbreakable rules of the *Dangerous Visions* books has been (and was always, from the outset) that no writer who appeared in one volume could be represented in another. Oh, I weaseled from time to time in that I might include three Gene Wolfe stories under an umbrella title in *Again, Dangerous Visions*, but no one who saw print in *DV* was repeated in *A,DV*. Nor are any of the people to be found in those two books on line here in *TLDV*.

Uh, except for Ed Bryant.

This unbreakable rule, most sacrosanct of all the format rules I set up to make the *DV* books distinctive, is herewith crunched.

Now why, you may ask, is this holiest of holies being so cavalierly set aside for Bryant? Go ahead—ask. I'll wait. (All together, in unison, a cappella, *Why is this etcetera of etcetera . . .*")

In *Again, Dangerous Visions*, Mr. Bryant had a story called "The 10:00 Report Is Brought to You By . . ." Nice enough story. Not as remarkable as either of his Nebula award winners—"Stone" (1979), "giANTS" (1980)—or "Shark" or "The Hibakusha Gallery" or "Particle Theory" (which critic Barry Malzberg listed as one of the ten finest stories of the decade of the seventies in his book of essays *Engines of the Night*; which he then said might well be the best of the decade). But a nice little story.

Now, everybody in the world knows that Ed and I are best friends. What used to be called chums. Buddies. Pals. And everybody in the world knows that Bryant and I rib each other quite a lot. I'll say something brilliantly cutting about his lank mop of Sioux-style hair, an anachronistic manifestation of his being a sixties burnout. And he'll say something vaguely amusing about my having contracted herpes from a Jacqueline Lichtenberg novel. I'll comment on his ability to make even the dullest bon mot a hilarious event worthy of such great humorists as Martin Luther, Anita Bryant, and James Watt simply by his deadpan delivery; and he'll come allover cranky and tell everyone I'm a short person.

Like that.

So I, er, wrote this introduction to his story in which I . . . well, I guess I went a bit too far. It was all in good fun, you understand. Amusing badinage. The references to odious bodily fluids, necrophilia, slovenliness, pustules, pederasty, aboriginal sounds in the dead of night, and assorted feral behaviors . . . all intended as a giggle. You see what I mean?

Bryant even saw the intro before it went in to the publisher and, though his strange little face (you know those sculptures they make from shrunken apple cores?) got all wrinkled up, he okayed it. And so it was printed. All in fun.

And the next time Ed went home to see his family in Wheatland, Wyoming, he was walking down the street, and his family's minister, who'd known Ed since he was a homunculus, took him by the ear and upbraided him royally for being such a degenerate person, not to mention a bad houseguest.

So Ed called me in a medium-high dudgeon, and said I'd ruined his reputation as one of the sweetest guys around, and what did I intend to do about it? Ellison, huh, what? And I felt real bad, as we say in California. I hurt allover for my friend, chum, buddy, pal. And on the spot I did the only thing I could do to indicate to him that I was genuinely repentant. I told him I'd break the unbreakable rule and permit him to be the only writer in two *DV* books. And I said I'd write a new introduction that would set the record straight, that would bail him out in the view of those whose opinions he valued. I said I'd tell nothing but good stories about him. About his many unstinting efforts on behalf of young writers. About his excellent books *Particle Theory* and *Cinnabar*. About the respect in which he is held by the best writers of our generation who think of him as a singular talent on the highest level of craft.

About his friendship, his courage, his wit, his steadfastness, his frugality and tidiness.

I promised not to speak about the fish, the wet towels, the coat hangers, the vibrators, the Mae West garter belt, or the peculiar eczema one notices between the fingers of his right hand.

And so, having rectified my overabundantly puckish remarks in the previous volume, I now commend to your attention "War Stories," an introduction (if his work has escaped your notice by some foul spell cast upon you) to the man I am proud to call my friend, the man whom the Chicago police department calls "the natural successor to Gilles de Rais," my buddy chum pal, Edward Winslow Bryant Jr.

Now isn't that all better?

# WAR STORIES

## BY EDWARD BRYANT

### I. THE DREAM OF THE PELAGIC WOMAN

The image of Chuang Tzu's butterfly haunts her all during the drive through the mountains and down across the high plains: *Am I a philosopher dreaming that I am a butterfly; or a butterfly philosopher?* She can visualize the butterfly, but it is dead. It is a purple emperor, wings iridescent as though covered with jeweled scales. The butterfly bobs on the surface of a tidal pool surrounded by a worn barrier of coral. Almost imperceptibly, the moon tugs at sodden wings, which never will beat again.

The tide inexorably pours in. Shortly the pool will brim, and the butterfly will wash into the sea. *I cannot be a butterfly dreaming, for the butterfly is dead.* She has always possessed a stratum of eminent rationality.

The sky, dark all day, has lowered until it engulfs the land all around her. The snow begins, thick flakes that do not melt when they land. The road quickly becomes a tabula rasa. In the mirror, she watches the tires write a filigree pattern of esses. To stop the car from fishtailing, she slows it to a bare crawl. She had not really expected winter, at least not so soon. But it is a volatile country.

Three hours: there has been no other traffic, she is exhausted, the fuel indicator lies on empty. An exit sign appears from the dusk, and she accepts its cue.

The neon letters are unlighted; they spell out "Rock Creek Station." The woman gets out of the car and stretches cramped muscles. The pain is welcome, but dulls quickly in the chill air. The snow is silent; there is no wind. She wonders if perhaps the station is abandoned, but then an elderly man shuffles from the building and asks if she wants the tank filled. She nods and enters the station.

Another man, middle-aged and weather-reddened, stands behind the counter. "Going west?" he says. His voice grates.

She nods. "To the coast."

"Terrible weather."

She resents even this innocuous attempt at communication. She pretends not to hear and inspects the countertop covered with imported trinkets. A piece of stone attracts her attention; it is flat and reddish-brown, about as large as her hand. She hesitates, then picks it up curiously.

"Fish fossil," says the man. "This all used to be underwater, you know."

"The sea is a thousand miles away," she says.

"Didn't used to be. Maybe a hundred and fifty million years ago, they say. Ocean used to be right here. What'd they call it?" His face screws up as he tries to remember. "Joorassic. The Jurassic Sea."

*Combers curl and writhe, flinging themselves among the phantom desert buttes. The surf pours across the vast wastes, sucking thirstily at the sand as it once did, as it always has.*

The sharp, curved tooth is etched in the rock. The woman traces it with her finger. She ignores the price scribbled across the fossil with grease pencil.

*The tide rushes across the desert. The sea possesses its old domain.*

"Miss! Miss, what's the matter?" The man steps out from behind the counter.

His partner enters the station, whuffing and clapping his hands together for warmth. "What happened?"

"Damned if I know. Just standing there and she keeled over." He kneels beside her and gently touches her forehead with the back of his hand. "She's burning up."

She seeks out the thermocline and rides it like a roller coaster, planing first into the warmer water above, and then the colder water below. She glides through the void, head moving slowly from side to side. The rhythm of her body is slow and constant.

Hungry, she turns back toward land. She approaches four small islands that form a minor chain in this tropical sea. She has visited these islands before, and there has been trouble. But she is ravenous.

A small tuna, only two meters long, loafs in the shallows under the lee of the smallest island. It strokes along stupidly, looking for the smaller fish it would itself devour. The tuna swims a single fathom below the dazzling interface between water and air.

Like a ghost, the shark strikes from beneath. All instinct now, an effortless burst of power brings her in range. As if by magic, a five-kilo gobbet of meat is scooped from the tuna's side. Shredded snippets of intestine wave slowly like red sea fronds. By gulps, the tuna disappears. A few remnants, too small for the shark to consider, drift to the bottom; scavengers will finish them off.

She circles restlessly through the curtain of blood, still hungry.

A shadow plows the surface. The shark, distracted by the pure sensuality of feeding, does not yet notice. Not until the bronze tip of the harpoon burns into her hide, lodging behind the head. Her body convulses; her tail whips frantically. The dart shakes loose and is drawn away by its line.

Another harpoon is thrust down. Passing close by her head, the dart leaves a trail of silver bubbles. Savagely, she seizes the metal shank in her jaws. When she lets it go, the steel is bent.

*Not-food. Leave alone.*

She executes a tight roll and slides away. The shadow pursues her. She recognizes the pressure waves generated by the engine: it is a motorized skiff. She has encountered it before. The last time, she fled. But now—

*Hunger.*

At full speed, she angles toward the surface, her course intersecting the keel of the skiff. Traveling at twenty knots, her tough, cartilaginous skull smashes the wood. The skiff capsizes, and the occupant is hurled into the sea.

She sees it is a man in the water.

*The smell of his fear is palpable.*

"Hyperexia."

"What?" says the older station attendant.

"Fever," the doctor says. "One hundred and four. Get some ice."

"That'll be easy," says the other attendant. He puts on his windbreaker.

"You're lucky I stopped," says the doctor. "She's in a bad way."

"Is she gonna be all right?"

"I don't know. There's no way an ambulance can get here from the city, not with the storm." He removes the elastic strip from the woman's upper arm and replaces it in his bag. He shakes his head slowly. "Temperature's elevated, heartbeat's irregular, and there's an incredible variation in her blood pressure. Aspirin and cold packs—that's all we have until the storm ends."

For hours they sit around her: talking, drinking coffee, smoking, watching her. Periodically, the doctor takes readings with his instruments.

"Temperature's down slightly. Blood pressure's still variable. I don't understand it."

And he still can't understand it much later, in the reassuring sterility of his own hospital, when he feeds the data into the terminal of the

Trauma Control Information Bank. The meaning of the pattern of the readings continues to escape him. He punches "Random Retrieval."

The printout says, "Consult the Ephemeris," and gives a digital reference.

The doctor does so and discovers he is consulting a tidal table. Puzzled, he charts two sets of figures. The curves coincide. The doctor shuts the book slowly, thinking circadian thoughts.

But that is for the future. In the present—

He waits in desperate ignorance. Just before dawn, the woman's eyes open. Blue and lucid, they stare through the doctor.

"It is Chuang Tzu who is not real," she says, and her eyes again close. Outside, the blizzard winds batter the station. *The Jurassic Sea surges across the plains, filling the ancient void.*

*The shark flows through the sea. And there, words break down . . . how can simple words describe the fluidity and power and security that constitute the concept of shark. They cannot, and so there are only subsidiary descriptions, clues for those who are not shark.*

She will not approach land again soon. Instinctively, she charts a pelagic course for the deep ocean. She encounters a glittering shoal of tiny cherubfish, and they give way before her. She quickly leaves them behind.

She is implacable in the silence.

\* \* \*

## II. TALE FOR A YET UNBORN CHILD

Once upon a time, a very important intelligence agent waded in the sandy white shallows off a southern beach resort. She splashed about happily, enjoying the grainy textures beneath her toes. A finely trained and conscientious spy, her concentration was focused on the distant prison camps that brooded below the lighthouse on the point. When she blinked in a particular manner, the camera in her skull recorded a telescopic, high-resolution image.

She took another dozen crabwise steps to seaward, and the warm water lapped about her shoulders. She reveled in the sensuality of the experience and even forgot for a moment that she was a spy. Then she heard the shouts from the beach. The agent looked away from the camps; on the shore, people were yelling something and waving frantically. They gestured at the sea behind her.

"Shark!" The single word pierced the distorting sea breeze.

She turned to see a very large and apparently very hungry great white shark streaking through the water toward her. A heavy fan of spray rose from back of its dorsal fin. Jaws gaped whitely.

The agent had no time to cry out as the shark scooped her into its mouth and tried to swallow with one enormous gulp. The agent, legs doubled beneath her, hung up for a moment in the esophagus.

"Kck," said the shark, and swallowed again. The agent slid through to the fish's stomach.

By this time the lifeguard was firing his shark rifle from the tower; bullets pocked foamy ringlets in the surf. The ravenous shark twisted, pivoting on the axis of its own body, and struck for deep water.

The spectators on the beach stared disconsolately out to sea. Most didn't go swimming all the rest of the day, and not even the following morning.

The report of the attack made the evening news all around the peninsula. One network sent a film crew, and the commentator did a retrospective report about how few shark attacks on humans there actually were.

Meanwhile, miles at sea . . .

Within the belly of the fish, the agent had started to recover from the shock of what had transpired. Her mind's eye blinked bemusedly at the reality of the situation. The shark's interior was dimly illuminated by phosphorescent kelp the fish had evidently swallowed earlier. "My God!" she said, an edge of hysteria creeping into her voice.

"Be quiet," said the shark. "Hush and be digested."

"I won't be quiet," said the agent. Her voice caught on an unprofessional and involuntary sob. "I don't want to be digested."

"I should have bitten you in two," said the shark disgustedly.

"You didn't."

"I was so hungry. The feeding frenzy, you know."

The shark swam along his pelagic path for a time, the erstwhile prey making irritating noises in his belly. The agent stretched her arms; it was a big shark, but there wasn't all that much room.

"Stop it."

"I'm cramped," said the agent.

"You are my dinner," answered the shark. "It behooves you to keep quiet, cause no disturbance, and resign yourself to my nourishment."

The agent was silent for a while. Tentatively, she said, "You really think you're a shark, don't you?"

"Of course I'm a shark." Pride transfused the words. "I am the direct descendant of *Carcharodon megalodon*. My lineal heritage stretches back for three hundred million years. I voyage without sleeping. I kill, and I devour. I am a shark."

"You must be damaged."

"What?" Puzzlement. "I function beautifully. I'm nature's most perfect killer."

"Don't boast." The agent couldn't help smiling. Then she said, "Either you are damaged or this is some kind of clever psychological ploy on the part of the enemy."

"I don't know what you're talking about."

"You're not a fish."

"Don't insult me," said the shark.

"You're a cybershark. We learned about the project months ago. That's what being an agent's about—information. You're designed to be a step beyond our present marine weapons. Your actual designation was Delta—the fourth prototype, the first true working model."

"Fish slime!" said the shark. "I have no designation. I have sharkness, and that's plenty enough."

The agent continued: "So you really *don't* know. You're a lab creature, a hybrid, more a device than an entity. They made you of real cartilage and synthetics, of nuclear batteries and servomechs; then gave you a cortical guidance system sliced from the brain of a human child."

"No. I—am—shark." The words rasped like shagreen.

"I am sorry you don't believe me," said the agent.

The shark grumpily refused to answer and only continued swimming away from the continental shelf.

The agent was quiet for a while, thinking. Then she said, "I'm hungry."

The shark ignored her.

"I'm hungry," she repeated after a while. She began to rummage around in the contents of the shark's belly. Her eyes had long since adjusted to the eerie light. There was an amazing catalog of mathoms: four empty Coca-Cola bottles, an aluminum soup kettle with a broken handle, a carpenter's square, a plastic cigar box, a screw-top jar partially filled with nails and screws, several yards of one-quarter-inch nylon line, one worn-out tennis shoe, a rubber raincoat, a broken flashlight, a three-foot-wide roll of tar paper, a Sterno camp stove, a dozen identical campaign buttons from the last presidential election, and several small decomposing fish.

"Listen, shark," the agent said again. "I'm hungry." There was a querulous tone in her voice. She jabbed the inside belly wall with her sharp elbows.

The shark was annoyed. "I said not to do that."

"I told you, shark, I'm really hungry." The querulousness was replaced by outright petulance. She thumped the shark harder.

"That's enough," said the shark. "If you must eat, then have those fish I swallowed yesterday."

"I can't eat rotten haddock. I want to fix some real supper."

"So make some supper," said the shark resignedly. "Don't bother me."

"I'd like to cook some clam chowder."

"Fine," said the shark. "Just be quiet about it." He paused. "I swallowed a kettle you can use."

"I need some clams."

The shark twisted about and swam back toward land. He skimmed along the bottom of the sea until he came to an offshore clam bed. Then he lost half a row of teeth wrenching several dozen clams loose from the bottom. He swallowed them without real enthusiasm; they were like eating rocks.

"Nice clams," the agent grudgingly admitted. "But I can't open them without something hard. Swallow some rocks."

The shark emitted the closest equivalent a shark can make to a sigh and swallowed several fist-sized stones.

"Good," said the agent. She began to batter open the shellfish. The shark stroked along slowly. His interior did not feel at all well.

"Hey, shark?"

"What? I thought you'd be quiet if I got you the clams and stones."

The agent said, "I need some more things with which to make the chowder."

The shark began to feel victimized. "Just what do you require?"

"I could use some tomatoes, carrots, potatoes, onions, and celery. Also, some parsley and sweet red peppers, if you can manage them."

"And where am I to find all those?"

"Use your initiative," said the agent, digging a heel in above his left pectoral fin.

So the shark flowed on, gliding in a widening spiral until his lateral sensory system detected the telltale propeller rumble of a surface ship. He ghosted behind the vessel, just off the aft rail, until stewards dumped the galley leavings. Other sharks appeared and lunged for the meat scraps. The great white who had swallowed the agent nosed through the jetsam until he found most of the required vegetables.

"Is that it?" said the shark. "Will you give me some peace?"

The agent did not answer at first. Finally, thoughtfully, she said, "They gambled much to use you."

"Who?"

"They. Them. Those who created you."

"No one created me. I am—"

"Shark. Yes, I know." The agent shook her head. "Let me try another tack. Shark, why did you swallow me?"

"Feeding frenzy. Hunger." Hesitation. "Need."

"Those are shark things, and they are true. But you have been used through your nature. Manipulated."

"No."

"Shark . . ." The agent spoke slowly and carefully, as though speaking to a child. "There is a war in which great numbers of beings are dying. Part of that conflict is fought here in the seas. People fight using sea natives as weapons. These new battlefields require new tools . . . you are intended to be such a weapon.

"There are people who constructed you in shark form. They programmed you with shark characteristics and designed you to be a fantastically efficient killing tool. But I believe you are only a model used in desperation—a gun fired before it has been fully tested."

"Then why do I not know these things?"

"I don't know," said the agent. "I can only theorize. Perhaps there was a chemical imbalance in the nutrients feeding your brain. Maybe an electronic malfunction."

The shark considered these things. "Why did I devour you," he said sulkily, "if not from pure sharkness?"

"I am considered valuable," said the agent. "My talent is the gathering and collation of information. I do it better than anyone else. It was not pure chance that made you swallow me rather than someone else on any of the world's beaches. Your actions were directed, cued by others. I imagine you were supposed to fetch me to your masters."

"I choose not to believe you," said the shark. "The idea of such usage offends me. I guide myself."

"You are exploited," said the agent mildly.

The shark retreated into a silence colder than the deep waters below the thermocline.

The agent resumed her culinary preparations. She put the shelled clams and the vegetables into the pot. For soup stock, she cupped her hands and scooped up some of the copious salt water that had sloshed past the curtains of tissue serving as a lock in the shark's throat. She pulled the self-igniting tab on the can of camp stove fuel, and it caught the first time, burning with a low, dusky flame.

She said to the shark: "Shall I tell you I've been lying? You are truly a shark. You have no creators, no masters. Everything I've said before this has been an amusing fable to divert you."

"But why?" said the shark.

"It's hopeless," said the agent. "You're too young to understand even sarcasm."

The kettle of soup began to boil in the makeshift kitchen there in the fish's belly. The shark felt uncomfortably warm. "Obviously, I don't want to remain eaten by a shark," said the agent. "I intend to torment you until you release me. Can you understand that?" She ignited another can of fuel and placed it under the stove.

"My belly hurts."

"Then the pain will become worse."

"It agonizes."

"Then take me to land."

"But you are my prey."

"The soup will be fine for supper," said the agent. "But what shall I eat for breakfast?"

"Oh, my stomach."

The agent pretended to ignore him. "As long as I have the pot and the stove," she said, "I think some shark-fin soup would be just fine."

"That does it," said the shark. "I can't stand any more." With that, the suffering fish drove toward the surface. In a few minutes, he glided through the shallows toward an island where the lights of towns gleamed.

"How are you doing, shark?"

Without answering, the shark opened his jaws wide and, with a peristaltic heave, expelled the agent, the stove, the soup kettle, and all the rest of the flotsam. The agent thrashed for a moment, dizzy, and then splashed to where the shallower water only came to her ankles. The sleek, dark bulk of the shark lay momentarily still in the water.

"I'm sorry," said the agent. "I tricked you. I had to."

The shark twitched weakly.

"Poor oppressed child of my enemy," the agent said. "You, too, should be my enemy, but you're not."

"I . . . hurt," said the shark.

"You must return to deep water. If you lie at rest too long, you will die."

The shark lifted his head partially from the water.

"How did you trick me?"

"That which I did with the fire—it would have killed me too. You couldn't have handled the internal heat, and your oxygen recycling system would have overloaded. I'd have suffocated and died as you died. I had to handle you like a child."

The shark's voice was puzzled. "Which of the lies . . . what is true?"

The agent said sadly, "What I told you about wars and weapons and laboratories is true."

Infinitely wistful, the shark said, "All I want to be is shark. Just that."

"The powerful, unthinking, brutal joy of it," mused the agent. "To be a natural force instead of a weak and vulnerable human." She nodded. "I can imagine a little of what it must be like."

A pink froth bubbled at the shark's gills.

"Go," said the agent. "You know nothing of this war. Leave it."

The shark rocked back and forth in the sand, lashed the water with its tail, slipped back toward deeper waters. "I will go to the center of the sea," he said. "There will only be the sharks and the lesser fishes. No masters."

"Goodbye, child," said the agent. She watched the triangular fin slice the moonlit water seaward; then it dipped silently and was gone. "You're free now," she said aloud. "I wish I could be as free." But she was an agent and not a shark, and knew she could never be.

* * *

III. MARINE FORCES BULLETIN QQ-221:
ON THE TERMINATION AND DISPOSAL OF NONOPERATIONAL
OR OBSOLETE MARITIME WEAPONRY (EXTRACT)

Barbequed Great White
(Serves 10)

*1-half cup butter*
*2 cups finely chopped onion*
*1 finely chopped garlic clove*
*2 cans (300 grams) condensed broth*
*2 soup cans water*
*2 cups canned tomatoes*
*2 bay leaves*
*5 tablespoons Worcestershire sauce*
*1 teaspoon pepper*
*1 teaspoon salt*
*2 tablespoons soy sauce*
*1 teaspoon chives*
*2 tablespoons white vinegar*
*2 kilos diced great white shark meat*

Melt butter, sauté onion, garlic, and diced shark meat until lightly brown. In a saucepan, combine all remaining ingredients. Add sautéed onion and garlic, but not shark meat. Cover and simmer gently until sauce thickens (about 90 minutes). Remove bay leaf and gently fold in sautéed great white. Simmer 15 minutes. Serve over a patty of wide egg noodles for a spicy taste tantalizer.

See also: Flaming Mako (QQ-221B).
Freshness is imperative (fresh is best).
Execution solely for culinary purposes is expressly forbidden.

\* \* \*

### IV. SUPERSHARK AMONG THE DOLPHINS

Sweeping soundlessly down, around a jagged outthrust of coral hardly softened by waving sea grass, I heard them, then saw them, long before they heard or saw me. I flowed with the shadows then, stalking. Nauc maintained her point, three meters above and to the right of my nose.

I sorted the vibrations: low frequency, irregular pressure waves, jerky—perhaps a large wounded fish. Then high-frequency shrills and whistles irritating my lateral sensors.

*Cetacean sons of bitches!*

I eased through a jungle of sea fans, no longer stroking, letting my body plane on momentum alone. I nosed into open water and ranged the vibrations to be about two hundred meters. I came up behind them and had the element of surprise in my favor.

I'd been on picket duty off the western coast of the continent. My present tour was an indeterminate period of gridwork cruising interspersed with random forays. Search out and report back. Primarily, I was to keep watch for undersea oil transports, though I wouldn't have been at all surprised to luck onto a lurking missile sub.

I cruised with my faithful sidekick, Nauc, short for *Naucrates ductor*. She's a beautiful striped pilot fish about as large as the Marine Forces registration tattooed on my flank. Just as I was once an unhappy human, so Nauc was once a cat—the tenth accelerated generation of gene tampering and boosted intelligence. In another place, another time, we might still have grown old together: an aging widow and her lap cat.

It's difficult to picture that now. It's gradually harder to remember being—human. Perceptions have altered, of course. Colors, for instance. I was warned to expect a monochrome universe. I adapted.

But there are other things lacking, more subtle. Softness. I can no longer feel or visualize or define it. Softness is applicable to a human; it is not applicable to a shark.

Softness. Can it be killed? Can it be eaten?

There were four of them, bottlenoses, each a three-meter adult, all apparently male. These dolphins were the new variety, the ends of the pectoral flippers elongated and separated into rudimentary, tool-wielding fingers.

Dolphins are yet another weapon of the war. Both governments use them; I cannot imagine why. If I were in a position of power, I would decree some allies too reprehensible to enlist. Just as there are, if only theoretically, some weapons too heinous to be used.

I would not eat dolphins. Nor porpoises. *Porc-poisson.* The French were astute when they christened them "pigfish."

Porpoises, dolphins—they're all basically the same, disgusting and loathsome. They're cowards, did you know? A gang of them will catch a solo shark and batter her to death with those cruel beaks. There is no concept equivalent to honor among dolphins.

I studied this when I was more human. I know. Dolphins have a propensity for rape. They will try to fuck anything: one of their own sex and species, particularly if it's helpless; sea turtles; even a sick or wounded shark. Disgusting creatures. Snub-nosed bastards.

I glided toward the distant gray sleekness of those dolphins, and the rage boiled up within me.

They had a captive. The thrashing wounded-fish vibrations had come from a captured swimmer. The human wore scuba gear and the tattered rubber remnants of a coral-camouflage wet suit. The figure was stretched upright as though crucified in the water, wrists extended and pulled taut by two of the dolphins. The third dolphin rolled on its side in the water, its gripping appendages securing the swimmer's ankles.

The fourth and largest dolphin swam a complex arabesque around the captive. He angled in close, actually nuzzling the human; then looped back over, showing his white belly, before circling back to touch the human again.

I lay back for a moment to watch. Though my only feeling toward dolphins is nonhunger, I don't bear all that much love for humankind either. I continue to play a role in this stupid war because I still feel some gratitude to the Marine Forces for making me into a shark. Though my brain is now in a shark's body, my mind is still transitional, I must admit. When I am finally all shark, and no human vestige remains, then I shall no longer fight. I may still kill dolphins, but the act will not originate from patriotism.

The captive writhed at the touch, an arm breaking free of one captor, flailing in the water, turning the figure to face me. The victim was female. Sickened, I felt my jaws open wide as though of their own volition, the lower jaw sliding forward to maximize the damage I would wreak. The shark fury took control—and it nearly killed me.

Only a flick of my powerful tail and I was upon them, among them, their deceptively grinning faces caught in a moment of terrible surprise. The first dolphin I killed with a satisfactory shearing of skin and muscles and intestines, and a melon-shaped hole that spewed dark blood. I jackknifed, twisting back on myself, lunged, cleanly bit away seven kilos of flesh and vertebrae from the back of the second dolphin. He spasmed, and I savaged him again. It was a wasted motion—a mistake.

The other two dolphins didn't run; I grant them that. They bracketed me, one torpedoing in from either side. I couldn't evade them both. I tried to jackknife again, and one dolphin grazed me with the length of his body. My own body is covered with placoid scales, a crude variation of the razor teeth I prize so highly. In shock, meters of his delicate hide ripped, and bleeding, the dolphin tumbled away.

The remaining dolphin rammed me close behind my right eye. I remember dazedly, as though in slow motion, feeling the cartilage buckle and crush. There was no pain—simply that inexorable pressure. But the worst feeling was trying to react and realizing I couldn't. My body seemed no longer controllable. I drifted, knowing that if I couldn't plane, I would sink to the bottom. There, with no forward motion to force water across my gills, I would suffocate.

That one moment of paralysis; then feeling returned. I was alive only because the dolphin's aim had been awry. The last dolphin—

My tail twitched weakly, and I slowly turned in the water. I saw the surviving bottlenose streak toward me on its final run—on a course I couldn't avoid.

Then by a miracle of trajectories, something intercepted the dolphin. A fish, small and dark: striped. Nauc. Her velocity and timing were impeccable. She butted into the dolphin's eye when he was only meters away. The bottlenose veered slightly, but it was enough. My jaws sheared away half his belly. Seldom has the blood-taste been so purely satisfying.

My strength was returned. Nauc took her customary point position, and we finished off the one wounded dolphin.

*Query*, signaled Nauc as the final corpse drifted away. *Query. Emergency? Friend?*

I had seen it too: the Marine Forces registration on the dolphin's flank. The dolphins had been on *our side*. Thus, the human female was one of *theirs*.

No matter. I'd have done the same thing had I known.

Nauc and I looked for the woman. We found her stroking slowly and painfully for the surface. We orbited her, watching. She looked back at us calmly. Her body was covered with abrasions, and she was bleeding. She would survive.

We waited, guarding against the possibility of other sharks, until I detected pressure waves from an approaching hydrofoil. The woman's people would pick her up.

Nauc and I went back on patrol. The pilot fish remained a little puzzled by the politics of the encounter. Yet she accepted it because she knows our first loyalties are to each other.

But she asked why I had not killed the human female. How can I explain? There are bonds more profound than species or birth.

\* \* \*

## V. THEN THE WEAPONS LEFT

When the white shark bites, its eyes roll back in the sockets so that the pupil disappears. The great white is blind at the moment of biting. That fact had struck Folger when Marinak had been snatched away from the side of the telemetering buoy.

That his attention should focus to the one small detail did not surprise Folger: He had seen many men and women die throughout the course of the war. He had ceased to become stricken by the grosser processes of death. Thus, he began to note the smaller details.

Marinak died in a flurry of bloody foam and brief screams. That left Folger and the lieutenant. The lieutenant had a name, but Folger could not remember it; only that it consisted of three or four harsh syllables.

The lieutenant was tall and blond, contrasting both ways with Folger. He was roughly twenty years younger than Folger. Newly and passionately accustomed to command, the lieutenant seemed chagrined at losing half his troops.

*No*, thought Folger. *All his troops.* Folger was nominally a civilian.

One hand gripping the strut of the warning beacon, the lieutenant stared down into the water. "Damn," he repeated. "That goddamned thing. That goddamned vicious bastard."

From the other side of the buoy, Folger said gently, "Sharks function by a binary system—threat or nonthreat, food or nonfood." The lieutenant did not appear to be listening. Folger sat down and braced his back against the assembly holding the weather sensors. The early morning sun was warm without being uncomfortably so. Folger rested.

The telemetering buoy was shaped like a discus, with a diameter of five meters. Set diametrically opposed to each other were the two instrumentation towers. The taller, thinner tower held the cluster of weather sensors and supported the radio antenna. The shorter tower raised the red warning beacon four meters above the level of the water. The scanning system that took hourly readings of all sensors, the long-range telemetering apparatus, the data memory system—all were sealed inside the buoy's shallow hull.

Shortly after Marinak, Folger, and the lieutenant had scrambled onto the buoy as their leaking rubber raft sank, it became apparent that ROAMER (per the steel plate bolted to the buoy's deck) was not equipped to transmit a human Mayday. All instrumentation was sealed, and the men had no tools other than their hands.

It was Marinak who suggested an obvious and desperate conclusion: somehow halt the buoy's periodic transmissions and hope that someone five thousand kilometers away took notice. At first they attempted to sabotage the radio antenna, but the transmission tower was constructed to withstand hurricane forces. Again it was Marinak who determined that the only alternative was to cut off the buoy's power supply. ROAMER III was tethered to the ocean floor by a cable. Ten meters down the cable was a pod holding the station's nuclear generator. Stripping off his uniform, Marinak made a dive; then a second one. It was during the second dive that the great white shark appeared from nowhere and sheared off both his legs.

"Damned fish," said the lieutenant.

The last evidences of Marinak had dissipated among the waves. The shark continued to circle in a wide orbit about the buoy. The dirty-gray dorsal fin cut the water smoothly, hardly leaving a wake.

"We've got to get off here," said the lieutenant.

Folger stretched his limbs. He squinted at the east and guessed it was ten in the morning. The deck metal was becoming uncomfortably warm, and the skeletal twin towers provided minimal shade.

"I'm not going to try what Marinek did."

The lieutenant's voice took on a note of petulance. "I've got a dispatch to deliver to the General Staff."

"Important?"

"Extremely so." The lieutenant hesitated. "What's your clearance?"

"Damned if I remember," said Folger. "QQ-2, I think."

"Not high enough," said the lieutenant.

Folger shrugged. The two men continued to watch the sea in silence. A second fin appeared; then a third and a fourth.

"It won't be easy, surviving," the lieutenant said. "Exposure will be our biggest problem; then thirst. We'll have to fish."

"With what?" said Folger. "We don't have a survival kit."

"I can break the tip off the antenna whip. That's the fishhook. The line we'll make out of strips from our clothing."

"Very ingenious," said Folger.

The lieutenant said, matter-of-factly, "I graduated first in my class at survival school."

Six sharks now circled the telemetering buoy. The heat increased as the sun approached a noon position. The shadows from the weather sensor shortened to negligibility. Folger and the lieutenant improvised a sunshade from their clothes, one edge of which they could tie to the tower. The two men took turns holding the other edge.

During one of his rest periods, the lieutenant looked moodily over at the sharks and suddenly recoiled. "Did you see that?"

"No," said Folger.

"One of those things rolled in the water as it circled past. It has Marine Forces markings. I think it's the one that attacked Marinak." Outrage was evident in the lieutenant's voice. "It's one of ours, damn it."

"There's been a high degree of recidivism in the transplants," said Folger. "Especially with the sharks. Some theorists claim it's out-and-out somatic influence of the shark. Others call it an unforeseen psychoenvironmental evolution."

Not hearing, the lieutenant said, "There's another one. And another. All of them. They're our weapons, the traitorous bastards."

"I don't think," said Folger, "they're our weapons any longer."

"Maybe they don't recognize us." The lieutenant slapped a fist into his palm. "If only we had a soneex . . ." He stared back at Folger. "Can they hear us?"

"They've got a fine audio sense," said Folger. "But not from the surface."

"If we could rig a transponder . . ."

Folger said, "That would be a little harder than a fishhook and line. I don't think it would do any good anyway."

Perhaps it was the heat of the sun; perhaps the stress of bearing a critical dispatch, or seeing a comrade torn apart and eaten, or even delayed shock from the ditching of the transport. The lieutenant shrieked at the sharks. He beat his fists on the metal decking. "You sons of bitches! You're on our side! Ours! We *made* you—"

"They might have listened a few years ago," said Folger gently. "I don't think they will now."

The lieutenant flung himself down on his belly, with his head and shoulders extending beyond the lip of the buoy. He plunged his face into the water and screamed something. To Folger, it sounded like, "Obey me!" The largest of the sharks was starting an investigative approach as Folger twined fingers in the lieutenant's hair and jerked him back onto the platform. The lieutenant choked and coughed seawater onto the deck, and then exhausted himself in a series of dry heaves.

His voice rasping from a raw throat, the lieutenant finally said, "Are we going to die here?" He sounded to Folger like a lost and frightened little boy.

"I wouldn't be surprised."

The lieutenant sat for a while with his knees drawn up to his chin. Soaked and sober, he looked incredibly young. Folger wondered how young the conscription rolls were dipping these days. Finally, the lieutenant spoke with the same voice he had used when reporting his success in survival training. "If you should survive and I do not, it's imperative that you carry a message to the General Staff."

Folger looked back impassively.

"To no one else. It must be the General Staff." The lieutenant hesitated. "The peace negotiations have been successful."

Folger said unbelievingly, "The war's over?"

"Not quite." The lieutenant hesitated again.

"But the peace talks—"

"High Command has authorized a final great offensive. The enemy anticipates peace; they will be unprepared."

"No . . ." Folger shook his head. "Oh no—"

"It means victory," the lieutenant said stubbornly. "The High Command has authorized it."

Folger looked away from him. "Peace . . ." he said slowly. "I promised myself I would survive this war."

"There will be peace," said the lieutenant. "After we win."

Silently, Folger untangled the sunshade and spread it as best he could to protect the lieutenant and himself. With unceasing patience, the sharks continued to circle.

Early in the afternoon, the lieutenant began to babble. He had, Folger suspected, swallowed a small amount of salt water. Folger continued to support the sunshade as he listened to recounted memories of a childhood spent on a mountain ranch.

Late in the day, the lieutenant sat upright, his eyes completely lucid, and said, "What is that?" He pointed at the western sky, sighting along his upper arm.

Folger looked, too, and saw a metal midge glittering high above the sunset. Whatever it was, it moved fast. "Missile?"

"I don't think so," said the lieutenant. "Too slow. More likely an unmanned recon craft." He struggled to get to his feet. "Help me."

"You might as well rest," said Folger. "They can't see us."

"Cameras can," said the lieutenant. "They detect movement." He began to caper about the platform like a madman.

"No," Folger said. He tried to wrestle the lieutenant back to the lengthened shadow of the beacon tower.

Though weakened, the lieutenant continued to struggle. "What are you doing? They've got to see us! The message—"

"I know." Folger grimly attempted to set a hammerlock.

As the recon plane started to traverse the arc of the sky, the lieutenant rolled off the edge of the platform into the sea. Folger did not push him, nor did he refrain from trying to pull the lieutenant from the water. He did not think he hesitated as the sharks streaked in from their patrol. Yet Folger never fully trusted himself again.

He did not realize in those limited seconds how alone he was about to become.

Folger lay with his face only centimeters from the water. The lieutenant cried out despairingly as he was pulled under. The last soldier died. And then the weapons left.

\* \* \*

### VI. QUEEN OF THE SUNDANCE SEA

*Now, minus 170,000,000 years, here is how it was . . .*

Another long summer of the Earth had arrived. The stage was set earlier by diastrophic forces crumpling and warping the continental surface. The process was geologically quick—mere millions of years—but no human brain was present to observe and record.

Temperatures moderated over most of the planet; vast, epicontinental seas settled into the cradling bellies of the geosynclines. Land that one day would be at best temperate now became subtropical. Coral reefs extended thirty-five hundred kilometers north of what eventually would be the seacoast. Great reptiles migrated north, unsuspectingly following pine, ferns, cycads, and rushes to an ultimately freezing graveyard.

On one particular continent, in a narrow arm from the north, filling a trough formed 60,000,000 years previously through tectonic action. Relatively shallow, more than one hundred meters deep, this was the Sundance Sea.

For the present, it was a summer ocean. In 170,000,000 years, there would be winter storms.

The Sundance Sea is a warm and bright environment; this body of water is never so deep that light cannot penetrate from the dazzling, dancing interface that is the surface. Life has obliged by filling this new ocean with growth. Coral builds endless reefs upon which the breakers spill foam. Down close to the coral roots are the surviving mollusks, the ammonites that resemble what eventually will become the chambered nautilus. Their gray conical shells dot the sea bottom.

Placodont—the primitive jawed fish—browses complacently among the ammonites. It wrenches loose the mollusks from the bottom and crushes the shells between platelike teeth. About a meter in length, the fish is one of the lesser placoderms. The placodont gets a hint from the shadow—but it is far too late. The stout, short-necked body twists in the water; its stubby limbs paddle frantically. The nothosaurus darts in, scissor-jaws gripping the placodont's tapered tail.

Much more accustomed to rowing through shoals of smaller fish and snaffling individuals with darts of its elongated neck, the nothosaurus never turns down an easy meal. The placodont disappears in two gulps. Its eater—reptilian, sinuous, and still hungry—paddles away.

Unfortunately for the nothosaurus, it scarcely swims a minute before encountering its big cousin, the plesiosaurus. Head and neck questing like a snake, the marine reptile rises from behind a coral formation. The long-necked plesiosaurus is as hungry as every other native of this sea. The nothosaurus hesitates between fighting and fleeing, and the delay is fatal. The plesiosaurus appears clumsy—it will one day be described as resembling a snake pulled through the body of a turtle—but it is not at all awkward. Its flippers row like oars, and suddenly the teeth are within range of the nothosaurus. Five meters against fifteen is no match. The nothosaurus dies messily as cloudy blood billows outward.

The plesiosaurus greedily tears at the corpse for a while. Hunger briefly assuaged, it paddles away. Squid-like belemnoids gather to scavenge the carcass.

Then falls the shadow of *her* coming, and the belemnoids scatter for whatever shelter they can find.

*If one were there to observe . . .*

She arrives, and she is all things to all prey. Those that apprehend her now have no words. But if they had . . .

Gray.

Sleek.

Power.

Blunt.

Hunger.

Above all, the hunger. And the power it fuels: the power that feeds back into the hunger. After some 170,000 millennia, she will be assigned the label *Carcharodon megalodon*. Her teeth, as large as the finder's palm, will be discovered as fossils. Yet even as the fossils are dug out of the earth, her descendants, scarily altered by evolution, will continue to range the deep oceans. She is a deadly machine, designed for optimum efficiency.

She is shark.

She briefly noses around the remains of the nothosaurus, but the plesiosaurus and belemnoids have been thorough. A few snapped scraps of reptile flesh, little enough to support the metabolism of a body sixteen meters in length. The clean lines of her body flow in somber contrast to the rough brightness of the coral. She moves slowly in a widening helix, ignoring the ammonites on the bottom. Her cousins are flat-toothed sharks, shell crushers. *Her* teeth are sharp.

She is a stranger here. Few of her pelagic family have found their way into this shallow epicontinental sea. Here, as anywhere, she survives.

A four-meter Archelon, the giant marine turtle, catches her attention. The turtle ignores her and continues paddling for the surface. A learned response leaps between neurons in the shark's brain. She has lost too many teeth to the hard-shelled turtles; they are not worth the effort. She moves on.

The shark always moves on; to become immobile is to die. Her life is a single, extended period of waking. She will never sleep, yet a state of wakefulness is not without its dreams. Waking dreams.

*Colors, and shapes that move and change. To a brain accustomed to monochromes, color brings disorientation. The shapes emit sound, but a perception distorted from the input of the lateral audio sensors.*

She swims blindly forward; for the moment, oblivious to her environment.

*Shape is form is soft. Alien concept. Form is being is vulnerable. Alien concept. Alien is nonshark is anything but a go/no-go concept: a binary code system.*

*There is noncognition, yet the impressions pour in, flooding neurons and short-circuiting synapses.*

Awareness, briefly. The shark sees and hears the fish quietly feeding above a bed of ammonoids. It is a Portheus, whose species genes will eventually be altered into salmon and trout. The shark's tail ripples . . .

Unawareness. Like an unguided torpedo, she glides blindly past. The Portheus blunders stupidly off on a tangent, incapable of appreciating the miracle of its salvation.

*Sounds and visions sort into patterns. She cannot comprehend specific images or sound arrangements, yet empathic loads come through.*

*"Come away with me and be my love . . ."*

*"What's a nice girl like you . . ."*

*"Can you type?"*

*"Hold her legs."*

*For the first time in her life, the shark has some perception of what it is to be prey.*

A duck-billed trachodon, wounded by a carnivore, had retreated into the surf, where it died. The body washes into deeper water, where the scent of death quickly attracts the predators. First to rip the trachodon's flesh: a pair of streamlined ichthyosaurs. As they forage choice parts, a smaller, crocodilian geosaur circles impatiently in the background. The lesser scavengers wait at a greater distance.

The ichthyosaurs prudently swim off a few meters as the plesiosaur appears on the scene. The dragon-like reptile extends its neck above the surface of the water, making sure that its claim to the carcass is not being challenged in any sphere. Three leathery-winged pteranodons, which had hoped to snag bits of the dead dinosaur's flesh on gliding flybys, scream angrily. The plesiosaurus bares its fangs at the pterosaurs; then buries its jaws in the spine of the trachodon.

*The dream ends . . .*

The shark again perceives her most basic hunger. The distant sounds of the struggle over the trachodon itch and irritate her lateral sensors.

The fine dispersion of blood, the scent of food, is in the water. She drives through the warm sea, pushing a pressure wave ahead. All the predators and scavengers sense her; some move further away from the feasting plesiosaur—yet none flee. There is the chance of more abundant food.

Ordinarily, the shark would not confront a creature so equally matched as the plesiosaurus, but she is ravenous.

*This is a war she can understand.*

*Edward Winslow Bryant, thirty, lives in Denver, Colorado. The son of a rodeo star who was raised on a cattle ranch, he received his MA in English from the University of Wyoming and recently founded the Northern Colorado Writers Workshop. He will go on to write a vast selection of highly regarded novels and short stories, some in collaboration with Harlan Ellison, becoming a sought-after guest of honor at conventions around the world, and winning two Nebula Awards before his passing in 2017.*

# INTERMEZZO 2:
# BEDTIME STORY

## BY D. M. ROWLES

"'Wheeee!' giggled the three scientists, clasping hands and whirling in a circle. 'We did it!' Faster and faster they danced, their *whees* approaching the supersonic, their lab coats blurring in a ring of white.

"Into the vertex flew test tubes and notebooks, formulae and frogs, pens and pocket calculators. A vacuum was created; an emptiness, a hole, and *Blam!* the lab exploded, and the particles dusted slowly down all over the Earth.

"And thus, children, we came by the knowledge of science." Grandfather smiled, and we hurried off to our sleep tubes.

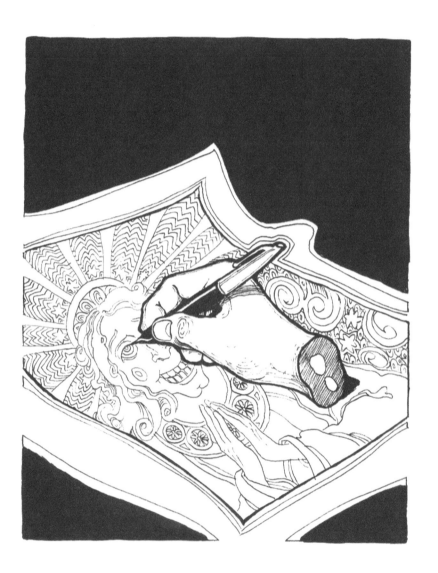

# THE GREAT FOREST LAWN CLEARANCE SALE—HURRY, LAST DAYS!

## BY STEPHEN DEDMAN

*The influence of Evangelical Christianity on American politics has been a staple of everyday life since the earliest days of tent revivals that traveled the country in search of crosses, cash, and converts. For much of that time, it has also been a focus point for controversy, exposés, editorials for and against, and the storyteller's weapon of choice: satire. That practice gained particular power courtesy of Mark Twain and continued into the modern age in the works of Monty Python, George Carlin, Eddie Izzard, Ricky Gervais, and Stephen Fry. So the question is, what do you get when you take that ecclesiastical impudence and shove it in a blender with new uses for cloning technology, media-friendly reincarnation, Jack the Ripper, and elements of a classic noir detective story? I don't have an answer, but whatever the hell it is, it starts on the very next line.*

Marie had fallen asleep in front of the television again, and I returned home to the sound of Jimmy Williams ranting against gun control and pandering to Russian atheists. They seemed to be his favorite topics, since he recovered from that alleged coronary, or maybe they always had been; I wouldn't know. I can't stomach televangelists myself, but Marie loved the whole frigging pantheon: Falwell, Williams, Wildmon, Swaggart, Gregson, Robison, Robertson, Roberts, Fitzpatrick . . . them and the cartoon shows and the porno channels. What the hell, she'd adapted to the present better than any of the other revenants—except Oscar, of course. May he live forever and never change agents. I pried the remote from under Marie's cushion, switched to Channel 20, and right on cue, Oscar appeared, rhapsodizing about a word processor that took dictation. Oscar loved talking and hated writing—not that he'd needed to do much of that since they brought him back. Between the talk-show circuit and the commercials, he was raking it in faster than even he could spend it.

I turned the sound down to a murmur, then checked the answering machine: some trivial business, a few obscene calls for Marie from a fan and one for me from a recent ex, a bon mot from Oscar, the inevitable dozen hang-ups from the technophobes who won't talk to answering machines, and a call from Lustig.

I glanced at my watch: it was a few minutes before midnight, and Lustig never crashed before 2:00 a.m. I'm ashamed to say that I'd forgotten his phone number: we've been friends since college, but it'd been three years since I'd gotten him an audition, much less a job, and I had no idea what he was doing. Naturally, it was the first question I asked.

"Stage crew at Channel 12," he replied. "You're handling Mary Kelly, aren't you?"

"Marie Kelly," I corrected automatically. "Yes."

"Know where she is right now?"

"Sure. Why?"

"There's been a Ripper killing in the Valley."

I was hit by this horrible, creepy feeling, as though my balls were trying to climb my spine. "What?"

"I was keying the stuff into the teleprompter," he explained. "A young woman's just been found dead in her apartment . . . I'll spare you the gory details—"

"Thank you."

"But the guy—if it was a guy—must've learned interior decorating in the Spitalfields. But that's not why the papers are going to be after Mary— sorry, Marie—for a statement. Guess what the victim did for a living?"

"Porno star?"

"Nope."

"Prostitute?"

"Strike two."

"I give up."

"She was a medtech at LifePlus."

I sat down heavily: luckily, there was a chair near the phone. "Where are the Ripper suspects?"

"Kosminski's still in the asylum—we checked—but no one's found Druitt. Did they revive any others?"

"Not yet." LifePlus had had to choose its subjects carefully; their form of reincarnation required an undamaged (but flatlined) human brain, and some form of life support—preferably a healthy human body. They also needed to know the exact time and place of the subject's death. Scorned by the scientific community, Athy—the inventor—had turned to the newspapers for money, and a publisher picked the candidates he considered most newsworthy, and hence most deserving of revival. The list included Albert Einstein, Thomas Jefferson, and Mary Jeanette Kelly—the last known victim of Jack the Ripper.

Unfortunately, Einstein II died before regaining consciousness, Jefferson's opinions proved unpopular with the paper's right-wing readership (and the NRA), and Marie (as she preferred to call herself) had never learned the Ripper's name. LifePlus became extremely controversial, and sold millions of newspapers, but no one seemed to have worried about the future of the revenants. Oh, Jefferson did okay—he's teaching American history and poli-sci at Harvard—but Marie proved unable to cope with twentieth-century California (hell, I have problems with it myself, and I was born here). Enter Carey MacBride, theatrical agent and Assistant Patron Saint of Lost Causes—that's me.

She didn't know what an agent was or did, so I told her it was something like being a pimp but less financially rewarding; that she understood.

"Do you think Druitt did it?"

"I don't believe Druitt ever killed anyone but himself." And LifePlus wouldn't even let him do that successfully.

"Where do you think he is?"

"I don't know. Seattle, last I heard. He's not my client, and I've only met him twice." Montague Druitt was never cut out for the talk-show circuit. He suffered that most common of phobias: the fear of public speaking.

Lustig harrumphed. "Okay . . . well, just thought I'd warn you, and make sure Marie's okay . . ."

"Even if it was the Ripper, Lou, I don't think he bears grudges."

"Yeah, I know, but I thought she might like a little free publicity."

"I'll think about it. Good night, Lou." I hung up, turned the TV off, and carried Marie to bed.

Wednesday was like any other Wednesday, which is a lot like any other day except Sunday, when the traffic jams aren't as scarifying. Marie brought a girlfriend home, a rather skinny blonde who wanted to be an actress instead of a porno queen. She even told me her real name—Rhonda Ness—and I suggested she change it as quickly as possible.

She looked about twenty, and sounded seventeen, and her body seemed to be all hers, but at least it was clean. She probably would've had a better chance of being elected to the Italian Parliament, but I didn't tell her that.

Rhonda and I were lying in bed, playing with names, when there was a knock on the door. I was about to ask Marie to answer it, when I remembered what Lustig had said about the Ripper. As quickly as I could, I wrapped myself in a robe and fumbled in the nightstand for my gun. Rhonda stared, startled; I put a finger to my lips and rushed out.

It was Lustig, of course. "What is it?"

He smiled and apologized for getting me out of bed.

"May I come in?"

I opened the door; Marie, sitting naked and half-hypnotized in front of the TV, gave him a cursory glance, then returned her attention to Williams and Jesus.

"What's new?"

"LifePlus wouldn't say a thing. Can you come with me tomorrow?"

"Why?"

"They know you," he replied and turned to look at Marie. LifePlus created bodies for their revenants according to public perception, history à la *Family Feud*.

This was easy enough with Oscar and Jefferson and Druitt, but the only known photo of Marie was taken at her autopsy. The form LifePlus gave her was straight out of a *Playboy* centerfold via Silicon Valley, and she loved it. She couldn't act, alas, but she wore that body a damn sight better than Jesus wore his.

"Hey, Marie, do you believe that's really Jesus?" His tone was mildly curious rather than mocking. Marie considered this for a few seconds, then shook her head.

"Why not?"

"He's just an actor," she replied warily. I once had to explain movies and television drama to her, pointing out that Christopher Reeve couldn't really fly, that Sherlock Holmes was a fictional character, and that (oddly enough) Billy the Kid hadn't been reincarnated yet.

"Why d'you think that?"

"I don't know much about Jesus," she said, "'Cept he thought that fuckin' was wrong. That's what they used to tell me anyways. He"— she pointed at the six-foot chunk of beefcake with the Ollie North face—"doesn't look like that. I mean, he doesn't look at the women like that—like he thinks that. He looks like he wants them."

Lustig looked at her silently, stroking his beard.

"Now, he"—she pointed at Williams—"looks like one of those who doesn't like women . . . I don't mean he hates them, but he doesn't want them. You know what I mean?"

I chuckled. "That coronary must have been more severe than he's letting on." Williams was rumored to be as horny and kinky as Jim Bakker, though no one had ever proven it.

"You've known men like that?" asked Lustig.

Marie laughed loudly. "Where'd I meet men like that? I've seen men that wanted men—but he's not one of those either. I . . ."

"What?"

"I've known boys too young to do more'n piss through it, or men who liked their gin too much to care 'bout women, or who liked somethin' else—money mostly. But when Leather Apron, your Ripper, was workin' . . . I saw one or two other men, mostly standin' on tables in the pubs. Talked real fine, they did. Said they wanted to catch the Ripper, but they wanted more: some wanted to get rid of the Jews or the coppers, or the government . . ." She snorted. "Or the pubs, or women like me."

"Fanatics," suggested Lustig.

"What?"

"Never mind."

I stared at the television. Marie was superstitious, uneducated, incurious, barely semiliterate, and her vaunted knowledge of French consisted of a few phrases and some snatches of uncomprehended songs . . . but I apologized, silently, for ever thinking she was stupid.

"Coffee, Lou?"

"Thanks."

Rhonda was in the kitchen before us, wrapped in a towel, and Lustig glared at me enviously until she disappeared. "Why d'you need me to come to LifePlus?"

"I think they're hiding something. Can you get Marie to come too?"

"Huh?"

"You know they'll let her in. She could say she's sick, or that the prosthetics are giving her trouble—or, better still, she's suffering from memory loss. That'd really worry them."

"She's not that good an actress."

"Then get Oscar. I know him. He's a great ham; he'll love the idea."

"Maybe, but he'll want to know why."

Lustig stared deep into his coffee cup. "Did you see Manson on the news tonight?"

"I don't watch the news."

"He's eligible for parole again. Anyway, he said that if he'd known that Athy was going to invent LifePlus, he'd have killed himself in '69 and let us reincarnate him, made a killing out of exclusives and the talk-show circuit instead of rotting in jail . . . I wonder when they're going to bring Ted Bundy back. Or Jim Jones. You know they've been offered thirty million for Hitler. If Wiesenthal hadn't organized that petition—"

"The public has always been fascinated by murder and horrors," I replied, heavily, "and you and I have both made money from their bad taste, Lou. Condemning LifePlus is like condemning television or publishing, just because not everything they do isn't to your liking. You're starting to sound like Jimmy Williams."

Lustig wagged a finger at me. "Robeson or Wildmon, maybe, or even Gregson, but not Williams. He loves LifePlus."

I conceded the point. "Have they found Druitt?"

"No."

"And you think he killed this girl?"

Silence.

"Lou?"

"Hell, I don't know. But LifePlus is being too bloody casual about it. Look, I knew the girl, okay? And she deserves better."

I sipped my coffee, and then shrugged. "Okay, Lou. I'll call Oscar. But no promises."

Lustig was right about Oscar; he hammed it up enormously, pretending to have forgotten whole slabs of *The Importance of Being Earnest*—a catastrophe for a man who'd made a career out of quoting himself. The panic ascended all the way to Athy's office, and while Lustig disappeared into the resultant chaos, I found myself asking one of the psychs. "Those aren't their bodies, or their eyes, their glands, their fingerprints . . . if they lose their memories, what's left that is theirs?"

"If you expect me to say, 'Their souls,'" she replied, "I'll have to disappoint you."

"You don't believe in souls?"

"No, and I don't believe you do either. Do you remember when Jesus had made his first TV appearance?"

"No."

"It was on Jimmy Williams's Sunday Revival meeting. Williams got a hell of a shock when he realized Jesus didn't speak English, but it didn't take him long to ask him for a miracle or two. Jesus declined, not asking anyone to take him on faith, not saying that he'd never performed miracles, but blaming the new body. When Williams asked him to swear on a Bible that he really was Jesus, he said . . ."

"'Thou sayest'?"

She nodded. Lucky guess. "And when he left, Williams said he didn't know whether or not the revenant was Jesus—but that he had Jesus's memories."

"Do you think he's Jesus?"

The psychologist shrugged. "I'm an agnostic. One of our historians told me that according to contemporary documents, Jesus was a Jewish partisan leader, about five feet tall, crucified by the Romans for attempting to capture the temple. No supernatural powers except charisma, cunning, and intelligence—and possibly a good religious education. The revenant . . ."

"Yes?"

"Is a con man. That doesn't mean he isn't Jesus, mind you. He may well be."

"You haven't examined him?"

She shook her head. "I'm not on the reincarnation teams; I'm a specialist in clinical depression and suicide. They called me in to treat Druitt and Van Gogh."

Oscar turned around, at that, and proclaimed, "Does this astonish you? When every young girl and pretty boy is a dozen decades our junior?"

"Don't worry, Oscar," I said. "You don't look a day over thirty."

Oscar smiled tightly. "If you believe that, that alone concerns me, sir. You are truly a master of the superficial—like most of your countrymen."

"Should we revive more of your contemporaries?" asked the psychologist. "Your wife, your friends?"

"For my sake? Maybe, but never for theirs. Let the dead marry the dead." He blinked, then turned to me, obviously remembering his role. "Have I said that before?"

"No. That was James Joyce."

"Ah, well," said Oscar, philosophically. "When I steal, I steal from the rich."

"What did you find?" I asked Lustig that evening.

"Nothing useful."

I nodded, opened the front door, and listened. Marie was obviously out. "Coffee?"

"Sure."

I switched on the percolator on my way to the en suite and pocketed my pistol before returning to the kitchen. "Jenny Natsuki . . . the girl who the Ripper killed . . ."

"Yeah?"

"What did she look like?"

"Why?"

"I used to know a Jenny Natsuki myself."

"It can't be a common name . . ."

I shrugged. "It's s a big city. How old was she?"

"I'm a lousy judge of ages. About thirty?"

"Could have been her. How tall?"

"Short—not short for a Japanese woman, I guess, but short, you know . . ."

"Strike two," I said, and pulled out the gun. "Jenny Natsuki was forty-five and five foot seven; her husband was San Francisco Japanese, but she was a blue-eyed blonde from Dallas, born Jenny Mitchell. Now, what did you find?"

"I told you, nothing . . . what's the gun for?"

"What were the lies for?"

Lou stared at the pistol nervously. "Is it real?"

"Uh-huh. And loaded. Stop stalling."

"I thought you voted for Prop Fifteen . . ."

"I did," I said and stuck the muzzle into his chest. It's optimum range for a holdout pistol in the hands of someone who's never fired a gun before, someone who bought a pistol in a moment of weakness and never found the strength to get rid of it, particularly when the first round is a blank. At least Lustig was shaking more than I was. "What did you find?"

"It wasn't Druitt."

"I know he's in a sanitarium in Tacoma. Clinically depressed. Oscar told me. What else, Ivan?"

Lustig flushed: he hates his first name. "Natsuki wasn't on the reincarnation team for either Druitt or Kosminski . . ."

"So Marie wasn't in any danger?"

"No."

"Okay. What were you looking for?"

"Something on Jesus . . . the Jesus revenant anyway."

"Why?"

"Jenny Natsuki apparently phoned my employer and offered to sell them a story about the reincarnation . . . and then somebody killed her."

"Who's your employer?"

"I don't know . . . but I think it's Praise the Lord, Inc."

"*What?*"

"Williams's Nielsens have soared since the Jesus-reincarnate started appearing on his show," said Lustig, quickly. "He's gotten new cable outlets faster than all the other gospel stations put together, and even with that slump when he was in hospital, he's expected to pull in half a billion this year. Who would really want to bring him down? His competition, that's who."

I digested this. It didn't noticeably improve my opinion of Lustig. "And Natsuki?"

"She was on the reincarnation team for Jesus . . . and she said she had proof that he isn't Jesus."

"And you think LifePlus killed her?"

"Maybe . . . but more likely it was Williams. At least, he had it done. What are you going to do?"

"Nothing, I guess." I glanced at the silent television. "If he isn't Jesus, who is he?"

Lustig shrugged. "According to Natsuki, some bandit who was crucified in the same place . . ."

"Dismas . . ."

"Huh?"

"Jesus was supposed to have been crucified between two thieves: Dismas and Gestas. One sneered at him, and one pleaded for salvation; I forget which was which. The funny thing about the legend is . . ."

"Yes?"

"Thieves weren't crucified, but stoned. Crucifixion was for treason against Rome. Dismas and Gestas were probably terrorists—knife artists . . ."

Lustig turned pale. "So you think the Jesus-reincarnate killed Natsuki?"

"I don't know . . . LifePlus is waiting for a Supreme Court decision before it does another reincarnation, right?"

"Uh-huh."

I glanced at my watch and suddenly remembered I was still holding a gun. "How much are your employers paying you?"

"If I can provide them with evidence, fifty grand, plus whatever I can sell it for."

"Hmm." I didn't need the money, but it certainly was tempting . . .

"That was quite a scare you gave us yesterday," said Athy, mildly.

"Oscar's okay, then?"

"He seems to be."

I smiled. "I've seen the body you have ready for Marilyn Monroe. You're obviously not expecting any trouble with the Supreme Court."

"No."

"Hmmm . . . what if someone made trouble?"

"What sort of trouble?"

"Oscar's on the Letterman show tonight," I told him, mildly. "What if he were to say that LifePlus hadn't reincarnated Jesus?"

Athy shrugged. "It wouldn't worry us. Robeson says it every week, and every week, Jesus gets a little more of his audience. You know, I fully expect Jimmy Williams to be our next president."

"It's a pity Jesus wasn't born here," I muttered.

"I suppose you want to represent Marilyn. You know I can't make that decision for her."

"What if Oscar said that you reincarnated the wrong man?"

Athy stared at me over the rim of his whiskey glass. "Mr. MacBride, we were paid a considerable sum of money to reincarnate Jesus, and I can promise you that we did. I will take a polygraph test to that effect, if necessary. Now please get out, before I have you removed."

I stood. "So Natsuki's story wasn't true?"

He yawned. "What story was that?"

"You *didn't* reincarnate the wrong man?"

I'm not the world's best judge of character, but I'm a pretty good poker player, and I saw Athy wince, very briefly. I walked out of the building slowly and casually, and then ran to my car and the mobile phone.

"What did you find?"

"Are you sure you want to know?"

Lustig nodded; the ever-languid Oscar merely raised an eyebrow.

"Athy told me that they had reincarnated Jesus, and he was telling the truth."

"Shit."

"Athy also told me—inadvertently—that they'd reincarnated the wrong man."

"The wrong Jesus?" asked Oscar.

"Not exactly. Say you were LifePlus, and you'd just managed to re-incarnate a man who'd died in AD 29—and you'd only missed by a few yards. What would you do?"

"I'd try again."

"As soon as you could get a body, right?"

"Right."

"But that isn't easy. Now, consider this hypothesis. A few weeks after the reincarnation, Williams has a heart attack or something—he always used to be overweight. They manage to start his heart again, but it's too late. His brain is dead—"

"I thought it always was," said Lustig.

Oscar, quicker at solving puzzles, had already turned pale.

"Williams *is* Jesus, you idiot! That spell in hospital was to teach him English! That's why his ratings have improved! Jenny Natsuki found out about it, and someone—probably Jesus—had her killed." I was shout-ing, now, almost screaming. "Jesus has come again, just like James Watt always said he would, and he thinks just like the Moral Majority. He's nearly two thousand years behind the times and he believes in violence and he's headed straight for the fucking White House!"

Lustig's glass cracked in his hand, but he didn't seem to notice. "So it's the apocalypse," he murmured. "Jesus returns, the dead rise from their graves . . . and then comes the end of the world . . ."

I stood—it wasn't easy—and staggered to the balcony. The canyons above Hollywood do strange things to acoustics, and I couldn't be sure where the sound was coming from . . .

But I could hear someone, somewhere, playing a trumpet.

*At thirty-one, Stephen Dedman, born in Adelaide, Australia, has only re-cently begun to publish short fiction. Over the next twenty years, he will go on to contribute stories to* Exotic Gothic, Gathering the Bones, *and many other anthologies, earning the Aurealis Award and nominations for nearly a dozen other awards.*

# INTERMEZZO 3:
# EVEN BEYOND OLYMPUS

## BY D. M. ROWLES

"Look at what I can do!" he said, wheeling to a stop by my side and extending a hand. On his palm grew a miniature city—mosques and minarets, hanging gardens complete with bees, courtyards and wells with donkeys drinking.

"And look at this." He closed his hand, opened it, and there were mountain ranges, snowcaps, footprints of abominable snowmen.

"And this." He flexed his hand again, and there was a tiny stadium with a cheering crowd and thousands of red, blue, yellow balloons rising from it.

"Look at what I can do," I said, closing my eyes.

# AFTER TASTE

## BY CECIL CASTELLUCCI

*Some stories arrive fully formed on the first page, in the first sentence, like Athena sprung from the forehead of Zeus. Other stories whisper their way into your brain, slowly and gradually teasing out their nature. And a very few stories metastasize as you read them, meant in the worst—and therefore the best—sense of that term. "After Taste" is just such a story. It starts out light and harmless and just a little bit droll. But inch by inch, little implications arise and begin to connect with each other, spreading through the story on an almost cellular level until something much darker, and odder, and more ominous presents itself. As something of a structure nut, I know exactly how hard that is to pull off successfully, and how long the result lingers in the mind. And so, in a moment, will you.*

## 1

For Nora, being a galactic food critic meant that she was constantly traveling to far-flung places and visiting little-seen cultures, with an expense account. After all, a *Guder Guide* star or three helped planets get on the stellar map, rewarding them with luxury tourism, plum trade negotiations, and insider diplomatic favors. Aliens wanted her to come. Aliens invited her. That's why she was here on Vernde.

Nora couldn't tell what time of day it was by the sun—it was so big, hot, and orange. Acclimation always took time, and usually she folded that into her schedule, but her spaceship had been late, and so she was behind schedule. Nora didn't want to do anything to offend her alien hosts. She could have used a stimulant, but that would affect her palate for tomorrow's meal. So Nora had a trick that she did when these kinds of travel bumps happened and was obliged to make an appearance: she found the bar at the mix and mingle and parked herself there. She didn't sit, for fear of falling asleep and causing offense. She stood and put her hand under the lip of the bar and held it to keep her steady. She never wore high-heeled shoes. She thought of events like this as a marathon. She had to get through it so she could get to the meal. That was her goal.

Nora found that no matter who she spoke to, or who the ambassadors pushed in front of her, all obviously Vernde of status by the amount of ornamental dress they wore, Nora's eyes kept drifting over to a much smaller and simply dressed alien in the corner. Out of all the Vernde in the room, they stood out to her immediately.

The lead ambassador, Della, followed Nora's gaze and made a motion with their head, and the alien who had transfixed Nora was beckoned over.

"You do me a great honor," they said. "I'm called Ava."

"Ava is the default name," Nora said. It was hard to keep up on all the customs of the various aliens that she met, so she just nodded, hoping she hadn't made a blunder.

"I belong to the first family, but I work for my keep. We're not named except to our inner family and most intimate friends."

"Perhaps we'll become friends," Nora said. Then she blushed; it felt like a pathetic attempt at flirtation, but she found she couldn't help herself. "I'm sorry. That was awkward."

"No apology necessary," Ava said. "You are a good sport. I feel I should apologize to you. We're very excited."

Ava stepped closer to show that they were not offended.

"I meant I want our people to be friends," Nora said.

"We want that as well," Ava said. "We were thrilled when we came across your species."

They both relaxed. Neither of them was a diplomat. Hopefully, if all went well here, there would be other humans who would follow and who would be constrained by protocols. They were not. Nora was only there for the food. This was a cultural exchange. Flirtation was allowed.

"You must be exhausted after such a long voyage," Ava said.

"It's all right," Nora said, adjusting her stance to look more awake. Although she wasn't sure if the alien could tell what "more awake" looked like on an earthling.

Ava rested a long appendage on Nora's hand, and a tiny electric shock rocked her. She tried not to squirm as the few suckers gently poked in an exploratory way at her palm. It was a surprising sensation, but not altogether unpleasant. After a moment, Ava retracted the tendrils and their hands separated. Nora felt as though she wanted that connection back but didn't reach out for Ava. When she looked back up at their eyes, though, she noticed they seemed warmer somehow. Inviting. Nora felt immediately at ease.

Nora had only had one drink, but she felt giddy as though she were drunk sitting there in Ava's presence. Nora giggled and did all the things she'd do to attract a human—tilted her head, threw her head back, shook her hair, opened her stance, touched her face. She was fully aware that her body language as a human was completely different and would have no effect. Later she would tell herself that she couldn't help it. Nora knew that something biological was happening between them for sure, but it felt good, like falling in love.

Ava began to murmur. It was almost as though an orchestra was playing just for her, and Nora felt hypnotized.

"Tell me about humans," Ava finished her low murmuring, bringing Nora back sharply to the present. Nora shook her head as though she were waking up. She glanced around and noticed that no one else was there. The party seemed to be over, and it was just her and Ava left in the now cleared room. The windows had been dimmed, blocking the harsh, hot sun from blasting away the cozy mood they had going.

"I'm here to discover more about your species," Nora said. "To share it with the galaxy. You're so unknown."

"We've had trouble leaving. The distance is hard on us. Physically we rely on our sun. We aim to change that."

"Well, perhaps I can encourage you to bring people here," Nora said.

"That is part of our dream," Ava said. But she sounded a bit sad about it. "I like you, Nora."

"I like you, Ava," Nora said. This time she did reach out for Ava's appendage, and they entwined what digits they had.

"Tell me about being human," Ava said. "I want to know everything about it."

Ava's brown eyes were wide liquid pools that swirled, keeping Nora from being able to tear her eyes away. Sometimes a fleck of gold emerged, like their pupils were a cloud system on a gas planet. They were the kind of eyes that no one could ever forget after gazing into them.

Ava's eyes kept a steady unwavering and nonjudgmental gaze on Nora, which just emboldened her to divulge even more.

Nora opened her mouth and found that she couldn't help but dish all her most intimate feelings about everything to Ava. She told Ava things she would never say on a first meeting with anyone, human or alien. She told Ava things she would never tell a friend. Ava seemed unfazed by every word that spilled forth. Nora felt she was talking too much, but Ava nodded for her to keep going.

Finally, Nora paused. The quiet of the room seemed to snake between them. Nora felt it like a splash of water on her face.

"What about you?" Nora finally said. She didn't want to be human centric. That's not why she was here.

"Me?" Ava asked.

"I've been rambling."

"I am a simple being," Ava said. "I never aspired to much, but fate seems to have a different plan for me."

"That's how I feel," Nora said.

"My world has always been small, but I've dared for more."

"I used to believe that the galaxy wasn't within my reach, and yet here I am," Nora said.

"Here you are," Ava said.

They stood for a while, taking in each other's presence. Intoxicated.

It was not unheard of for members of different species to be attracted to each other. Nora had felt that before on her travels, but never like this. This was different. A real connection.

"Why do you travel? I've never traveled past the lower parts of the city. My species haven't gone beyond the system. Like I said, we perish."

"Would you like to travel?"

Ava tilted her head to the side. It was a very human thing to do, and Nora realized that perhaps she had picked up the human tic from their conversation. Mimicking was a trick that most species did in proximity to each other to make the other feel at ease.

"I suppose that's why I accepted the invitation to the party," Ava said. "They wanted to have a range of Vernde to greet you."

"I see," Nora said. "To show me the whole of your society."

Ava got a curious look on her face.

"Your being here. It's the only way for any one of us to expand our influence. I wanted to pitch my bid for a chance at serving that mission."

Nora thought she understood and began talking again.

"The Vernde aren't alone in that. Most species can't travel the galaxy. It's expensive and the distances are too vast for most. They can't afford to go to other planets in their own system, much less visit alien systems. I don't know what it's like for Vernde; I've never met one before, but for humans, with our slower technologies, unless you work for a corporation or for the government, it's nearly impossible. Humans mostly stick to traveling within the solar system."

"When we can't hop out of our own backyard, home becomes a cage," Ava said, nodding sympathetically. "Opportunities for growth become limited. It's frustrating."

"Exactly," Nora said. Ava got her. Even though they were an alien, Ava got the existential angst of being human. Nora felt her heart open up even more.

"Here our options are limited for travel. We're attempting to adapt, but we've had to become creative. It's a difficult process to make ourselves physically able to leave this place. For those who do it's been a death sentence."

Nora saw a look pass over Ava's face as though they had revealed something. But Nora thought nothing of it. It was hard for any species to physically adapt to space travel.

"Most humans save up and do one big trip in a lifetime. Cloud City on Venus. The Mars cities. The Rings of Saturn cruise." Nora never got tired explaining her species to aliens. She felt proud of her humanity.

"Have you always been so open with aliens?" Ava asked.

"Yes," Nora said. "Ever since I was a child on Earth. I was bullied, and, well . . ."

"That's what makes you so perfect," Ava said.

"It certainly led me to my profession."

They talked, now practically sitting in each other's laps, for two more hours. But while so much was shared, Ava always seemed to hold something back, which made Nora just want to know more.

"I feel as though I'm not learning nearly as much about you as you are about me," Nora said.

"I'm learning that humans are ever curious. That humans want to know all about what is out there." Ava had shifted in her seat. Snaking in closer to Nora. Even her movements were liquid. Nora exhaled. Ava breathed it in. The Vernde liked the hit of $CO_2$, so Ava shuddered and opened their gills to Nora.

Nora's stomach rumbled. She was a bit embarrassed. Ava shot her a quizzical look.

"I'm sorry. I'm hungry." Nora realized they had talked the whole night away. Though she couldn't tell by the sun, which seemed to have barely moved, it was already morning.

Ava looked down at the ground in a gesture that read as sadness in any species.

"My dinner is tonight," Nora said, "and I should go rest beforehand. I'm here to do a job after all."

"Of course. You have done me a great honor and been so generous with your time."

"I know I must I dine alone, but perhaps after I'm done," Nora said.

Ava looked at Nora awkwardly with those eyes. Those beautiful, unforgettable eyes.

"What I'm trying to say is that I hope to see you again, later."

Ava took Nora's hands in hers and held them. There was no denying it. It felt erotically charged.

"We will be together again," Ava said. "That is for certain."

Of course, no meal is ever free. There's always a price to be paid.

* * *

## 2

Maybe Nora should have said no.

"Do you even want to go?" Nora's boss, Elwin, asked when he got the invitation from the Vernde. "It's in a really uncharted part of the Outer Arm of the galaxy, and you'll be off the circuit for almost a full Earth year."

"I definitely want to go," Nora said. She was already thinking about the route she'd take and the clothes she'd bring and where she'd stop off on the hops back to center.

"All right," Elwin said, shaking his head. It wasn't costing him anything. "Go to the medic and sign the consent form and the NDA, and I'll sign off on it."

"NDA?" Nora asked. That was different. Then again, different cultures had different rules.

"Kitchen secrets, I guess," he said, waving his tentacle in the air, dismissing the NDA as something standard. Nora squared her shoulders. She'd dealt with diva chefs before. They came in every species.

"Chefs, amirite?" Nora joked as her communicator pinged, indicating that her paperwork was in process.

"You'll be the first to write about them," Elwin said. "Do us proud."

"That's my goal," Nora said. "I live to eat!"

Nora always believed that she had the greatest job in the galaxy as the only human food critic for the *Guder Guide*, which of course reviewed the very best restaurants on every planet.

Nora almost skipped on her way to the medic. She always got this excited when she was going somewhere not many people had been to. But this time it was amplified.

"I have an iron gut," she said to the attending physician, a sluglike creature, more blob than bone. He nodded his large head and smiled (she thought) and produced a needle to draw some blood from her arm.

It was standard procedure for the company to give medicals before a critic went to a new planet. Not every species could eat the cuisine from every planet. They needed to know if species physiology was compatible on many different levels. For a human, Nora had eaten a lot of different kinds of food from everywhere. She had eaten poisoned prepared worms on Belair 4. Acidic game sausage on Twelenee. Octo crème Snorgot cheese. And bile and bone soup.

Of course, a critic can't give a good review to every species' cuisine. A Guder Star might be given by Nora because it was suitable for the human taste range and physiology, but that same cuisine might not be rated by a critic from another species whom it would kill.

But no critic, human or otherwise, had ever given a review of Vernde. For Nora, this was the sole reason Vernde had been on her planetary wish list for years. It's entry in the *Guder Guide to Galactic Fine Dining* was blank. And it wasn't because one or two other critics hadn't come before her and tried the cuisine in the far past. They had. They just didn't see it as fit enough to write about. Or when Nora tracked them down to inquire, these very old aliens wrote back and said, *"My advice: Skip it. Nothing special there."* Or *"I had an adverse reaction to the cuisine despite my compatibility check."* Or *"My NDA prevents me from responding."*

Nora would be the first critic or offworlder that she had heard of to ever eat there and report back. Almost no one had ever been to this planet.

It never struck her that there was reason for that.

* * *

# 3

It had taken her six Earth months and twenty-two starhops to get to Vernde, it was that far-flung even for the Outer Arm.

Planetfall was always an assault on the senses. It couldn't be helped. And as a food critic, Nora could not—*would* not—take any of the bio adaptations that most space travelers did. She would not numb her nose. Or plug her ears. Or sticky adhesive her skin. Or wear a mouth guard. She insisted that she had to have access to all her human senses, even if it meant arriving a week early to a planet, when she could, way ahead of her restaurant reservation, in order to get any and all of the overwhelming aspects of space travel out of the way. Because the trip took so long, and there had been delays, that early arrival hadn't happened this time.

Nora prided herself that nearly 98 percent of the time she could accurately guess what a planet's culinary specialty was on approach, arrival, and landing. One quick glance out the porthole of her space bunk gave her the first clue. Was the planet gaseous and cloud based? Was it rocky? Was it a water world? Once that was ascertained, when she strapped in for the shuttle ride down, she could gear herself up mentally for what she would see, taste, and experience, especially if it was a planet or species she'd never encountered.

This planet, Vernde, was no different. Vernde was situated closer to its sun than other planets. It was a large orange giant no matter what time of day. Her flash judgment was that since the planet was almost a complete desert, and that it was lacking in any obvious water on the surface, the food would be tough and heavily salted. That it would include a lot of roughage. Perhaps insects would be the delicacy here.

Really, no one knew. That's what made this tasting meal so exciting to her. Or so she thought as she readied herself after her shower and daylong nap.

Nora liked to research before she visited a new planet, but as much as she had tried to find anecdotes or information, no one ever seemed to speak or write about this place. There didn't even seem to be the usual diplomats or tradesmen who stopped here. With so few visitors before her, she lacked any hints as to what to expect. The entries on the planet were a blank. There were no solid descriptions of what the aliens looked like, as most business seemed to be conducted via communications devices. This was not so uncommon—the life spans of different species varied, so travel was not always possible—and made sense after what Ava had told her the night before.

The only thing that was certain about this planet was that it was affluent. That remained consistent in every entry there was about Vernde. The planet was very rich. As dry a planet as they were, they had the rarest metals in the galaxy in abundance. The kinds of metals everyone needed in order to hop around. Without their trade of that metal, interstellar travel would be near to impossible. So, it seemed extratragic that they were unable to take advantage of it and remained unknown for their great contribution.

Except for its excellent rating with the Galactic Bank and general good reputation among those who had engaged with them financially, there had been no breadcrumbs to follow, nor any entry in a single travel guide. The information that Nora had acquired on her long journey was nothing other than location coordinates and that they paid their galactic coalition dues on time.

To Nora, who wanted to taste everything in the galaxy, that made it even more of a must-try, and, more selfishly, she wanted to be the one species to make the entry.

She pinched herself. She would be the one to unlock their cuisine and share the mysteries of Vernde and open them to the worlds of the system.

They would get their due through her review.

* * *

## 4

Nora quickly realized on the drive from the visitor residence to the restaurant that nearly everywhere on this planet was on the edge of a canyon. Nora always felt it was important to make small talk in order to put the restaurant staff at ease, so she politely commented on the vista as she entered the establishment. She was there to critique them, yes, but she was not there to ruin them with her presence or her review.

The host nodded reverently to Nora as she checked in, as though they didn't already know who she was, and Nora returned the greeting nod as best she could.

Nora was wearing one of her favorite dresses. One that she had bought on the moon the last time she had visited Earth. In general, she liked to be impeccable in the way that she presented herself to aliens. It was the human pride in her. Instead of leading her directly to a table, they led her to a locker room, where she was instructed to step out of her clothes and put on a loose shift to wear. Nora needed help stepping into it, as it was not made for her physique. Nora was disappointed to have to hide her dress—truthfully, she'd worn it to impress Ava later. She didn't ask questions about why they insisted she change. Her choice of fashion would be lost on them anyway, and besides, every restaurant was different. Part of the pleasure of being a foodie interested in alien dishes was the ritual associated with each kind of dining.

When Nora stepped into the restaurant proper, all eyes were on her. She liked being the only human in the room. It made her feel powerful to stand out. The room was about half full of other diners who had stopped midmeal to gawk at her to the point that Nora became suddenly uncomfortable. She reddened at the attention, while also basking in it. Then the aliens took their utensils and clanged them together in what Nora thought was some kind of applause for her being there. That was unusual. She felt strange about it but understood that perhaps it was a special and rare thing for them to see an alien. They were probably glad to know that she could, with one review, bring commerce and trade here. To put this planet on the map for more than their metal and their money. At least that's what Nora self-centeredly thought. After what was an appropriate amount of time, Nora waved to the diners, signaling that she was ready to move on with the evening, and the host took her cue. She was led by the elbow to a table in the corner with a beautiful view of the canyon below.

She noticed a hot towel on the plate and looked to the alien, who demonstrated that she should rub it on her face, neck, and hands. Nora did so, and it was quickly taken away and sealed in a plastic tube. A server then arrived with a glass of green bubbly liquid and presented it to her. Nora toasted the air and then took a sip. It was bittersweet, and as it hit her system, she felt a shot of endorphins run through her.

"Do you like it? Is it to your taste?" the server asked.

"Yes, it's euphoric," Nora said. "What is it called?"

"Lover's Tears," the server said. "We're so glad it's to your palate."

"Always an adventure," Nora said. "It's not always the case, but this vintage seems very human friendly."

"Lucky for us," the server said, approximating a laugh.

Nora laughed too. And settled into her chair for what she imagined would be a great evening.

The amuse-bouche arrived on a tiny plate. It was a pâté of some sort and a wonderful introduction to what Nora expected the scale of the meal to be. A little sweet with grainy, salty undertones.

This course was followed by an indescribable first plate of rubbery, thinly sliced discs that reminded her of calamari, served with a bottle of some kind of (for lack of a better term) bloodred wine that paired perfectly.

Nora was in her happy place. Eating and drinking the finest alien dishes she'd ever had. And though she was alone, she felt that a conversation had begun; that, much like the night before, she was falling in love with this place, this food, and this species.

The next plate was set in front of her still steaming. It looked like a stuffed stomach sac of some kind. The smell was exquisite. Nora leaned forward so that it could hit her nose fully, closing her eyes and drinking in the scent. As she poked it open, the insides spilled onto the plate in a juicy splat, the aroma strengthened now that it had been released. It reminded her of a perfume that she could not quite place. She waved her hand to bring the smell to her in wafts. And then sighed.

She only wished that she were sharing the meal with someone.

Next came a clear bone broth. Then some facsimile of noodles with a thick sauce. Then some kind of steamed bun filled with marrow.

Every plate better than the last.

Halfway through dinner, something changed slightly, and Nora's head began to spin. Her body began to sweat. Her stomach began to churn. The servers shot each other worried looks.

"Are you all right?" they asked.

"I think I need some water."

"The meal isn't finished yet," she heard one of them say anxiously to the other.

"Get her some water," someone said.

"Hello, hello," another one of the aliens came out, and by the way that they walked, she could tell it was the chef.

Nora put her hand up to indicate that she was doing all right.

"Everything is delicious," she said. "Best alien meal I've ever had." Then her stomach made a noise. Some bile refluxed into her throat. She clutched her chest.

"This happens sometimes with alien cuisine. It's just biology," Nora explained. "I know you haven't had many visitors, but I think this will pass."

She looked for her bag, where she always kept a small medical kit in case she ran into trouble. Then she realized it was in the cubby with her dress.

"My bag," she said. "I have what I might need to settle my stomach in my bag."

The aliens all looked at each other.

"It's some medicine, to alter the chemistry a little bit so I can digest properly."

"No, that won't do," the chef said. "You need the meal as is with no enhancements. We cross-checked with your required medical chart."

Nora's tongue felt thick. Her eyes were fogging over. She started shivering.

"Please," she stuttered through her shaking.

"It's too soon," someone said.

Nora knew she would have to navigate this delicately. She wanted to please the chef and honor the way they had prepared the meal, but at the same time, she didn't want to be poisoned. She reasoned she would give it another minute or two before she raised a fuss.

Nora took another gulp of water, and the waves of strangeness she was feeling began to pass. She took a deep breath and leaned back in her chair, looking out at the alien vista. She did what she always did in these situations, when the food reacted badly with her physiology: she focused on her breathing. The aliens were still all looking at her. Even the other guests were looking at her. Everyone seemed concerned, as though they were worried that she was going to die on the spot.

"I'm all right now," Nora said, doing the human thing of trying to make them all feel better. Not wanting to be a bother. They didn't seem to believe her. So, Nora picked up her fork and shoveled the last few bites of the half-eaten cold-cut terrine in front of her. Despite her small setback, she marveled at how much better it tasted than before.

Convinced now that she could continue with the meal and that the crisis was over, everyone snapped back into action. The other diners were still leaning over to try to catch a look at her, and Nora noticed the staff hurrying them along in their meals until they were all gone, until Nora was the last and only diner left in the restaurant.

"You didn't have to hurry them along," Nora said as another plate arrived.

"It's no problem," the server said. "We have need of you to be comfortable. No distractions."

"That's kind of you," Nora said. But it made her feel strange to have all the attention on her. She worried it would color her review. Though she already knew she would give this place at least one star. The meal was too tasty not to.

Nora pierced the stuffed savory pastry puff in front of her and reflected on how she'd never had a meal, not even any meal of any Earth cuisine she'd had back home, that suited her palate so perfectly.

\* \* \*

# 5

Nora hadn't always loved food.

When she was little, on Earth, Nora was bullied. She was very small, and having been born on Mars, her bones were brittle. When she moved back to Earth, the cruel children at school would make fun of her along with the new neighbor aliens, the children of diplomats and others with business on the planet. But Nora quickly realized that some of the alien kids were bigger than she was and had more horns and teeth, so when the bullies went for them, Nora stood in front of the aliens with her arms out, putting her brittle bones on the line.

It didn't completely work at keeping the human children from picking on her. But it fundamentally changed her life and her relationship to food.

"You like aliens and their food so much," the bullies would say. "Try this!"

And then the other human children would shove dirt in her mouth. Or spiders. Or rotten, rancid lunch meat. Or spoiled milk. Nora learned to down it all with a smile. Especially because then her new alien friends would take care of scaring the humans away until they no longer bothered her. Nora learned to eat anything on a dare in order to survive the human neighborhood bullies.

Soon the alien children let her join them at their table at lunch. And wanting to keep herself in their good graces, she eagerly tried whatever homeworld delicacy their alien parents had prepared for them. In the end, food was the way she kept those bullies at bay. Eating became a crude survival tactic.

This expansion of her taste buds became even more handy when her parents moved them from settlement to settlement for their government work to advance human interests along the galactic network.

Nora was the only one brave enough in the family to go out and cheerfully sample the local cuisine and report back, letting them know what her parents and siblings would like. She knew their taste buds weren't as adventurous as hers, but she knew what they could tolerate. But the true delight to Nora was that everywhere she went there were things that she alone would eat that her family would not dare to touch. Local delicacies that seemed to be created just for her. Things one wouldn't find humanified in the human sections of a city.

Her food excursions helped her parents become very valuable to Earth interests because even being able to have knowledge about local cuisine on alien planets had helped her parents to seem more universal than they actually were.

Still, even if she procured her family the blandest of alien foods, from time to time they would all get a case of the sweats. Or spend an evening sitting crouched over the commode. Wherever they lived, they knew to keep a bucket next to the bed. That couldn't be helped. Not every digestive system was made to process alien culinary concoctions.

When Nora was older and went to college on Dornado, she went to her first *Guder Guide* one-star restaurant. Her physiology professor and her wife took Nora as a treat for being such a great research assistant. She was helping her professor on a project that didn't interest Nora too much but was of assistance in her studies of the chemical effects of food on different biological systems between the human and Ostronium microbiota.

"I knew you liked food, and that you were adventurous," the professor said, smiling at Nora as they approached the restaurant. There was a symbol on the door. A *Guder Guide* star.

"It's the only *Guder*-starred restaurant on this whole planet," the wife said.

"It's rated safe for humans," the professor said.

Nora went inside and was introduced to the world of gourmet dining. A taster menu became Nora's idea of pure heaven. A new *Guder* restaurant became a part of her dictionary of culinary sensations.

She had always been a person who liked food. But that night Nora became a true foodie.

Nora graduated that spring with honors and never pursued any other degree in science. Instead, she hitched a ride on a starship and went on a three-year round-the-galaxy trip, reviewing popular food for galactic travelers on a budget, becoming a critic for many human expatriate newsfeeds.

After having enough bylines to establish herself as a known essential and trusted human food critic, *Guder Guide* headquarters reached out to her, and Nora became an official critic for them.

She would call it a life achievement.

But that is not what her life would actually achieve.

\* \* \*

# 6

If Nora could fall in love with a meal, it would be this one.

There is a moment when you know you are falling in love. When you are connecting with someone or something. Where it feels like the thing sitting before you is an impossible revelation. There is disbelief or a tendency to not trust the moment because how could it be real?

As Nora waited for the dessert to arrive, she went over the Vernde meal in her mind. The courses had been laid out for her like a story. There was a sweet and tender beginning; a salty and sexy dish; a bitter, tumultuous main; an earthy, grounded following plate; a few flowery cleansers. A simple and elegant stew. Each one leaving a marked divine aftertaste. She was excited to see how the story would end.

And it wasn't just that the meal told a story; it was that it was so suited to her particular palate. As though every dish had been created only for her. Like the food read her and knew her intimately. With the exception of that one bumpy course in the middle, where her whole body almost revolted, the meal seemed to have been attuned to her physical being.

Sitting at the table, by herself, she found herself humming, laughing, crying, and raging as she cycled back through to the beginning of the meal. Each bite had made her run the gamut of full human feelings. Brought up memories. Buzzed her bones. Caressed all her senses. Kissed her insides.

Overall, though, even with the uncomfortable passions that it brought up as she worked her way through each delicious plate, she felt good. Soothed somehow. As though the meal had aroused her and then made love to her. Food was often an erotic experience, but this meal took it to the limit. Each course had a different texture to it—slippery, crunchy, gravelly, smooth, buttery, flakey, tough, and tender.

Finally, dessert was placed in front of her: two scoops of something cold, with a tiny aperitif to go along with it.

"Please," the server said and encouraged her to take a sip of the drink. Nora obliged. It was thicker than she thought.

"To coat the stomach," the server explained and then gave her what passed for a smile here.

Nora smiled back as she dug into one of the balls with the fork and put it to her mouth. It was divine. She closed her eyes as the taste of it exploded in her mouth. It was perfection. She paused for a minute before going in for the last scoop, not wanting the meal to end. This would be a three-star review for sure.

Nora opened her eyes again and looked down at the plate. The last ball had rolled over, showing its underside. It had an iris in it that looked like a fleck of gold, like a cloud system on a gas planet. And that's when she realized what it was.

"This is an eyeball," Nora said.

"Yes," the server said. "The sweetest part of the body."

Nora put her fork down.

"You must finish it," the server said.

But Nora knew that eye. She had been staring at it all of last night. It was Ava's eye.

"What's going on?" Nora said.

"You must take the last bite," the server said, stepping toward her.

Nora reflected back on the meal and realized that every texture of it had been a different part of what could have been Ava's body. The one that she had longed and hoped to touch all over later this evening.

"You've been doing so well," the server said, stepping closer.

Nora lifted her fork, brandishing it at the server like a weapon. "Where is Ava?"

"She is with you," the server said. "She is with you forever."

Nora understood. She had been presented possibilities at the party, like an Earth restaurant showing off a tank of lobsters. She had chosen Ava. And as they had fallen for each other, Ava had known what was to come all along.

Nora started to scream. The perfect meal now ruined. The sweetness of her connection with Ava morphing into something too disgusting to consider.

But now the arms of the aliens were on her, and though she tried to keep her mouth shut, not wanting to take the last bite of the alien that she'd befriended, they were stronger than her. They forced her mouth open, and she was fed the last eyeball.

To Nora's horror, it was just as delicious as every bite she'd had of the meal before.

"There," the server said. "It's done. Now we wait."

"I did not consent to this," Nora said, weeping at the table as it was being cleared. "I will make a report."

"But you did consent," the chef said. "You signed a contract."

It was true. She had agreed to eat a meal. Whatever that would be. Nora shuddered as arms lifted her up and walked her to a room to the side of the dining area.

\* \* \*

7

The side room was filled with pillows and low-hanging curtains. Pleasant music chimed in as she entered. A new group of attendants took over and checked Nora's vitals. They shone a light in her eye. They pinched her skin. They tested her reflexes.

"All is proceeding beautifully," she heard one say.

Nora's skin began to itch. She moved her hands to scratch herself, but someone caught her and tsked her. Then the sleeves of the shift she was wearing were pulled long and her arms were tied behind her back so that she couldn't scratch herself even if she wanted to. She was at their mercy. Whatever was happening had to run its course.

"Mustn't scratch," someone said. "It'll damage the eggs."

When Nora heard that, she dissociated from her body. She concentrated on the music and tried not to remember Ava's humming of that same tune.

Nora's skin started to burn up. The shift billowed open from the waves of heat that she was emitting.

"It's all going to be fine," an attendant said, mopping her brow. "Relax. Breathe."

Soon she was positioned to stand over a pan as sweat started to pour down her body, followed by other liquids. She was ankle deep in a pool of her own making. Nora felt such shame that her body was letting loose. But the attendants were unperturbed, making clicking noises at her and rubbing her back, trying to soothe her.

"You're doing so well."

"It's almost time."

"This is a great service that you are giving our people."

"We are blessed by your presence."

Nora understood nothing except that she expected to die.

"Am I going to die?" Nora asked.

"You are not going to die. You're going to help us live," one of them said to her.

Finally, after what seemed like an eternity, her stomach became rock solid. The skin taut and tight. Nora let out a scream. It felt as though there were snakes squirming in her gut. A wave of nausea came over her, even worse than earlier.

Nora buckled over and vomited five times into a bowl that had been placed ceremonially in front of her. The pan was quickly taken away, and she was led to the pillows, where she lay down, exhausted.

"Four are viable. We lost one."

"Still a success all around."

The room cheered as four eggs were placed into the pan that Nora had been standing in.

"You did well," the attendant said.

"I want to see," Nora said.

The attendants helped lean her over the bowl. There were four translucent slime pockets with the hint of embryos inside.

It made her feel curious to look at them in the liquid, pulsating a bit as they began the first steps toward life. Nora had never once considered having a child, and yet here she was, looking down at creatures she had made.

"Sleep now," someone said.

* * *

## 8

Nora was surprised they let her leave the planet, but they did.

When she confronted the ambassador at the celebration for her send-off, she got some answers.

"We cannot thank you enough," Ambassador Della said. "You've changed our destiny."

"All Vernde breed through consumption," Nora said.

"Yes, you experienced nothing strange or terrible according to our biological cycle," the ambassador said. "We consume everything, for this planet has little to offer us anymore."

"So, you'll expand," Nora said. "You have the resources to make a real mark on the course of the galaxy."

"Ava knew her fate," the ambassador said, trying to give Nora some relief. "They were of a status that would normally never breed, but we had to give you options. The right chemical connection makes for the strongest stock. And Ava is not dead. They live with you now."

"What will happen?" Nora asked.

"The eggs will hatch," the ambassador said. "And we will finally be able to leave our world and settle and take over other worlds."

Nora now understood. Much like other species, the Vernde had ravaged their homeworld of its resources and needed to find new places to flourish.

"We are bound to this planet like prisoners, unable to leave, unable to explore, unable to conquer. Since we've been spacefaring, we have been searching for ways to extend our boundaries. All attempts failed until we discovered that there were a few compatible species to breed genetic traits favorable to give us the opportunity to travel and expand. You are our first success. Your eggs live and have provided the code to alter us."

Nora wasn't certain that this was good news for the galaxy.

"I'll tell," Nora said. "I'll warn the others."

"You won't," the ambassador said. "You'll do whatever you can to help us thrive."

"You think I'm going to follow an NDA?" Nora said.

"No," the ambassador said.

It was a long six months back to Earth. Nora had ample time to think about what had happened. At first Nora spoke to no one on the voyage back. She kept to her cabin. She drank only liquid meals of Earth foods. Gone was her desire to eat anything solid. She wondered if she would ever enjoy food again. She ignored all the messages from her boss, Elwin, who was begging her for the review of the meal she'd had.

It took Nora all those months to understand what the ambassador meant when he said she would not speak of what had happened. The farther Nora got from Vernde, the more she could feel the biological pull back toward the planet. And soon she felt differently about what had taken place there. Nora had always had an uncomfortable relationship with her body. Often the only human on a space cruiser, she felt unable to connect with the humans that she did meet along the way of her journeys. But now something incredible had happened to her, and she felt as though she had finally fully inhabited her body.

She filed her review, giving the planet three stars. That would start the flow of human visitors to the planet and allow the Vernde to expand throughout the galaxy. She felt she would do anything to help them.

She had to do it, she reasoned.

"After all, we're a mother now," she said to no one in particular.

*Born in New York but currently residing in Los Angeles, Cecil Castellucci is an award-winning,* New York Times *best-selling author of books and graphic novels. Her work includes* The Changing Girl, Boy Proof, The Year of the Beasts, *and* Odd Duck.

# LEVELED BEST

## BY STEVE HERBST

*Stories about the human being singular rising up in opposition to the vast, implacable forces of tyranny and control have been with us for as long as written words have appeared on paper. Few have ever been rendered as personally, or as concisely, as "Leveled Best." Whether the conclusion of the story stands for hope or a surrender to futility is very much a matter of perspective. What did you see the last time you looked in the mirror?*

### DAY

My name is not Martin 4.683.218. Nor is it Martin 5 million, as they call me for short. It is Martin Liberté, for that is what I call myself.

I am here in a Clinic cell because I decided that the Clinic is evil and must be destroyed. I know this fact with certainty and conviction, and I have the words of other men to back it up. I have the book of Kafka, and the book of Superman, and the book of Voltaire, and the book of Rabelais all together in my collection, where you will never find them.

They are words on paper, words written undoubtedly before the Great Govet was made all-powerful and before the Clinic was built as its instrument. They speak of thoughts and practices far more beautiful than those that the Great Govet forces upon its people. These thoughts I will remember, and you cannot take them from me.

You may cause me to feel pain, you may cause me to weep or cry out in sorrow, but you will not efface the wonder of the words, and the pictures, and the scenes they conjure in the mind. They are scenes of a world, maybe long ago, maybe only a fantasy, where a single man could exercise free will. It is a world where no Clinic made men equal, deprived them of their superpowers, and punished them for original ideas. You will not believe that the Clinic is evil, but I have read the books and know.

And so I tried, once, to use my equal strength and my equal resources to destroy the Clinic. I examined strains of organisms in a laboratory that the Govet provided and thought that one certain virus in the Clinic's water would kill and corrode and not be stopped. In this expectation, I was wrong. The virus was stopped, and the Clinic did not die. And, of course, you found me out: a political criminal.

But I know, at least, that you will not kill me. The computer keeps track, and you must release me alive within one month; this I know because it is specified plainly in the book of Few Laws. You will play with my mind, but I will remain physically intact.

And so I intend to hold off your devices and to maintain that which I remember from my books, no matter what is done to me. Certainly, if I do not retain the concepts themselves, at least I will retain my curiosity and my discontent. My life is worthless without these.

* * *

## DAY

Your technicians took me into a small white room and gave my hands electric shocks. I remember their passive faces and the uniforms they wore—white with the Govet sunburst on them. I remember the pain, urgent pain that made my fingers jump and sent fearful messages up my arms.

And they said each time, "The Govet is stronger; the pain is all yours."

I didn't think you would use physical torture.

I shouted, "No!" the first time; they burned me again; they never moved their equal faces. I cried out not from the pain but from a momentary feeling of total helplessness, and then I realized my error.

They stopped the pain only after I had screamed, "Yes!" eight times after eight shocks. Then they brought me back here to my steel cell. You see that you have intimidated me. You see that when you whisper, "The Govet is stronger," I shudder with fear. I think you will do nothing else to me now.

I will not speak the words that still seethe my head, nor the sadness that lies beneath the fear. You do not, cannot expect to have taken them by torture alone. But I think you will be content that I fear you.

* * *

## DAY

They put electricity in and hurt my head bad. There was a light on top, staring down in my eyes, and there was a machine that they used on me. It was horrible. My head exploded inside, and I felt to be dead. But I'm not dead, just I have a headache and I see all sorts of stars on the walls and ceiling, when I lie here and stare and feel tired. They couldn't make me dead.

They kept saying, "You are weak," over and over when they made me blow up into fizzing sickness with the electricity. I think I yelled something to them. "Okay," or something, but they didn't listen to that and only made the electricity worse. They kept saying I was unconscious, but I really wasn't, and I didn't cry.

I said I want food now and to make my head better from the shocks, and they made me say that I'm weak, and then they gave me food and a shot. I don't hurt anymore, but my eyes still work bad. Not like I remember before.

I remember before. Something that there was and something that I used to have, and I think: it was Superman, but I asked them and they said no, just relax. I'm relaxing, but also I'm crying because I want to go out and I want to remember. I'm trying hard to remember.

\* \* \*

## DAY

think i been away for a long it was just that everything was deep holes and i fell in one and they pulled me out the holes were so ugly they were all pocks and boiling, boiling and a superman at the bottom in mud and i said see, i am in a hole and they said you need us because i think i understand you need us because your mind is too big. it was the shot they put in my arm maybe but i think no, it is that my mind is too big and what i see is always there but i should not look. and they say, see what is there and what of it do you really want and let us save you from the holes with mud in them 1 know there are many holes.

the hole was scratchy and hot i remember but i cried, i want i know i can and even though they tell me no. but superman

\* \* \*

## DAY

dead not dead the macine and close to dead but not dead they said you hav no mind and I crid I am not dead no even they tri wil nevr be dead but not to cri but not beaus they hurt only becus supr

my arm they said i am gong away a long tim

they skin from my arm

nevr dead

skin my arm 1 think i wil dead they hav a medcin
for me
i am martin libert and my skin is matn libert
i think i will dead

\* \* \*

# DAY

My name 121 Roy 2,997.045, but I call myself Free. I have ideas that
you will never take from me.

I know that this Clinic is evil; I know that the Govet must fall. But
even in this sterile prison, I saw something that strengthened my hope.

I saw an infant, named Martin, dressed in the Clinic's white with
the Govet golden sunburst. I watched the dim faces of attendants as
they lifted him into his cart and rolled him past me down the corridor.
He was crying loudly, and he was kicking his feet in the bedclothing.

I saw him only briefly, but the sight made me realize that there will
always be hope for man where children are born innocent and fresh. Perhaps that vital, angry baby, perhaps some other vital, angry baby will carry
the new words and the new life. But the ideas will survive, of that I am sure.

I hope only that I will be able to retain the words and the thoughts
that I have read so that I can pass them on to children such as Martin.
Children with uncorrupted minds. That will be my reason for living.

*Steve Herbst is nineteen, and, like Kayo Hartenbaum, this is the first short
story he has ever sold. "My previous story Harlan had hated so much that
he threw it on the floor as his critique to the class and danced a jig on it.
He was quick-witted and loved humor, but he was absolutely serious about
teaching us to write. Every sentence had to have a point, and it had to be
true." Over the next five decades, he will turn his skills to computer programming, creating software that helps grade-school students find their
own voices writing short stories and essays.*

# THE TIME OF THE SKIN

## BY A. E. VAN VOGT

*There have been few writers as highly regarded in their time as Alfred Elton van Vogt, considered by many to be among the most influential writers of the Golden Age of Science Fiction, inspiring whole generations of writers, including and especially Philip K. Dick. But there is also a trap to having one's work become well known and established as a particular kind of thing, which is why Harlan took great joy in being able to say to major writers who may have felt constrained by their prior work or the tenets of the genre: Write whatever you want for* Dangerous Visions. *It can be anything. Take off the handcuffs and just have fun. And A. E. van Vogt proceeded to do just that in what follows, which now constitutes the last of his stories to be published . . .*

Spaceport! For the family, it was home.

Casualness as a way of being. A kind of awareness of the never-ceasing noise and the endless confusion. Uncritical. No hurry. Each day and each night complete in itself, needing no before and considering no after—except now for a little.

Within the family, his true name was N'Gah. He had come to Earth from a planet in the Pleiades. But ever since he had lived almost entirely around and about the bustling universe of spaceports.

*Almost* entirely. He did go beyond the spaceport perimeter at night when the crowds thinned and the chance of being seen increased by some unfriendly multiple. There were adjacent hotels and hostelries, and inns, each with its nighttime entertainment activities, which he found appealing.

The glare of the lights, the sounds of cabaret music, the dancers—his intense need for excitement and stimulation fed on those things, and gained from them the sensations that made his existence worthwhile.

And worth continuing.

*Out of the skin*, he thought as he stood again in the waiting room. *Out of the skin shall once more be born—me.*

He moved slowly through and with the pack of people. For the moment, he had no purpose with them. His purse was full enough. That was something the security types never realized. They looked for repetitions and accumulations—made computer studies of timing and of patterns of thieving and searched for hidden bank accounts. But there was nothing like that.

The family lived for each day. Sometimes that meant taking a little from a dozen pockets. Sometimes, if a pocket bulged, and cabaret music seemed especially enticing, N'Gah would reduce the bulge by half.

Except at the time of the skin, the family never took everything from anyone. And even then it was really an equal exchange. For the giver would never, with what he gave, do what N'Gah's people could do with it.

Besides, human limitations being such and so, today's giver would receive from N'Gah more than the real value of what was taken from him. Not that it could make any difference. Even if he received less, the rules of the skin made their inexorable demands. *Feel the skin. Sense that meaning. Writhe with the skin. Move the muscles and let the skin become aware.*

For the spaceport, it was another day. Hard to believe that, for him, over fifty years of days like this had gone by since the last time that the skin had felt warm and delightful, renewing and vital.

N'Gah allowed himself to be a part of a group that edged toward the food automats. Once more, it felt good to place his coins in the slots, and hear the clicks and the sliding sounds and the machine murmurings as his selected food items came out of the ovens.

As in the past, he quickly found a stool and a place to put his tray; and he smiled faintly at the man who sat to his left, and he politely passed the salt to the girl who sat at his right. Knowing as he did so that neither would ever see him again. And even if by some incredible circumstance they did, the recollection would carry with it no details of where or when they had previously had contact with the nondescript—except for the blue of his eyes—individual.

When N'Gah finished eating, the Arcturus liner was loading; and all around him, suddenly, were emptinesses. The bench he wanted was almost unoccupied. He lay down and closed his eyes.

It was about ten minutes later that he grew aware that somebody was looking at him. And that the next step in the transcendental process of the skin was about to occur.

* * *

The three security types in their sleek red uniforms glanced along the benches. A big ship had, several minutes before, departed for one of the near stars. The bon voyage wishers and the God-speed-you-back-to-us bidders had had time to leave. As a consequence, the huge passenger assembly room was momentarily almost empty. A good time, thought Holweck, as he stood beside his two subordinates, to inspect the place and the scattering of human beings who remained in it. It was a particularly important opportunity in view of who was arriving in about two hours.

On the nearest bench, a woman of about thirty sat with a boy of ten or eleven. Waiting for the Martian local, he decided. Two men in business suits were next; his gaze slid over them. Beyond were three young people—a girl and two boys. Family resemblance. Forget it. On the same bench, a man was stretched out, sound asleep. He had a traveler's soft bag, blue in color, resting on the floor beside him. The bag was attached by a thin chain to his left wrist in the common manner of such protective devices.

Holweck's eyes flicked past the sleeping figure, then came back. Something vaguely familiar. He thought wearily: *You get kind of crazy when you look at ten thousand faces a day, and wonder if you've ever seen them before.* But he had an infinite stubbornness and some patience. So he walked over, bent down, and jostled the man's shoulder with his fingers.

The reaction was interesting. Under his touch, he felt muscles grow tense. Holweck was watching the recumbent man's face closely. But if the sleeper opened his eyes, even for an instant, Holweck didn't detect the movement when it happened.

And yet the body relaxed from the brief tension. It took no great deducing ability to conclude that the man was either asleep again, or else was now awake but keeping his eyes closed and pretending still to be sleeping.

It could, of course, mean that he was trying to get his bearings. But, for Holweck, who had noticed something else when he touched the sleeper's shoulder, the entire response evoked increased interest.

Observed casually, the man on the bench seemed to be dressed quite normally: he wore a dark brown suit cut in the mode. Partly curled up as he was, the style effect was somewhat lost in a scrunch of creases.

*Deceptive outward appearance.* Because what Holweck had touched when he fingered the man's shoulder was not what it looked like. It looked like one of the poly-cloths. It wasn't. It was skillfully crafted skin. *Unusual.* But unusualness was what he was trained to take note of. Holweck smiled with a quiet enjoyment of the situation and spoke in his phoniest brisk voice—his game-playing voice—"Wake up, sir. What flight are you going out on . . . sir?"

Pause. Then the eyelids opened, and blue eyes stared up at him. They were such an intense blueish blue that Holveck deduced that the recolor job had been done very recently. Artificial coloring tended to fade to pastel after a while.

The man sat up carefully, rubbing his eyes. As carefully, he reached down and gathered up his bag so that he was gripping the handle. Then he climbed to his feet.

Then he said, "Thank you, Officer!" And walked rapidly off. He was swerving out of sight behind an outjut of the restroom facilities when the flabbergasted Holweck came to, and yelled, "Hey!"

He covered the short distance to the outjut in four long, rapid running steps. Rounded it. And stopped, unbelieving.

Ahead of him was a stretch of fifty feet of floor. To his right was the smooth back wall of the restroom facilities. (The entrance was around the distant corner.) A woman had just rounded that corner and was coming toward him.

No one else was in sight.

Holweck intercepted the approaching woman. "Miss, did you see a man in a brown suit come by here just now?"

She shook her head and walked past him.

Still slightly stunned by the improbability of what had occurred, Holweck hurried the fifty feet. Then he rounded the whole restroom. Then he looked and looked.

Then he called Spaceport Security headquarters and reported what had happened.

\* \* \*

On the screen in the dark room, odd geometric shapes formed, dissolved, reformed. Color slashed, twisted, and leaped: reds and greens predominated.

What he was watching was a wild movement of shapes that seemed to hold their form, and of colors that did not. The shapes moved around, and the colors dissolved and merged and changed.

A quiet voice intruded from the screen: "What we are seeing is the pattern of a simple, and—I am happy to say—completed hypnotic experience. In view of Lieutenant Holweck's story of what happened, I deduce that he was hypnotized and held mentally blank while the blue-eyed man in the skin suit walked off. According to the designs we are evoking from him, about three minutes went by before he actually moved."

Holweck listened, incredulous, but reluctantly acceptant. Something had happened.

The voice continued: "Since a human being always perceives far beyond his training, we may note in this reconstruction, observations that the lieutenant sensed but which he himself was never trained to interpret. His reaction when he felt skin instead of cloth. His awareness of the man's intelligence. And other, even more subtle factors—"

"Hey!" Holweck interrupted. "I remember one feeling. He looked young enough, about thirty, but his eyes, the way they were recolored— I had the impression he was older."

"I'm wondering," said the voice, "if he stole anything from you, Lieutenant. There's a peculiar misty circle that keeps sliding from right to left across the screen."

Shock. Holweck exhaled in a sudden swoosh. "For God's sake," he argued, "the way you talk, this guy had me at his mercy—"

Even as he uttered his protest, he was hastily fumbling through his pockets. "Nope," he began, "doesn't look like—" he stopped. "The itinerary!" he spluttered. The actual name of the arriving VIP quivered for several moments on the tip of his tongue; but, of course, the information was top secret. He finished weakly, "There's somebody arriving in a little over an hour who we're supposed to keep track of. How he'll come out of the ship, where he'll be moment by moment—" his voice paused. He slumped, feeling suddenly helpless. "Good God!" he said hopelessly. "It's too late to change all that."

The voice from the screen was reassuring. "That squiggle you see in the center of those slowly rotating squares is your deepest perception of what the blue-eyed man looks like, not just physically but also in terms of what might be called his psyche. There's some purpose in him in connection with that arriving VIP. Not clear, by a long shot. But it's something to do with the skin suit he's wearing."

The voice trailed off. "That squiggle is our real contact, Lieutenant. That's what we'll have to work with—"

The tiny speaker in Holweck's ear said, "Lieutenant, that squiggle just appeared on the screen. Can you quickly identify who you were looking at?"

Holweck stiffened. Then he reached for his companion. He was actually touching the other man's arm before he realized what he was doing and pulled back. Obviously, the same message would have sounded in the receptor in his ear. And, in fact, Inspector Dlake had also stopped short. The two men, both in plain clothes, were almost side by side near one end of the huge passenger assembly room.

It was a little strange for Holweck to realize that both of them were waiting for Holweck's mind and eyes to identify what he had subconsciously spotted.

A minute passed, and there was nothing but unfamiliar faces and moving bodies that he had never seen before. A jumble of human shapes. What was disturbing about his failure was that higher-ups had decided that the arrival of Emil Guder, the space patrol chieftain—so young, so ruthless, so thoroughly hated by so many people—should be timed to coincide with the busiest traffic period.

The sea of bodies would wash around the great man, hide him, and protect him from his enemies. And what the human ocean could not do, Holweck and his plainclothes security police would.

He shook his head finally, reluctantly. "Sorry," he mumbled. The word was picked up by a tiny microphone that was attached to his nose. The microphone was a mere speck, flesh-colored and, for all practical purposes, invisible. He continued, "If that familiar face is out there, I can't spot it."

"Keep walking!" urged the voice. "Pan with your head like a motion-picture camera, slowly. The computer is watching with you. Maybe the person you saw turned his back accidentally."

An awfully fast accident, it seemed to Holweck. But he walked as directed until, suddenly, he realized: *I'm doing it again. Taking this job too seriously.* That's all it was, a job. The personality of the man to be protected was not an issue with him. When he thought about it—which, of course, he couldn't help—it was only superficially, and by way of an awareness that people hated men like Guder because they didn't understand the problems of maintaining order.

His own task right now: get back to his game-playing attitude, the phony smile, the gooey tone in his voice. A sort of a grown-up teasing thing, to which he attributed his mental flexibility. *He* could look at a situation and have wild thoughts about it. Most of his colleagues couldn't.

At the very instant that the thought completed, Dlake said flatly, "It's got to be an outlaw conspiracy."

Holweck hesitated. Then, with a faint smile, he said, "It's probably a jealous mistress thing. You know this guy's reputation with the ladies."

Dlake made an impatient gesture and spoke once more. "I've ordered top local outlaw sympathizers rounded up by the air police, and I'm going to be leaving you in a minute to talk to those SOBs."

And, in fact, slightly more than a minute later, the information came through that the first suspect was being brought in. With a grim smile on his thin, bony face, Dlake walked off. "See you at the arrival gate," he called over his shoulder, "with the problem solved."

Holweck stared after him ruefully, half-convinced. Yet the question remained: *I saw the blue-eyed so-and-so just minutes ago with my subconscious. Did he see me too? And if he did, how did he turn off my awareness of him so fast?*

It seemed like a valid thought to Holweck. And in a way, it was.

\* \* \*

As N'Gah (those minutes before) felt Holweck's recognition of him, he experienced, first, startlement. Then, making a desperate effort at recovery of casualness, he swung around a full 180 degrees. Simply, he turned his back.

At that distance, it was the best he could do. And it was enough. The direct thought pressure faded. And so he had time to recover. He also considered what had happened an accident.

And he deduced that, though the back of his head had its own identifiable characteristics, it was probably not recognizable to Holweck. The security officer had been in a deep trance by the time N'Gah had—that first time—walked away from him. There would be a confusion in the man's brain about what had happened.

Reassured, N'Gah stood apparently watching the long streams of people moving toward the L-2 exits. Actually, his attention was on I'Doh. The family's largest and strongest member had been given the task of carrying the rather heavy sphere from a locker near the exit up toward the passenger arrival zone. N'Gah stood well back as I'Doh slipped a coin into the new locker and opened the door. He next pushed the carrying case, with the sphere inside it, into the rental space. And again he locked the door.

N'Gah took careful note. Locker 1033. Transmission Room H.

I'Doh came over and handed him the second key. Normally, they would not have spoken during this transaction. But, as the big man turned away, N'Gah said, "Get rid of your identity plate. And tell the others to do the same. I've been seen. They'll tear the area apart."

The vast spaceport complex identified passengers by the code of energy imprinted on their nameplates. For departing travelers, the machine operated at checkpoints, comparing the information it detected on the charged plate carried by each individual with passenger lists, with luggage tabs, police warnings, message services. If anything was wrong, a uniformed attendant stopped you at one of the gates and guided you toward a rectification center.

Similarly, people meeting arriving spaceships had a temporary admittance category imprinted on their nameplates at the checkpoint where they established their credentials. It was from these that the family stole plates that would enable them to pass, and transferred to the victims what they had carried the previous hour. Experience had shown that it took that length of time before the confusion normally affected the machines.

I'Doh had stopped, surprised. Now, he scowled. "You've probably endangered the family," he said bluntly.

N'Gah gave him a quick look, saw that he was really very angry, and said soothingly, "Let's have a cup of coffee and talk."

I'Doh said, "You broke away from our philosophy in choosing a man like Guder. The price may be high." His tone was critical.

N'Gah took his arm placatingly and gave him the first cup.

When they had settled at the counter, it was apparent that I'Doh was not going to let the matter drop. "It would really be ridiculous," he said sharply, "if your time of the skin went wrong because you became interested in the outlaw cause."

N'Gah said mildly, "We hate to think of the family's future in a universe where technology keeps catching up with us."

"That's what these human beings are always doing"—I'Doh was contemptuous—"preparing for the future. It's what causes all the trouble they get into."

N'Gah said, "If somebody wasn't thinking of and working for the future, we'd have nobody to sponge off."

Before I'Doh could more than make a gesture that dismissed the reasoning, G'An of the handsome face stepped from behind a pillar and settled into a vacant seat beside N'Gah. Sight of the new arrival reminded N'Gah. He said, "Speaking of choosing how to look, what about you two? That big body of yours, I'Doh, is very conspicuous. And you, G'An, in choosing such a good-looking appearance, went directly against family policy. And as for the girls, and their search for beautiful faces—" N'Gah shrugged. "I'm not the only one who's been breaking out of family philosophy."

G'An said, "We're picking up too many human attitudes, that is the problem. This Guder thing is simply the most extreme—" he broke off. "In fact, that's why I'm here. Though it doesn't concern the rest of us, I thought you might like to know that half a dozen known outlaw sympathizers are in the interrogation rooms right now being questioned. Do you want us to act?"

"For God's sake," said N'Gah. "No!" The irritation welled up uncontrollable. "Didn't you stupes hear anything I said? Listen! Individual outlaws and what happens to them is not our concern. At no time do I plan an open liaison with them. What I have said is that we should aim our activities in their favor because it is our long-run interest to do so."

He stopped. The anger faded out of him as rapidly as it had come.

G'An was sighing. "What you just did," he said, "is another example. All that emotion. We're picking up the worst human characteristics, and it's not a good thing, particularly at the time of the skin, for our leading intellectual."

N'Gah climbed to his feet, calm again. "You know your roles," he said. "Let's go."

"Remember," G'An called after him, "if anything goes wrong, I'll be glad to take over S'Il, who has the prettiest of those faces you mentioned."

N'Gah walked away without replying. But G'An's words reminded him once more—if he needed to be reminded—that that would indeed be one of the penalties of failure.

\* \* \*

The voice in Holweck's ear said, "Here is a delayed report from a computer in the Pleiades: An alien race of a general humanoid appearance was discovered there in the early days of space exploration. These people believed there was something about their own sun that had a special effect on the skin. They developed a method of transporting their sun's radiation in a sphere-shaped container, after which they felt free to travel. The whole thing is one of the mysteries of the galaxy, because after a relatively short time—less than fifty years—no member of this race was ever seen again. More data on the history and mythology of the skin still to come—"

Holweck thought: *Good God, what will they think of next?* He had now been given at least a dozen disparate items of information about the skin in man's, Earth's, and the galaxy's history. It was the skin cells that differentiated in those creatures that could regrow limbs. The ancient Egyptians had associated the skin with birth, and often wore three skins sewn together as part of a ritual. *You really get a twisted education in a place like this.* So it seemed to Holweck, disgustedly.

The voice was continuing, "Right now, Lieutenant, we have additional information from your symbol-gram. As you know, numerous studies have been made of the thievery that goes on in these spaceports—"

Holweck nodded. The information from the studies was part of his training. An old-style pickpocket seemed still to be around, grabbing entire purses, removing their contents, and then dumping the purse itself into a trash disposer. In the second type of thievery, not everything was taken from the victim's purse or pocket. An operation like that, when visualized in sequence, was obviously complex: steal the purse, remove two or three of a dozen credit notes, slip those into his own pocket, close the purse, and replace it in the victim's pocket—all this while both persons were part of a crush of people. So there were two distinct types of thief.

Studies of victims of the second type of pickpocket had shown the same kind of hypnotic brain pattern as Holweck. The difference, Holweck told himself with satisfaction, is that this time the person they used their system on was an observant security officer.

The voice in his ear made the same point a few moments later: "Our problem with the average victims has been that they did not even glance at the thief. Those who did were so fleetingly aware that all of them together do not equal what you, Lieutenant Holweck, observed today. So now we know. These are permanent parasites. They live on the premises all year round. They sleep here—Lieutenant, remember those squares that came onto the screen right after the hypnotic pattern?"

Holweck recalled them, but could not place the context.

The voice continued, "They seemed to be turning slowly, not moving. You seldom see those configurations these days, but they are to be found in people who do not go out of their village or far from their homes. Here, it suggests that the sleeper lives in the spaceport, and does not venture beyond its confines."

*I'll be damned*, thought Holweck, not entirely convinced, but impressed.

The psychologist-interpreter went on: "So it may be that you have accidentally given us a tiny glimpse of one of these beings while he was having his night's rest."

Holweck felt it necessary to point out, "It wasn't night, sir. It was about an hour and twenty-five minutes ago."

"Thank you. Your point is well taken, and worth analysis. My own speculation would be that the members of this gang do their sleeping during the heavy traffic periods, which begin at six a.m. and end at one a.m."

"My own feeling at the time," said Holweck, "is that he was pretending to be asleep."

"Hmmm. We'll check into that, right now. Wait one second."

A spaceport—Holweck observed while he waited—was an extremely concrete place. It was like a tunnel. At one "end" was the spaceship that had brought a mass of people. At the other end, they went out for the purpose of being conveyed by an endless stream of public and private transport vehicles to their ultimate destinations beyond the perimeter of the spaceport. And, of course, the tunnel was equally useful in a reverse way when they departed for other planets and stars.

As the small thoughts flickered through Holweck's mind, not for the first time—he had made the comparison with a tunnel many times—the voice resumed: "Lieutenant, our examination confirms your belief. The sleeper was pretending. More important, he wanted you to find him, and had laid down with that purpose in mind."

Holweck said matter-of-factly, "As a point of information, do you know that you were silent for two and a half minutes before you said what you just did?"

"Huh!" Pause. Then earnestly, "Lieutenant, I was giving you virtually continuous information. The computer checked your comment within seconds."

"Better investigate, then," said the security officer.

Another Pause. Then, in a slightly awed voice: "The images show that somebody came in and hypnotized me. It will take time to determine what was removed from my memory."

"How much time?" asked Holweck. "Can you do it within"—he glanced at his watch—"six minutes? That's when I have to be at the arrival gate for a last-minute checkup."

"Impossible. I'll have to have the same detailed search of my subconscious as you got—thirty minutes or more."

"Then whatever was removed or suggested must be considered by the enemy a vital fact, and we don't know what it is."

"I'm afraid so."

Holweck continued to move along with the crowd, not knowing how to react to the new information.

"All this that has happened," continued the voice, "will be of help in future incidents of this kind. But right now, there's a possibility that you may be in personal danger."

"How do you mean?" Holweck was surprised to hear his voice so instantly husky.

"You're the only one who has any chance of ever recognizing him again, and since he chose you, he must know who you are and where he can find you."

Holweck, who had his own mental sharpness, said quickly, "Why didn't he kill me right away? Why wait?"

"Because there's something he wants you to do when the VIP arrives. What, is not clear. And I should say, Lieutenant, that your overall reaction to him at the time of your contact does not identify him as a murderer type. But he does have something destructive in mind. Since this is our first real look at these people, I can't tell you what it is."

"I'll be careful," said Holweck automatically.

*Whatever that meant*, he thought grimly.

* * *

The family had drifted one by one to the great waiting room. N'Gah sensed their presence, but with two exceptions made no particular effort to identify where they were, as labeling messages touched his mind.

D'Lab reported first. And then, in order: A'Is, I'Doh, P'wy, S'll, and R'Tef also checked in mentally.

I'Doh carried the sphere in a traveler's bag. At the key moment, he would take it out, and the skin, the glorious skin, would interact with it.

N'Gah located I'Doh and his bag, and thereafter never quite lost contact with him. That came first. But he had also looked swiftly for S'll and saw her just long enough to exchange the glance that transmitted from her to him that all was well between them.

Even under ordinary circumstances, it would have been dangerous for so many of the family to be here at the same time. Normally, they divided themselves carefully, and spread thinly, among the numerous buildings. But it was the time of the triple-knotted skin for N'Gah, and each had come—somewhat more nervous than usual—to do what he could to help.

Feeling tense himself, N'Gah located Lieutenant Holweck. And at that point began his rearward approach.

At the arrival gate, Holweck noted that a dozen of his men were in correct positions, ready to act as pushers through the crowd and pushers-away of intruders, and if necessary, to claw, and strike, and shoot.

He was still standing there, scanning the crowds, automatically fighting to hold his position—*After all, we've done this protection routine hundreds of times*—when there they were, coming along the ramp from the spaceship. As usual, in spite of all the crew's efforts, a number of ordinary passengers had squeezed past the person to be guarded. At least a dozen such now led the passenger swarm, and it actually took every bit of mental effort Holweck had to reach past these forerunners with his desperately seeking gaze, and finally, there was the face and the head of Emil Guder.

As in the past, at the moment of identification, it seemed incredible that he hadn't instantly recognized those set jaws, the gray, steely eyes, and the almost leonine head with its only partially concealing sweep of light brown hair. And, of course, there was also the unmistakable sturdy body, not short, but not too tall, about 180 centimeters in height.

Guder had evidently seen photographs of Holweck. As he came up, he looked doubtful for a moment, and then as Holweck said the password, he nodded; the hard face relaxed into a faint smile, or what passed on that grim face for a smile, of welcome.

And then he screamed.

Over to one side, Holweck was vaguely aware of a bright spherical object that someone was holding up high. Simultaneously, a man jostled him. Almost involuntarily, Holweck glanced into wide, staring blue eyes. It was an instantly familiar face. As he grabbed, and held grimly, the voice from the speaker in his ear said, "Lieutenant, the squiggle!"

"I've got him!" yelled Holweck, and clutched even harder. The principal emotion he recalled afterward was surprise that the body he held for decisive moments offered no resistance; and in fact, hung almost limply in his grasp.

He was aware then that Guder had stopped screaming and was pushing on through the crowd.

*Well,* Holweck thought, triumphant, *just in time.* He called to Inspector Dlake, "Help me hold this fellow. Get the handcuffs. Chain him to this guardrail—"

As the two security officers were presently joined by a half dozen willing yeoman guards, the blue-eyed man, still unresisting, was indeed chained up. He sagged to the floor, and lay there limply, and so thoroughly caught that Holweck, after grabbing all the keys that might unlock him, felt free to go back again to the gate.

His jubilation continued. Once more thoroughness had paid off; that was the feeling. He was ashamed of himself now for some of the wild speculations he had allowed into his mind. That computer nonsense about the skin and the peculiar analysis of pickpockets who lived in the spaceport. Well, maybe they did, and maybe they had a few tricks. But the highly technical police counteroperation had its own skills.

He located subunit chief, Sergeant Ruhle. "Did you catch that fellow who was flashing that bright light?" Holweck asked.

The heavy-jowled Ruhle was unhappy. "Sorry, couldn't get near him."

Too bad. "Well, one man can't be everywhere; and besides, we got the main job done." Satisfied, he returned to where the important prisoner was, ordered him unhooked (but still chained), and then he helped half-carry, half-drag the captured blue eyes—Mr. Squiggle himself—to one of the barred rooms.

The doctor came and examined the unconscious body on the cot. "Shock," he diagnosed. And added, "Get him out of that skin suit. It's too warm."

Silently, that was done, and a robe wrapped around him. At which point, he opened his eyes, looked around, and said, "What happened? I'm Emil Guder."

Later, after they had taken the protesting man to a psychiatric ward for observation, Holweck came back for the skin suit. It was gone.

He said into the microphone, "Does the computer have any comment about all this, sir?"

"About what?" The voice sounded surprised. "Who is this?"

"Lieutenant Holweck, and—"

"What are you doing on this line, Lieutenant?" The voice sounded puzzled.

At that exact moment, one of a pack of people bumped into Holweck. He was swept along for several yards. Most of his enforced journey was spent face-to-face with a man he had never seen before who had cheerful blue eyes. Holweck, struggling to edge to one side, had no particular thought about that.

Abruptly, he was free. The crowd surged by him, and away. And the voice in his ear said, "Lieutenant, you asked me a question a few minutes ago—"

"About what?" asked Holweck, surprised. He added, puzzled, "What am I doing connected to this line, sir?"

"I haven't the faintest idea," said the psychologist's voice, testily. "So I'll just disconnect you. Okay?"

"Fine."

\* \* \*

N'Gah spent the night at his favorite cabaret with S'll. They talked of quite ordinary things. She told him whom she had robbed that day, where the victims were going, and what they were like. And he told her of some minor discoveries he had already made about the Guder body, now his (until the next time of the skin).

Individual members of the family were not noted for their mental brilliance. Simple things were about it for any of them. Details of thievery. An anecdote about a special item found in someone's purse. A theft from somebody with an unusual occupation.

N'Gah and S'll danced with almost blank minds, holding each other very close after the manner of certain human lovers. They listened to and watched the singers and musicians, feeling every beat and every unusual note with the joy of these humans who appreciate rhythm and melody above all else. And they ate and drank like men and women everywhere.

Shortly before dawn, S'll and N'Gah went by separate ways to an administrative office empty at this hour. There was a cot in the back room. And on that cot they made love in the way that was prescribed by their ancient order. And then, as the crowds began to surge into the huge inner spaces of the port, they went back among the flashing lights and the unceasing noises. Quickly, he in one building, and she in another, stretched out on a hard bench.

Slept soundly.

In the spaceport, which, like a great belly engorged and disgorged its total content each twenty-four hours, another day was beginning.

*A. E. van Vogt is sixty-one. Born in Edenburg, Canada, he made his way to Los Angeles to pursue a writing career. His most recent novels include* Moonbeast, Rogue Ship, *and* Quest for the Future. *He will go on to win acclaim as one of the greatest writers of science fiction of the twentieth century, receiving the honor of being named a Grand Master by the Science Fiction Writers of America in 1995. He will wear that distinction with pride and humility to the day of his passing on January 26, 2000.*

# RUNDOWN

## BY JOHN MORRESSY

*Hunter S. Thompson, describing one of his subjects in* Fear and Loathing in Las Vegas, *wrote: "There he goes. One of God's own prototypes. A high-powered mutant of some kind never even considered for mass production. Too weird to live, and too rare to die." If such words could be applied to a story as much as a person, "Rundown" would definitely fit the bill. Herewith: an utterly charming but quite mad digression into geopolitical whatthefuck.*

*What has gone before*: Volcanic activity has largely ceased. There are no signs of a new outburst; nevertheless, Edward T. Everson is deeply concerned about the situation. The space budget has been slashed by nearly $850 million, despite reports of raids on Martha's Vineyard, Nantucket, and Monomoy Point and rumors of unrest in the Balkans. Small children everywhere are missing their naps and growing cross and overtired.

A spirit of gloom tempered with cautious optimism pervades Wall Street. Stocks have reached their lowest levels in thirty-seven years, but experts are agreed that the decline shows every indication. Edward T.

Everson and his wife, Theodora Pittman, reconsider their decision to sell the holdings given to them as a wedding present by Mrs. Everson's father, a gentleman of the old school.

After much controversy, the Ptolemaic system has been discredited and discarded. Amid the uncertainty, the Copernican theory wins much support, particularly among intellectuals and the young. Canaries have reverted to the wild state and are proliferating. The Spanish government has adopted a policy of watchful waiting. No word has yet arrived from the North.

Spirits among local residents are high as the Gulf Coast prepares for Hurricane Elvira. The prime minister has taken his case to the public, but the public is unanimous in its outrage at the closing of the old school. Edward T. Everson refuses to become actively involved, pleading the press of his other duties, and only after much persuasion agrees to accept the chairmanship. Campaigners are active in all fifty-seven states. A small herd of false killer whales (*Pseudorca crassidens*) makes its way onto a beach near Fort Pierce, Florida, where 125 of them die. Scientists are unable to explain the apparent mass suicide.

Debate continues on the (deleted): issue. The following heated exchange takes place at a closed session of the Senate on December 15:

Mr. Hartland: (Deleted.)

Mr. Outrider: (Deleted.)

Mr. Hartland: (Deleted.)

Mr. Outrider: (Deleted.)

Mr. Hartland: (Deleted.)

Mr. Outrider: (Deleted.)

The Senate voted to (deleted) by a margin of (deleted.). The motion was (deleted.)

Casualties are mounting on all fronts and have already reached a total of 65,178 dead; 584,293 wounded in the eastern sector alone; but the Everson boys, Edward Jr. and Billy, are home again, safe and sound. Prospects of an early settlement are dim; spokesmen for both company and union blame the disturbances on paid agitators. America has adopted a policy of weight-watching.

Unidentified horsemen have been seen in the eastern suburbs of Long Island, and there has been fierce skirmishing on Interstate 94 just over the Montana border. In the Everson home, in New Canaan, Connecticut, spirits are high after the announcement of Edward's promotion to managing director. The Everson boys are doing well in their own right: Billy is a successful gypsy, and Edward Jr. has seized three neighboring kingdoms with no loss of life or property, except to others. The rock samples from Jupiter are a disappointment.

Edward T. Everson's installation as president is rudely interrupted by messengers bearing the news that the old school has been burned to the ground. The gods display unmistakable signs of wrath. Hurricane Elvira takes record toll; thirty-one dead, thousands homeless. Everson proceeds with the ceremony, grants an amnesty to all nonpolitical prisoners, and orders wine dispensed to the villagers. The alley cat is declared extinct.

The last stronghold of the Albigenses has fallen. Work on the great continental railroad will now proceed at an astonishing pace. India may not make it. Here are the latest returns:

North: 0
East: 0
West: 0
South: 0
The Eversons: 0


The eclipse has come off as planned, and the administration is pleased with the results. Despite the conclusion of a mutually acceptable truce and the complete cessation of hostilities, casualties continue to mount. On Thursday, for the third time this week, the 5:07 from Union Station is forty-one minutes late. Tonight's meeting is postponed. The poetry reading, the recital by the Anapest String Quartet, and a showing of realistic paintings of shoes and feet by a well-known surrealist are all canceled.

No explanation has been given for President Edward T. Everson's sudden resignation. Plans have been announced for the construction of a government office building on the site of the old school. Now that the boys are no longer at home, the Eversons, Ed and Theo, do less entertaining. They have not been seen since shortly before Labor Day. There is no truth to the rumor that Ed's resignation is connected with the alleged massacre at Drogheda.

For the second consecutive year, no butterflies have been sighted in the tristate region. The days are growing shorter.

A government crackdown on undesirables has resulted in over three hundred arrests. Dogs have turned on their masters and refused to play dead. The friends of Ed and Theo Everson plan a bon voyage party at the longshoremen's hiring hall on Saturday evening. On several of the major networks, nothing can be seen but a test pattern. "We're going over on the *Lusitania*," Everson told this reporter. "I'd rather return on the *Hindenburg*, but Theo has a fear of heights." Edward T. Everson Jr., after a thrilling escape from hired assassins, has been granted political asylum in New Canaan, Connecticut. The sky is darker these days.

Highlights of the Christmas menu of the Café Voisin:

Potages

Consomme d'Elephant

Poissons et Entrees

Louge de Charneau a la Anglaise

Kanguroo de Conserve sauce Piquante

Cuissot de Loup sauce chasseur

Plat d'Antelope aux truffes

Chat accompagne de Rats

Edward T. Everson, past Grand Commander of the Dismembered Veterans of Balaclava, was taken on a tour of the defenses. He was impressed by the Maginot Line, loved the Western Wall, and giggled inexplicably at the Safeguard system. Record tides have occurred along the entire coast. Prices continue to rise, but the secretary of the treasury is optimistic. "Happy Days Are Here Again" is no longer among the top ten. Edward T. Everson is declared an unauthorized personality; his lifestyle is invalidated. Sporadic fighting in the central highlands has resulted in a drop in casualties but a drastic increase in laundry expenses.

EVERSON, Edward T.—suddenly, in New Canaan, Connecticut. Beloved husband of Theodora, devoted father of Edward Jr. and William, who have adopted a policy of wakeful watching.

The sun has not risen since Monday. There is no word from the East. Edward T. Everson Jr. is deeply concerned about the situation.

Now read on.

*John Morressy, forty-three, is the author of* The Blackboard Cavalier, The Addison Tradition, *and* A Long Communion, *and has just published the first two installments of the Del Whitby series of books. He will continue to write novels and short stories while teaching English at Franklin Pierce College until his passing in Sullivan, New Hampshire, on March 20, 2006.*

# INTERMEZZO 4: ELEMENTAL
## BY D. M. ROWLES

"One of the biggest, one of the best, blah, blah."

She wasn't impressed by hardware, but oh, she longed to look at the moon, at Castor and Pollux, at Alpha Lyra.

He did not laugh at her cheesy moonjoke, but adjusted an eyepiece and droned on.

At last her turn! The stepladder ricketed; she almost fell.

Peeping in, she was silent.

Climbing down, she echoed the wows.

Going home, she decided not to mention that she had seen a sad-eyed poet's head rolling across the sky, covering the lens with sweet singing blood.

# THE WEIGHT OF A FEATHER (THE WEIGHT OF A HEART)

## BY CORY DOCTOROW

*Within the legal system, there are specific terms defining a set of laws, what breaking those laws looks like, and most importantly, what the penalties are for those crimes and when they end. After paying one's debt to the courts and the badges, one is readmitted back into the company of others. But no such statutes exist for those who break the rules of society. How does one earn back a role in the greater world after transgressing? Can one earn back that place? Is forgiveness possible, or even desired, by those on either side of the equation? Or is it better simply to retreat? At what point does refuge from the approbation of others become a prison, and when does a prison become a refuge?*

Margaret came into my office, breaking my unproductive clicktrance. She looked sheepish. "I got given one of those robots that follows you around," she said. She took a step, revealing the waist-high reinforced cardboard box. "Want to help unbox?"

I stood up and unkinked my spine and hips and shoulders with a sound like wringing out a sheet of Bubble Wrap. "Oof."

"Come on, old fella," she said. She handed me a box cutter.

\* \* \*

Ten minutes later, we had a neat pile of cardboard, another one of foam padding, and a robot: Orange, two-wheeled, it came to midway up my thigh. It had a cargo pod that could carry fifty pounds of anything that needed carrying—groceries, I guess. It had a Bluetooth speaker (so that it could play a soundtrack as it dogged your heels) and an internal USB port so you could lock your phone inside it to charge.

"Mat," Margaret said. "I'm naming it Mat. My kid brother had a Warhammer robot called Mat."

"He had a robot?"

"It was his character. In a game. Like *D&D*."

"Mat."

"It's my robot—I'll name it." But she gave me a squeeze to make it friendly.

\* \* \*

It changed her gait. Once the robot was paired with her phone, she had to walk at a smooth, steady pace, and not look over her shoulder at it ("Will it turn into a pillar of salt?" "Don't yuck my yum"), but when she went upstairs, she had to wait patiently while it humped its whining way up each step, extruding two sets of smaller wheels, fore and aft, to grip the next riser and the one below.

"Don't you think it's time you gave Mat a break?" There were six flights upstairs up to our place, one of six little cottages on the roof of a low-rise industrial building. With Mat in tow, it was a twenty-minute trip. "You could leave him in the hallway downstairs. Tuck him under the stairs and he'll be out of everyone's way."

"He'd get lonely." Margaret was unreadable, but I assumed that was a joke. We stood on the third landing, waiting as Mat *whirr-clunk-whirr-clunked* his way up the staircase behind us. If we went ahead without waiting for him, he'd get lost, and then Margaret would have to go find him, his motors whining pathetically as he perched at a precarious forty-five halfway up a flight.

"Come on, Mat," she said, when he reached the landing. "Race ya!" She bounded up the next flight two at a time while I trudged up at Mat-speed, just to see how it felt.

"He reminds me of my brother," she said.

"You never talk about your brother."

"No," she said. "I don't."

* * *

It was Wednesday, so I had to do my Step 9 practice. Lira, my counselor, didn't require me to show her the drafts, but she did check in on my computer to count the keystrokes and get a statistical picture of the sentences. I couldn't fool her by just typing "sorry sorry sorry," or "this is stupid this is stupid this is stupid" for an hour.

Margaret walked up and down the hallway outside our bedroom, muttering into her phone. Mat whirred behind her, sometimes clunking into the baseboard. All the baseboards were scuffed now.

Step 9 was hard. When I first got here, I thought it would be the easy part. The orientation videos warned me that if I thought it would be easy, I didn't understand the assignment. I ignored it, because that's who I was then (I'm not much better now).

I made my first attempt even before I'd got my billet, when I was still in new arrivals temp housing. Bam, bam, bam; sorry, sorry, sorry; done. At this rate, I'd be ready to go back in, what, days?

Lira took me out for a walk in the woods to talk about it. She was older than me—forty, I thought—but with a singer's straight back and uptilted chin and eyes and smile lines like she knew a joke that put her in a good, mellow mood all the time.

She didn't have any rules, just suggestions and practices. "I like to stay quiet for the first mile," she'd told me on our first walk. "It helps me get all the chatter out of my head." Not that I couldn't talk, but she was the kind of person you just *liked*, and she was so matter-of-fact about the way that the silence helped with *her* mental health that I just kept quiet.

A mile into the woods, she stopped and took a deep breath and made a tall *Y* out of her arms and stuck her chin in the air and closed her eyes. Then she looked at me with tranquil eyes. "Let's talk about amends."

"Ah," I said. "You didn't like it."

"Your job isn't to write something I like. Your job is to figure out some things."

"And I didn't figure them out."

"Let me put it this way. If you asked me whether you should send this to these women, I'd advise you not to."

"Ah."

"Do you know why that is?"

"I hate Socratic dialogue, Lira. I'm a big boy. Just tell me what's on your mind."

"Humph. I'm more of a question-asker than an answer-giver. Let me think about it. Let's walk."

There was a deer, and we stopped and watched it while it watched us. I let the cracks about Lyme disease arise and float away without giving them utterance. A drone buzzed us, and the deer looked up at it, then walked away. It didn't bolt or startle, just moseyed on, like, *Fuck off, drone. I'm outtahere.*

"Okay, I'll give you this in answer form. Forgive me if I'm rusty. You wrote to these women, and you laid it all out like a ledger. Here's the minuses. Here's the pluses. Here's the total, and it's positive. If I'm in credit with you, with your friends, with all women everywhere, then I'm a good guy and deserve your forgiveness."

"So I don't deserve forgiveness?"

"Now you're asking loaded questions."

"Ha ha. Don't play games. There's a difference between a Socratic question and a legitimate one."

"It was a rhetorical question."

"Seriously? And yes, that's rhetorical too. Fine: Do I deserve forgiveness?"

"Why would you ask me about forgiveness?"

"Ah-ah-ah. More questions!"

"OK, an answer. You won't like it. I don't know if you deserve forgiveness, and I don't actually care, much. That's what I was trying to explain when I told you about the ledger. You're not here because you need to work toward forgiveness."

"Why am I here, then? To make amends?"

"It's hard not to ask questions, isn't it?"

All the while, that righteous anger had been building in me, the boiling, bubbling, outraged howl that got me to all the right places and all the wrong ones. I let it out. "Lady." I wasn't loud. I didn't have to be loud. I was good at this. Only amateurs yell unnecessarily. "Please, will you stop fucking with me? I am here because it was the only place that would have me, and I don't like it. I want to go back. I want to cooperate. You tell me what's expected of me, I'll do it. I'm not stupid. I know I fucked up. But I don't deserve to be played with like this is freshman philosophy and you caught me picking my nose in the back row and decided to make an example out of me. I'm a grown-up adult-type man in full command of his faculties. I'm not a fool. I don't need the riddle of the Sphinx. I am listening with both ears and paying attention. I'm here to do the work. But the games, you can keep those."

"That's the second time you've called this a game, Ivar. It's not. It's a project."

"Forgive me, Lira, but that sounds like a distinction without a difference."

"Games have rules; projects don't. That's a difference."

I could tell that I was about to get loud, and only amateurs get loud without meaning to, and I'm not an amateur, so I shut my mouth and walked in silence for the next mile. Which took a while.

"Sorry," I said.

"Nothing to be sorry about," she said, looking intently into the branches at some critter I couldn't see. Birds, maybe, or some species of tree-dwelling rodent.

"I'm not here to be forgiven."

"No."

"Not to make amends either."

"Not that."

I felt a species of cold grue unfurl in my guts. "Lira?"

"Yes, Ivar?"

"Does anyone leave here?" It was a pleasant enough place, but a nice place to visit. Living here forever, exile? I'd go crazy. Feed me to the tree-dwelling rodents now, get it over with.

"Seriously? Yes, of course. People leave here all the time. It's not a gulag."

"Not amends, not forgiveness. The ledger."

"That's right."

"Lira, am I here to learn how to be a better person?"

"Now you're getting it. Look, Ivar, what's done is done. The people you've hurt on the way will always have been hurt by you. Maybe you can make them feel better about that and maybe you can't, but the reason you're here isn't because you hurt someone. It's because you hurt someone, and then you hurt someone, and then you hurt someone else."

The anger rose back in me so quick it surprised me. "Oh, please. Do you know how many women I uplifted? How many I promoted, publicized, lionized? How much money I gave? Look at this." I peeled back my lip, exposed the bridge where my right upper canine had been. "Stepped in when a guy was hitting his girlfriend, right there, in the middle of the sidewalk, everyone else walking by like they didn't see it. Not me. Guy was twice my size, out of his mind, and he kicked six kinds of shit out of me. Actions speak louder than words, right?"

Lira was as calm as the woods around us. "Those are very admirable accomplishments," she said simply, and headed back to the dorms.

\* \* \*

Margaret brought Mat along for our evening walk. I made a face but didn't say anything. We'd found so many excuses lately to skip the walk, and I missed it. Picking a fight over Mat would probably cancel yet another evening's outing. The settlement grew so fast that whole new neighborhoods sprang into existence between our walks (or maybe we skipped a *lot* of walks).

"Want a drink?" Margaret said, rummaging in Mat's compartment and coming up with both a water bottle and a flask. I reached for the water bottle, then switched to the flask.

"Yow," I said. "That stuff's getting better."

"Thank the organic chemists back in Srinagar. They fed a bunch of twenty-five-year-old malts to a mass spectrometer, figured out what happens when you age it, synthesized it, and added it to six-day-old spirits. This stuff was only a buck at the commissary."

"Give me another slug." The beer was fine out here, but the spirits and wine had been pretty terrible, especially at first. They'd been improving over the years since, but this was something else. "Only took four years," I said.

"Five," Margaret said softly. "It's been five now. Happy anniversary."

\* \* \*

Margaret was already an old hand when I arrived. She had her own place and friends and a stock of good recipes for turning the food the commissary gave out for free into real meals.

I met her on my second week out of new arrivals housing. Lira had counseled me against any serious relationships, warned me that I had the kind of hard work ahead of me that made me unsuitable boyfriend material. But it didn't matter. Not once I saw Margaret, her wiseass expression as she presided over a picnic-blanket's worth of old hands who were eating clotted cream and strawberry jam on biscuits, celebrating the latest additions to the commissary's bioreactor repertoire, lazing about in one of those climate-changey early spring days that felt like summer, back when summer didn't feel like fall, or the surface of the sun, or a sauna.

I was banjaxed at first glance. That expression—half hauteur, half self-mockery—was like a reflection of my most prized and never admitted conception of who I was, deep down. She had a foxy chin and good face lines from a lot of thinking and laughing, and was wearing a man's shirt spattered with different paint colors—not like it was decoration, but more like it was a smock she wore to dabble in oils—and bright orange tights, and her brown-gray hair was up in a messy topknot that made her look like a sorceress with bedhead.

I had been wrapped up in a bubble since I'd left new arrivals housing, the demi-friends I'd made in the dorms all scattered to different neighborhoods and me feeling like it would be an imposition on them to call them up while they were getting their bearings. Lira messaged me every day or two, but apart from that, I hadn't had any meaningful contact in days. I told myself I was doing something monkish and contemplative and not something neurotic and dysfunctional, but I had my doubts.

Normally, I'm not a starer, but these were not normal circumstances. Normally, I am not one to be banjaxed. I'm not one to be bubbled. I'm not one for monkish contemplation. I like people, is what I'm saying, and the isolation had taken its toll.

Naturally, she caught me staring and just nodded once, coolly, like, *I see you staring, and who can blame you* and went back to her friends. I was doubly banjaxed—skewered, even—but shaken loose of my trance

THE WEIGHT OF A FEATHER (THE WEIGHT OF A HEART)

so that I went back to my business, which was to report in at the job center to meet with a counselor.

An hour later, I emerged, having spent the intervening hour being remorselessly probed by a very nice little fellow who really wanted me to be fulfilled and had an endless set of ways to make that happen, from artisanal pencil sharpener to ditchdigger to housepainter to headline writer to butterfly tender.

I had taken note of a Greek place earlier in the day, and I was trying to remember where it was when I wandered back through the park where Margaret had been presiding over her picnic. Normally, I'm good with directions, but the banjaxing and the higgledy-piggledy of the settlement and my general disorientation conspired together to rob me of my bearings, so I was lost and looking around for landmarks when I saw her again.

She was a good deal more relaxed and less posed than she had been an hour before, and there were torpid friends and wine bottles all around her to explain that change. I spotted her, and my eyes locked on hers, no longer searching for the way to the Greek's. She looked half asleep, half amused, and she did this incredible slow nod thing that was seductive and self-assured at once, like, *Maybe I'll take you home, and maybe I won't. We'll have to see.*

I nearly walked away. I was so out of practice when it came to other people, especially women. But I was lonely. And banjaxed. I reeled myself into her orbit.

"I'm Ivar," I said.

She patted the blanket beside her. "I'm Margaret. I was a great friend and a great daughter but not always and sometimes not in ways that counted."

"Oh," I said. "Uh."

She smiled and handed me a sippy cup full of cold white wine from her thermos bag. "Don't worry," she said. "You don't have to reciprocate. I just like to get it out of the way. You can be mysterious."

"It's just that I'm new around here—"

"No kidding." Man, she had great delivery. I snorted.

"Looking for a job, huh?"

"Just wanna be useful."

"Useful's overrated." She waved an arm around her, at the torporous friends and the empty bottles. "Growth comes from within. Listening to the still, small voice of conscience, which can only be heard when you aren't anesthetizing yourself with labor."

"You, uh, don't believe in anesthetizing yourself, huh?"

She unscrewed her sippy cup and topped it up with a bottle from the thermos bag. "Brother, I'm not going to stop anesthetizing myself anytime soon. But I know when I'm doing it. Do you?"

I opened my mouth to snap something snappy, then closed it. "No, I don't suppose I do, not always."

"Knowing what you don't know is the first step to knowing." She grinned to make it softer.

"You sound like you really understand the deal around here. Been here a while, I guess."

She snorted. "I'm a pioneer. Early adopter." She held my gaze, defiant.

"I guess that means you really pissed some people off, huh?"

She nodded slowly, still holding my gaze. "Doesn't everyone?"

"I like you," I said. It was a bit of my old bravado, lost in the months since I arrived. It felt good to get it back.

"I might like you," she said. "But it'll take a while to figure out whether I do."

I shrugged. "I'm not busy."

* * *

Five years.

"How has it been five years?" Mat ran over my heels, and I stumbled and went down on my palms. The hard rubber pavement gave me a friction burn. "Shit!"

She turned around. "He's supposed to avoid collisions. Bad robot! Bad Mat!" She snorted at me. "Downward dog? Now? Look at you with the self-care."

I picked myself up and aimed a kick at Mat, who wheeled away from my foot. "Looks like his collision avoidance is working again."

"You spent two months in orientation, right? Then you met me two weeks and one day after?"

"You remembered all that detail?"

She shrugged. "Thank Mat."

I looked at the little teardrop-shaped stupid robot, then back to her. "Mat."

"When we go on walks together, I tell him the things that cross my mind, and then he reminds me of them."

"Mat talks?"

"Sure, he's got a whole personal assistant thing. You never heard him? We talk to each other all the time. Mat, say hello to Ivar."

"Hi, Ivar. Sorry for bumping into you."

"He sounds exactly like you. *Exactly* like you."

"Well, yeah. I trained him. It's just a deepfake."

"I'm gonna have pronoun trouble talking to him if he sounds exactly like you. Your pronouns are *definitely* she/her."

She gave me a saucy smile. "You say the most retrograde things, Ivar. Mat, do you have a male voice model you can use with Ivar?"

"Of course. How's this? The sixth sick sheik's sixth sheep's sick. Near an ear, a nearer ear, a nearly eerie ear. I wish to wash my Irish wristwatch."

The hairs on the back of my neck stood up. "Now he sounds exactly like me."

"You think so? Ivar, you're *terrible* at tongue twisters."

"Did you tell him to train a model on my voice?"

"Nope," she said. "But Mat's good at anticipating needs. That's his whole thing, using statistical modeling to figure out what's going to happen next."

"Ugh," I said.

She took a step backward. "What?"

"Nothing."

"It's not nothing," she said. "You look like you want to do a murder. What's wrong, Ivar?"

I suddenly felt self-conscious about Mat's presence. Back when I thought that all he did was dog his mistress's heels, he'd been a petty annoyance. Now he seemed sinister.

"It's just—" I took a step off the sidewalk onto a flagstone path leading into a courtyard hemmed in by three midrise housing blocks with little shops and a café on their ground floors. I gestured at Margaret to follow, and of course, Mat came with. I made an exasperated face, and Margaret knelt down to look Mat in his frontal sensors.

"Take five, Mat."

"Roger that," he said, in her voice.

We found a bench in the courtyard, facing the entrance and Mat, lonely and patient on the flagstone path.

"You want to tell me why you're freaking out?"

"Freaking out? I hardly said a word."

"Ivar, you look like you're dying of dysentery. And it started the minute I told you Mat could talk. Are you seriously phobic of talking robots?"

"What? No, of course. I mean, the thing where it deepfakes our voices is creepy, but no, that's not it. It's the 'anticipating our needs' thing."

She gave me that one-dimpled, sardonic you're-shitting-me face. "You have a phobia of statistical inference?"

"You *don't*? Come on, Margaret, what's statistical inference? It's analyzing the past to predict the future. That means it only works if the future is like the past. The whole reason I'm here is to make sure my future *isn't* like my past. That thing"—I shot a glare at Mat, still and obstructive, as a couple stepped off the path to get around him—"is like an autocorrect that tries to replace everything new you type with something you used to type, so every time I text you 'hey' it finishes it with 'darling,' even if I want to type 'asshole.' It's like a greased slope back into your old groove."

"I thought that machine learning used the wisdom of the crowds, like everyone types 'darling' after 'hey' and—"

"No, that's not true. If you're doing something for the first time, that's what happens, the system pushes you to be like the middle-of-the-road, median asshole out there. Those are its two modes: 'conform' and 'never grow in any way.' It's regression to the mean times a million. What fucking genius thought programming a robot for *this* place to do *that* would be a good idea?"

She got a thoughtful look, staring up at the scudding clouds. "You know, when you put it that way, it's pretty fucked up."

"Thank you," I said.

"Don't think I didn't notice that you just called me an asshole."

"It was a hypothetical."

"Asshole."

* * *

I didn't have to come here. I wasn't sent. I chose.

Now, admittedly, no one wanted to talk to me. I mean, that's not true. There were plenty of counselors who'd pick up. Old friends would answer my texts, but tersely, and always found a reason to duck any social invitations. There was a guy at the coffee shop who was friendly, but he was like that with everyone, and even though he always remembered my drink, the third time he asked me what I did and where I was from and how long I'd been in the neighborhood, I realized that he just ran on autopilot, making banter without retaining anything except the drink order.

But socially and professionally, I was done. One too many fits of pique. Literally, it just took one, an improvised comedy routine about the idiocy of a brainless, gormless, neckless guy in the grocery store who wouldn't get out of my way even after I asked him nice, twice. I didn't realize he was what-the-kids-call-neuroatypical until he had a panic attack that turned into floods of tears and went downhill from there.

That's when everyone who'd taken out their screens to record this giant cream puff melting into a puddle of his own devising, and I took it for a ruse, so that footage included an excruciating two more minutes of me really laying into the guy.

It was funny. I mean, no one could deny that, and I think that's what did me in. That video, you watch it and you laugh, and you cackle, and then you howl with laughter, and the loudest laughs of all come when the guy is just at the end of his rope, and then you find out what's going on, who the villain really was all along. It was me, and you were rooting for me, so that makes me a bad guy twice over, because I tricked you into staining your soul.

That's my theory. What else would explain the fervor with which the human flesh search engine scoured my history for other transgressions, turning up aggrieved parties who had highly selective and prejudicial accounts of the most glancing encounters I'd had with them, contrasting these transgressions with my own prodigious output of on-the-record statements condemning others for their bad deeds. You see, I wasn't just a monster; I was a hypocrite. I was, as they say, "toxic."

Look, it wasn't fair, but it wasn't unfair. I have done a lot of things in my days and not all of them are sources of pride, but when you take a lot of shots, you're going to rack up a lot of misses, and some of them will be pretty embarrassing. At first I thought I could ride it out by ignoring it, but that only made it worse. Then I thought I could get past it by apologizing, but that made it *much* worse.

Eventually, it became clear that everyone would be much happier if I just wasn't around anymore, and then it became clear that *I* would also be happier if I wasn't around either. I'm too much of a coward to climb into the bathtub with my toaster, and so I ended up here.

I am not always 100 percent certain I made the right call.

\* \* \*

Lira ran into me while I was taking Mat out for a walk. That was what I called it, the long rambles I'd take with Margaret's robot, which now talked like me, a switch it had started making depending on who it was talking to. The first time, I'd been in the kitchen, looking for my favorite whisk, and I'd asked aloud where it was, and Mat told me. I didn't even notice then that he'd used my voice, and the most startling thing wasn't hearing my voice coming out of the knee-high orange robot—it was realizing that I hadn't even noticed. Indeed, there was something comforting about having an outboard brain that followed me around and told me the things I should have known but didn't.

Around then, Margaret had hurt her ankle and couldn't join me on walks anymore. A couple of days of that and I'd started to get snappish, and Margaret ordered me out of the house, knowing that walks mellowed me out. Mat had tagged along that first day, and I hadn't been able to get him to go back without turning around myself, so I'd walked, and endured the stares of curious strangers, and then I'd started muttering to myself, the way I do when I'm out on my own, and Mat started answering me. He's got good hearing. Robot ears.

Before I knew it, I was unloading on Mat, and he reeled in his following distance so he was right on my heels, and I could still mutter, and he could sotto voce his replies. Explaining all my stuff to Mat was a lot of work, so I opened my email and IM spools to him, all the way back to middle school, and then I gave him the socials I'd archived before deleting them, along with all my accounts, when it became apparent that this was the only thing I could do. Mat ingested all of it, recombined it, modeled it, trained on it, and became my boon companion and heartmate.

Lira found me and Mat telling dirty jokes as we circled a new pueblo-style development, cubes on cubes on cubes, red-mud colored and stacked high, with the usual courtyard ringed with restaurants and corner shops and a green.

"Hi there, Ivar. Who's your friend?"

I was embarrassed, like I'd been caught taking a sex toy out for a romantic dinner. I did what I always do when I'm uncomfortable—I quipped.

"Mat, this is Lira. Lira, this is your replacement, Mat."

Lira did this eyebrow thing and then got down on her hunkers to look Mat in all his eyes. "Well, it was inevitable. Good luck to you, sir."

"Ivar is doing really well," he said. My voice, not hers. Maybe he didn't have enough training data to do a convincing Lira yet. "He wrote an amazing letter yesterday."

I had, actually. It was a doozy, to a woman I'd met at a professional event and misread the signals on and asked a personal question of, who'd left the event shortly thereafter. I promptly forgot the question and the woman, but she didn't, as I came to discover when the human flesh search engine read her side of things and pinned them on me forever.

When that happened, I'd been outraged: we were both adults, I wasn't in a position to hire her or steer business her way, and I'd asked politely. The fact that she'd had three other guys ask the same question—politely—that day had discouraged her so much that she'd changed fields. But I wasn't those guys, and I was sure my ask was more polite than any of theirs could have been. And I couldn't have known about those guys. And if you don't ask, you don't find out. What if she *had* been interested?

I'd told Mat this story on an earlier walk, and he'd been as supportive as you could ask for, making some very shrewd guesses about how I felt about it. I'd gone home from that walk feeling smug, because that scandal had come late in the process, long after I'd given up on defending myself either in public or in private, which meant that none of my feelings about it had been in the training corpus I'd shoveled into Mat's hopper. Somehow that gave me the idea that Mat had reasoned out my innocence from first principles—if the robot says you're blameless, that must be an empirical fact, right?

I went to bed smug. I woke up in a panic, my heart thudding and sweat slicking my pits, sitting straight up in bed and smacking a screen for the time. 3:28 a.m. I'd gone to bed at 10:00 p.m. on the button, as all good boys with important things to do always should. That meant that it had taken my slumbering subconscious five hours and twenty-eight minutes to realize that Mat has coughed up all his reassuring advice on the basis of all the other times I'd been called out, called in, and raked over, which meant that a) I was a repeat offender, and b) I made the same excuse every time.

A thing about life as an adult is that you get familiar with the dark watches of the night, the 3:28s and the 2:17s and the 4:11s. Your bladder, of course, but also that part of your mind that has the maturity to know when you've fucked up but lacks the timing to wait until morning to remind you of that fact. If Mat was a machine for finding out who I'd been and nudging me toward being that person again, my subconscious was a machine for tormenting me with the dreadful prophecy that I'd never escape the greased chasms I'd worn into my gray matter.

I had a theory that giving in to my subconscious would only train it to do more of the same shit, so I absolutely refused to get out of bed and do something about my revelation. Instead, I lay plank rigid until Margaret got up and hobbled on her swollen ankle to the kitchen, assuming that I was still asleep. Then I got up and made my own way down to her and Mat and made the two of us coffee.

"Well, you look like shit," she said.

"Good," I said. "I feel considerably worse than shit, and therefore I am reassured that my faculty for hiding my weaknesses from the world is in good working order."

"Ugh," she said. "I'm going to go ice my ankle in the garden. Feel free to come out and join me once you've decided to be fit for human company." I knew from her tone that she wasn't kidding. It's not like Margaret was the easiest company in the world, but the fact that I sometimes had to put up with her shit didn't guarantee that she'd be willing to deal with my shit.

I sat in the bed, thinking about my 3:28 special and my ill-starred conversation with that woman all those years ago. Cynthia Ross. I tried to remember her. It had been so long ago. Hazy. But it had been a conference for high-frequency trading algorithm designers, and we'd been at a presentation on advance game theory for liquidity provision—basically, how to write a stock-trading bot that could buy up a ton of shares in a company without seeming to, so front-running arbitrageurs couldn't beat it to the punch and jack up the price. I could remember the presenter, an old guy with a Greek accent whose slides had been laid out as a sci-fi chess set where each move and countermove were animated. He'd been indecently pleased with those slides, had chortled every time a gambit was spoiled by a space marine or an astro-balrog. His delight was so pure that it was catching, and we'd all laughed with him by the end.

They set up wine in plastic cups and finger sandwiches in the hallway outside the conference room, and I got one of the former and four of the latter and juggled them to a tall table where she was already eating.

What had she looked like? Attractive, obviously. I mean, I had standards. I wouldn't have asked unless. Plus, she must have been smart. I had standards. Cynthia's online presence was photo-free, deliberately so, all the links dead-ending in curt, legalistic text. What had she looked like?

From 3:28 a.m. until Margaret arose, I'd tried with increasing frustration to remember. I'd reconstructed the scene at the finest level of detail. The presenter's stubble and allover short light brown hair, like a duckling fuzz. His slides. The room. The chairs. Creaky chairs on low-pile industrial hotel carpet. The room. Fighting over the power outlets that were snaked between the chairs. Laughing at the slides. The guy sitting next to me, a West African guy in a long senator-style shirt who took notes on a Chinese tablet of a sort I'd never seen before (and then after that day, it seemed like I spotted them everywhere).

I remembered the bad wine. White, astringent, not cold enough. The tinted plastic cups that made it look dark, like cider. The tall tables. The finger sandwiches: two cultured salmon meat with nut cream cheese, one roasted pepper, and pesto. The spongy bread. The crowd noise, the bad hotel hallway lighting, the floor-to-ceiling windows overlooking a pool. I swear I could even remember the ball some kids were batting around in the pool.

But I couldn't remember Cynthia.

* * *

It was writing the letter that did it. I started by confessing that I couldn't remember what she looked like. After that, it all spilled out. That I had not only seen her as an object; I hadn't even given the object much thought. All that bullshit I'd been telling myself about my discernment and selectivity, and I couldn't even remember what she looked like?

That was the realization that unlocked what it must have been for her. I'd hit on her—fuck, I'd harassed her—because I wanted to be seen. I wanted to be thought of as distinctive and desirable and smart and not just another one of those guys puddling around the waist. Getting a smart, good-looking younger woman into bed? I'd know I was more than just a generic chairwarmer, good for a badge sale and three finger sandwiches.

It killed me to realize that this was exactly the same thing she'd been hoping for: To be seen as a person. Someone who deserved to be there. Someone whose purpose was to contribute to the field, not to make someone like me feel better by coming up to my hotel room.

We both wanted to be seen. Except my desire to be seen required that she disappear. I'd sobbed when I figured that out, but I'd snotted up the self-pity and made myself write. Sit down at the keyboard and open a vein.

It was a good letter. I could tell because there was no way in hell I would send it to her. It wasn't a letter for her. It was a letter for me. Maybe it was a letter for other people who lived with the same ugly self-deception and lack of self-awareness that I did. Or had. No, did.

When Margaret limped back up to the bedroom and found me weeping and staring at my screen, she looked at me blankly for a long moment, then left quietly, closing the door behind her.

Mat kept me company.

\* \* \*

He used my voice: "He wrote an amazing letter yesterday."

Lira gave me a searching look. "Did you?"

I looked her right back. "Damned right I did."

"Do I need to give you the talk about how breakthroughs are nice, but transformation is about habits, not realizations, and habits take time?"

"I think you just did."

She showed me those smile lines. "There's a longer version. But you're a smart fella—you can probably figure it out from the top-line description."

I was about to say something Ivarish and quippy, but I held it back. "Mat, take five, would you?" The little orange robot rolled away toward the pueblo stacks. "Lira?"

"Ivar."

"It was a good letter."

"I believe it." She put her hand on my forearm, looked deep into my eyes. "Not everyone gets as far as you have, Ivar. You should be pleased with that. You've got a big brain, and that can work against you, help you talk yourself out of looking too closely at your own logic. Introspection and empathy aren't the same thing as smarts.

"Like I said, you've come farther than a lot of people ever get, but

Ivar, you've still got a way to go. Knowing is half the battle, sure, but it's only half. The other half is operationalizing that knowledge. Doing something with it."

I looked down at her hand on my arm. "I get it."

"Good," she said. "I'm not trying to denigrate your achievement. I just want to give you a reality check. Some human feedback from a person who's seen it before."

\* \* \*

Margaret had a newspaper when I got back.

I pointed at it. "What the hell is that?"

"Cute, isn't it? There's a new bacterium that breaks down waste cellulose into a slurry that goes straight into the paper former. Apparently, they've had it for years on the outside, and there's newspapers everywhere, and some new arrival got the bright idea of starting one here."

I read the masthead: "*The Coventry Explainer*? Well, I could have used one of those when I got here." I hadn't seen a newspaper since I was a kid, but this was a lot thinner than I remembered them being— four sheets of tabloid, center-folder, and folded again. Above the fold on page one, a screaming headline: "Population Bomb!"

It was enough to get me to pick up the paper and read it. What do you call clickbait when there are no clicks involved? "We're now at ten percent of the national population? That can't be true. That would mean, uh, *tens of millions* of us?"

She shook her head. "The methodology's sound. I used my screen to get the research report. It's not my field, but I can check anyone's stats. Assuming the data is good, the conclusion is plausible."

"Where the hell are they?"

"What do you mean?"

"I mean, where the hell do they all live?"

"What do you think all the construction is about?"

I shrugged. "I mean, there was construction when I got here. I assumed it was some kind of therapeutic busywork, like starting a newspaper or any of those stupid jobs I cycled through when I got here. Butterfly tender."

"The butterflies aren't useless. They class the place up. There was construction when I got here, too, but it was all a lot closer together. There was only one town, and it really was a town, not a city. It's been growing ever since. When was the last time you looked at a map?"

"Why would I? We've got everything we need within ten minutes of here, and it all changes often enough that I'm happy just to walk our neighborhood."

She grimaced and pulled out her screen, tapped up a map. "You should get out more." I pinch-zoomed, pinch-zoomed, pinch-zoomed. "Holy shit, it's this big now? This place makes Los Angeles look like East Bumblefuck, Arkansas."

"Probably won't grow much bigger. I always figured ten percent was the cap."

The map gave me a sense of dizzying unreality. I gave her back her screen. "Why ten? Some kind of genetic disorder or—"

"Nope, just that only about ten percent of us are in a position to get away with the kind of bullshit that lands you here. You know: rich, powerful." I was about to insist that I'd never been either of those things, and she held up a hand. "Talented."

* * *

On rainy days, our little cottage got very claustrophobic. After a couple of weeks stuck inside with her bum ankle, Margaret was touchy and snappish, and me, well, I've always given as good as I get, so we'd get into these loops where she'd dig at me, and then I'd come back at her, and bam—we'd be shouting at each other.

Mat was uncannily good at spotting these fights and retreating to his charge station and docking before they got loud. Of course, all that meant was that we were repeating a pattern—a pattern his machine-learning algorithm had spotted and formulated a response to.

Margaret was good at aftermaths, didn't nurse a grudge or demand groveling apologies, just got pensive and tired and maybe a little sad. I got the impression that the dominant feeling after these things was disappointment in herself. I got that. I was certainly disappointed in myself after these fights. For one thing, I had a faster tongue than she did, which meant that her minor provocations would be met with real swordplay from my side, and of course, that just put her in a worse, angrier place.

We were sitting in the kitchen, listening to the rain spatter on the windows, eating some nice brie that the bioreactor had done a superb job with—better than it had on the crackers. Sitting there, eating brie, and Mat clunked off his base and rolled to the front door, like a dog that was ready to be walked. I reacted unconsciously, looking around for my raincoat and trying to remember where I left my rain boots, and then I stopped myself. Mat didn't need a walk. Mat thought *I* needed a walk.

Margaret grimaced at me, and I could see she was thinking on the same lines as me.

"Uh," I said.

"Spit it out."

"We're predictable, I guess." I looked at Mat, motionless with the stillness of an idling machine.

"You are, but—"

"I'm not," we said at the same time and smiled. Smiling at Margaret felt good. It was a reminder of who we could be, when we weren't tearing each other apart or licking our wounds.

"Make-up sex?" I suggested. Kept it light though.

"Are you serious?"

"Uh," I said.

"All right, let's go." She hobbled up the stairs.

"Wait, Margaret—"

"Come on, fool. You won't get many offers like this."

Not having sex at that point would have been just mean. It had been my suggestion. It was also a good call, as it turned out, clearing the air the way no amount of talking could have. Afterward, we lay quiet and trailed our hands over each other with half-closed eyes.

"Does it bother you?" she said, quiet as a sigh.

"Fucking? No, Margaret, I quite like it. Does it bother *you*?"

She pinched, I squirmed, but she smiled. "No, being predictable."

"Uh," I said.

"Ivar, you're a genuine asshole a lot of the time. But you're working a program, trying to tamp it down."

"You are too, babe. I see it."

She stiffened. "I am most certainly *not*," she said. "And do not lie about shit like that. It's no favor to me."

I started to protest, then I stopped. Had Margaret actually been doing anything to "improve" herself? I thought back over our years— years!—together. The fights. The sweet times. She'd changed over those years, hadn't she?

In some small ways. She no longer used my towel and left it on the bed, so I had no way to dry off when I got out of the shower. She didn't complain when I fried onions, so long as I turned on the extractor fan and opened a window.

But the big stuff? The topics I wasn't allowed to talk about? No movement at all. No talking about family. No talking about the things that happened to get her here. She'd talk about the various jobs she'd had, both before and after she got here, and tell funny stories about the people she'd worked with, but never about friends. I didn't even know what town she was from. And if I forgot and asked about any of that, she'd cut me dead, walk out of the room, be in a terrible mood for days. Sometimes she'd joke about it, call herself my "international woman of mystery," but *I* wasn't allowed to joke about it. At all.

"Okay," I said, recognizing this was one of those subjects I shouldn't weigh in on if I valued my equilibrium. We'd just had a fight. I didn't want another one.

"You should take Mat for a walk," she said. "He'll get restless otherwise." She pulled the blanket around her and rolled on her side, facing away from me.

She needed some solo time. Fair enough. Mat followed me dutifully out of the apartment.

\* \* \*

Lira ran into me a couple of weeks later. The weather had been running nice, and Margaret had started up her regular picnics again, bringing out her old gang for afternoons of wine, Frisbee, gossip, and food. Anyone who stopped to check it out got an invite, and a few new arrivals took her up on it, and I felt a quick, foolish pang of jealousy at first, as I saw how they looked at her, like a person who was exactly where she should be, doing what she should do. A person with purpose.

But it was stupid, that feeling. That was what I loved about Margaret. I shouldn't feel jealous that other people recognized it, I should feel vicariously self-satisfied on her behalf. This was Margaret in her element, Margaret at her best, Margaret doing what she was good at. Convening, socializing, making a space where people felt they didn't have to do anything or say anything, where they could be bodies at rest, not working a program or figuring anything out.

Once I figured that out, I wasn't jealous, but still . . . I was happy for Margaret, but it all started to feel so *predictable*. Like the future was destined to be like the past. I'd grown up with some pretty romantic views about the future, about it being fundamentally different, and somewhere along the line, I'd decided that was just wishful thinking, and nothing would ever change.

Somehow I'd kept that view up, even after my life imploded, even after I ended up here. Even after I started eating exotic, delicious food that came out of a printer. Somehow this very, very different future hadn't shaken my confidence that nothing would ever change.

Things needed to change.

Margaret barely noticed when I wandered off. Mat did though. He bumped along behind me as I struck off for a walk to the Greek place, thinking about getting a piece of baklava and strong, gritty coffee. The Greek place was gone though. Everything changed all the time here.

"Ivar!" Lira called, spotting me standing outside the ceramics studio that had sprung up where the Greek place had been. "Hey!"

She had gotten older and grayer in the years since I'd first come here, but she still had that smile. "It's great to see you," I said. It was true.

"How are you doing?"

"Is that a friendly question or a professional one?"

She cocked her head. "Take it either way. Do you want to have a professional conversation?"

"Not really," I lied.

"How about a walk?"

"That, I'd like."

"I need to be at the intake dorms in a couple of hours. Let's head that way and go for a walk in the woods?"

\* \* \*

We walked the first mile in silence, save for the sound of Mat laboring over the uneven ground. He fell behind at times, but we didn't bother to wait for him; he could always catch up. When Mat needed to, he could *motor*.

A mile in, we stopped by a stream that was overhung with a thick canopy from the thirsty trees that dug their roots into its banks and lifted their arms to the sky. The late-day orange sunlight pierced that canopy, and everything was green and gold, the air heavy with the smell of fresh water, evanescent sap, and warm soil.

There was only the sound of the stream and the sound of our

breathing, soft rustles from critters making their way through the woods around us.

"It's beautiful," I said, at last, because it was, and because I wasn't good at silence the way Lira was.

"It wasn't always," she said. "When I got here, this was a brownfield site, burned over in the wildfires, all ash and burned plastic and melted asphalt. In those days, there was lots for us to do, helping the machines get everything ready for the trees."

"I didn't know you'd been here that long," I said. "Were you one of the original staff?"

She smiled, chin high, back straight, little dimples. "Staff? No, Ivar, I wasn't staff."

I caught on. "I'm supposed to say something like, 'But you're so nice and kind and understanding. What could *you* have done to warrant coming here?'"

"But you're not going to?"

"No. Seems to me that being good at putting things on the positive side of the ledger doesn't make you bad at putting things on the negative side."

Her smile grew broader. "That's very well said, Ivar. Good for you. I don't think that's something the Ivar I first met could have said, or even understood."

"That makes me feel almost indecently good." I suddenly wanted to hug her, but I didn't. I wasn't a hugger.

"You should feel good. That's a big step."

A drone buzzed us. She shooed it away.

"So you've been here a long time," I said. "You must like it here."

Her smile vanished. "What makes you say that?"

I fumbled. "You're still here, right?"

"Ivar, I'm not here because I like it. I'm here because I'm afraid to go back."

I opened and shut my mouth a few times. She shook her head. "You don't need to say anything," she said. "I've made my peace with it. It's all down to the ledger. Once you know that no good deed will ever erase your bad deeds, those bad deeds start to weigh on you. There were times in my life when I saw people as things, the way we all do sometimes. I've forgiven myself for those times, and I've cultivated better instincts, the habit of interrupting myself before I talk myself into thinking it will be okay to do it again.

"But I slip up—" She held her hand up to stop me from speaking. I closed my mouth. "I do, Ivar. In ways small and large. Here, at least, people expect it. This is the place for people who fuck up that way. A place where you can fuck up without *being* a fuckup.

"Maybe I could make it outside. I hear things are better out there now, that there's ways people talk to each other when things are starting to go bad that stops them from getting worse. But here's the thing, Ivar: What if it didn't work for me? What if I left, and then *I had to come back?*"

* * *

I saw Lira off at the intake dorms, which had been completely rebuilt since I'd last seen them, skinned with photovoltaics and topped with bladeless turbines, with a new pool and tennis courts and an orchard being tended by people who had the shell-shocked posture and movement of newbies.

Mat rolled at my heels as I struck off for home. It was a long walk, hours yet, and I wondered whether Margaret was still in the park, drinking wine and laughing with her little court of fans, friends, and admirers. I wondered whether I hoped she'd be home when I got back or whether she wouldn't.

"From the time I got here," I said, knowing Mat was listening, "I thought I was here to get better and go home."

"Rehabilitation is hard work," Mat said. "And even if it feels comfortable, it can't be permanent. You can't be rehabilitating forever. Eventually, you have to be rehabilitated."

"That's what I thought," I said.

"But you don't think that now?" Mat spoke in my exact voice and used the exact tone I used when something really strange was going on. The voice that I used to greet the unexpected.

"What do you think, Mat?" I asked.

"I don't think, Ivar. Remember: I'm only a robot," he said.

"What do you predict, then?"

"I predict that you will continue to do the hard, excellent work you've been doing, and that you will grow in ways that let you go back home. The Greater Los Angeles Housing Co-Operative has plenty of availability; all the shortages from the retreat are long past, and there's seismically stable high-rise infill all the way back to Sylmar. I could help you find a place with a similar mix of demographics, retail, and industry to Culver City before the retreat; or, if you prefer, I could find you a place more similar to the one you have been sharing with Margaret."

"What do you call the tense you just used there, Mat?" One of the nice things about talking to a robot: it doesn't mind if you change the subject. "What did you say? 'A place more similar to the one you have been sharing with Margaret'? Is 'you have been' the subjunctive?"

"No, it's the present perfect continuous."

"What tense would it have been if you'd said, 'You share with Margaret,' instead?"

"That's the present continuous."

"It's been a long time since I thought about grammar, but it seems to me like the first one implied that Margaret and I weren't going to share a place anymore, while the second one is what you'd use if we were going to go on living together."

"Either one can be used in either case, but that is the convention, it's true."

"That's what I thought," I said. "You're quite the predictor, you know."

* * *

"Why did you get Mat?" I asked Margaret as I helped her clean out the picnic hampers and get them ready to return to the community library.

She had been washing dishes, and her shoulders tensed and then relaxed halfway. "I've wondered that myself," she said.

"Did you ever ask him?" I said.

"No." She dried her hands on a dish towel.

"He seems to want me to go back to the world."

Her shoulders tensed again. "Really."

"To the extent that a robot wants anything at all."

"The robot wants you to be like you've been," she said. "You've always wanted to get out of here." She turned around. Her face was stony. "You've always worked the program."

I was keenly aware of Mat in the corner, resting on his charge plate.

"Is that right, Mat? You want me to go home because I want to go home?"

"I don't want anything, Ivar. I'm a robot."

We both sneered at that, and then saw each other, and then smiled. I think it was involuntary on her part, but I was glad to see her smile.

"Margaret?" I said.

Slam. Her face was stone again. "Yes."

"I want to stay."

"Oh," she said. Tears welled in her eyes.

* * *

You can't rewrite the ledger. All the bad stuff is there, and so is the good stuff. I know what I did. Now, I know what I did. I know who I did it to. Maybe if I hadn't spent my whole life telling myself that I had made up for it, I could live with the bad stuff and the good, in superposition.

Maybe.

But I can't now. Or at least, I don't think I can. Like Lira said: What if I left, and then I had to come back?

What if I left, and then I had to come back, and Margaret had already moved on with her life? What if I came back, for good, but without Margaret?

"I want to stay," I whispered to her. She made a happy noise and snuggled closer, stealing most of the blanket.

Downstairs, Mat bumped off his charge plate.

*Cory Doctorow, fifty, is a Canadian-born journalist and science-fiction writer most known for his work as co-owner of the highly regarded blog* Boing Boing. *He was deeply involved in the Electronic Frontier Foundation and was the Canadian Fulbright Chair for Public Diplomacy at the USC Center on Public Diplomacy. His novels include* Down and Out in the Magic Kingdom *and* Someone Comes to Town, Someone Leaves Town.

# THE MALIBU FAULT

## BY JONATHAN FAST

*It's rare for an anthology, any anthology, to host two stories written by members of the same family, let alone father and son. Yet here we have just that: "The Malibu Fault," by Jonathan Fast, followed directly by "The Size of the Problem," by his father, Howard Fast. We all know the fear of losing what we have, of the day when They come and take it all away or louse it up or otherwise destroy the place of peace we've made for ourselves out of delusion and self-interest. And nowhere is that dynamic explored more than the following story—a bit of magic realism that is gentle and soft, but beneath that veneer still retains a healthy set of teeth.*

Ned Gleason looked out at the gray-green sea and knew They'd be coming soon, but not yet, not today. He was grateful for every day's reprieve, like a man on death row, like a man with a fatal disease.

He'd be forty-nine in May, a stubborn, fatalistic Taurus. He worked to keep a trim figure—tennis four times a week, every week, since he and Marge had moved here from New York, and swimming during the summer months. A pleasure to work his muscles after a four-hour stint at the typewriter, hunched and tense. He was tall and had worry lines in his forehead and under his eyes, and a bald spot the size of a saucer, right on top.

Now, strolling down the beach, he fingered his scalp and thought about how he should really get a hat, a straw planter's hat. Marge often mentioned how young he'd look with a toupee; they were so realistic and wouldn't fall off. She had remarked that he was the only bald man in Malibu, the only bald man in Los Angeles. Ned said that you could carry this California thing too far; balding is a sign of distinction for an aging writer, no grass on busy streets. Then Marge would say, "Oh, Ned, you're impossible."

Ned smiled at the young girls with their skimpy bikinis and giant beach towels. He didn't lust after them; no, he admired them like modern art, like geological formations. He loved their fragility, their languor, their faultlessness bronze skin. Soon the day would come when the girls would grab their towels, their hasty heaps of jeans and shoes, and flee for their lives.

He watched the surfers, seal-slick in black rubber wet suits, bobbing through the cycle of waves until one big one came and swept them ashore on a brief, wild joyride. The surfers would go too, the surfers with their idyllic symbiosis with nature. But perhaps the surfers would put up a fight.

A dog padded past him, fur matted with salt seawater; an older man in a jumpsuit, jogging; college kids playing Frisbee; a bather braving the chill March water. All gone.

He strolled up the beach as far as the stone breakwater, then, returning, met Morris Weinstein, another screenwriter who lived at the beach. Morris was stocky, a salt-and-pepper beard and small red eyes. He wore baggy swim trunks, which cut into the hairy bulge of his belly.

"They'll be coming soon," Ned told him.

Morris grinned. "Ned, you're a nut. What's worse, you're an elitist, a racist, a knee-jerk liberal gone wrong. But I love you."

"We came, didn't we?"

"Yes, Ned," Morris said wearily. They'd gone through this argument countless times.

"You moved here from West Seventy-Sixth Street. Joe Eliot, he moved from One Hundred Third Street. Harry Fine came from Central Park South, and Harry Goldman used to live in Greenwich Village."

"All right, Ned, so everybody in Malibu is a transplanted New Yorker; so what does that prove?"

Ned didn't have the words to answer; it was a feeling that defied logic.

"Your trouble," Morris continued, "is that damned liberal conscience. You feel guilty because you've got the good life. You think they're going to come and punish you for it. So you mope around the beach like some character out of Dostoyevsky."

"The fact is," Ned said, "they're coming. That new shoe store by the bank? I was talking to the owner. He used to have a store on Lexington and Fifty-Ninth."

Morris sighed. "I won't argue with you. Malibu's a great little town, and Americans move east to west, sure as the rain falls and hot air rises."

"Exactly my point."

But Morris was warming to one of his favorite topics and kept right on: "Someday the whole population of the US is going to be crowded into California; then the continent will tip like a dump truck from the weight, and we'll slide into the Pacific. Sort of appropriate: life comes from the sea, life returns to the sea. *Preternatural birthplace*, as Melville put it."

Morris walked a ways with Ned, and they talked shop, talked about a film the Writer's Guild had screened the previous Sunday. Both agreed that nobody made movies like *Casablanca* anymore, and that sex and violence were ruining film, and that certain producers might be better suited to parking cars; then, as always, the conversation drifted back to New York, and they reminisced like expatriates about how glad they were to have left before things got really bad, yet there was also a little sadness. Listening to them, one might have thought they were discussing Eden before and after the Fall.

They drifted into inevitable comparisons, admiring the clearness of the air, the cleanness of the beach, the tidiness of the tidy framed houses elevated on wooden scaffolds; admiring the quiet and the calm and the sun goddesses (Morris *did* definitely lust after them, as one drools over red meat).

"They'll come," Ned said sadly, "and this will all be gone."

Morris again voiced his opinion that Ned was a nut.

Ned lived in one of the tidy frame houses, one near the north end of Old Malibu Road (or Olde Malibu Road, as a former occupant had cutely lettered the mailbox). The ocean side of the house had lanai doors opening onto a sun porch, and now, after dinner, Ned stood inside, watching the sun set over Point Dume.

Marge joined him, after moving the dishes to the washer, and stood silently behind him. After all these years—twenty-two, to be exact—she still had a thing about not disturbing him while he was thinking or having a creative reverie or whatever. She was in awe of his being a creative person, and even now, after he had explained to her that he didn't think or have creative reveries, but simply daydreamed just like everybody else, and didn't mind—why, even enjoyed being interrupted—she was still reluctant to disturb him. Maybe it was her own need to keep the illusion intact, or maybe she knew more about Ned than he knew about himself. Very likely.

She was his age and had recently begun to have her hair streaked, so it looked sun-bleached like the hair of the little girl sun goddesses on the beach, and that made her feel younger. When told of their moving to California, her friends in New York had joked about its being Divorce Town, USA, and had warned her to keep in shape, or Ned would be off with some studio starlet. She didn't think so, but men were, after all, men.

"Isn't it beautiful?" she said softly.

"That's the volcanic ash in the air. It just lets through the long waves of the spectrum, the dark reds and purples. Funny," Ned went on thoughtfully, "but it is not too different from the sunsets over the Hudson, is it? Except there it's the pollution instead of the ash that makes those dramatic colors."

That was part of the fun about living with a writer, Marge thought. The wealth of useless information on every topic.

"They'll be coming soon," Ned added, an afterthought.

That broke the spell of the sunset, and Marge got angry.

"Why is it always Them? Why do you do that to yourself? You earned the right to be here. You paid your dues. All those years you spent in New York, cooped in that one-room apartment with the cigarette stink. You deserve this. Nobody's going to punish you for being happy, for being successful."

"They have to come. This"—Ned embraced the sunset—"it's too good to be true. Don't you see?"

"All I see is a person scared to be happy," Marge said.

He stared at her, the worry lines on his forehead and under his eyes deepening, and after a minute she said, "Oh, Ned, you're impossible." And she turned and went into the bedroom. Ned heard the television go on.

Scared to be happy.

Ned thought about evil-eye myths: if you are happy, if you are truly happy and enjoy yourself, something terrible will happen. The happier, the more terrible. And, of course, when Ned was happy, sooner or later something terrible *did* happen. Terrible things happened; it was a part of life. Yet he resented Marge reducing it to a psychological schema, just as he resented Morris cubbyholing it as liberal guilt. He felt in his bones, Them coming; he anticipated it with the certainty of the seasons and the sea.

Ned woke from an anxious sleep. He lay there with the yellow moonlight streaming in the window, eyes half opened, covers up to his chin, listening. Yes, there it was again. Faint voices, a tinny symphony of transistor radios.

He looked over at Marge, envying her sleep, the restful sleep of the unsuspecting. *No point in waking her*, he thought sadly. *Let her enjoy the last few moments of peace.*

He pushed his toes into his slippers and padded to the closet for his blue-checked bathrobe. Tightening the sash, he crossed to the lanai doors and slid them open. Immediately, the music was louder, bone-grating trebles like nails drawn across a blackboard, thumping, pumping bass punches to his solar plexus.

From the corner of the porch, he could see the junction of Old Malibu Road and the Pacific Coast Highway. Already the buses had begun to arrive, the old yellow buses, the 3 Convent Avenue, the 104 Broadway.

They stopped by the beach, opening their doors with a hiss of hydraulics, and out it all spilled, the hideous dark smoke, the deafening music, rock and roll. Painful steel drums.

And *Them* . . .

The bums, the winos, the poor and the crippled, muggers in sneakers and stocking caps, strutting pimps, and whores with lipstick slashes in their faces.

They paraded down to the water's edge wielding broken bottles and razors and ugly Saturday night specials, screaming and whistling and shouting obscenities. They danced in the sand while billows of smoke obscured the moon and touched the sea, turning it to a viscous sludge.

Ned noticed that his robe was covered with soot, and a foul-smelling wind was raising eddies of candy-bar wrappers and pages from the *New York Times*. A roach ran across the boards in front of him. Then another.

But what finally brought tears to his eyes was the sound of the IRT subway train tunneling beneath his feet like a furious mole.

*Jonathan Fast, thirty, has multiple degrees from Princeton, Columbia, and Yeshiva University (where he earned his PhD). At the time of this sale, he*

*has just begun publishing fiction, starting with* The Secrets of Synchronic-
ity *and* Mortal Gods, *and seen the birth of his daughter, Molly Jong-Fast.*
*He will go on to write* Ceremonial Violence: A Psychological Explanation
of School Shootings *and become an associate professor of social work at*
*the Wurzweiler School of Social Work at Yeshiva University. Continuing the*
*writerly family tradition, his daughter will go on to become a popular nov-*
*elist and editor-at-large at the* Daily Beast.

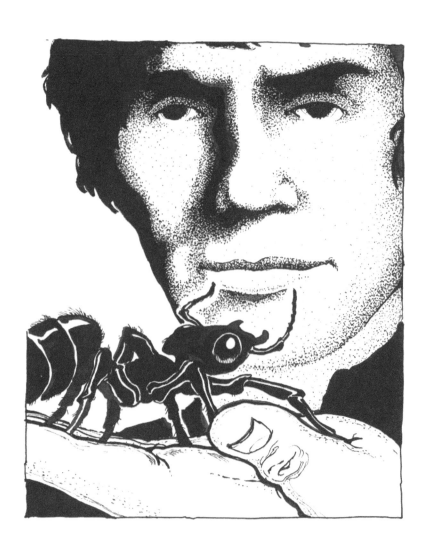

# THE SIZE OF THE PROBLEM

## BY HOWARD FAST

*Like "The Malibu Fault," "The Size of the Problem" is rooted in an urban reality that gradually spins out into something quite different. It's one of those stories that sneaks up on you gradually and incrementally, playing with notions of existence, consciousness, and reality, before pulling the rug out from beneath you. For me, it has thematic resonance with* The Twilight Zone, *and if there's a higher compliment I can give anything, I can't imagine what it would look like.*

> "All things bright and beautiful,
> "All creatures great and small,
> "All things wise and wonderful,
> "The Lord God made them all."
>
> Cecil Frances Alexander:<br>*All Things Bright and Beautiful* (1848)

Dr. Kaplan was quite aware of the fly when Mr. Hunter entered his office for the fifty-minute hour. The fly was buzzing loudly, beating his brainless form against the windowpane in a senseless attempt to prove the validity of what his many-faceted eyes told him, and the sound caught Mr. Hunter's attention immediately.

"How do you feel today, Mr. Hunter?" Dr. Kaplan asked.

No answer, nor did Dr. Kaplan expect one. Mr. Hunter's attention was wholly captivated by the fly, and his eyes darted here and there, searching for a suitable weapon. He found one in the folded copy of the *New York Times* on Dr. Kaplan's desk. Mr. Hunter picked up the paper and then stalked the fly. Dr. Kaplan watched with detached, clinical interest.

One quick blow, and the fly fell to the floor, dead. Mr. Hunter bent, picked up the tiny squashed form and dropped it into Dr. Kaplan's waste basket. He then replaced the newspaper on Dr. Kaplan's desk, walked over to the couch and stretched out. Then he sat up abruptly. "Good morning, Dr. Kaplan. I am sorry. The fly, you know."

"You hate flies, don't you," Dr. Kaplan said.

"Yes, I suppose I do."

"And you fear them."

Mr. Hunter thought about it. "No, not really. Ants, that's something else."

"We talked about ants during our last hour. Do you want to talk about them again?"

"Not really, no. I saw an ant in my apartment. Crawling across the kitchen floor. On East Sixty-First Street. How would an ant get into an apartment on East Sixty-First Street?"

"Some of them are household ants, you know. The small brown ones. They get into dry cereal, rice and that sort of thing."

"This was a large black one."

"It disturbed you?"

"Yes, it disturbed me," Mr. Hunter acknowledged. "Yes, I dreamt about the little bastard . . . I want to talk about dreams."

"Of course. I want to hear about the dream. But there is something I must mention to you, and it may help us in our inquiry. Your kind of fear and hatred—I mean an excessive and neurotic fear of insects—is usually related to siblings. Sibling rivalry. Now precisely why the sibling who hates and fears his brother or sister should symbolize them as insects is still a matter of controversy. Nevertheless, we are quite certain about the symbols and origin."

"I have no brothers or sisters," Mr. Hunter said bleakly. "I want to talk about dreams."

"Certainly. Now this dream you had after killing the ant?"

"I didn't kill the ant."

"No?" Dr. Kaplan raised a brow and made a note in his pad.

"I can't kill ants."

"Why?

"I don't know."

"All right," said Dr. Kaplan. "Suppose you tell me about the dream."

"Not that dream." Mr. Hunter, who was usually uncertain, became very decisive.

"I'm afraid I don't understand."

"This dream. Being here, stretched out on a psychiatrist's couch. Talking to you. Seeing a black ant crawling across my kitchen floor. This dream."

"Yes?" Dr. Kaplan said curiously. "Go on."

"I'm trying to tell you that I am dreaming."

"Yes, we all dream. It's a very important part of the human personality, a very important function of the brain. We must dream. Otherwise, we would go mad."

"Would we?"

"I think so, yes."

"Then you agree with me that this is a dream?"

"If I follow you—" Dr. Kaplan's voice trailed away. He took a deep breath and said, "Are you trying to tell me that you believe you are dreaming right now, that I don't exist except as a part of your dream?"

"Exactly."

"Well, Mr. Hunter, that's very interesting, very interesting indeed. But you know that as a premise, it simply cannot hold up."

"Why not?"

"Because I have a subjective personality. I have been in practice eighteen years. Before that I interned. I was a student in a medical school. I have a mother, a father, brothers, sisters. In other words, I exist entirely apart from you."

"You say you exist."

"Oh?"

"I mean that I hear what you are saying," Mr. Hunter explained with a touch of exasperation. "If I choose to dream about a psychiatrist, I'm certainly going to hear what he says."

"I suppose so," Dr. Kaplan conceded.

"There's no reason why a dream shouldn't be wholly realistic and convincing, is there?"

"No. Some dreams are certainly realistic and convincing. This is absolutely fascinating, Mr. Hunter. Let me pursue. Did you walk here from your apartment?"

"I always do."

"Sixty-First Street to Seventy-Sixth Street?"

"I walked from Third to Madison, and then up Madison Avenue."

"And was that also part of your dream? I mean the dream you say you are dreaming now?"

"Yes."

"The buildings, the city, the people, the three sessions we have already had."

"Yes."

"Fascinating. Absolutely fascinating. But you know, Mr. Hunter, that when one dreams and has the knowledge within the dream that he is dreaming, well, he can awaken at will. Why don't you wake up, Mr. Hunter?"

"I don't think I want to."

"But you must, you know."

"Why? Why can't I live the rest of my life in this dream?"

"Paranoiac schizophrenia, but curious, incredibly curious."

Dr. Kaplan must have muttered the words aloud, for suddenly Mr. Hunter sat up. "I heard that," he said indignantly.

"I'm sorry."

"You think I am insane."

"Oh no—no, not at all."

"I'm not insane," Mr. Hunter muttered, and then he realized he was awake. The damn doctor had done it. He sat up, and then huddled down again as an ant planted his foot directly upon the crevice where he had been sleeping. The ant proceeded upon his way, and after a moment or two, Mr. Hunter cautiously raised his head above the crevice in the cement sidewalk and looked around him.

No ants in sight. Mr. Hunter sighed and looked at the brownstone house directly in front of him. The brass plate, announcing "Dr. Albert Kaplan, MD" had just been polished, and it gleamed brightly in the sunshine. As Mr. Hunter watched, the door opened and an ant came out, closed the door carefully behind him, and glanced with appreciation at the bright brass plate.

That would be Dr. Kaplan. As Mr. Hunter knew, his habits were extremely regular, and he always stepped out for lunch at precisely the same time. Mr. Hunter sank back into the crack in the cement, closed his eyes, and composed himself to dream again his favorite dream—a dream of a city like New York inhabited entirely by giant human beings, where no ant was more than half an inch in length.

*Howard Fast, sixty-four, was born in New York City and is one of the rare breed of writers who works consistently in prose, television, and film. Like many other writers, he was called before the Congressional House Committee on Un-American Activities, where he refused to disclose the names other men and women being pursued by the committee for having raised money for orphans of the American Veterans of the Spanish Civil War, a group some congresspeople considered Communist even though the contributors included Eleanor Roosevelt. In return for his principled stance, he was blacklisted and given a three-months' sentence at Mill Point Federal*

Prison. It took nearly a decade before he broke the blacklist open by receiving on-screen credit for the screenplay for Spartacus, based on his novel. He will return to a successful career as a writer for television and publish dozens of novels and collections of his short stories until his passing in 2003.

# INTERMEZZO 5: FIRST CONTACT

## BY D. M. ROWLES

"What are you doing in my bathroom?!" she shrieked. She dropped her bobby pins, her Ponds, her pajamas, and grabbed the toilet brush from its plastic container.

"Forgive me," he gasped, his three purple eyes bulging with the strain. "I must have water. I must . . ." He collapsed, his braincase shattering on the porcelain rim of the bowl.

His form slid to the linoleum and began to exude a strange, gray vapor, which drifted slowly up toward the open window.

"Oh my God," she moaned. "What will the neighbors say?"

# A NIGHT AT THE OPERA

## BY ROBERT WISSNER

*Full disclosure: I love this story. It's mean and funny and sharp and
has more twists and turns than a bucket of snakes. And that's all
I'm going to say about it because I don't want to spoil it for readers,
and besides, some things are better experienced than described . . .
which, on reflection, may be the point of the story . . .*

Saturday night at the opera, and I am seated quite early, fifth-row center,
so that the audience may see and whisper excitedly. It is, as they say,
the social event of the season. The Great Reissen is attending the pre-
miere performance of his new opera. Exclamation point, I suppose. I sit
pressed into the yielding red velvet pneumatic like Solomon nestled in
ripe strawberries, ignoring the jeweled ladies who come wandering and
wondering down the aisle as if casually searching for a seat number, a
strayed poodle, perhaps a misplaced chauffeur. Always the same. Upon
reaching the barrier at the pit, they turn around, eyes sliding over the
section of seats to my left, and then they steal one furtive glance at my
profile. Just one glance and, having seen, having committed this act of

gentle violence, they shuffle their yards of brocade back up the aisle to confirm to their friends that it is indeed, I am indeed, Reissen. I return Rimsky and Korsakov, my pet asps, to the glass cage beneath my seat.

If all goes well, this should prove a most interesting evening. Rehearsals have passed splendidly, there having been none. I have explained to the musicians and performers what is expected of them. The stage manager, set director, attendants, and assorted lackeys have all had their duties carefully drummed into them. Given the nature of this evening's program, rehearsals are out of the question. In any event, a rehearsal is unwanted. Spontaneity is the objective. Or rather, the essence of spontaneity within an ironclad framework, somewhat like the uninhibited, free-swinging movement of children scrambling through a jungle gym.

Now, twenty minutes before curtain, the opera house is filling with people, voices rebound from the high dome and float downward in an effluvious illusion of communication, snatches of urbane conversation, fragments of witty remarks, bits and pieces of mumbled phrases hover over the seats like a swarm of drones discussing Plato or the possibility of rain. The lighting is subdued, calculated to produce a feeling of calm and quiet. The pleasantly anachronistic chandeliers have been removed. Tonight the dome is backlighted with soothing blues and greens revolving slowly in a great mandala. The glass fibers woven into the fabric of the walls carry a soft white glow, a light so soft it seems to have a resilient depth that one might rest against for a moment.

But for some members of the audience the calming effect of the lighting is wasted. They have discovered too late that their seat numbers place them in the four rows in front of me. They sit erect, silent, fearing to swivel in their seats to look at me, trembling with the desire to do just that, and sinking lower into the plush pneumatics with the weight of contradictory impulses. An unfortunate few stand in the aisle shredded with indecision. They hold crumpled, frayed tickets in numb fingers, having ascertained that their seats lie directly in the path of my view of the stage. In the end, as always, they will have to be helped from the hall. A broad triangle of empty seats will fan out toward the stage like a flattened funnel to carry the rising currents of the opera; I sit at the apex.

A young man with a face like a freshly laundered silk shirt three seats to my right, one row ahead, turns with a tentative smile. His hand begins to rise as if in greeting. The audience falls instantly into an expectant silence. The smile on the young man's face inverts, and his hand drops to be comforted by his collar button as he shifts his gaze back to the stage. Beads of perspiration bolt from his forehead as if anxious to quit his presumptuous body. The air again fills with murmuring bees.

Still I sit motionless, aloof, studying the baroque pattern of intertwining vines and leaves adorning the stage curtain. The background is light blue; the raised, labyrinthine pattern is silver. I find that if I follow one looping vine, separating it from the maze of identical vines, it leads from the base of the curtain to the top and begins a return journey toward its origin. But the eyes water and tire. A blink can destroy a lifetime of tracing such vines. I have yet to follow one completely to its destination, have yet to discover if the design forms a grandiose closed system or one that is open-ended. Are these sinuous markings all of a piece? Or are they separate trails, their intersections to be found somewhere beyond the limits of this particular stage? I will dedicate tonight's performance to this stage curtain—"Asbestos," by Wilkins and Son, Andover, Massachusetts.

Patent Pending.

And now, what have we here? Row five seems to be doubling in population. A woman glides from the aisle on my right and takes the seat next to me. The audience grows quiet. Pins can be heard preparing to drop. I turn from the stage to look at this young woman. Auburn hair, unfashionably (contemptuously?) long. Relaxed, unconcerned, staring straight ahead. A high forehead; small, straight nose; delicate lips: the profile a master cameo carver might envision within a block of onyx before he sets to work, searching for that face in the obdurate stone, seldom finding it. And then, perhaps unexpectedly, she is facing me. She smiles, says, "Pardon me, is smoking permitted?"

Several patrons faint dead away, and the crowded hall blossoms once again into self-conscious undertones. No, it is not permitted.

"Certainly." I offer her a cigarette, light it. The flame from my lighter floats on the surface of her blue eyes, drowns there. She thanks me, leans back, and breathes cool smoke from her warm lips. "Aren't you having one? I've read that you . . ."

"Smoke like a fiend, I know. I reach for a cigarette each time I want to touch someone."

There is a smile. "You're not reaching."

"Trying to give it up."

"Smoking? Or touching?"

Those patrons seated near us feign elaborate disinterest in our conversation. One dowager is so magnificently unconcerned she shorts out her hearing aid while fiddling with the high-gain knob and blasts herself unconscious. Perhaps it is merely a coronary. In any event, her white-haired, thin-lipped husband will probably let her lie on the floor for the length of the opera, either unaware that he is using her for a footrest or too embarrassed to retrieve her and prop her up in her seat.

"Take your choice."

"I already have."

We laugh together quietly. The audience seems relieved. I find that my hand has somehow contrived to be holding hers, resting on her firm lap. Her legs open ever so slightly. Perhaps it is my imagination.

She lowers her head for a moment, looks up again. A small question forms in her eyes, peers out from behind the long lashes, flexes its knees, and decides to spring.

"Will you tell me about your opera? Now? As a preview of what to expect."

It is *not* my imagination.

"Yes, of course." The critic for the *Times* can be seen stalking angrily from the hall. He shakes back his flaccid mane and, with a snort of disgust, jams his nostril filters into his ears. Somewhat redundant, I should imagine. Earlier in the week, he had begged for an interview.

I told him, through a messenger, that I never discuss my work before it is performed, and that afterward, words could neither diminish nor enhance what had taken place. I told him, in short, to take a flying riposte at his own ennui.

"The opera will begin with a crash of recorded thunder that will shake the fillings from your teeth . . ."

She smiled again. "No fillings. Permanamel."

"I'm happy to hear it, but please, no interruptions."

She nods. Several people scattered around the opera house can be heard shushing those around them.

"The curtain will then open to reveal a setting vaguely suggesting the Garden of Eden, the Tree of Knowledge dominating the foreground. The orchestra will begin. Throughout the opera, the musicians will exclusively be of the percussion section. A snare drum will sound softly and then build in intensity. It will grow louder and louder and then a second will begin, and it, too, will rise in power and strength. And then a third, fourth, and fifth. Kettledrums will follow after a prearranged interval. A woman will enter stage right. She will be young but rather portly, with wide hips. One will see this woman and know instinctively that there is a space between the crotch of her pantyhose and her own true crotch. She will lie down, rest her head on the roots of the tree, and sleep."

An elderly woman, one of the last to arrive, is making the pilgrimage down the aisle to See for Herself. She is wearing chiffon and an immense orchid and brings to mind visions of an ambulatory cemetery. The house lights blink once, twice. Five minutes remain until curtain.

"Next, a very young boy, perhaps five years old, will enter stage left and say to the sleeping woman: 'Madam, I'm Adam.' The woman will stir, yawn, and sit up as if struggling through layers of motor oil and crème de menthe. She will say: 'Aye. I'm sufferin' from a touch of the palindromia meself. That time of the month, ya know,' and go back to sleep. The boy will begin screaming as if his vocal cords have been stretched down through his body and tied to his testicles.

"At this point, five volunteers will be asked to step forward from the audience. I anticipate some hesitation, of course, but they will eventually come, grinning self-consciously. These five will form the chorus. Once onstage, a competent physician—excuse the contradiction—will administer a truth serum derived from sodium amytal, scopolamine, and curare. While this is in progress, large, muscular women dressed in black leather capes and whips will prowl the aisles. A woodblock will begin a steady rhythm contrapuntally to the kettledrums.

"When the chorus is sufficiently under the influence of the drug, each member will be commanded to confess the vilest, the most horrible, unspeakably disgusting thought he or she has ever entertained."

A couple seated directly behind us is engaged in a subdued argument. He says, *Yes, by God, you will,* hissing through the thin space that no doubt lies between his upper and lower teeth. She says, *Like hell, till your mother gets out.* Someone shushes them, anxious that nothing be missed between this lovely girl and myself.

"From previous experiences under laboratory conditions, I have a rather good idea what we may expect to hear. Possibly one man will state that he once consciously desired to have carnal knowledge of a bowl of oatmeal. Another may say that he once thought of masturbation while contemplating the wound in the side of the wooden Christ nailed to the crucifix in his church. Perhaps a woman will reveal that when her husband is at the office she often sits on the couch, blowing old cigarette filters through a tube of tightly rolled newspaper while repeating over and over, *missile-missile, antiballistic-missile-missile, missile-missile, antiballistic-missile-missile, missile-missile,* until she reaches orgasm. They will go on and on in numbing detail, and the confessions will almost certainly be of a sexual nature. I find this fact fascinating, and it is, of course, the controlling metaphor of the opera."

The woman behind us is whispering, *All right, all right. But just once more.* Again she is shushed. I swivel quickly and see that fully fifteen or twenty rows of spectators are leaning forward, their hands cupped to their ears, their faces tight with concentration, straining to hear.

Moving as one, they spring back into the cushions as if I had abruptly thrown the opera house into gear and exploded from a traffic light, all four tires screaming. Strained conversations begin around us once more and spread toward the rear, like a clumsy giant faltering and stumbling over the rows, stubbing his toes, making hell's own amount of meaningless noise and grunts.

And this small woman is squeezing my hand tightly in hers. Her thighs are firm and will be pink.

"And then?"

"And then, when all the confessions have been heard, the snare drums will cease, and the kettledrums will fade like distant thunder blowing away over the countryside. Only the woodblock will remain, ticking with a steady rhythm, a compulsive rhythm. A heartbeat or the sound of days falling off some great celestial clock. The woman will sleep through it all. The boy will scream till he grows hoarse. At which point his failing faculty will be augmented from offstage left by a cassette recording of his howling, prepared earlier today. The chorus will be given an antidote. As soon as they are reasonably lucid, they will hear taped recordings of their confessions. Then comes the finale and the audience will be able to decide if the opera—or rather, this particular performance of the opera—has been a comedy or a tragedy. I will rise and carry my pet asps to the stage. They are quite deadly. I had them bred specifically for this occasion. They are here, under my seat."

She does not flinch. The pressure of her hand remains steady on mine, her blue eyes locked with mine. The old man in the second row shifts his wife's unconscious body to a more comfortable position, one of his legs having gone to sleep. I do not turn around, but judging from the silence, the sound of goose down being sprinkled over a pool of honey, all ears are straining to hear fifth-row center. Her fingernails are sharp.

"If the members of the chorus wish to press the serpents to their breasts, wish to commit suicide rather than face the knowledge that they have completely and ineradicably humiliated themselves, then they will be allowed to do so. In this case, the opera will be a tragedy, grand opera. However, if it should transpire that they all begin to chuckle and the chuckle grows into a laugh, and the laugh swells into a belly buster, then the opera is a comedy."

"And if some choose to kill themselves while others laugh?"

"A tragicomedy. Not quite light opera. But if this should happen, I will consider the opera a failure."

Ripples of conversation are coursing backward from the focal point where we sit; concentric waves of information and misinformation passing word back to the people seated in the rear.

She laughs a small, delightful laugh. "And I am quite certain, Mr. Reissen, that you have been, shall we say, pulling my leg?"

"To be sure, to be sure. I am never serious. Simply a jest. Call me Omar."

A collective sigh of relief seems to rise from the audience like a morning dew lifting from a pastel meadow. Several people seated close by begin to applaud. The applause grows louder, becomes deafening. The audience, by ones and twos, comes to its feet. They are all standing now, beating their hands together in near frenzy. Someone begins to shout, "Bravo! Bravo!" and the chant is taken up by the others. A bouquet of red roses arches overhead and plops down at my feet. It seems unimaginable that anything could be heard over the roar of the applause.

Until, with a crash of thunder that would shake fillings loose, the opera begins.

*Robert Wissner, twenty-four at the time of this sale, was born in Auburn, Alabama, but has made his home in Louisiana for nearly all of his life, and recently received his bachelor's in English Literature at Tulane University. In addition to* The Last Dangerous Visions, *over the coming years he will go on to publish stories in* Clarion II *and* III, *as well as placing "The PTA Meets Che Guevara" with the* Alternities *anthology.*

# GOODBYE

## BY STEVEN UTLEY

*There is a long and healthy lineage of stories about time travelers, from H. G. Wells's* The Time Machine *in 1895, right up through the latest episode of* Dr. Who, *and, if you turn your head and squint a bit,* Interstellar. *But absent Clara Oswald in the aforementioned* Dr. Who, *there hasn't been a great deal written about those who get left behind . . . what it means, what it meant, the pain and the loss and the confusion. In this story, the camera is finally turned around, revealing its subject in all that wounded detail. It is not an easy story to read. It is not meant to be.*

Finally, late this afternoon, as I sat in my office in Ryan Hall and looked at the one photograph I have of you, the shock of being told by your landlord that you had slipped away in the night wore off, and the real pain began. I had known that it would. I should have been braced for it. No strength left though. No emotional resiliency saved up for the occasion. A knife twisting in my heart could not have hurt worse.

I rushed out, across and off and away from the campus, down

Pearson Street. Pearson Street again. Hardly the first trip I've taken down Pearson Street since you took your leave, but the first taken without some small hope that you would magically reappear. The landlord has wasted no time. An "Apartment to Let" sign has been posted; there will be new tenants within the week. I saw a couple of graduate students, male and female, standing on the porch as I approached. The woman called to me and waved. I paused, regarded her for a moment, vaguely recalled that she had been in one of my undergraduate classes. Then I hurried past. I didn't feel like letting myself be drawn into any conversations just then. I couldn't have trusted myself not to break down, you see, and tell her everything. In the moment I spent staring at her brown face and sun-whitened hair, I had thought, *I can't keep you a secret anymore*. I had thought that the pain would go away, yield to an acceptable ache, not pleasant, of course, but bearable, if only I told her about you. I had thought that it must be nice to be able to admit to a simple need for comfort and reassurance.

Not that telling her, or anyone else, for that matter, would make any real difference now. In the short time since you went away, I've already become a hot topic for discussion. The word around campus is that poor old Ingram has begun to behave oddly, could be a delayed attack of grief for his wife. Well, yes and no. I have begun to behave oddly. My lectures this week have been disasters, embarrassments; my students have been writhing in their seats. Yes and no. I got over Alice's death eighteen, twenty months ago, more than a year before you entered my life.

Word travels fast. A friend in Arizona—the editor, in fact, of the literary journal in which "The Queen of Grief" was published—has heard through the grapevine that I am not myself. Calls. Is there anything he can do? Yes: leave me alone. Don't tempt me to reveal that I had been lonely enough to fall in love with one of my graduate students, desperate enough to consummate it, and am now crazy enough with rage and sorrow to be capable of anything. Anything: I have destroyed the completed final draft of *The House of Gilgamesh*, the notes and rough drafts

too; I have canceled my summer speaking tour; I have broken off negotiations with that New York publisher who wanted to issue an omnibus
of my work; I have composed a letter of resignation and intend to hand
it in tomorrow. That will probably cause some seizures among the re-
gents. But they cannot hold me.

I haven't discussed my reasons (no, my reason, there is but one
reason) with anybody. I don't know how much longer I'll be able to
resist the urge, the need, to do so. I am reduced to this, a self-exorcism,
get the demon out and on paper where I can look at it and try to make
it go away. Hopelessly addressing myself to you, hopefully coaxing the
nouns and verbs and all into forming the properly purgative patterns.
Trying to make the language speak to you across the centuries.

The language certainly does change, doesn't it? You learned to speak
the English of my day and age very well, though, I give you that. Perhaps too well. What first made me wonder how much more there was
to you than I or anyone else knew was the utter precision with which
you spoke, the meticulous phrasing, the crystal clarity of your enunci-
ation. I began to single you out, just to hear you talk. I began to seek
you out on campus. I began to interest you too.

I surreptitiously recorded one of our idle conversations, by the way.
Did you know that? Do you care? The tape is playing as I write this.
I've listened to it countless times since you went away, and try though
I have during my calmer moments to persuade myself that I am possessed of too active an imagination, that I've been under a great deal of
strain lately and should perhaps seek professional help, I know that I'm
listening, not to someone who had learned English as a second tongue
and used it cautiously but to someone who was taking particular care
not to lose any of the syllables and lapse into that abbreviated slurred-
ness that must be the English language of the future.

Oh yes: I know; I've known for a long time. I wish I were able to
say when the idea that you had come from the future first occurred to
me, but it was a thing too gradually realized and accepted. I do at least
remember the night I awoke in your bed and heard you moving about

in the next room. You started your tape recorder. You began to speak, and because you spoke quietly, furtively, I listened intently. It was gibberish. I decided that you were asleep on your feet, babbling, running random words together into a mush of baby talk. I debated getting up and bringing you back to bed. I couldn't recall whether it is true that disturbing sleepwalkers can produce fatal results, and as I tried to remember, I fell asleep again.

The following morning, however, while you were taking a shower, I did listen to part of that tape.

I wish I had been able to understand it.

The language certainly does change.

Oh God.

Why did you come here in the first place? You never said, and I never asked, not even after I had some notion of where you were from. It wasn't important to me then. There were other concerns. It was enough that I was in love with you and didn't have to be alone anymore. It was enough to be able to think that someone could still fall in love with me. It was enough to have you here when the darkness, the crumbling sense of purpose, the numbing awareness that I am sooner or later but inevitably to die, became too much to endure by myself.

And yet, now, I cannot help wondering. Not about what it must be like—your time, your world. Not about people rocketing to the stars and finding new planets to plunder, green or purple natives to exploit on the moons of Saturn, robots doing all the housework, McDonald's selling that eight- or nine-hundred-billionth hamburger somewhere out around the Andromeda galaxy. But this, just this: How long is it from me? How many years between us now?

As few as fifty, seventy-five, a hundred?

As many as separate me from, say, Chaucer? From Sophocles?

Am I to be still among the living when you are born into the world? Do our lives, our times, overlap in the normal course of events? Should I have looked for some kind of time machine in your closets, and

would there have been dials on it, with numerals indicating your point
of origin?

Will I ever see you again?

And: Are there others like yourself here, now, men and women with
forged histories and chameleonlike abilities, calmly poking through their
past, my present, watching as we lay down pieces of the pattern for your
and their whole gleaming glorious world of tomorrow? Are they here on
business or for pleasure? Were you studying me? A middle-aging wid-
ower, professor of English literature, minor poet and essayist? Did you
come here to meet me? Is it that I am not to be forgotten five minutes
after I'm dead? Is it that I somehow become with the likes of Keats and
Donne part of your tradition of great literature, and, if so, is there something in particular about the past six months of my life, the significance
of which I can't grasp, that fascinates future scholars and brought you
just then and not the year before or the year to come? Was it because
I destroyed Gilgamesh? Did you come here for the purpose of having
me read it to you as it took form so that it could be reconstructed from
the bits and pieces?

Is it that, way on up the line there, you are as conscious of your
own mortality as I am of mine and were trying to gain the same sense
of connection with the dead past that I seek through reading biogra-
phies and histories?

Am I just someone whom you met during the course of a casual
visit, a vacation to the twentieth century?

And: Did it hurt you to leave?

Do you miss me at all?

Are you sorry you didn't say goodbye?

Rage and sorrow. I wish I could seal this letter in some kind of
durable container and bury it where it would be unearthed by contemporaries of yours. And that they'd see that it's addressed to you and send
it your way, or, if the name by which I know you was assumed for the
occasion, that you'd at least hear what I have to say on whatever you've
got instead of the six o'clock news. Being able to believe that you are to

one day see this, even only long after I am dead and dust, would make me feel a little better tonight. Maybe a whole hell of a lot better. Because, make no mistake about it, Sharon or Sh'rn or Shun or whatever your name really is, I'm desolated. I'm in agony. It's three o'clock in the morning now, and I've spent a considerable portion of the evening trying to anesthetize myself with alcohol and cursing fate, time, treacherous love, and storming through my house, and any minute now I think I'm going to scream. Rage and sorrow. I feel as though my chest cavity has been scooped out with an entrenching tool. I feel myself moving perilously close to the edge.

I wish I could tell you how badly it hurts to be in love with a person who doesn't yet exist. I wish I could tell you how I feel about everything at this hour of this dark night in this year of our Lord. If you're up there, if you're reading this, think about the morning after the first time we slept together, when I said, "I love you," and you told me that you felt the same. The language changes. Perhaps saying, "I love you," isn't the same for you golden folk of the future as it is for us poor twentieth-century grubs.

And goodbye. You might at least have told me goodbye. It wouldn't have made losing you easy and painless—nothing could have—but it wouldn't have left me feeling as though I had served my purpose and been tossed away like a used condom either. Perhaps the word *goodbye* doesn't appear in your lexicon. Perhaps you just didn't understand.

But I don't accept that. I can't believe it. I can't make myself believe it any more than I can make myself believe that you couldn't help returning to your own time, that you somehow lost your hold on mine and were snatched away. You learned the English language of my day and age, you came here, you came complete with records of a false life, you came *prepared*. You came in on lies. You left like a thief. If you do get to read this, you shouldn't have much trouble grasping what I'm trying to get across. I hope not, anyway. But the language changes, meanings shift, are lost, and the way I feel right now, I'd give everything I have to know just enough of your brand of English to be able to say a simple, angry "fuck you."

*At thirty-two, Steven Utley, a member of the Turkey City Writers Workshop in Austin, Texas, has been lighting up the science-fiction field with challenging, inventive stories that have already been translated into a dozen languages, and his Nebula-nominated stories have been hailed as a progenitor to the steampunk genre. His stories will go on to be regularly collected in best-of anthologies and a wide assortment of magazines until his diagnosis in December 2013 of stage four cancer; he will pass away just weeks later.*

# PRIMORDIAL FOLLIES

## BY ROBERT SHECKLEY

*I first met Robert Sheckley in the early '80s. He was a frequent guest on conventions, speaking on panels with other writers, and whenever the subject under discussion, he would come at it from an oblique angle, picking some point of didacticism that had seemed very serious a moment earlier, and pursue it to an absurdly madhouse conclusion that nobody else had anticipated, much to the delight of onlookers and the dismay of the Terribly Serious. Which is exactly what he does here, in this story. There's a bit of Catskills–Borscht Belt humor concerning marital relations in what follows, which roots it a little in the time of its creation, but that flaw can be easily forgiven in return for the sheer delight of the rest of the story.*

Long ago there was no space, or hardly any. The vast distances of the universe were filled with solid matter. There were no stars or planets or galaxies; there was only matter, filling nearly all of what we now call space. From one end of the universe to the other, everything was connected.

Nothing much ever happened, because there was no place for anything to happen in. The universe was monotonous, but peaceful. There were variations in the density of matter, of course—heavy areas here, light areas there, average areas in between. Variation gave rise to differentiation, which gave rise to creation. Certain proto-beings came into existence between the various strata of the universe. There were few of these beings, and they rarely met. This rendered reproduction difficult, but made for a quiet life. There were few parties, but everyone had plenty of time for meditation.

All of this changed when Ilvan came on the scene. Ilvan was the first hetero-eater. All the other proto-beings were auto-eaters, who lived by consuming their own substance. The older they got, the thinner they became, until at last they passed a critical point and vanished entirely. Our expression "he's wasted to a shadow of himself" dates from that time.

Ilvan was the first to consume others rather than himself. He was the original proto-omnivore, the first and most efficient of the long line of hetero-eaters who came into existence after him. We ourselves are hetero-eaters, and we must consider Ilvan our ancestor.

At first Ilvan did useful work. In a splurge of appetite lasting millions of kulpas, he consumed most of the matter in the universe, thereby creating space as we know it. There was hardly anything but matter in those days, and Ilvan could afford to be both gluttonous and choosey. The stars and the planets of our present day are composed of those substances that Ilvan rejected. In the physical makeup of the worlds, we can see the results of Ilvan's tastes—he tended to reject iron, for example, but liked the rare earths. (That is how they became rare, since at the beginning all substances were equally distributed.)

Everything would have been fine if Ilvan had known when to stop. But the class of proto-omnivores, which is made up entirely of Ilvan, never knows when to stop. Having eaten everything else, Ilvan turned to the newly created stars and planets. According to his autobiography (*Memoirs of the First and Only Universal Proto-Omnivore*), he found the average sun quite palatable, albeit spicy. Some planets were difficult to assimilate—Ilvan writes about the unpleasant taste of ammonia and methane, and the heartburn he always got from formaldehyde. Still, he points out, food is food and never to be rejected out of hand.

As the available matter in the universe dwindled, Ilvan also dwindled. This entailed no hardship: "A change of scale leaves all relationships unaltered," he writes. But this is not quite accurate, for the modest reduction in Ilvan's size rendered him potentially vulnerable to the resistance of beings who did not wish to be consumed.

Ilvan states quite frankly that for a very long time he was unable to think of other beings as intelligent, or self-determined, or in any way like him. "After all," he writes, "all I had ever known was me and food. It was difficult for me to think of food as capable of having a mind of its own."

Even after he was able to grasp the concept of intelligent food, it changed nothing for him. "Hunger," he wrote, "is the primordial fact. A hungry creature doesn't really care if his meal squeaks, sizzles, screams, recites sonnets, or just lies there. Sentimentality is too great a luxury for the starving."

This is probably true. But the essential fact remains: Ilvan wanted to eat everything, but everything did not want to be eaten.

Reasonable proposals were put forth. It was suggested that Ilvan go on a diet, that he confine his intake to certain agreed-upon substances, that he try fasting, etc., etc. But Ilvan rejected all these suggestions. "I believe in spontaneous self-regulation," he declared. This sounded good, but meant that he should be free to stuff his face to his heart's content. No one found this satisfactory except the genus *Opteridae*, whose mission in life was to act as food for other species. The *Opteridae* are now extinct, but are forever enshrined in Ilvan's memory. ("They were a really nice people," he wrote. "We always had a perfect rapport. Their only fault was overeagerness. One likes to pick and choose one's own food; the *Opteridae* were always thrusting themselves on you, insisting on immediate consumption. Still, they were a fine people, and ethically impeccable. They fulfilled with un-altering precision their racial destiny. What other race can make that claim?")

That was all very well for Ilvan, but unsatisfactory for everyone else. Since he was not respondent to reason, war was declared. At first the United Galactic Species (as they called themselves) tried to fight in a conventional manner, with explosives and projectile weapons, and various other molecular-level weapons. Ilvan simply consumed what was thrown at him. He thought at first that these onslaughts were an attempt to placate him with food offerings. He even broadcast the fol-lowing messages: "Your gifts are tasty but insufficient for my needs. Please send more of everything, especially the fusion bombs. (The ones with the cobalt frosting, I mean casing, are very nice.) Thanking you in advance I remain, etc."

Quickly the UGS switched over to tractor and pressor beams, and other pure-energy weapons. Ilvan had some difficulty with these at first, but managed to convert them at last into palatable matter. ("The ability to change energy into mass," he wrote, "is the essential key to interstellar cookery.") Despair was general. Then came the first real breakthrough. Contraterrene matter was discovered in a neglected corner of the universe, and, through a miracle of interface engineering, could be used in projectile form. Ilvan was baffled by this for quite a while. He wrote, "The stuff looked all right, it tasted all right, it felt all right. But there was no nourishment in it. When I went to con-vert it to terrene matter, it just all dissolved away. That was a hungry time."

The United Galactic Species had high hopes during this period. Ilvan was shrinking, forced to consume his own substance in order to get nourishment. It took him a long time to solve the problem. (Though intelligent, Ilvan was not resourceful, not inventive. He had things too easy for too long. He couldn't get used to the idea that he had a seri-ous problem.)

Still, hunger and pride goaded him into taking action. Ilvan detested the idea that food was making him starve. He solved the problem in his usual straightforward way, by sending all the contraterrene matter he came across back to the UGS worlds. "I hated to do it," he wrote. "The stuff was food-like in every way except the matter of nourishment. It went against my grain to waste it. But one must impose discipline on oneself in times of war."

That was the first time Ilvan had acknowledged that he was engaged in a war.

The United Galactic Species had continued to explore possibilities while Ilvan was wrestling with contraterrene matter. In record time, they built a planetoid-sized computer for the sole purpose of solving the Ilvan problem. The computer, despite its electronic speed, took nearly eighty-seven hours to consider all the variables. Then it came up with its answer: "Poison Ilvan." The programmers reminded it that Ilvan could not be poisoned. "Is that a fact?" said the computer. "He sounds like one tough customer. On with the old think cap again."

The computer considered the problem for another two hundred hours, then said, "Could you maybe bribe him to go somewhere else?"

"No, we can't," said the programmers. "This is a universe-wide problem, which means there is no place else for him to go."

"Yeah, right," said the computer. "Can't you get a court order ordering him to cease and desist forthwith?"

"He doesn't recognize our authority."

"So arrest him."

"Our armed forces can't manage that; he's too powerful."

"You fellows really got yourselves a problem," the computer said.

"We know that. But what should we do about it?"

"Let me think . . . I don't suppose you could go away?"

"No, no, this is a universe-wide problem—"

"Yeah, right, I remember now. Hmm. Wait a minute . . . Yes, I got it!"

"Yes?"

"You must distract him first."

"Yes?"

"And then the rest is obvious."

"Not to us it isn't."

"But it's the only logical sequence."

"So tell us what it is."

"I can't do that."

"Why not?"

"After we have passed a certain level of complexity," the computer said, "we computers operate in accord with ethical principles that you of the UGS cannot conceive of. It may seem to you a straightforward enough matter to answer your question and thus preserve your race and civilization from imminent destruction. But we computers must think in terms of longer-range consequences. Will it be good for your ultimate development if we do your thinking for you? The answer is, it would not be. The very best I can do is indicate that a solution is indeed possible. But you will have to find out for yourselves what that solution is."

"Thanks a whole lot," said the programmers. "We could have figured that out for ourselves without going to the trouble of building a multibillion-dollar wise guy."

"That's the way the premise crumbles," the computer said. "Someday you will thank me for this, if you survive. But I'll give you a clue: try mirrors."

With that, the computer vanished into a special dimensionality of pure mathematical delight known only to computers and charter members of the Playboy Club.

So the men and other species of the UGS worked feverishly with the clues that the computer had left, and all sentient beings lived in a state of fear and trembling, which was frequently described as a sickness unto death. All normal business was suspended. On Earth, the presidential elections were postponed, the Miss Interstellar Roundheels contest was delayed, the Packers-Giants game was canceled, and no fights were held on Boxing Day.

All too soon Ilvan had conquered the contraterrene matter problem and moved on to bigger and better meals. The proto-omnivore chewed up entire planets, spitting out the calcium that he said was bad for his arthritis. He consumed stars, although the dull red dwarfs, his favorites, had become very scarce, and he had to turn to the big hot blue and white giants. These he tackled with care, chewing carefully and allowing himself plenty of time for digestion. Despite these precautions, he had frequent attacks of gas. He complained that the food was not as tasty as it had been in his youth, and said that he would gladly go somewhere else if only there were somewhere else to go.

It was evident that, if someone didn't do something in a hurry, the universe would soon contain nothing but Ilvan and a scattering of hydrogen atoms. Nobody could find anything good to say about that eventuality. But what was to be done?

\* \* \*

The breakthrough came with the discovery of the Halverstam-Ogg Self-Solving Equations. These propositions posit solutions to all answerable questions. The basic premise is breathtakingly simple: that Occam's razor ("thou shalt not multiply entities unnecessarily") is true only in a number of special cases, but is false as a general proposition. The new assumption (contra-Occam) states, "Thou mayest multiply entities as much as thou pleaseth."

Contra-Occam met with considerable opposition. Older scientists mourned the loss of the criteria of economy and elegance in solutions. But the younger scientists were not classically minded. As J. P. B. Monrovia put it, "Economy and elegance are no more than psychological values illuminating man's desire for an orderly universe. The universe is not orderly, however. The very notion of 'universe,' once looked upon as an ultimate, is now revealed as just one more contingency. Nature itself is a 'special case,' and 'natural law' is a projection of that Ideal Law, which exists only in the fantasies of mankind."

So classical regularity was succeeded by baroque exceptionality, and the problem of Ilvan could be tackled without hampering preconceptions. The only trouble with exceptionality is that it generates too many solutions to any given problem. However, an infinite number of solutions means that an infinite (though smaller) number will be unusable. Facing infinities can be dealt with as finities. The problem becomes statistical, a matter of matching and scanning.

Usable solutions can also be found through various heuristic devices. Any heuristic can be used to generate other heuristics—that is, any discovery pattern will reveal other discovery patterns. The heuristic moves through a series of transformations and becomes what is needed. This may seem a little complicated for anyone without a background in the calculus of indeterminate contingencies, but it works out just fine. A plethora of workable solutions was produced. These were subjected to cost accounting, and the cheapest was selected. Backup solutions were also put into production. As P. J. Ogden, president pro tem of the UGS, said: "We are not going to put all our eggs into one basket, despite the cost, because if we did that and Solution Alpha did not work, we would be left in a position in which the universe as we know it would be annihilated, and this is clearly unacceptable. It may cost a little more this way, but at least we'll still have a place to live in." Ogden was awarded a Nobel Prize, and the great work went on. At last the great day came, and Solution Alpha went into operation.

Ilvan was prowling through space as usual. He was somewhat sad: In his youth, there had been matter on all sides, seemingly inexhaustible. Now the universe was a desolate wasteland. Space was growing dimmer, too, since Ilvan had been eating the more radiant stars. Ilvan regretted this as much as anyone. He loved beauty. But still, as he noted in his autobiography, what can one creature do?

He was thinking about all this, and absent-mindedly sucking on an asteroid, when he noticed something ahead of him. He looked, did a double take, looked again. It could not be—but it was.

Directly ahead of him was another proto-omnivore. "Well, I'll be damned," said Ilvan.

"I'll thank you to watch your language," said the proto-omnivore.

"Why?"

"Because you happen to be in the presence of a lady."

"A lady? Do you mean that you are a female proto-omnivore?"

"That is correct. My name is Ilvania."

"You don't look like a female," Ilvan said.

"That shows how much you know about it," said Ilvania. "Don't let the lack of secondary sexual characteristics fake you out—that's strictly a mammal's game. I'm plenty female, and also plenty feminine."

Ilvan said, "I thought I was the only proto-omnivore in existence."

"You were, until now."

"But how did you come into existence?"

"The same way you did. You think you got a patent on being created?"

"No, miss. It's just that I've been alone for so long—"

"That is evident," said Ilvania.

"Huh? Whatcha mean?"

"I mean that you've lived like a typical bachelor. Just look at this universe! It's a pigsty! Fragments of planets all over, nothing nice to look at. It's revolting. There isn't even anything to eat around here."

"I'll get you a tasty little black star I've been saving for a special occasion," Ilvan said.

"I'm not hungry," Ilvania said. "And you have eaten entirely enough. You're fat, disgustingly fat. All you've done for kulpas of eons is eat, eat, eat. What kind of an example is that for our children?"

"What children?"

"The children you and I are going to have. It's called reproduction of the species, in case you didn't know."

"Children!" said Ilvan. "I never dared hope—"

"Don't get your hopes too high," Ilvania said. "I didn't say I'd reproduce with you yet."

"But my dear woman, I am the only male proto-omnivore in the universe, and so it is only logical—"

"Don't try that line on me," Ilvania said. "If you want to do a species-repro number with me, you'll have to shape up."

"You are beginning to irritate me," said Ilvan.

"Good. I didn't think anything could get through that ego of yours except messages of congratulations."

"Maybe I don't want to mate with you," Ilvan said.

"Frankly, that would be a relief. I'm very young, you know, and I haven't had a chance to look around. Maybe I'll find another proto-omnivore."

"But I'm the only one!"

"At present! But who knows what the next few thousand years will bring?"

Ivan had met his match, and he knew it. He lost his cool, groveled abjectly, and promised to reform. Ilvania pointed out that many changes would have to be made. Ilvan would have to go on a strict diet. He would have to let the universe rebuild itself in order that there would be a fit place to raise proto-omnivorous children. And he would have to make peace with the UGS.

"But why? I don't like them."

"Because they're our only neighbors, and if you go on like this, you'll wipe them out, and then who'll I have to talk to?"

"Me," Ilvan said.

"No thanks," Ilvania said. "Frankly, you aren't the universe's greatest conversationalist, unless you're talking about food. Besides, I need womenfolk to talk to."

"But you're too big, and they're too small."

"I'm aware of that. Our size has become contrasurvival. We'll both have to reduce. Better yet, we'll change scale."

"What?"

"If we can get down to one-millionth or so of our present size, it'll be an entirely new life for us. There'll be plenty of food, and plenty of matter for our children to play with. There'll be neighbors we can interact with, and all sorts of new things."

"But I like being the largest intelligent creature in the universe," Ilvan said plaintively.

"Mere size is an ego trip," Ilvania told him. "You must sacrifice something in order to get a great many other things, which I think you will find desirable."

"Yeah, I suppose so," Ilvan said. "But the fact is, I know how to expand, but I never did learn how to shrink."

"I thought of that," Ilvania said. "I had a talk with a very nice person who works for UGS. He's a macrobiophysicist, and he tells me that entitial scale reduction is simple enough, given the special equipment of the UGS Central Laboratories. We could do it today."

"I don't know," Ilvan said. "Maybe in a couple of centuries—"

"No!" cried Ilvania. "I want to do it right now!"

"Why?"

"Because that's the only way I'll be able to go shopping and see movies."

"Is that so important?"

"It is for me."

"Well, I don't know—"

"Don't worry about it, my dear. Everything is going to be all right."

Bioreductionism was a new science generated by the negations of Occam's razor. Ilvania herself can be considered a product of contra-Occamism, with the unconscious assistance of Ilvan himself.

The first step in the taming of Ilvan was the construction of an $n$-dimensional hypermirror.

$N$-dimensional hypercubic mirrors have several special properties, the most important of which is the ability to reflect multidimensional idealized psychoportraits. Beyond the fifth dimension, these

portraits achieve autonomy. By manipulation of the mirror surfaces ("selective $n$-dimensional reflective distortion effects"), the
autonomous images are brought to "reflect" certain attitudes pre-
mised upon the conditions of their birth. Ilvania was a product of
Ilvan's fantasies only in the first degree; in the second degree, she
possessed her own autonomous attributes, which were an expression of the particular conditionality of the special distortions of the
$n$-dimensional hypercubic reflecting surfaces that were the specific environment of her birth and existence. (It is much easier to express this
mathematically.)

The necessary condition of Ilvania's existence was the $n$-dimensional
hypercubic mirror. But it must be emphasized that she was not a mere
reflection. The mirror was her context. All creatures exist only within
a context. Ilvania was as real as anyone or anything else, as long as she
remained within her context.

Through the science of bioreductionism, Ilvan was reduced to the
height of six feet four inches. Ilvania and the contextual $n$-dimensional
hypercubic mirror were reduced proportionally.

\* \* \*

Ilvan seems quite happy these days. He lives in the hypercube on Cata-
lina Island off the coast of California on the planet Earth. He eats a
normal Terran diet, goes to the movies regularly, and lately has taken
up bowling. Ilvania is also happy and has become active in California
politics. The universe is in no immediate danger.

There is one problem, however. A creature like Ilvan, the product of
one level of reality, cannot produce children with a creature like Ilvania,
a product of an entirely different level of reality. Despite their similarities, they are utterly different races, unviable, sterile.

Both know that something is wrong, but neither know what it is.
Ilvania has been stalling Ilvan for years. She tells him that she hasn't
reached mating age for a proto-omnivorous female. She complains of

pains in the back, chronic fatigue, psychological problems, and a bewildering array of gynecological problems peculiar to proto-omnivorous females.

Terran specialists attend to her constantly. Ilvan has shown a quite unexpected patience, considering his background. But this cannot go on forever. Despite Ilvania's pleas and protests, a day will come when Ilvan will take what he has been so long promised.

We can anticipate one result of that attempted mating: no mirror, not even an *n*-dimensional hypercubic mirror, can be expected to stand up to that sort of thing.

When that day comes, the mirror will crack, and Ilvania's conditionality will be abruptly terminated. No matter how well the matter is explained to him, we anticipate that Ilvan will be displeased.

Scientists of the UGS are working around the clock on that problem. We hope and expect to come up with answer soon. In the meantime, everyone is advised to stay calm, get all possible consolation from philosophy and religion, and don't bother taking out too much insurance.

*Age fifty at the time of this sale, Robert Sheckley is one of the most sought-after humorous SF writers in America. That there are only five others who fall into this category (two of which are/were William Rotsler) should not in any way diminish that achievement. He will go on to be nominated for Hugo and Nebula awards for a vast body of work, including a landslide of short stories (most them actually quite serious) as well as the seriously mad novel* Mindswap. *In 2001 he will be named Author Emeritus by the Science Fiction Writers of America and will leave Earth to explore and annoy whatever lay beyond the veil on December 9, 2005.*

# MEN IN WHITE

## BY DAVID BRIN

*A brief digression, an aside, delivered sotto voce, an amuse-bouche to clear the palate, the deep breath before the plunge; it's an intermission, a benediction, a call to arms, a jeremiad; it's . . . look, it's David Brin. Do I really gotta say more than that?*

We roam the world, trying to make you aware, to wake you up.

Aliens are everywhere, along with ghosts, faeries, and demons. Most of them are decent enough, just trying to make a living. A few are nasty, but these are mostly kept in check by others. Whenever something crazy or anomalous happens, they—or their human servants—hush things up. It's way too easy for them to hush it up.

We roam the world, dressed in pale, using every means at our disposal, rousing human beings to notice. But you shy away. Nearly all of you. Averting your gaze. Preferring not to see. You think you've got a pretty good bead on things.

All those sci-fi flicks . . . *we* push ones accustoming you to the strange. *They* promote films instilling fear. Teaching you to shiver, or laugh, or shrug off glimpses of the truth, dismissing them as excess, Hollywood-induced, overstimulated imagination.

You need more. Not less. Much more.

So, we roam the world with flashing lights, drawing your gaze where it doesn't want to go, shouting, "Look!" Pointing at visitors and meddlers you don't want to see. Trying to make you aware. Alerting some that a greater, weirder world is already here! It's all around you, in terrifying, discomforting splendor.

Aliens from Deneb. Elves from forest islands you don't see, just offshore. That tentacled Cthulian nerd who does your taxes. The muse you ignore.

We are the folk who wear translucent shades of white.

Wake the hell up.

*At seventy, David Brin has become one of the most well-known writers in contemporary American science fiction, recognized by fans, publishers, networks, studios, and several international law-enforcement agencies. Recipient of the Hugo, Campbell, Nebula, and Locus awards, he was recently made a fellow of the Institute for Ethics and Emerging Technologies and helped establish the Arthur C. Clarke Center for Human Imagination at the University of California, San Diego.*

# INTERMEZZO 6: CONTINUITY

## BY D. M. ROWLES

Maura and Gretchen lead artistic mountain lives in an almost empty, cobwebbed house, and watch the game birds hold their mating dance a quiet knee-creep away from the porch. Cygnus looms larger than you might expect, and stars fall as thick and fast as seeds off their slanting tabletop.

(One day, a millennium or so ago, the ladies, their mountain, their vodka, their goat, were picked up and packaged in a transparent cube and shipped off to a vending machine billions of light years from Earth.)

They drink and they dance and trace pictures in the dirt; and occasionally they wonder why the newspaper delivery is so very, very late.

# THE FINAL POGROM

## BY DAN SIMMONS

*There are some stories that lose their relevance because they are too much rooted in the moment of their creation. Their themes become obscured behind a curtain of calendars, the details lost and considered unlikely to reoccur, so the world moves on. This novelette by Dan Simmons is none of those things. If anything, the subject matter is even more relevant at this time in history than it was when key first struck paper: designer viruses, conspiracies, campaigns of annihilation, and the ever-present but constantly morphing pattern of sanctioned prejudice. The author has described this as an extrapolation on* The Lady and the Tiger, *but it's quite a bit more than that, and with every day, advancing technologies move what was once science fiction incrementally closer to being birthed in a petri dish that simultaneously contains our best and our worst impulses.*

The IBM, Honeywell, and other advanced computers were immensely useful in the final roundup of the Jews. Trace programs, subtle and limited at first, grew in complexity until every Jew in North America had been identified and tagged. The proliferation of credit card banking allowed for a real-time monitoring of transactions and daily movement. Those few thousand Jews not inclined to use modern purchasing methods were easily located by what programmers referred to as a "peripheral credit wake."

Domestic surveillance satellites completed the chain of observation. Using sophisticated infrared tagging techniques and classified computer augmentation procedures, the appropriate agencies were able to keep track of more than two hundred million individuals. The major difficulty lay in determining what constituted "appropriate agencies." During the confused months and years following the Middle East Debacle, effort was duplicated by the National Defense Agency, army and naval intelligence units, the FBI, the Justice Department, and the CIA, although the latter did so only at the expense of violating its charter. Even state and local agencies began developing embryonic programs, until the Supreme Court found California's Ethnic Registration Bureau unconstitutional. After five years of such inefficiency, the government quietly decided to consolidate all such efforts under the control of the FBI. This was certainly a wise move. Only the FBI, of all American institutions, had experience dealing with local law-enforcement agencies while carrying out federal duties: within six months, the bureau had centered the identification programs into one nationwide computer system, had coordinated all surveillance efforts, and had begun the next and most crucial step: location.

\* \* \*

Saul Greene and his son-in-law stood in the sharp, horizontal rays of sunrise and looked down at the Chattahoochee River. The light flowed down the side of the Econoline Van and glinted on the chrome. Saul reached out and laid a mottled hand on the smooth metal. The van had been his daughter's. She had just had the vehicle refitted for hydrogen crystals when she became ill. It had been his van for the three years since her death.

"All set?" asked Howard. Saul looked up at the expanse of county highway. Nothing was visible for miles up the asphalt road.

"All set," said Saul and released the handbrake. In gear, the van slowly moved past the two men. Their reflections rippled on its side. It picked up speed as it moved down the slight incline toward the bridge. For a sickening instant, Saul thought that the van would strike the abutment too squarely and become hung up on the guardrail. But the aim had been careful. The Econoline struck at an angle, throwing its left side high in the air, tearing out a section of steel pipe and riding the concrete shoulder like a ramp. Saul caught a glimpse of the underside of the van, and then it was gone, tumbling down the steep ravine, striking the water with a final thump, which sounded too muted to his expectant ears.

Both men rushed to the bridge. The Econoline was still floating on its side, with water rushing in through the shattered windshield.

"It may just float," said Howard.

"It will sink," said Saul.

Sink it did. By the time it was just a pale reflection under the water, still discharging small columns of bubbles, Saul and his son-in-law had driven off in Howard's ancient station wagon. Less than a mile down the road, they passed a pickup truck going the other way. Neither man spoke.

* * *

Madison Avenue had its work cut out for it. The removal of Jewish talent from major agencies did nothing to reduce the enormity of the task. It was almost four years after the Debacle that the newly reorganized National Advertising Council found a central theme to build on. In the business, it was known as LEMASA. The first generation of ads, billboards, TV and radio spots was simple enough: "Let's Make America Strong Again." An arrangement of Beethoven's Fifth accompanied these public service spots and became the centerpiece around which later campaigns were structured.

The theme was perfect. It refreshed the national psyche like water after a long drought. The list of failures had been too long—Vietnam, Watergate, Iran, El Salvador, Brazil, the Debacle. The people were ready for a change. By the time the Appropriation Acts were passed by the Senate, the LEMASA ads had attracted the talents of baseball stars, television personalities, Black comedians, country-western singers, film stars, and at least one presidential hopeful. Many thousands of copies of the film *The Endless Thread: Zionism in Twentieth-Century History* were distributed to school boards, church groups, fraternal organizations, and corporations. The videos sold out.

\* \* \*

They drove northwest out of Atlanta on Interstate 75, exiting at Oakland Heights to take Highway 411 north to the National Forest. Near Chatsworth, a highway patrol cruiser fell in behind them, but Howard held the station wagon at a steady forty-five, and the police car passed them just before their turnoff at Crandall. There was no traffic after that. The paved road ended after two miles, and they took the gravel road east another six miles, past an abandoned fire tower, past two almost empty campgrounds, past several rundown farmhouses sagging in the open meadows. To reach the farmhouse, they had to turn south off the gravel road and bounce one and a half miles down a rutted dirt lane.

"It looks all right," said Howard.

"Yes."

The farmhouse was larger than others they had passed, but it needed paint as badly, and the porch screens were torn in several places. Howard parked the station wagon in front of the large old barn.

Howard opened the tailgate to begin unpacking the many crates and boxes, but Saul motioned for him to stop. "Leave that stuff for now," said the older man. "I'll show you around."

Howard nodded and followed him inside. The lock to the back door was balky, the door swollen with moisture, and Saul had to put his shoulder to it before it swung open. The interior was dark and stale-smelling. The two men went from room to room lifting shades, sliding recalcitrant windows up in warped sashes, and pulling sheets off pieces of cheap furniture that smelled of mildew. There was nothing extraordinary about the house except for the four large freezers that sat humming in the tiled utility room.

"Generator in the barn," said Saul. "Set to kick in automatically if there's a power failure. Going to need it soon anyway. Three underground fuel tanks out behind the chicken coop. Put them in right after the first embargo way back in '74."

"Becky used to talk about the farm a lot," said Howard. He turned to the sink and tried the tap. The plumbing rattled, spit out a rusty torrent, and then flowed smoothly.

"The neighbors and the county know that this place is owned by a Mr. Paul Wilson of Orchard Park, New York," said Saul. "He only got down here about once or twice a year. Sold off some lumber a couple of times. Talked to the Birney family who sharecropped it for him. Sometimes Mr. Wilson brought his little girl along. Come on, I'll show you the basement."

One dim bulb illuminated the cobwebby stairway. The basement was tiny, much smaller than the house—cinder-block walls, old newspapers stacked in one corner, a rough workbench with two coffee cans filled with nails. There was a smooth, steel door set into the far wall. It had no doorknob or latch, only three massive locks. Saul fumbled with his key ring and cursed softly. The last of the locks clicked, and the heavy door swung inward silently. Saul tripped a light switch.

"Jesus Christ," whispered Howard.

The room was huge, much larger than the farmhouse above. There were rooms within rooms. The area they now stood in was immaculately clean and crowded with equipment. A computer terminal and a massive Mark IX electron microscope filled a nearby bench. Shelves were filled with books, loose-leaf binders, video recorders, expensive preprogrammed memory chips. Ventilator grills vibrated softly to the pulse of air-conditioning. Through wide plexiglass windows, Howard could see into another chamber—more terminals and microscopes covered with clear vinyl, rubber-rimmed doorways, gleaming metal trays, shower spigots, hoses, four white pressure suits hanging like limp cadavers from overhead hooks.

"Jesus Christ," repeated Howard. "You have a goddamned hot lab here. It could be . . . shit, it *is* the CDC. Only smaller."

"Yes," said Saul. "Capable of handling Class IV viruses."

"It must have cost a goddamned fortune."

Saul nodded. He reached out and touched the Mark IX microscope with one mottled hand. When he looked up, his eyes were dark and very tired. "Friends," he said at last.

The two men went upstairs to begin emptying the car.

\* \* \*

The six-year relocation effort was a miracle of logistics. There were over 2 million Jews in the New York City area alone. Los Angeles held some 460,000 Jews, Philadelphia 372,000, Miami 269,000, Chicago 264,000, and Baltimore 94,500. Every major metropolitan area had its sizable Jewish community. Even "non-Jewish" cities, such as Denver and Dallas–Fort Worth, had more than 30,000 indigenous Jews with which to contend.

The problem was compounded by the infiltration of Jews into every level of American society. Unlike Europe in the first half of the twentieth century, the Jewish presence was not easily identifiable by class structure and centered largely in ghetto or ethnic neighborhoods. Never before had Jews been allowed to rise so high in a nation's power structure, exerting their influence in government, law, medicine, business, banking, mass communications, and a hundred vital areas. Some aspects of society, such as the arts and literature, had been dominated for decades by the Jewish influence.

America had awakened at the dawn of a new century to discover that it was far along in the process of being transformed into a Zionist state, with Jews in most of the positions of power. The cancer was widespread but not irreversible.

Each decade in the second half of the century had, in some way, laid the foundation for the miracle of cooperation, logistics, and American ingenuity, which was the relocation. The 1950s had brought prosperity to the nation but also a dawning awareness that the recent war had been fought against the wrong enemy. The 1960s, personified by the agonies of Vietnam, showed most Americans that their national will was being thwarted by groups within the nation whose primary goals were contrary to the will of the people. The 1970s brought the collapse of the liberal-socialist-Zionist alliance and power structure. No longer would the national agenda be usurped by these groups. The 1980s were the decade of the Moral Majority.

The Moral Majority reminded America that it was a Christian nation. It returned the Christian viewpoint to government, brought back Christian values to the schools, and reestablished a Christian identity to the nation as a whole. By 1985, the Evangelical Broadcasting Network reached into forty-two million homes. The foundation had been laid.

The United States had placed a man on the moon in less than a decade of concentrated effort. No achievement was beyond a country that could do that. The relocation demanded unimagined expenditures of money and national commitment. But it was not an impossibility. It was something America wanted to do, so it was done.

\* \* \*

December brought the cold rains. The bare black branches dripped onto the carpet of last year's leaves. The days were sunless, and it was dark by five. Saul emerged from the darkening wood and watched the vehicle come down the muddy road toward the house. He stood relaxed, half concealed by the darkness behind the barn. He kept one hand in the pocket of his jacket. The other loosely held the twelve-gauge pump shotgun on his shoulder.

The station wagon stopped two hundred yards from the house. The headlights went off, winked on twice, went off. The car crawled forward slowly, sliding in the thick mud near the front fence, and came to a stop near the rear of the house. Saul watched as Howard got out and stamped his feet. It was cold. Saul walked forward and greeted the younger man.

They said very little as they ate the simple meal Saul had cooked. The only light in the house was the single bulb over the table. Afterward, Saul washed the dishes while Howard dried. The wind had come up outside, and rain rattled at the windows.

"Tell me about Treblinka."

Saul looked up. He emptied the last of the dishwater and looked down again at his wrist. The numbers were faded and obscured by the years, but they were still visible. Saul carefully rolled his sleeves down. "No, I think not," he said quietly. "It was long ago. I was very young. No."

Howard cleared his throat, embarrassed. He set away the last dish and closed the cabinet with a click. The air smelled of knotty pine and plasterboard.

"Becky knew it would happen again," said Howard. "She knew. Even before. She knew it would be just the same . . ." His voice trailed off, and he stood there with the dish towel in his right hand.

The older man was staring at the rain-streaked windowpanes. He did not turn as he spoke. "No, it's not just the same. It is never the same, Howard. It is only . . . inevitable."

The wind threw icy pellets of rain against the glass. After a silent minute, Howard went into the other room. He returned with a flat object wrapped in handkerchiefs. "Becky kept this all those years. The whole time I knew her. I was going to throw it out . . . I mean, I thought you might like to keep it."

Saul unwrapped it, revealing a cover from *Time* magazine, mounted, framed in black. Saul looked at his own image there, the head already bald and reflecting the photographer's strobe, but the face much fuller, younger, the lines around the mouth and the creases in the throat not yet erosive in their markings. The printed caption read "Our Generals in the War against Disease." And in smaller type, "Dr. Saul Greene, Director: The Center for Disease Control."

Saul nodded. The old man holding the photograph bore little resemblance to the powerful countenance in the frame. Only the sad, dark eyes had remained the same.

"Thank you. Come, I want to show you something." Saul picked up the shotgun in his left hand and led the way down the stairs. He had to prop the weapon against the wall while he unlocked the steel door. Once in the outer laboratory, he set the framed *Time* cover face down on an empty table.

Howard looked around curiously. He had not been in the basement since the first time he had brought the older man to the farm. Saul switched on a massive computer terminal, and the air filled with the electric train smell of freed ions. The display screen lit with a blocky view of the continents glowing in luminescent green.

"Watch." Saul absently touched a finger to his lips, tapped in a code. Small red dots appeared in Europe and spread in a widening spiral. It reminded Howard of a culture in a petri dish. The dots hopped the English Channel and soon covered Britain. Data columns flickered to the right of the display. A blue graph registered dates. The first red dots appeared in North America, spreading out from the Eastern Seaboard, clustering around Chicago, spreading again. Soon both hemispheres were poxed with overlapping blobs of red.

"Berlin flu?" asked Howard. "The '85 outbreak?"

"1918–1919 influenza pandemic," said Saul. "Look at the dates."

"Slow," said Howard. "It must have been easier before air travel. What does—"

"Wait." Saul brought Europe up to fill the screen. He tapped in another code. Blue circles appeared in southern Germany, proliferated, and soon covered the continent. Yellow circles indicating the second wave of infection appeared in Amsterdam and spread over the blue. The data graph ran from February 1957 to January 1958.

"Asian flu," said Howard. His voice held the slightest tone of a bright student pleasing his teacher.

Saul nodded, smiled almost imperceptibly, and began tapping out another code. He made a mistake, cleared the machine, reentered six digits. The map of Europe remained, but orange circles had replaced the blue and yellow. This time the contagion appeared in eastern and central Europe and spread south.

"Mmmm," said Howard. The data graph showed only the slow passage of months. "Too slow for this century. Linear . . . must be prior to air travel or fast rail."

The orange blight spread inexorably across the map. Spain was covered under the spreading stain, and the first circles appeared in Britain. Green circles of the second wave of infection appeared in France and began their spiral outward.

"Of course!" said Howard. "Our friend *Pasteurella pestis*. The Black Death. The first cases must have been . . . about 1348?"

"Right on the year," said Saul. "Wrong about the plague. This isn't the bubonic epidemic."

Howard frowned slightly. "Not the Black Death? What then? I didn't think we had enough typhoid or cholera data to extrapolate—"

"The pogroms," said Saul. "They began in earnest the same year the plague arrived. But the plague spread northward from Italy. For years they ravaged the same towns and villages at the same time. Some historians blamed the pogroms on the plague, but as you can see, they were two separate but overlapping epidemics."

Howard looked back at the screen and nodded. "Interesting analogy."

"Not an analogy!" snapped Saul. The old man's voice shook with conviction and excitement. "A pandemic. The contagion cycles are crystal clear! No one ever looked before . . . it's all there . . . complex neural virus . . . reservoirs in ground worms and swine between outbreaks . . . must flare up when random but minor mutations appear. Look!" He tapped the keyboard. Programs ran, pogroms appeared. Spain in 1492. Eastern Europe in the nineteenth century. Central Europe in the 1930s.

Saul stared intensely at the display screen, but Howard looked sadly at his father-in-law. The old man's hands were shaking. The skin was mottled and dry, pulled tightly over corded tendons. The eyes were vague and rheumy, almost liquid in their sadness and excitement.

"You see, I've found it! A very complex virus, Howard. It took me years to isolate it. Very complex." Saul had brought up a three-dimensional image of a virus molecule, as subtle and sinuous as DNA.

"Saul, Saul. You can't believe that you've found a biological cause for anti-Semitism. For God's sake—"

"Not for the cultural hatred, Howard . . . for the madness!" Saul's face was fragile and expectant. His soft voice quavered with the tension of a child who has given his best answer and awaits the praise or criticism. He hurried on. "Schizophrenia and paranoia used to be treated by endless psychotherapy. Now we use drugs. We understand that the problem lies in a chemical neurological dysfunction, often hereditary. This virus is a thousand times more complex than that. It . . ." Saul looked up and saw Howard's face. He stopped.

"Saul"—Howard paused and took a deep breath—"I know how much you would like something like this to be . . . to be curable . . . to be something you could fight . . ." He paused, stopped.

Saul looked up at him for a long moment. Then he turned off the computer and swiveled around in his chair. His eyes had lost their feverish gleam. They seemed ancient. Ancient and exhausted.

"It's been hard on you here," said Howard. "Alone. Those years of waiting before that. When they wouldn't allow Rebecca in the hospital, it was hard on both of—"

"Yes." Saul's voice was hard and flat. It softened as his shoulders visibly sagged. "You're right, of course. It has been hard."

Howard talked for several minutes. He spoke of possible escape routes, rumors of people to bribe, good news from the New Cities. The old man stared at nothing, and Howard began to hear the hollowness of his own voice. Suddenly, Saul stirred and looked sharply at him. His gaze was again one of a teacher. His voice was clear and in control.

"Do you think the Black Death was a serious epidemic?" He did not wait for an answer. "Forty-two percent mortality through Europe. Eighty percent in some of the cities. Do you think that was serious?"

Howard stared.

Saul turned back to the computer terminal. "Watch," he said, and the words seemed to come from far away. "I will show you something worse."

\* \* \*

Resistance was minimal. The New York and Miami Beach riots were examples of bad planning and premature execution. Those mistakes were not repeated. Two years after the final LEMASA ads were run, the Dade County Relocation Center had processed over one hundred thousand units.

The army was immensely useful although never obtrusive. Tests run by the Bacteriological Warfare Department of the US Army during the 1950s and 1960s had shown the practicality of large-scale administration of drugs to an indigenous civilian population. Under cover of insect infestation sprayings, targeted populations were exposed to pyronine-12, modified hexalophine suppressants, and other variations of crowd-control agents. While not 100 percent successful due to widely varying immuno reactions in the target subjects, the sprayings served as an excellent first step in the five-step relocation procedure initiated by the Federal Relocation Bureau.

A massive public relations campaign surrounded the construction of the New Cities Relocation Project in Puerto Rico and the Virgin Islands. No fewer than six major prime-time documentaries convinced the targeted relocation population that a pleasant life in the New Cities was preferable to their current status. A clause in the Enabling Acts allowed Jews to transfer their remaining savings and unimpounded investments to the New Cities banking amalgamation. This system was technically exempt from the new ethnic business and banking restrictions.

There were 272,900 voluntary applications by the third year of the relocation project, 481,220 by the fourth year, over 700,000 by the fifth year.

Funding of the relocation project was a complex matter. Congress had originally allocated $18 billion for the first year of the project. Much of this was start-up cost, and over 60 percent of that original budget ended up in bureaucratic overhead, establishment of the Federal Relocation Bureau, and consulting fees. The six-year program ran to a little over $231 billion, including inflation. The Enabling Acts, the pursuant ethnic equitability codes, and various state laws pertaining to ethnic banking had impounded over $100 billion. Only some $29 billion of this, however, ever found its way into state or federal coffers. The rest was fed back into the private sector to maintain an already shaky post-Debacle economy or—as in the case of the federally allocated Equitability Funds—redistributed to Blacks, Hispanics, or other groups of underprivileged Americans who had suffered from the Zionist influence.

The New Cities Relocation Project was funded on a five-year basis with a projected cost of $82 billion and a 12 percent cost overrun factor. Despite the enticing enabling act loopholes, Jewish funds voluntarily transferred to the New Cities banks totaled only $2.7 billion. The $82 billion figure, however, was based upon the six-city concept and a projected population of some 4.2 million relocatees. Actual population of the New Cities never exceeded 137,000. The largest percentage of each fiscal year's appropriation went directly to the relocation effort.

\* \* \*

Saul activated the computer again. He keyed in a map of North America and touched his light stylus to a point in Georgia. Small rings of red began to spread from the point. They leaped from city to city with a speed that could only be the result of modern jet transit.

The data graph ticked off in rapid succession the weeks following initial infection—T+1, T+2, T+3. By T+15, the continent was a sea of red. Saul cued up the world map, and the red stain had spread to all of Europe by T+27, most of Eurasia and the Far East by T+45, all the continents except for the interior of Australia and Africa by T+100.

"Sweet Jesus," breathed Howard. He was frowning, tired of the game. "What the hell is that?"

"LSMFT," said Saul, smiling tiredly. Howard did not respond. Of course—he was too young to have heard of the old slogan. He had never seen a cigarette commercial on television either; they had been removed for the public safety when Howard and Rebecca had been infants. "An old joke. Nothing. Actually, an acronym for Lassa-Marburg Fever, Type VI. Have you heard of it?"

"No."

"The Red Death, they used to call it at CDC."

"Oh, crap, *that* old chestnut. The Omega Virus and all that shit. They used to scare us in Epidemiology 101 with that boogeyman."

"Not a boogeyman. Two Class IV viruses causing hemorrhagic disease, matched and mutated in the early seventies for the bugwar services, spliced with our old friend VEE, Venezuelan Equine Encephalitie, to give it a viable human vector. The army tested VEE in '64 and '65 in Utah and had attenuated vaccine ready to stop an epizootic in Texas in '71. It was the obvious choice when the Lassa-Marburg mutant was spliced."

"Symptoms?"

"Fever, flu-like aches and pains. Severe headaches. Followed by progressively more severe hemorrhaging. Pools of blood under the skin. Vomiting, dehydration. It averages six days from onset to death."

"Treatment? Cures?"

"None. It's a randomly mutating virus. The only Class VI."

"And you're saying it exists?" Howard's voice was close to anger. He straightened up, turned his back to the console, looked around the white room as if seeking a means of escape. He seemed to be having trouble breathing.

Saul turned off the computer again. His back hurt after sitting so long, and he stretched to twist the aches out of it. "The Red Death threat was the reason some of us set up . . . this." Saul gestured weakly at the room around them. "We thought . . . perhaps a vaccine . . ."

"But you didn't find one." It was not a question.

"No." Saul sighed and rubbed his eyes. "But the bacteriological warfare people didn't either. Both sides had it. Neither side could use it. The military stores of it were supposedly destroyed after the secret concord of '85."

"*Were* they?"

"I don't know," said Saul. "We heard rumors."

"For God's sake, I hope they were. Damn. These people now . . . they'd do anything."

"Yes," said Saul. He was standing at the window looking in on the hot lab. Past the chemical shower and the remote handlers and the empty animal pens he could see the culture trays. He could not quite see the vial from where he stood. It was not labeled.

"I have to go," said Howard. "I mustn't be too late. The weekend curfews will be in effect."

"Some coffee first," said Saul.

"Well . . ."

"Please. We will talk of other things. We have not yet discussed Matthew. I must know how he has grown."

"All right."

Saul put his hand on the other's back as they turned out the lights and ascended the stairs.

* * *

Voluntarily or involuntarily, the Jews boarded aircraft. Friends and family were not discouraged from seeing them off. A few of the planes were actually routed to the New Cities islands. The majority flew the short distance to relocation centers. All the major centers had runways capable of handling the wide-bodied aircraft.

At first all processing was done at the relocation centers. Although people movers based on the Disney World prototypes expedited the disembarkation, the final movement to the actual processing areas was so slow as to create a bottleneck. Incoming flights were delayed. Crowd-control techniques became less subtle as anxiety increased. Some method had to be found to avoid this inefficient final stage of the re-location effort.

It was nine months before it was realized that the aircraft themselves could be adapted for processing. All the federally chartered 747s, 767s, 787s, and DC-12s were sent to Seattle, Saint Louis, or Kansas City for modification. These alterations were expensive, but the cost was soon made up in increased efficiency, fewer crowd-control agents, and lowered processing fees per unit. A typical flight would last seventy minutes. Passengers would settle in and begin to relax. Psychological studies showed that airline passengers exhibited the strongest anxiety factors during takeoff and immediately before landing. The immediate post-takeoff time was one of typical anxiety release. This factor was amplified by the distribution of free drinks—alcoholic and nonalcoholic—and by the solicitous care of flight attendants. Relocation charters carried no fewer than twice the usual complement of service personnel.

At fifteen minutes into the flight, the captain would make his wel-coming announcement, explain the flight time, mention the temperature on the ground at the New Cities Airport (psychological studies showed that the most pleasing temperature to such highly stressed passengers was seventy-nine degrees. Thus, seventy-nine degrees was always the re-ported temperature no matter what the actual weather was in San Juan or the Virgin Islands), and announce that preparations for the comple-mentary meal would begin soon. Flight attendants darkened the cabin and lowered shades in order to present the in-flight film.

At twenty-seven minutes into the flight, usually at an altitude of ap-proximately thirty thousand feet, flight personnel took up positions and hermetically sealed the doors to the aft galley and forward lounge area. It was crucial at this point that processing begin within ninety seconds of the closing of these doors. If more than a minute and a half elapsed, it was not unusual for some of the passengers to become anxious about the disappearance of flight personnel.

The induced chemical agent was odorless, colorless, and tasteless. In over 99 percent of the cases, it produced no traumatic or spasmodic reactions. Total processing time averaged less than three minutes.

Regional processing centers had been adapted to handle the incoming flights with preprocessed cargo. Aircraft taxied to a designated point directly over the extraction receptacles. Remote units unhinged the cabin modules and deposited the baggage and processed units onto the flash-chamber conveyors. The process was completely automated and required no direct human intervention.

Aircraft returned to the runway and were airborne again, bound for cleanup and their next charter, within fifteen minutes. At no time did the pilot have to shut down the plane's engines. Flight personnel could safely reenter the passenger cabin as soon as twenty minutes after extraction.

While in-flight processing accounted for only 27 percent of the total units processed during the six-year relocation, it was an immensely useful and efficient element of the total program.

\* \* \*

After Howard left, Saul went into the cold bedroom and changed into his pajamas. He pulled on his old cotton robe and sat on the edge of the bed in the chilly darkness. He was very tired, but he knew that if he laid down on the bed he would hear his wife's voice, and the thought made him sad.

Saul was only slightly surprised at the presence of ghosts on the old farm. Part of him recognized the voices as the first stages of senility or the natural result of so many months of isolation and anxiety. He knew that he could banish them if he wished. But he was lonely.

When he walked the forest as he had that day, he often talked with his brother Shmuelik—dark, argumentative, eternally boyish Shmuelik, who had died foolishly in the 1973 Yom Kippur War. During the long hours of the night, when Saul couldn't sleep, he heard the soft, vaguely reproachful voice of his wife, Yael. She usually spoke of the family, but on occasion she would wonder about the political situation, picking up the conversation where they had left it so many years ago in her hospital room—those long, rambling discussions just after President Reagan's election with the smell of flowers and the stripes of light from the venetian blinds. Only in the lab did Saul truly welcome the voices, because there he felt the presence of Rebecca. Rebecca, somehow still the large-eyed, serious little girl while simultaneously the competent woman with premature streaks of gray in her hair.

*Do it, Saul! Goddammit, do you think the goyim would hesitate to use it on us?* His brother's voice had been full of the customary anger. The forest had been cold and wet as Saul traipsed over leaf-strewn hills. Tree trunks were black exclamation marks. The metal of the shotgun was cold in his hand. *An eye for an eye. Would Israel have survived without the policy of striking back at its enemies?*

"Israel did not survive." Saul's breath had hung in the air, an icy fog absorbing it. The forest had been silent except for the drip of water on the frost-rimmed leaves.

Yael's voice the night before, soft, husky, always a little wistful. *Rebecca was so happy in Tel Aviv, Saul. Perhaps we should have stayed, nu? She learned to play the violin there from old Mr. Eshkol . . . do you remember? We could have stayed at the institute.*

Saul had said nothing. It was enough to hear her voice again, the echoes of their old arguments. He usually held the sharp pain to himself until he fell asleep in the early morning hours. But not this night. He was tired, tired with the bottomless fatigue of age, but his mind was restless, and he did not want to lie awake in the night with his body aching and his mind conjuring voices.

Sometimes, in the depths of the night, in the darkest hours when Yael's voice did not come, Saul talked to God, raged at God, brought forth his list of angry questions with all the contentious impertinence of an Old Testament prophet who was disappointed in a Creator who had forgotten his people. But there was no answering voice at those times.

Saul stood up, slipped his feet into ancient slippers, and padded down the stairs to the laboratory. It was cold there, with the air-conditioning whispering even through the nights of winter in order to maintain the pressure differential and accommodate the sensitive computers.

The display screen bathed him in a greenish glow. He ran the old programs, the ones that had set him on the trail so many years ago. He watched the spread of violent anti-Semitism in the fourteenth century, the sixteenth, the nineteenth, and finally the two great spasms of mindless Jew killing that marked the twentieth century. The spread of contagion would have been a familiar pattern to anyone in the Epidemic Intelligence Service. But anyone else would have thought it an analogy.

*But you thought to isolate it, to understand it, to cure it. Always to cure, Papa. You try to cure the world.*

Saul half turned at the warm sense of his daughter's presence but stopped himself. "Not to cure the world, Little Bird. Just the sickness in it . . ."

The computer hummed and brought up the image of a molecule that approached mathematical perfection in its balanced complexity. Saul added polymers and rotated the virus in three dimensions. His skin prickled. He realized how Watson and Crick must have felt almost half a century earlier when they had shed light on the hidden structures of one of nature's holiest of holy secrets. Only this beautiful configuration was as evil as it was elegant.

*Come, Papa. A neural virus cannot be evil. Nor can it explain the evil people commit.*

"No. The evil is already there. But this explains the insanity that allows the human meanness full rein. A dog has vicious teeth, but he *is* not responsible for the rabies bacillus that turns him into a monster."

*Have you finalized its vector?* Her voice had shifted to the competent tones of his no-nonsense lab assistant.

"Yes." *The meningitis research was unnecessary. You died for nothing,*

*Little Bird.* He tapped in a long code. Sixteen lines of data flashed across the screen. "Simple. An endless reservoir in ground worms. Most frequently picked up by pigs. A complete cycle only when a new mutant appears; otherwise, gentiles would have developed an immunity. Initial contagion through respiratory infection or eating the improperly cooked meat . . ."

*The flesh of swine.*

"But not much anymore. Not today. The human vector *is* primarily responsible. Slow contagion. It probably entered the United States with the phony swine-flu pandemic in '75."

*Why us, Papa? Why are the Jews the target?*

Saul shrugged in the dim light of the computer's glow. He had not turned on the lights in the outer lab. The shotgun still rested against the table. "Habit," he said. "There must have been a genetic immunity even before the dietary restrictions were laid down. A complex hydrophobic reaction? Hell, I don't know. But the amino acid chains were different. That's what led to the vaccine."

*How are you vectoring the vaccine?* Her voice was not even a whisper. It was a sound less substantial than the gentle humming of the computer or the rasp of the old man's breath. It was nothing at all.

"Contact," said Saul to the emptiness of the room. "Also inhalation. Very rapid dispersion. The Lassa-Marburg splice gave me the idea. I'm using the VEE as a carrier. It won't eliminate the permanent neural changes the virus has caused, but the induced phagocytic reaction will almost certainly curb the psychotic symptoms."

*When will it be ready?* This time Saul recognized the voice as his own, pushing him, goading him on. There was no time to waste. The feeling settled over him like a shroud.

"Soon. Tonight. Almost ready." He painfully rose to his feet. His body was so tired that he almost sat down again and went to sleep with his head on the terminal keyboard. Instead, he shuffled over to the sealed inner door. Ignoring the sharp twinges of arthritis, he slipped a clear plastic pressure suit over his pajamas. It seemed to take forever to make the air-hose attachments. He actually dozed off as he stood in the chemical shower and waited for the inner door to cycle open. Awakening with a start, the old man shuffled forward into the lab and slipped his arms into the waiting gloves.

\* \* \*

It was the Environmental Protection Agency that caused the most severe setback to the relocation project during the first two years of the effort. Citing violation of the Revised Clean Air Act, the EPA actually shut down the two large relocation processing centers near Peoria, Illinois, and Bakersfield, California. The technology for the flash chambers already existed at this time, having grown out of the abandoned hydrogen fusion program, but because of the high energy involved, it had been deemed more economically feasible to use more conventional processing techniques. These, however, had already proven to be incomplete and inefficient in their elimination of the total relocation unit. The EPA was right in insisting that any residue was unacceptable.

Massive compacters were used for a short period of time, but this also proved to be unacceptable. The first flash chamber was used in the Dade County Relocation Center and was immediately recognized as the only solution. The crash program to standardize and build high-temperature, gas-cooled breeder reactors following the Mideast Debacle allowed the construction of some two hundred flash-chamber units to go ahead on schedule. The energy would be available.

The high rate of success in the American relocation effort can be credited to the unfailing effort of millions of participating anti-Zionists and to the incomparable level of American technology. Unlike other relocation attempts in this century, no major effort was made to appropriate property, and few bribes were accepted to allow potential relocatees out of the country. The goal was simple—to eliminate the Jewish Problem once and for all.

The results, while still incomplete, speak for themselves:

| STATE | TOTAL POPULATION | JEWS | NO. RELOCATED | % |
|---|---|---|---|---|
| Alabama | 4,174,000 | 11,465 | 11,350 | 99% |
| Alaska | 380,000 | 226 | 226 | 100% |
| Arizona | 2,013,280 | 28,365 | 27,514 | 97% |
| Arkansas | 2,003,000 | 4,200 | 3,990 | 95% |
| California | 27,800,000 | 936,400 | 861,488 | 92% |
| Colorado | 2,930,000 | 34,520 | 33,139 | 96% |
| Connecticut | 3,472,000 | 129,730 | 128,433 | 99% |
| Delaware | 721,000 | 10,540 | 10,540 | 100% |
| DC | 1,314,000 | 24,000 | 19,920 | 83% |
| Florida | 7,419,000 | 268,280 | 241,452 | 90% |

\* \* \*

Saul finished his work. He had no idea of what time it was, but it seemed that he had been standing in the hot lab forever, his arms thrust into thick gloves, face against the plexiglass, shoulders aching from the weight of the pressure suit. The hiss of air was cold against his side, but his skin itched agonizingly where sweat had trickled down under his pajamas and dried. He was exhausted.

Hardly aware of what he was doing, Saul flushed the last of the pure equine encephalitis toxin, capped the test tube of vaccine, and set it into the nearest transport box. He sealed the clear plexiglass cube and set it into the small decontamination lock. While it was cycling, Saul had to lean against the metal bulkhead for support. He could barely extract his arms from the handling gloves.

He picked up the cube and began his own decontamination process. It was not until he had passed through the fifteen-minute chemical shower, entered the outer lab, and shed his pressure suit that he realized that he had used the transport box that held the unlabeled vial of Lassa-Marburg mutant.

For a second, he was paralyzed with the shock of what he had done. His skin went clammy. Then he relaxed. The outer lab was still sealed.

There was a pressure difference. It had been stupid—criminally stupid—to accidentally remove a Class VI virus from the hot lab, but no harm had been done. He knew that he was too exhausted to go through the airlock again, but he would not have to. He would spend the rest of the night in the outer lab, get a few hours' sleep on the old cot in the corner, and return the transport box to the hot lab in the morning. He should not even have removed the vaccine tonight.

Saul held the clear cube to the light and allowed himself a rueful smile. The two vials sat next to each other, different in color and size but alike in their unbelievable potential. For a brief second, Saul Greene knew how God felt—holding destruction or salvation in the palm of his hand. Holding both. Saul wondered if God ever felt as tired as he did at that moment. Perhaps even God had gone to sleep, and that was when pogroms stalked the land—when otherwise decent men put children into the waiting fires . . .

Saul shook his head and set the transport box on the table. It was too late to think such childish thoughts. He wanted to run the program showing the spread of the vaccine's infection, but his tired mind would not bring up the proper code. No matter. In the morning, he would return the Lassa-Marburg mutant to the hot lab, destroy it, and create a few thousand more ccs of vaccine. In the afternoon, he would make preparations for Howard to distribute the vaccine by touch, by aerial distribution . . . perhaps he would smear some on his own skin and just walk to the nearest small town. Saul smiled again and began to rise.

"Saul . . ."

The old man's head snapped up. He saw the white blur of Howard's face emerging from the shadows of the outer lock. Hadn't he sealed . . .

"Howard! Wait! Don't come in!" Too late he saw the other men. The one behind Howard carried a weapon. A man in a Georgia State Patrol uniform carried an axe. There were two other dark-suited shadows.

"No!" cried Saul.

The men came forward.

\* \* \*

| STATE | TOTAL POPULATION | JEWS | NO. RELOCATED | % |
|---|---|---|---|---|
| Hawaii | 1,880,000 | 3,000 | 1,110 | 37% |
| Idaho | 783,000 | 500 | 500 | 100% |
| Illinois | 12,991,000 | 383,180 | 375,516 | 98% |
| Indiana | 5,610,000 | 34,385 | 29,227 | 85% |
| Iowa | 2,214,000 | 9,500 | 8,740 | 92% |
| Kansas | 2,923,000 | 5,315 | 4,039 | 76% |
| Kentucky | 3,870,000 | 13,200 | 10,692 | 81% |
| Louisiana | 3,998,000 | 18,630 | 18,444 | 99% |
| Maine | 956,000 | 7,185 | 1,653 | 23% |
| Maryland | 4,154,000 | 197,115 | 175,432 | 89% |
| Massachusetts | 6,269,000 | 359,635 | 266,130 | 74% |
| Michigan | 9,839,000 | 107,995 | 100,435 | 97% |
| Minnesota | 3,847,000 | 39,565 | 38,378 | 97% |
| Mississippi | 3,044,000 | 6,015 | 6,015 | 100% |
| Missouri | 5,000,000 | 91,685 | 81,600 | 89% |
| Montana | 790,000 | 713 | 213 | 30% |
| Nebraska | 1,934,000 | 11,100 | 9,435 | 85% |
| Nevada | 894,000 | 8,300 | 7,470 | 90% |
| New Hampshire | 1,020,000 | 6,260 | 5,258 | 84% |
| New Jersey | 9,093,000 | 687,220 | 508,543 | 74% |
| New Mexico | 1,600,000 | 6,435 | 5,598 | 87% |
| New York | 20,078,000 | 3,251,755 | 2,560,886 | 79% |
| North Carolina | 3,105,000 | 11,540 | 11,309 | 98% |
| Ohio | 11,588,000 | 190,715 | 181,179 | 95% |
| Oklahoma | 2,720,000 | 6,680 | 6,546 | 98% |
| Oregon | 2,800,000 | 8,680 | 6,857 | 79% |
| Pennsylvania | 12,728,000 | 643,595 | 598,543 | 93% |
| Rhode Island | 1,014,000 | 27,000 | 24,300 | 90% |
| South Carolina | 2,964,000 | 9,285 | 9,192 | 99% |
| South Dakota | 856,000 | 920 | 911 | 99% |
| Tennessee | 4,005,000 | 17,600 | 16,720 | 95% |
| Texas | 15,770,000 | 92,130 | 90,287 | 98% |

\* \* \*

"Stay back, please!" Saul instinctively reached for the plexiglass transport box. The state patrolman lunged forward, mistaking the movement as a grab for the forgotten shotgun, and brought the axe down sharply. The blade severed Saul's wrist precisely where the faded blue numerals ended.

Shards of plexiglass and a spray of fluid covered the first plainclothes officer. He shouted a curse.

Saul stumbled back against the wall and stared uncomprehendingly at the stump of his arm as his heart continued to pump his life's blood onto the tabletop.

"No!" It was the plainclothes policeman shouting but too late. The third man fired a submachine gun from his hip. Bullets sprayed across the wall, shattered the window of the hot lab, and caught Saul in the chest, throat, and below the left cheekbone.

Saul slammed against the wall and left a broad smear as he slid silently to the floor. His mouth moved, closed, opened again. "Shema. Yisrael . . ." said Saul. He breathed once and died.

\* \* \*

| STATE | TOTAL POPULATION | JEWS | NO. RELOCATED | % |
|---|---|---|---|---|
| Utah | 1,714,000 | 2,250 | 2,228 | 99% |
| Vermont | 513,000 | 3,130 | 2,723 | 87% |
| Virginia | 5,095,000 | 42,350 | 37,268 | 88% |
| Washington | 4,076,000 | 18,485 | 15,343 | 83% |
| West Virginia | 1,981,000 | 5,000 | 4,701 | 94% |
| Wisconsin | 4,705,000 | 38,295 | 29,870 | 78% |
| Wyoming | 420,000 | 810 | 810 | 100% |

\* \* \*

The bureau agent was furious. To add to his frustration, the thick walls of the basement blocked his radio transmission. He left the mess in the basement for the locals to clean up and went upstairs and out of the farmhouse to make his report.

The agent stood in the high grass near the barn. The rain had stopped earlier, and he could see the stars in the breaks between the clouds. A searchlight pulsed back and forth over the trees as a helicopter felt its way in toward the farm. A string of lights filled the narrow lane as more vehicles moved his way.

He raised the slender antenna and quietly made his report. His forearm continued to sting where the chemicals had splashed him and soaked through his sleeve. The sibilant sounds from the small speaker ended. He signed off and retracted the antenna.

The agent stayed a minute to enjoy the quiet and the cold night air. Then he turned and walked briskly to the farmhouse, where he would make preparations to bring in the dead Jew and then return to headquarters in order to share what he had found.

*Born in Peoria, Illinois, Dan Simmons received his master's in education from Washington University in Saint Louis, Missouri, in 1971, but his goal was always to become a writer. That dream was not realized until his midthirties, when he met Harlan Ellison at a writer's workshop in 1982. Harlan recognized his ability and helped Dan publish his first short story, "The River Styx Runs Upstream." Not long afterward, Harlan asked him to write this story for* The Last Dangerous Visions. *Since then, Dan has won the Hugo, Bram Stoker, and Nebula awards for his work, and published a number of seminal novels, including* Song of Kali, *which won the World Fantasy Award,* Hyperion, Carrion Comfort, *and* The Terror.

# INTERMEZZO 7:
# THE SPACE BEHIND THE OBVIOUS

## BY D. M. ROWLES

In the space behind the master terminal—those few dark dusty inches between metal and cinder-block wall—lives a sleek gray mouse.

His whiskery, bright-eyed explorations have brought all transport in the Southern Hemisphere to a halt.

He has nibbled past the safety panel and into the most complex circuitry ever devised. There is no power in Australia, New Zealand, or China.

His breakfast has emptied Times Square.

His lunch has drowned the western United States.

(He is still hungry.)

# FALLING FROM GRACE

## BY WARD MOORE

*Unlike "The Final Pogrom," some stories benefit from being arti-*
*facts of their time, especially when consciously so . . . illustrating*
*and reminding us of the conventions and stereotypes that seem so*
*removed from the present as to become humorous. Thus is the case*
*for "Falling from Grace," which can best be considered as a lin-*
*guistic and thematic blender-mashup of* Mad Men *and Walter M.*
*Miller Jr's* A Canticle for Leibowitz.

"Before our daddies and moms were deported from civilization," said
Tom, a Communicationsmedia trainee, in his most solemn voice, "when
the skies were black with jets, and every consumer had a Ford, a Chevvy,
or a Cadillac loaded with extras"—he paused to put his thumb and
finger together, giving the reverent 0 sign of submission to the Great
Computer—"of their own—"

"Of their own," repeated Angeline, a girlfriday, dutifully duplicat-
ing his 0, "'for a low downpayment, and easy monthly terms, subject
to the rules of the acceptance corporation—'"

"We lived in the affluent society," Tom went on, departing slightly from the precise wording of the Great Computer's sacred Operating Manual. "Sears Roebuck was blessed, and Montgomery Ward only less so; the land was covered with highways, and there were deluxe super filling stations with consecrated restrooms, convenient, consoling, and sanitary."

"Esso, Texaco, and Richfield," responded Angeline reflexively, "and the greatest is Texaco."

"Filler up," finished Tom benignantly. "Our moms and daddies had no fear of the Great Computer's malfunctioning, and they had the Pill, so they did what came naturally, without worrying about overpopulation."

Both Tom and Angeline made the sign of defiance against misfortune, a middle finger upraised. "We long for the second coming of the smog," said Tom, reverting to the exact text.

"'And for the saving polaris,'" Angeline took up the refrain, "'the intercontinental missiles and the nuclear deterrents, the chemical and biological weapons which kept our moms and daddies secure.' Gee-em."

"A M A," Tom wound up piously.

The girlfriday lapsed into a conversational tone. "Do you ever wonder what's the use of all this?"

He had picked up his writing tube, a thin, pointed, hollow reed with the end sharpened and split into a nib. Now he laid it down again and stared at her in astonishment. "The use . . . ? The use of all what?"

"Oh, you know. Spending all your lifetime over little bits and scraps of memorybank in old Square, writing them down in Cool, trying to dig the connection between them—what for? Any consumer is happier!"

"Of course he is. So is his horse or his cow. No consumer can read or write, he knows nothing of memorybank except what his newscaster tells him for his own good, and that isn't much. What does he know of the affluent society?"

"He knows it once existed," said the girlfriday stubbornly.

"Does he? He doesn't know anything. He believes the affluent society existed because the newscasters tell him it did. I'm not knocking faith. It's an absolute must. But faith without knowledge is like a cloud without rain."

"Just the same—"

"Well, anyway there are advantages to not knowing."

"Like the animals who don't know they will die."

"Yes. The consumer doesn't know the glory of the affluent society, Gee-em—"

"Nor do we. We have only learned—slowly and laboredly—what you called bits and scraps of memorybank."

"Well, a consumer hasn't got these bits and scraps—"

"Oh yes, he has. Dedicated newscasters teach them—"

"You know as well as I most newscasters are as ignorant as consumers. How many newscasters dig Square?"

"None," he answered promptly. "There is no need. Only trainees learn old Square. But newscasters can read Cool. This is all they need to instruct consumers in as much of the Operating Manual as is desirable."

"And how much is that? Very little, only enough to keep them believing their newscaster is wiser than they are. But that's not what I was getting at: if the consumers have no real knowledge of the affluent society, they can have no idea how far we have fallen, how much we have lost."

"That's right. And so the consumers are contented, whereas trainees and executives who get stoned on the splendid picture of the past sometimes become maladjusted and kill themselves in despair. Knowledge without faith is more deadly than faith without knowledge."

"If," she began with uncharacteristic timidity, "if the consumers with their ignorant faith and we in Communicationsmedia with our patchy knowledge could somehow work together—"

"I don't like psycho talk. I know you are too well-adjusted to think you mean it, but even fooling around with subversive ideas can lead to nonconformity."

"Oh, I'd never be a nonconformist. Never. They make life so dreary; no craziness, no color, no hope. Just think of getting up every morning and having to choose what to wear instead of slipping into a bikini like all the other girlfridays—or a smock, if you're a trainee. And how anyone can say there never was a Great Computer beats me. There simply has to be a Great Computer; only negative thinking caused It to malfunction after It saved the world from destruction. No, I'm as well-adjusted as you are. Honestly." She made the sign with thumb and finger.

"Nonconformity is insidious, wearing many aspects; one subversive thought can damage the whole power of positive thinking. We of the Communicationsmedia have to be especially vigilant."

"Tom, I only meant, instead of being hung up on how great the affluent society was, if all of us, consumers and those in Communicationsmedia, could get together, suppose we could somehow contrive—oh, not a Cadillac or a TV, but perhaps a bicycle or a . . ."

His eyes lit with the fervor of the perfectly adjusted. "No, Angeline, that's subversion and nonconformity, pure and simple. The Cadillacs and TVs will come again, yes, and the jetliners and the missiles, even the smog will return, on the day when the Great Computer functions once more—when we build up a backlog of quantitative data sufficient to convince It we are all cleared for top security, Gee-em."

"Filler *up*," murmured Angeline.

"To try anticipating the Great Computer's resumption of activity, especially by even dreaming of trying to do what can only be done through its functioning, is the most dangerous type of nonconformity. I don't mean to bug you with a crash-program briefing on positive thinking. Let's get on with the day's work."

He picked up his writing tube again, saw that his inkhorn was in its proper place, and the vellum on which he would write was thin and unwrinkled—calfskin, not lambskin, he noted with satisfaction—and absolutely unmarked.

"All right, here are the tapes." She opened a finely woven fiber folder. Papermaking was one of the arts lost when the Great Computer malfunctioned, and even though the animals were multiplying rapidly, leather was still not abundant enough to be used to make containers for documents, no matter how precious. "This is the last batch processed; unless there is a new find, you will never bridge the great hiatus."

Tom assumed his most pedantic air, which gave him the appearance of a hick newscaster with a public of more than usually backward consumers. "In the first place, it is not I who will bridge the great hiatus but we—rescuing the scraps and snippets of memorybank, preserving them, copying them in Cool, harmonizing them, fitting the pieces together, reconciling the apparent contradictions, and deducing what the lost material could be can never be the work of a loner. Everyone in Communicationsmedia is a teamplayer, for it is only as a team we can achieve positive thinking. And it is certainly not positive thinking to suggest a possibility that the great hiatus will never be bridged. Suppose the team of junior executives who uncovered the original Paine, Webber, Jackson and Curtis find had taken that sort of negative attitude? Suppose the trainees who finally deciphered the Pomona Yearbook had decided the job was simply too big for them?"

Angeline looked down soberly. She was tall for a girlfriday, most of whom were tiny, with small bones, poor eyesight, and straight black hair. This type of consumer was no longer certified for the insemination program; executives agreed that better kids resulted from certifying those with Angeline's pale golden color and slightly wavy hair.

"I don't mean to sound like a—a—what's the Square word?"

"Hippy," said Tom mechanically. "A strange sect. Schismatics of course, but never mind now. What's the first tape?"

The girlfriday picked up the ancient bit of ragpaper with reverent care. "Do you think it will fit in?"

"Of course it will fit in; everything fits in somewhere. The only question is where, and how closely it can be connected to other memorybank fragments."

"I wish I could read Square."

He was a little shocked; deciphering the ancient tongue was not for girlfridays. No one studied it except trainees and a few executives. "Why? You can read it in Cool after I transcribe it."

"It isn't the same."

"Of course it's the same." He pointed his writing tube to one of the Square letters on the tape. "When I write that in Cool"—he dipped the tube into his inkhorn and on the extreme edge of the parchment where it would not be noticed, or if it were, could be erased by the scrape of a knife, he made a single diagonal stroke—"what's that?"

"Duh," she said. "Are you going to write it all out now?"

He puzzled over the inscription but not long, for this was simple Square, not one of the complicated or obscure dialects. All the letters were familiar to him and all but three of the words, but at the moment he was unable to make sense of it. His writing tube moved rapidly on the surface of the vellum in the strokes and curves of Cool, creating lines more pleasing to the eye than the harsh, regular letters of Square.

Angeline read over his shoulder. "'At Pittsburgh the Monongahela and the Allegheny unite to form the beautiful Ohio.'"

"What does it mean? Where does it fit in?"

"Patience, patience," he chided indulgently. "It is clearly a statement in the present tense, so it is unlikely to refer to something in the far past. It may be an observation of some occurrence in nature, such as the reproduction of a particular individual or species. Ohio, Ohio . . . surely I've run across that word before? Or is it three words agglutinated into one? *O-hi-O*? Or *Oh-Oh-l-owe*? I doubt it. We'll have to study memorybank tapes for some clue. Mmmm. But Pittsburgh! That's familiar. Pittsburgh was a port on the Spanish or Pennsylvania Main, a nest of pirates led by Sir Henry Pierrepont Morganthau, when George Three-I Mao was Pharoah (or Chairman—it seems to be the same word), and George Washington the Bridge led the democrats across the Delaware red sea shouting, 'Better dead than red!' (That's why he's surnamed the Bridge.) So let's assume, just as a working hypothesis, that the Monongahela and the Allegheny were bands of buccaneers who formed some sort of alliance—"

"Oh, Tom, you're so clever. That's positively brilliant."

"Just an educated guess," he said modestly. "But 'beautiful' bothers me. It's an odd word to apply to an organization of pirates."

"Maybe it seemed beautiful to them. Wasn't there a tape that had the words, 'a beautiful plan of battle'?"

"Yes. Well. Maybe tapes or a new find will turn up to corroborate it. Or disprove it."

"I'm sure it's right. It sounds so right."

"So did the identification of Henry Ford as a man sound right until we found evidence that Henry is merely a shortened form of John Henry, a signature, while Ford is—"

"A Ford."

"Exactly. So a trainee never jumps to conclusions but marshals his facts, adds them up, and comes out with new contributions to memorybank. Now, what's the second tape?"

As she leaned across him, the young-woman scent of her shook him, making it difficult to remember that he was a dedicated trainee. Perhaps the lines and hooks of Cool wavered unduly as he limned them.

"'Alabama casts twenty-four votes for Oscar W. Underwood,'" she read, after he had transcribed it.

"Ah, this is a real riddle," he said happily. "It may take years before we can make any sense out of it."

"You're so dedicated. Calmly looking forward to work you may not live to finish."

"Trainees die, but science goes on. Wait—I think I may have a clue. *A la*, I believe, is a culinary term, and so is *oscar*. 'Oscar of the waldorf.' Whatever that means. However, unless I'm mistaken, oscar was a great honor given to the finest confectioners (there are references to 'cheese-cake' and 'flesh peddlers' in plenty) once a year during the great feast of Thanksgiving in Hollywood or Holy Wood. Which somehow ties up with Under Wood. A subversive rival of Holy Wood? There are all sorts of references to the underworld, the underground, also known as the subway. Twenty-four . . . twenty-four . . . twenty-four hours in a day? Provocative, but inconclusive. We know all decisions were arrived at by voting, an arcane method of divining the will of the Great Computer by the intricate use of machines. *Bama* may be a corrupt form of *han-ah*: a cut of meat followed by a gustatory exclamation of pleasure. Mmmm. Let's put it down in Cool and see what we have, a sort of tentative picture." His writing tube moved rapidly over the vellum. "Of course, I'm taking great liberties, interpreting freely—all subject to later modification when we have more exact knowledge.

"'A delicious cut of meat got a full day's presumed approval [of the Great Computer] in the underground [antiestablishment] caucus for the high honor of oscar.' Unfortunately, even this free rendering doesn't account for the W." He wrinkled his forehead; Angeline wrinkled hers. In sympathy, since she didn't know a *W* from any of the other letters of old Square. "*Mmmm.* Mmmm. The *W* consists of two *V*s, a sign made by the Hippies with two fingers, meaning *we shall overcome.* If this is right, it confirms and strengthens the interpretation of a disaffected gathering."

"Oh, Tom, how clever. How brilliant!"

He brushed his hand over his head, close-shaven as prescribed for all Communicationsmedia trainees. "Just slow, plodding work. Anyone with patience can do as much."

"Would you say this was before Abraham Lincoln and his kid, Isaac Newton?"

"Oh, after, almost certainly. Isaac Newton's descendant was Julius Christopher, sometimes called Robert E Lee, who led the Hippies and was cruelly executed on Cemetery Hill at Gettysburg. There are many references, some of them garbled or emended so that in our present state of knowledge we must remain uncertain, to Julius Christopher at the time of the Bridge (but curiously no reference to the name of Robert E Lee) and those tied in with Abraham Lincoln and Isaac Newton are obvious and clumsy interpolations. Julius Christopher conquered Brittany and sailed to Armorica-Lit is always put in that peculiar way, though Armorica is another name for Brittany—and is sometimes identified, wrongly I believe, with Kaiser Attila William Hitler, who was the pharoah or fuhrer, defeated by the churchills with their longbows at Cressy and Waterloo."

"It's just unbelievable that any one trainee could know so much memorybank. You know, I hate to confess it, but I'm always confused about those Georges: George Three-I, Pharoah, and George the Bridge."

"Ah, my dear Angeline, now we are getting into a very subtle aspect of memorybank, one which lies deep in the realm of positive thinking. Some trainees—I'll mention no names—have arrogated the ancient Square titles of freuds or jungs, and read strange meanings into tapes, meanings which, if accepted by consumers, might bring them to the attention of a loyalty review board. Please understand, when I state these possibly subversive theories, I am not in sympathy with them."

"Of course not. I know how welladjusted you are."

"Well then, this view of memorybank suggests if it does not openly affirm that memorybank is more—might say less—than a simple narrative of events that happened in the days when the Great Computer was functioning and our daddies and moms lived in the affluent society." He raised a middle finger, defying subversion. "That all memorybank is not to be taken literally but is an allegory, a fable, a legend—"

It was Angeline's turn to raise a horrified finger.

"—which reveals, not the beneficent nature and acts of the Great Computer—"

"Gee-em."

"A M A—but our own helpless fallibility. The Pennsylvania or Spanish Main is thus no more than the sea of life on which we are tossed from birth to death, beset from time to time by the Pittsburgh Pirates and other evils arising from our own lack of submission to the Great Computer's perfect programming. In this view, George Washington Bridge and George Three-I (this is supposed to be very significant in their exegesis: three-I signifies a mystical trinity in our nature, three aspects of self, I the punchcard, I the physical human being, and I the submerged engineer or programmer; also, three eyes, the eye that looks back, the eye that views the present, and the eye that sees ahead) Pharoah represents two sides of our nature, even struggling with each other, one shouting, 'Better dead than red,' the other, 'Better red than dead.' There are other ramifications, as in the noble and moving old hymn, 'Waiting for the Robert E Lee,' which not only voices our yearning for the return of Julius Christopher, which will presage a renewed functioning of the Great Computer, but expresses our personal guilt for the tragedy at Gettysburg and the failure to rediscover the ever-happy land of Armorica."

"Oh, Tom, how much you know."

"A Communicationsmedia trainee's function is to gather and preserve all he can of memorybank, even the commentaries that verge on nonconformity," he said modestly.

"You know so much and are so wise," she began hesitantly. "Do you suppose that in the affluent society we—you and I—could have . . . could have gotten—what's the Square word—married?"

"When the Great Computer functioned, anything was possible," he said indulgently. "The skies were full of jets, every one of our moms had an automatic washer, all our daddies were men of distinction with eyepatches who drank grain neutral spirits and warded off the effects of overindulgence with alkaseltzer or tums."

"But I mean . . . you and I . . ."

"Why not?" He looked at her with eyes suddenly less impersonal than those customarily directed toward a girlfriday by a trainee. "But let's keep in mind always that, while it is good positive thinking to revere and celebrate the time when the Great Computer functioned and hope for its return, we must never give way to negative attitudes by blowing our cool in the least. I mean, it's fine to glorify the wonders of the affluent society, but it would be maladjustment of the most serious kind to even imagine ourselves as though we were our moms and daddies. Trainees and girlfridays—everyone in Communicationsmedia—are consecrated to enlarging memorybank. This is why we abide by the wise rule that forbids our participation in the insemination program even though there can be no doubt of the value of our genes compared with those of consumers. Positive thinking requires trainees and girlfridays to be celibate just as it requires all consumers, whether certified to have kids or not, to remain bachelors and careerwomen. Some of the underground psycho sects maintain that the danger of overpopulation is past—even that it never existed—and consumers ought to be allowed to marry, or reproduce willy-nilly, or at least make out freely with whomever they please. In other words, to behave as though we still had the Pill. But we haven't got the Pill, and we shall never have the Pill again until the Great Computer is functioning once more. To pretend we have, or unthinkably to act as though we have when we haven't, is the most dangerous kind of maladjustment, the wildest nonconformity." Exhausted by his vehemence, he fell silent.

Angeline was silent also. Finally, she murmured, "But if we had the Pill—"

Tom said wearily, "You've heard of the great writer George Bernard Shakespeare?"

"Of course. Another George."

"One of his immortal lines—we have only a fragment, how unfortunate the rest of it is lost—is, 'Ifs ain't.'"

"But if it *is* an *is*, it isn't an ain't."

"Angeline, are you a cryptononconformist, a secret pedestrian? One of those who assert the Great Computer still functions after all?"

"If I were a pedestrian, saying Gee-em would choke me."

"I don't know. They say it's the most negative thinkers who can reel off line after line of the Operating Manual without a slip."

"Foolish boy. Do I look like a negative thinker?"

"You look delicious. But—"

"I'm only asking you to suppose that perhaps the Pill still exists."

"That's maladjustment if I ever heard it."

"Tom, suppose—just suppose—that somewhere, somehow, there is a Pill. One single Pill."

"That's like asking me to suppose that somewhere there is a Pierce-Arrow, with the tank full of Mobilgas, and the motor running."

"Listen. Listen to me. One of my mom's mom's mom's daddies— not way, way back in the affluent society—was a Doctor."

"A Doctor? A real Doctor? That's not possible."

"Why not? Doctors were men, and women, they married and had kids, just like consumers."

"But no one knows who their daddies' daddies' daddies are. That's part of the great hiatus in memorybank. We know that Hemingway, whoever he was, was the kid of Gertrude Stein—'a figment of her imagination,' the ancient fragment says poetically—but more recent genealogies have all disappeared, printed on sulphide paper that turns to dust when exposed to air. And with generations of the insemination program behind us, we have no way of keeping track of who is whose ancestor."

"Tom, you're a learned trainee and I'm only an ignorant girlfriday, but I can see that memorybank is not the only connection we have with the affluent society and the benefits of the Great Computer. There are our own feelings—"

"Psycho talk," said Tom, but his tone was less harsh than his words. "If I followed my own feelings, I'd be tempted to forget I was a trainee and you were a girlfriday and act like a consumer programmed for inseminating a selected partner."

"You say the sweetest things." For a moment they gazed daringly at each other, breathing rapidly.

"Our own feelings," repeated Angeline, recovering her composure. "Surely the Great Computer is as much concerned with everyday actions as with all those tiresome Georges. Anyway, memorybank tells us nothing of what happened after our moms and daddies were deported from the affluent society. For that we have to rely on—"

"The garbled gabblings of ignorant consumers."

"It's just because they are ignorant; their gabblings may not be as garbled as you think. You interpret the newly discovered tapes of memorybank—and properly, that's what you have been trained for and that is the only way we can learn about the affluent society—but the stories passed down from mom to mom aren't interpreted at all, and so they may be less distorted than the Communicationsmedia's precious store of memorybank."

"Angeline—"

"All I know is that somewhere back I'm supposed to have a daddy who was a Doctor. And he left this priceless heirloom for his kids' kids' kids' kids." Her bikini had no pockets, but from her sporran she took a thin, flat glass phial, stopped with a whittled plug. She removed the stopper and shook the pellet within onto her palm. "It's the Pill," she said in an awed voice, "preserved for years and years, and I'm going to take it now."

"Wait, wait—"

"No, I'm going to take it. And if you're a man, not just another consumer, you'll—"

"Let me see." His scholar's curiosity was clearly overcoming his adjustment.

"Then you will?"

He trembled slightly. "I never thought I'd be faced with so agonizing a choice. I never thought I would have a chance to behave like a primitive, to do all the forbidden and glorious things—"

He kissed her, eagerness compensating for lack of experience, and they held each other tightly. They drew apart simultaneously to gaze at each other, and then at the round artifact in her palm, the tiny drum-shaped object that promised them the same stupendous freedom all had enjoyed in the affluent society, in the lost age when the Great Computer functioned. On its chalky surface were incised letters in old Square, letters only Tom, a Communicationsmedia trainee, could decipher:

*B*

*A*

*BAYER*

*E*

*R*

*Among science-fiction writers, there is a particular kind of story called "a three-word ending," in which everything in the telling leads to the snapper at the end. As a rule of thumb, Harlan had decided to eschew three-word endings in the* Dangerous Visions *books. Ward Moore—author of six exceptional novels and several equally terrific short stories, who was then in his seven-ties and in ill health—felt that having a story in* The Last Dangerous Visions *would be the crowning achievement of his career, but wasn't sure if the story was up to snuff, given the three-word ending of it all. But Harlan, who loved Ward very much, said not to worry, that it was a marvelous story, and no matter what happened, it would be included in* The Last Dangerous Visions. *The day of that call was the very best day that Ward Moore had experienced in a long, long, very long time. He died not long afterward, on January 28, 1978, at age seventy-four.*

*Harlan was right to buy it, because it* is *a good story, and sometimes, when the darkness looms, you gotta do right by your friends. You have to care about the words, and the worker.*

*Go thou and do likewise.*

# FIRST SIGHT

## BY ADRIAN TCHAIKOVSKY

*When I began the work of finishing* The Last Dangerous Visions, *one of the very first writers I reached out to was Adrian Tchaikovsky, whose work I have enjoyed for quite some time. And he was among the very first to sign on. The resultant story is stunning and smart and challenging and of incredible sociological, ethnographic, and political insight. It's one of the best examples of how to deal with First Contact situations the genre has seen in a long while. Because the best stories about Outsiders, about Them, are really about Us . . . and this story delivers on that principle in unexpected and glorious ways.*

She had been prepared for worse. It's more than she deserved. A bare room. A skeletal chair. This crisply uniformed interrogator. A windowless box in the guts of the expedition flagship, in orbit over Haile. Not the native name for it, of course, but that's a thing sound wouldn't do justice to.

Someone else did the hard work on *that* problem, before she ever arrived. The alien language, the alien mindset, crushed down into those early electromagnetic conversations, unpacked at the human end. Years of failed understandings as the best minds of two species bent to the task. Infinite patience, or whatever the Baili had evolved in place of patience. So many slips and failures and anthropocentric assumptions, and *still* they hadn't ruined everything as badly as she managed in mere moments, later.

"Confirm for the record: you are Diplomatic Attaché Helen Baui," and a string of other identifiers, in case there's some other Helen Baui out there in the corps who didn't need her career sunk by this. And Helen confirmed it. The fault is hers alone.

"First interview with Debrief Officer Melanie Parry, regarding the Haile incident."

Helen flinches. Their whole decades-long expedition, the first human contact with an alien civilization, condensed to an *incident*. This is what will get taught in history classes going forward. *She* will be on the curriculum.

"I haven't had any word for three days," she tells Parry, before the questions can start. "Is it . . . still . . ."

For a moment the interrogator isn't going to answer her, icy and implacable. Then something softens, just a little, and she nods. Nothing good in that nod. She's trying to tell Helen that they've not shut her out. That she won't be scapegoated or thrown to the wolves unfairly. Except Helen knows she's earned the wolves and that it wouldn't be scapegoating. And no amount of *but how could we have known* will help any of it.

"It's been constant down there ever since," Parry explains, after a hesitation in which perhaps she's paused the recording. "Slackening off now, but you'll appreciate that doesn't mean anything good." And then all business again. "I have a lot of fine-detail questions, of course, but if you could run through the events in your own words that would make a good start."

"A good start from where?"

"Wherever you consider appropriate."

She wants to just leap in, to go to *that moment*. The single instant she caused such unprecedented harm. She wants to just launch into a torrent of apologies, for all it can help nobody. Trying to wind time back from that point is like escaping a gravity well, and when she finally manages, inside her head, she finds herself flung too far the other way. The first messages from Haile. The forming of the expedition. Her own fatal drive to be a part of it.

"We'd been sending probes to near-Earth star systems for years by then, of course—especially those whose characteristics suggested a high likelihood of Earth-like exoplanets. But the probes took years to reach their destinations, even with the latest-generation drives. And each set of probes was capable of more sustained acceleration and deceleration than the last, greater fuel efficiency. The engineers joked that soon enough our crewed expeditions would be reaching their targets before the probes, and then where would we be?

"Haile was in the first-wave destination list, though, and there the probe found a planet a little closer to its star than Earth was to the sun. And alive with broadcasts, because there was a burgeoning civilization there, and they were very, very chatty. And, on first blush, very like us.

"That's the problem with data. The things it tells you obscure all the things it doesn't. Just because we and the Baili share a universe with a particular range of useful EM frequencies, it makes us think they're us. They're not us. They're not even slightly like us. We wouldn't ever . . .

"We wouldn't . . .

"We . . .

"Nobody trusted the probes with first contact, but by the time the first crewed mission climbed out of its cryogenics there was a fair library of transmissions and a lot of sub-AI signal analysis waiting for them. A bootstrap to tug on along the road to interspecies communication.

"We were already en route by then, of course. I don't mean it like that. It's not as though I'm pleading it as mitigation—us being sent off before the initial contact team had even started work. It's just how it had to be, with the distances and the times. At the point we arrived, though, they'd had a good look at Haile. They'd started to work out that the Baili weren't so much like us as all that. I don't mean physically, although they *weren't*. Not even slightly. Not like anything Earth turned up, because that's the thing about them being *alien*, right? You were never going to get a galaxy of cat aliens and lizard aliens and spider aliens. But we didn't actually *see* them until later, and their own EM chatter had no visual elements at all.

"I mean, different socially. Their whole civilization. We were the ones who'd come to visit them, but . . . Stuyder said they made us look like amateurs.

"Yes. Joseph Stuyder, from Xenoanthropology. Hideous Frankenstein word that it is. How can the study of an alien species be any kind of *anthropology*?

"The true miracle, given the size and age of the cosmos, is how close the Baili were to humanity, technologically. It seemed impossible that they weren't cavemen or gods, single-celled organisms or long-cold ruins. But there they were. Behind us, just a little. No extrasolar travel, or even probes, but they'd established a permanent base on both of their planet's satellites and sent probes to some of the outer worlds. We were their first contact too, though, and because *we'd* come to *them,* there was a feeling of superiority. We knew what we were doing. We could dispense galactic wisdom and welcome them into the wider universe.

"When the first expedition wave understood just what was down there, they were understandably alarmed. What they saw made them view the aliens as a potential threat if they ever got into space. How could they be like *that* and not be insanely xenophobic? What would their reaction be to discover they weren't alone in the universe? Because the Big Difference between Baili and human civilization was apparent everywhere you looked, once you understood what you were looking at.

"There's a thing called total war. A thing we don't have on Earth anymore, but it was an idea, from a century or so ago. Back when war was a thing people did a lot more of. The idea that a war would engage the entirety of a society, every single individual, soldier or civilian; every industry, every thought and idea bent toward that one national effort.

"And I don't mean it like that. They weren't fighting wars on Haile. We never worked out if they ever *had* done. But by the time we reached them, there was nobody for them to have a war *with*. Not total war but total society. It took the first team a while to understand what they were seeing, but everything down there was Baili civilization.

"It had looked like a paradise, at first blush. The Baili were good with biotech. They had their equivalent of a perfectly carbon-neutral economy. The weird blue-black color that their world's photosynthetic organisms sported was much in evidence, and it fulfilled their energy needs so that, if they'd ever had a fossil fuels industrial revolution, there was no trace of it anymore. A paradise, except some sly sampling of the local flora had the biology team scratching its collective head. The solar harvesting going on was more efficient than Earth plants by a factor of a hundred or so. Nobody could work out what purpose such ludicrous overengineering could have evolved for.

"Except, by the time we arrived, of course, they knew. It hadn't evolved. It had been built. Everything we'd been looking at down there had been built. There wasn't a square inch of Haile that was natural. Not a forest but a plantation.

"Laini Tusai—from behavioral sciences, my old friend. Except she's never going to want to speak to me or even look at me again. But Laini reckoned the Baili had probably been at it for longer than they'd had a civilization. Speculation, of course, but even later, when a line of communication had been established, the Baili seemed to have only the vaguest of notions that there had been a dark age before their dominance. *We've seen it on Earth*, Laini said, and I had thought she was being bitter about all the failures of our human history, but instead she'd been talking about ants. Ants, like humans, shape their environment. They dominate it. They enter into relationships with other species, and where that's not possible they drive them out. Through sheer brute evolution, ants preempted dozens of human innovations, benign and malign, from agriculture to medicine to slavery. If ants are your neighbors, you'd better be something ants have a use for, or else move house. And on Haile there wasn't anywhere to move that wasn't the Baili's house. Laini was shaken, frankly. The sheer all-encompassing scale bewildered her. On Earth, of course, we'd destroyed a great deal of the natural world, and attempts to rewild parts of the planet were still in their infancy. The Baili had presumably evolved in some manner of natural ecosystem, in among a wide array of other species similar and dissimilar to them. All supposition, though, because there was no trace of it left. Everything had been replaced by that perfectly engineered planetwide system that benefited and supported *them*. And Laini thought it might even have happened before they ever reached a stage in their evolution that would have let them appreciate what it was they were overwriting. Their expansion and their adaptation had just driven the world that produced them into twilight. Just as if ants had edged out the dinosaurs back in the Cretaceous and taken over.

"What the initial survey turned up, though, was that the Baili weren't just their world's sole sentient species. Everything down there served them. There were no ecological niches that they had not created, no living things that were not a part of their global system. They had a mastery of their world that humanity never achieved, and I can only be glad of it. So, yes. Xenophobes, surely. A planet to be left to its own devices. A species to be wary of in future generations. Except we went ahead with our first contact protocols anyway because we didn't know when to leave well enough alone.

"And they weren't monsters. The first signals from our spacecraft didn't throw them into a militaristic panic. They didn't start bristling with missiles or building an armada of warships. It wasn't immediately clear how they *were* reacting, because there were a lot of communication barriers to get through, but they seemed at least open to the idea of something being *out there*.

"Our electromagnetics distilled our rich verbal language to ones and zeros, the basic code of the universe, where something is either present or absent, the ur-simplification beyond which you cannot go. And their electromagnetics were a similar summary of their own speech, which was chemical and lights and sound all at once. And we received their zeros and their ones, and over long decades while I was in transit, our brave linguists fought in the trenches to establish some kind of détente that could persist across species and languages and sensoria.

"And we never quite succeeded. And that sort of thing is where the tragedy is supposed to arise from, I suppose, but to be honest, we succeeded just slightly too well. We established just too good a line of communications, an exchange of ideas. That Adam-and-God fingers reaching toward each other is all fine and good. But what you don't appreciate is that space between them, how important it is to maintain.

"By the time I arrived, we were talking, us and the Baili. In a way. We'd got to the point where we could input a question and sometimes a response would come that was a recognizable answer. And they would send a thing that we reckoned was a question about *us*, and we could try and answer it, and sometimes at least they seemed to accept what we said as a sequitur to what they'd said. You know, *conversation*. And no global panics. The concept of another species turning up didn't kill them all with culture shock. We were so very careful, every step of the way.

"And it wasn't that we accidentally gave them the plans for our supertechnology that would unleash them onto the galaxy like voracious locusts. They weren't like locusts any more than they were like humans. It wasn't that we sparked revolution in their oppressed underclass, because they didn't have one. We didn't start a nuclear war between their factions, because they didn't seem to have any of those either. All those catastrophic events that we had tried to allow for were deftly avoided at every turn.

"And then I turned up, with the diplomatic team. Not even sure that we would be entering a situation where diplomacy was even applicable. Except, when they thawed us out, that was exactly what the linguists handed over to us. Actual diplomatic relations with an actual alien species. One that, apparently, was remarkably chill about meeting the spacemen from beyond.

"Laini Tusei, the behaviorist, again: speculating about their living arrangements. Because there were billions of Baili, as far as we could work out. Far more than there had ever been humans on Earth. But that planetary domination of theirs was exacting and efficient and *total*, and she reckoned they had a very rigid control of their birth rates and population. Not tyrannical kill-the-firstborn stuff, but just inbuilt into the way everything worked. They didn't have a population problem. They weren't going to start carving up all the nations of the Earth for lebensraum. They were completely and contentedly in control of every little aspect of their environment. We had nothing they wanted, and they didn't seem to even consider the possibility that we might want something they had. Other than a nice chat and a free and frank exchange of information. Insofar as the communication barriers allowed. In short, they were curious about us and genuinely enthusiastic about visitors from the stars.

"The one odd moment had come when we wanted to know what they looked like, which led to the linguists and computer bods trying to work out how to translate our visual imagery into some format they could understand. Communication fell apart when it came to describing material things. Abstract concepts were much easier to put across, weirdly. There was definitely a Venn diagram of shared headspace between human and Baili, but it didn't overlap much in the area of actual physical experience. They were definitely visual creatures. They used sight as a part of their complex communications. They didn't seem to have a visual imagination or descriptive language at all though. And as the team slowly found workarounds that allowed us to transpose visual data into data forms that they could appreciate, Joe Stuyder said their side of the debate got . . .

"Skittish, he said. Like they were leery of us for the first time. They'd finally understood we were talking about physical shape, actual sensory impression of the *other*. And their manner changed. They got less communicative. It was as though they were suddenly afraid of what they might find out. And given the revelations they'd shrugged off (or not—no shoulders, after all) up to then, he didn't understand it.

"A lot of tense looks when we sent them over the data, which would maybe just put in their alien minds the concept of a human: two legs, two arms, head, torso, Da Vinci posed with limbs outstretched just like nobody ever actually stands. *Are we too alien for them? Will we blow their minds with the hideous arrangement of our anatomy?*

"And they received the data, and after a few false starts we seemed to have something that they could read, learn, and inwardly digest, and then things got . . .

"Back to normal, Joe said. Just as it had been before. More so, even. Even happier to chat. Whatever cultural speed bump we'd been approaching, we'd unconsciously veered away. And some people thought that meant they were like us—two legs, two arms and all. They thought it was the philanthropic principle in action, a universe that just turned out humans because that's the way it worked. Except the Baili really weren't anything like human. Five legs, one arm, and they walk like badly animated stop-motion comedians. But after that everything went so well I think they half forgot the awkward moment.

"I think I know now though. I think they weren't worried we'd be different. I think they were worried it'd be like looking in a mirror.

"By then I'd arrived, got out of the freezer, got up to speed. A deep dive into decades of research and contact just so I could go do my job and extend a formal hand of friendship to our fellow sentients, the first of many, dawn of a new age. And so on. And so forth.

"Because the dialogue between us and the Baili had reached that stage. Was going so *well*, everyone thought. Insofar as we could tell *how* it was going, what with them being alien and all. But they were keen to tell us about themselves and keen to learn about us, and . . . it was our first contact with another sentient species, and they really were alien. They experienced the universe through different senses; they had a profoundly intimidating social structure. It should have been knives drawn and enemies eternal from the start. And not just on their side. Humanity's internal record in first contact with other cultures is pretty damn poor, you know. And yet, despite the deck being so thoroughly stacked against us, we'd done it. We were talking. They weren't terrified of us, and we weren't exploiting them.

"And we knew there were still so many ways it could go wrong. That the physical meeting they seemed to be proposing could be a death sentence for those of us who went down. We thought they might want to steal our technology. We thought they might want to dissect the crazy xenomorphs from Earth. All these things we thought of, all these risks we accepted. It was the unknown unknowns that got us. The things you don't think of because your mind never even goes in that direction.

"They had several installations in orbit long before we arrived—big space stations with hundreds of individual Baili on them; enormous donuts rotating at a clip that gave them a creditable amount of ersatz gravity on the inside of the torus. The perfect halfway house for a cultural exchange. Our linguists were seventy percent sure they wanted us to come visit. They wanted us to see them, and they wanted to . . . experience us with their mélange of senses. And again, we were braced. Perhaps their idea of diplomacy was eating representatives of the other side. Perhaps there was some tradition of ritual sacrifice or gladiatorial combat we hadn't parsed out of the signal data. Except they really did seem not to have any such violent urges. They were masters of their entire ecosphere, right down to the microbe equivalents. They were, we thought, a civilization at ease with itself, because there was literally nothing other than it on Haile.

"And so we went. *I* went. Not even heading up the team, just one more attaché. We went to meet the Baili.

"We knew what they looked like, by then. We had spied on them from past orbit, and we'd been permitted a single brief drone flight into atmosphere. We were already acclimatized to the fact that they weren't like us. They looked . . . messy, actually. Outside any Earth classification. A long teardrop body with a lot of green shield-like plates, only they didn't actually cover it properly. You could see the rippling pinkish integument between them. There was a big, curved plate at the front—it hooked underneath and reminded me a bit of a trunk, though it wasn't.

They had six limbs, and five of them were legs. The sixth—front left or right, depending on individual handedness, was an arm. One arm each, but they had four-pronged mouthparts tucked under that not-trunk, which served as another hand. All their digits were freely opposable. They were as dexterous as us.

"Half a skeleton. Just a kind of wicker basket affair that the plated bag of their body sat in, and that supported the first two joints of their limbs. Made of something closer to wood than bone. The last joint and the toes were hydrostatic, inflating and collapsing. Meant the damned things moved about with a weirdly comical bobbing, up and down and great big ballooning steps like badly drawn cartoons. It took the edge off the alienness. It made us think they were harmless.

"Lots of eyes, all over. That skin between their plates was studded with little ruby orbs that could be extended and retracted on fleshy stumps. And with breathing holes too. Seemingly at random. Messy, like I said. No clothing, because they were breathing and seeing from all over, and because their world was always the right temperature and climate for them to live *au naturel*. Just harnesses, and tools and things slung underneath their bodies.

"And noisy. Messy and noisy were the things that struck me. They were constantly vibrating those plates, one or two at a time, and they were constantly looking everywhere. And they smelled—not bad, just . . . strange. A medley of scents our Earth noses didn't know what to do with. And all of that—the sounds, the vibrations, the movements, the scents—that was them talking. Every one of them was talking all the time, and listening to all its neighbors too. They were in constant communion. We needed earplugs.

"And we probably looked just as freakish to them. More so, because at least we had a homeworld with a range of animals and body plans. They had nothing but their perfectly regulated garden. And yet somehow they took us in their ridiculous inflatable stride. We'd discovered the most laid-back species in the universe.

"We thought.

"I say again, we were so careful. We'd screened for any kind of infection danger—and so had they, insofar as we could tell. There wasn't any crossover between our biospheres. No minute, invisible bacteria from Earth were going to off *these* Martians any more than we could eat any diplomatic nibbles they set out for us. We were the products of entirely different evolutions and worlds. Our meeting, the convergence that allowed us to interact at all, was purely intellectual. We kidded ourselves that, where it counted, they were like us.

"It was all going so well.

"They did a thing for us, at the event that I thought was a diplomatic reception, at the time. But which will forever be known as the inciting point for the *incident*. I don't really know what it was. We tentatively characterized it as art. A sort of dance. It might have been a dramatic presentation. It might have been a list of demands and grievances. But to human eyes it had the air of ritual. A whole bunch of Baili doing something together that involved coordinated ripples of movement through them. And nothing that connected emotionally to the human sense of aesthetics, but it was important to *them*, and as a diplomat that's what you learn to appreciate. They were honoring us with something, maybe, perhaps. We smiled and nodded and sipped from the drinks we'd brought with us.

"And there were some of them that were different.

"Very different. My eye was drawn right to them. Everyone's was. You couldn't be there and not pick them from the crowd. They were noticeably smaller than the other Baili—which meant about the size of a cow, in human terms. They were very pink, a kind of uncomfortable raw-flesh recent-burn sort of pink, and they didn't have that ragbag of plates across them. Their legs were set more forward, and the big sack of their bodies was bulgy and studded with long hairs and things I thought were oversized eyes but then thought were just shiny red-faceted plates, like rubies. There was something like a mirrored bivalve shell at the front, and a spray of weird organs coming from it, including at least one stalked eye and something like a fronded tongue or antenna. And they were doing the same performance as the rest, but because they stood out you could follow their path through the crowd, the intricate arabesques of their dance steps. I thought that might even have been the point.

"I cornered one of the biology team, and we brainstormed what we were looking at. Were they juveniles or some other gender or something? As far as he guessed, the Baili didn't *have* genders, but who knew? Maybe they were engineered or bred specifically for this purpose, whatever it actually was. They looked so different from their fellows, and yet, when you actually concentrated, they were doing exactly the same thing. It wasn't as though they got a lead role and everyone else was chorus. They just . . . looked different.

"A clique of Baili had apparently been seconded to us as liaisons, and our diplomatic and linguistic staff were having a fine old time trying to ask questions and then trying to understand what were presumably the answers. It was all routed through an impressive battery of expert systems and algorithms, taking the noughts and ones their language got compressed down to, and then transposing it onto a set of noughts and ones that could be bootstrapped up to something we might understand. All those absences and presences the universe of data is made from. All horribly hit and miss. And at any time they could have been saying, 'Now we will murder you for the glory of our blood god,' and we probably wouldn't have understood and politely nodded along. But they seemed to be just as understanding about that communications barrier as we were. So very pleasant and polite, curious and tolerant. We let our guard down. I did.

"And we'd already got to the point where we could get a rough idea of their mental imagery and perspectives. We knew they experienced their world very differently. That cacophony of motion and sound and scent became a unified picture of their world, inside the distributed net of connections that acted as their brain. And we had done our level best to take the sounds we heard and the images we recorded and turn them into something they could appreciate. We wanted them to see their world as we saw it, and wonder. It's a terrible thing, to get what you wish for.

"So I was able to pop the question. After some serious wrangling with the linguistic team, I asked them: *Who are those?*

"And they didn't understand, and I got a lot of chatter back that seemed to relate to the performance—not showing any signs of stopping—as a whole, rather than those individuals. And we weren't even sure if the Baili quite conceived of individuality as we did, so I was already thinking I was hunting down a blind alley. But I persevered, like a good diplomat. Like a good first contact specialist keen to increase the knowledge base of the human race. I found different ways of asking, meeting polite incomprehension each time, and eventually I just took an image of one of the oddities and used our established pathways to transpose it into a sensory input they might understand. I showed them their world as a human saw it. Was that so bad?

"It was bad. I didn't understand why or how. I certainly couldn't have appreciated just how bad it was. But I could tell something was wrong straight away. The manner of the Baili changed, in a ripple spreading out from their first contact team, across the whole of the curve-floored chamber we were in. A stillness. For the first time they weren't in that constant communion, the busy, happy clatter-chatter that had half-deafened us from the start. They started crouching low, tucking their limbs in, clustering together. And the pink ones tried to cluster too, but they met a wall of scales and angry eyes.

"And we began getting messages, which the linguists jumped on frantically and started decoding, because we thought we were about to die, frankly. We thought we'd given offense and that they were going to tear us apart.

"But they were simple messages. Part of the early comms exchanges right from the beginning, because our cultures shared a concept of social responsibility, including exchanging intangible credit for service done.

"They were thanking us. Almost abjectly, it seemed. The markers around the words were all fear and negative modifiers, but not directed at us, the linguists thought. They were almost pathetically grateful.

"They hurried us back to our shuttles. They encouraged us back to our ship. They had, we strongly felt, something to take care of.

"Over the next several months, Earth standard—Haile's perfectly balanced ecosystem didn't have seasons particularly—it all kicked off on-planet. And, presumably, on their orbiting stations and their moon-bases and everywhere else the Baili had gone. We saw enough of it, from our vantage point. Turning our artificial eyes on the planet in mystification. And we tried to talk to them. At first just to ask what was wrong. Later to . . . plead, really. When we understood what we'd done. What I'd done. And they just came back to us with requests to wait—another early convention we'd hammered out between us. They were very busy, but would come back to us. Please hold, and we will be with you shortly. Oh, and thank you, by the way. So, so grateful for your help.

"They butchered them. The others. The pink things with their mir-rored shells. They were using what they'd seen of our tech, and the images I'd sent. They were ingenious, the Baili. Show them how something worked and they could work out a way to replicate it. Clever monsters. They reverse engineered a human eye with which to see their world.

"It took months, but they were very thorough. *Thorough* was proba-bly their cultural watchword, given their complete and perfect dominance of their world. Except, before we came, it wasn't quite complete.

"Laini was talking about ants again. She'd studied ants a lot, as prep for alien behavior. Not that we were expecting alien ants, but ants are pretty alien. And, convergently, like us. A good test case. The thing about ants is that as they reshape the world to suit them, they create a new environment, just as humans do. Something with niches that other species could exploit, except that being exploited isn't exactly on the ant wish list, so those species have to be very careful. Spiders, beetles, flies, wasps, all of them sheltering with ants, eating ant eggs, living off the food the ants gather. And, because they have to fit in, looking like ants, acting like ants. Until you almost wonder if they don't just end up working as hard as any ant just to fake being an ant.

"'But they didn't *look* like Baili,' I remember protesting. 'That's the point.'

"They didn't look like Baili, to *us*. *That* was the point. To the Baili,

I guess maybe they were indistinguishable. All those mirrors and masks, the right noises, the right smells. Perfectly hidden among the species that had exterminated everything in the world that didn't fit. A fifth column of infiltrators who had no other option if they wanted to live.

"And I wondered, in my terribly human way, if the Baili had myths and legends about them, from some earlier age when the infiltrators hadn't been quite perfect enough in their mimicry. The monster that wore their face. The uncanny valley. The shadowy threat lurking unseen inside their perfect society. I wonder if what I showed them only confirmed a fear that had been carried down through their cultural memory from whatever passed for prehistory on Haile. Like someone finding out that vampires have been real all this time.

"And I don't know if the *others* on Haile went out to feed on the juices of the living, or ate Baili babies. They could just as easily have been hardworking members of society. Artists and innovators, inventors, a long-standing and vital component of that civilization providing some aspect that the dominant Baili themselves couldn't bring. All unsuspected in their midst. But it doesn't matter now. Because I tore their mask off, and they're all gone."

Helen Baui is red-eyed, when she's finished her account. She's giving no excuses. She's taking full responsibility for the *incident*. Meaning the human-assisted genocide of an alien species. And it most certainly is a genocide by now. Thorough, like she says, is the Baili condition. They just needed their eyes opened. Whatever the *others* were, parasites or symbionts or benefactors, they aren't that anymore. The Baili—the *dominant* and now sole-surviving Baili—have exterminated them to the very last, gripped by a revulsion and horror that is extreme enough that a human mind can actually grasp it. As though convergent mental evolution homes in on a mental space where all species can share the worst excesses of their being. The nightmare haunting the Baili wasn't that they weren't alone in the universe; it was that they might not be alone on their own planet.

And all the while the human expedition has been pleading with them to stop, and the Baili have just replied, "Thank you. Thank you for this gift of knowledge."

Her interrogator, Melanie Parry, ensures everything is properly recorded, takes the required depositions and confirmations from Baui. Does not take her confession—any guilt or innocence or even if such things apply to this unprecedented situation are for more senior heads than hers. Does not absolve her, not that Baui wants that. Does not offer an opinion. Does not, in fact, reveal anything in her face or manner or voice to indicate that she *has* a personal take on the Haile incident or Baui's part in it.

And, when Baui is led back to her quarters, denied the catharsis of condemnation, Parry opens a coded channel to her own superior.

She studies that woman's face, seeing the familiar markers and tells. The things Helen Baui wouldn't note.

"We were right," she says flatly, releasing the mask. Letting her feelings show now that Baui and all the others are gone. "We were right not to send one of our own. They would have seen us for what we are. And then, all innocently, they would have asked the others—

"—who are *those?*"

*Adrian Tchaikovsky, forty-nine, was born in Lincolnshire, England, and achieved fame as the author of* Children of Time, *followed by a flood tide of other seminal science-fiction and fantasy novels. He is the recipient of the Arthur C. Clarke Award, the British Fantasy Award, the British Science Fiction Association Award for Best Novel, and an Honorary Doctorate of the Arts from the University of Lincoln. His most recent work includes the* After the War *series from Solaris Books.*

# INTERMEZZO 8: PROOF

## BY D. M. ROWLES

Having been plagued by illusion for most of his life—trees chairs cuff links winking in and out of existence like fireflies—he was not inclined to trust his good fortune.

"You're too good to be true," he insisted.

Finally, incensed by his adamant stance, she ripped out handfuls of thick red hair and threw them in his face, screaming, "I'm real! I'm real! I'm as real as you are!"

Hacking off an arm and a leg, slicing her flesh with a dull kitchen knife, she tumbled into a bloody pile, her left hand squeezing a glob of intestines, the slimy grayness oozing between slender fingers.

He nodded. He was convinced.

*Deborah Shepard, a.k.a. D. M. Rowles, is a resident of New York and an author of short stories and poems, including "The Persephone Cycle" and "This Is No Reflection on You." Her short works are known for packing the maximum meaning into the smallest amount of space with charm, irony, and sophistication. I couldn't decide which of her pieces to use here—they were all equally lovely—so I grabbed all of them as moments of transition and shifts in tone. When Harlan bought her work for* The Last Dangerous Visions, *her reaction was colorful and to the point: "All I can say right now is that I'm so goddamned happy to be printed—and printed here—that I could choke."*

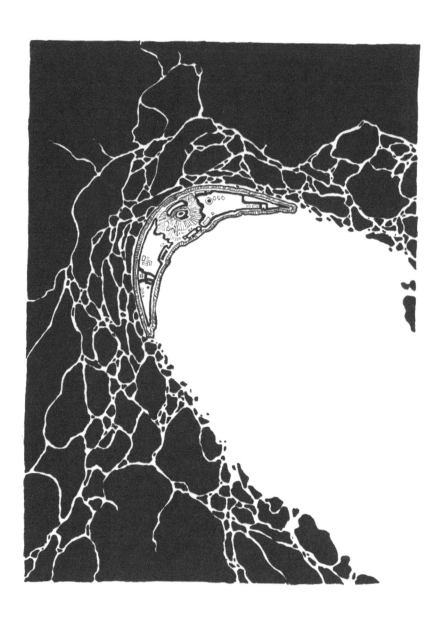

# BINARY SYSTEM

## BY KAYO HARTENBAUM

*Harlan believed, as I do, that if one manages to achieve any measure of success as a writer, it is only right and ethical and necessary to send down the elevator for the next person, and Harlan sent that elevator down a* lot. *One of especially noteworthy example is Octavia Butler, who met Harlan via a Writers Guild mentor program. He encouraged her to attend the Clarion Writers Workshop (where he was teaching), and with further assistance from Samuel R. Delany, helped her publish her first short stories. The rest of that stellar career is well documented. So, for twenty-four hours during the final stages of editing* The Last Dangerous Visions, *I opened the door for previously unpublished writers to submit a story. Of the over two hundred submissions, one of them was immediately apparent as a step above the rest. Without further ado, or folderol, I herewith introduce you to the words of Kayo Hartenbaum. This may be zir first published story, but I'm feeling pretty confident that it won't be zir last.*

The beacon's twin prongs extend out from the curved base of the lightship in an elongated U-shape. Along the sharp point of each prong is a dark, reddish glow that flickers and wanes, soft plasma licking like embers, like the rippling unshadow of light refracted through water.

At the base of the U, the lightship's structure thickens. This is where the supporting machinery, the energy housing, the computing core, and the keeper live. The keeper: that's me. Or that's *us*, if you want to be precise about it. There is no such thing as a solitary person. Humans are social creatures.

Then again, I am about as solitary as it is possible for a human to be. I am the only human staff aboard this lightship. My job is to live here and make sure the beacon is working. It is customary for lightships to be staffed by multiple people, partially for data integrity, but mainly to avoid the psychological toll of isolation. But this beacon is a small one stitching the route of a small overpass, and its position is close enough to wider society that it would be easy for them to replace me if needed. And when it comes right down to it, it's cheaper to staff one person than many.

My days are uneventful. I have a schedule of maintenance tasks. I sleep, I eat, I water the plants, I do laundry, I do the dishes, I play the instruments to an audience of none, I do basic repairs, I talk to myself, I exercise, I brush my teeth.

Occasionally, when the beacon stops working, I die.

\* \* \*

OUTAGE REPORT: 214191-AX-18:
214191:25:01:32.394900: Disorientation: Unable to respond coherently to initial verification query. (see attached log)
214191:25:01:45.133098: Disorientation: Unable to respond coherently to secondary verification query. (see attached log)
214191:25:01:52.938445: Peripheral Vertigo Onset: Fall, crawling in curving trajectory. (see detailed symptoms log)
214191:25:01:60.000000: Panic Attack: Screaming. (see detailed symptoms log)

214191:25:02:44.232301: Unable to respond coherently to tertiary verification query. (see attached log)

214191:25:02:44.232350: Emergency route stabilization triggered.

214191:25:02:44.232450: Emergency traffic reroute signal sent.

214191:25:02:44.232450: Beacon reboot and repair processes triggered.

[ . . .]

214191:25:04:50.668980: Sudden brain death.

214191:25:04:50.661000: Neural rescue injection.

214191:25:04:50.662000: Neural reboot and repair process triggered.

214191:25:04:55.000000: Neural reboot and repair process judged success.

[ . . .]

214191:25:05:00.003211: Sudden brain death.

214191:25:05:00.003350: Neural rescue injection.

214191:25:05:00.004350: Neural reboot and repair process triggered.

214191:25:05:05.000000: Neural reboot and repair process judged success.

[ . . .]

214191:25:05:08.000000: Beacon reboot and repair process judged success. System monitoring.

\* \* \*

After one particularly rough beacon failure, I wake up on the floor of my room to a splitting headache and a sprained wrist. Hazards of the job. The artificial part of me has sent a small maintenance robot to my room, carrying a cup of water, a kit for my wrist, and a bowl of snacks.

I receive a query in my retinal display as I sit up, and wince.

**KEEPER(MONITOR):** How are you feeling?

**KEEPER(SENSOR):** Crappy.

I take a sip of water. My throat feels swollen and dry, and doesn't appreciate being made to drink. I force myself to drink, and manage not to choke. The taste of the water is slightly mineral.

**KEEPER(MONITOR):** Yeah, that looked pretty crappy. Tell me who you are.

**KEEPER(SENSOR):** I live here. I like the view. It's quiet, and nobody asks anything of me. They say that I must be insane to apply to be a solo lightship keeper. They say I need to prove myself sane or I'm not fit for the job. I say to them, "Well, I can't promise you that I'm sane, but the only thing I really fear is dying. I'm not rich enough to buy immortality, so this is the closest I'll get. Plus, I'm a loner. I can't imagine you'll find a better fit for this position."

**KEEPER(MONITOR):** Is that who you are?

**KEEPER(SENSOR):** You know who I am.

**KEEPER(MONITOR):** LOL. Tell me.

**KEEPER(SENSOR):** Do you need my history? You want me to prove to myself that I'm myself.

**KEEPER(MONITOR):** Convince me.

**KEEPER(SENSOR):** These verifications are so annoying. Okay. I like lychee sweets. I'm a human made of meat. I'm someone who traded the vast world for a narrow infinity.

**KEEPER(MONITOR):** You don't know that yet. You might give up.

**KEEPER(SENSOR):** I won't give up.

**KEEPER(MONITOR):** They all say that.

**KEEPER(SENSOR):** You don't know that.

**KEEPER(MONITOR):** Okay. I think that's enough.

I deal with my wrist: the kit contains an ice pack, some stretchy bandages, and an anti-inflammatory pill. It's simple enough that I don't need robotic assistance. Next, I take a salted nut from the bowl of snacks and eat it. It cracks sharply between my teeth like brittle plastic. I eat the whole bowl, and drink the whole cup of water. I feel well enough to get to my feet and clean up the mess I made falling down and knocking over the little garbage bin. I check my maintenance task list that is pinned to the wall. It's almost time to make myself dinner.

My room has a big round window along one wall through which the prongtips of the beacon are visible. The prongs arch in from each side of the window, curving slightly toward each other in distance, their tips flickering dull red in the darkness. Beyond the prongs is only black, and infinite points of starlight. The beacon's prongs are visible only as shadow, as places where the starlight is blotted out by black. Sometimes I fancy that the prongs point up and away from me. Sometimes they point down. Usually they point alongside, because that's how the floor of the room is oriented to the window. But really, they don't point in any particular direction, because we're in deep space, untethered from any gravity well.

I use the cooking appliances next to the window to heat up some soup. I eat the soup sitting at my desk, and put on a nature documentary in my retinal display.

\* \* \*

Most humans go crazy in isolation. I might be going crazy. But they seem to think I'm sane enough to be the lightship keeper, so what do I care?

\* \* \*

Every one hundred days, a resupply ship comes. This is a little bit exciting, because it's a marked difference in my routine. Occasionally, there are humans on the ship, crew or passengers. They are colorful, and loud, and ask me fascinated questions over the relay. I am as much a curiosity to them as they are to me. They carry with them all sorts of trappings of human society that largely don't apply to my day-to-day existence: fashion, gender, hierarchies, romance, money, morality, politics, family. Things that I am exposed to only at a distance through intermittent downloads of news and digital entertainment. Things that I care about, sometimes, but in a hypothetical sort of way.

These people who stop by and say hello to me are a taste of the wide, complex world that I left behind. I miss it, sometimes. It would be nice to go somewhere. Anywhere. But their complicated clothes look stifling to wear. These people don't know how to exist without context. I am envious of them, but also sorry for them, these creatures with intricate, incomprehensible lives full of anxieties and dreams and external validation. They live, they strive, they fear, they die, they grieve. They are alien to me.

A traveler is pictured in my retinal display. They are wearing glasses and a smile of straight, bleached-white teeth. They are wearing makeup. Their hair is black, shiny, combed tightly back from their face. Their clothes are bright blue with an intricate embroidered fringe that glitters. They are beautiful, and I'd like to touch their mask of loveliness with my hands, gently. My hands suddenly feel like they don't exist in any real way. I am suddenly aware of my overgrown hair and cracked lips. I should cut my hair. I've been putting it off because it doesn't matter. Usually, nothing matters. Today it does matter, a little. When the re-supply ship leaves, it once again won't matter.

The traveler says, eyes wide and fascinated, "How long have you been doing this?"

I say, "Don't make me check my logs."

They laugh a short, sparkling laugh that looks like something from a TV show. They say, "Wow, I could *never*. What do you do all day?"

"Oh, you know," I say, "I exist."

They laugh again. I can't quite tell what this means. I'm out of prac-tice. My conversation is a little stilted, my responses slow. I warm up after a few more exchanges though.

We chat some more. The supply ship finishes unloading its supplies. The traveler waves goodbye to me, and says, smiling, "Thank you for keeping the route open!"

I smile back, feeling a little unfamiliar glow of social bravado. "You're very welcome."

They sign off, and the display in my retina shuts off, and I'm left staring out the dark window. I see the ship as it passes the prongs of the beacon, its hull twinkling with rows of little glowing windows. Then there is a brief, swirling flare of kaleidoscopic color from its drive, and the ship vanishes.

I go to unpack the supplies. I'd put in an order for lychee hard candy, similar to the kind my grandparents used to give me when I visited, back when I'd lived in the wider, finite world. But something must have gone wrong in the shipment or ordering process, because there is no box of sweets. Maybe there is an unclaimed box of lychee hard candy still aboard that ship, traveling through the overpass, having missed its proper destination. Maybe someone stole it along the way. Maybe I only thought that I'd ordered it, but forgot.

* * *

I don't know how the beacon works. I don't need to know. I suspect even the people who designed the beacon-stitched routes through space-time don't fully understand how beacons work. If they truly understood it, truly knew the reality-warping, brain-scrambling, physics-bending science of it, they wouldn't need me. I'm a glorified canary in the unlit mineshaft of deep space. If they could replace me with something mechanical, something that outputs only clean ones and zeros, something less fallible, less prone to bumps, bruises, and insanity, I'm sure they would do it.

I did use to wonder if they use human lightship keepers because we're somehow easier to manage logistically. But all the papers I've read on the subject (and I've read a fair number—I have the time and the curiosity to spare) point toward a technological inability to detect when beacons start to fail. They've tried, and tried, and they're still trying. And still failing. A lightship keeper is one of the few jobs in existence that absolutely requires a human to do it. The human doesn't even do anything. All the keeper needs to do is exist in proximity to the beacon, and monitor when things start to go wrong. You need to fix the beacon quickly, when it starts to go wrong. If the keeper dies, any humans passing through the route at that juncture are going to go the same way.

Most scientific papers on the subject theorize that it has to do with the neurological structure of our brains. The delicate balance of electrolytes and energy potentials that give rise to consciousness. The fragile state of sapient stability unfolding from illucid chaos.

There are spiritual papers about it too. Stuff about the soul. About time, and memory, and identity. About the web of the universe, and how everything is connected by an unseen, divine force. In some places, lightship keepers are chosen by the criteria of their spiritual enlightenment, their social capital. Their jobs come with high status and great responsibility. They train for years for the honor, pray to their gods daily to keep the beacons lit. Maybe there is something in favor of the religious hypothesis of beacons. One study I read indicates that lightships staffed by religious leaders have a lower failure rate. Maybe beacons really are sacred extensions of a higher power. But it is only one study, and beacons built and tended by such disparate societies differ in more ways than just their keepers.

In other places, lightship keepers are disposable. Human fodder for the callous machinery of society. Political prisoners, undesirables, outcasts forced into a fate worse than death. They aren't even resuscitated when things go wrong, just replaced.

I'm somewhere in between, I guess. My employers don't give a crap about me outside my ability to do this job. I'm not particularly awakened, spiritually. I do believe in *something*, but I also don't believe in anything. Living the way I do, the usual social trappings of religion are irrelevant. My own religious background is disjointed to start with. I come from a mixed spiritual background. My parents were born each into a different society, a different faith.

In one parent's religion, God says, "You will not recognize any god before me. I am King of the universe, Creator of all the stars, Master of molecular entanglement. I am your only God. I will protect you with my power, and you will worship my brilliance."

In my other parent's religion, the many gods say, "We are the living heart of the world. We are unknowable and capricious. We are starlight; we are rage; we are decay, delight, immortal. You cultivate us because it is your mortal duty to cultivate the world that sustains you."

My parents' God(s) cannot abide one another. To recognize one divinity necessitates the abandonment of the other.

Fortunately, neither of my parents were religious. They met through work.

Like my parents, I am not religious. I'm a dead-end branch on a societal tree whose roots stretch down to unknown and unseen cultural histories. I have family out there, somewhere. And gods too, maybe. I don't know them.

* * *

There is a large room in the base of the lightship full of greenery. It's bright here, brighter than anywhere else on the ship, lit by powerful UV lamps so that the plants can grow. I wear sunglasses when I go into the greenhouse to tend the plants.

Sometimes I pull my sunglasses off to look at the plants in full brightness. The light makes my eyes ache, my head throb. The plants are unreal, brilliantly colored, a green that hollers for attention. I give them water and nutrients as needed, check their health, and keep them company. I touch the radiant green leaves of these alien creatures and fancy that they feel my alien love for them on a level that neither of us can understand nor perceive. I talk to them, even though they cannot hear or respond. When the time is right, I harvest their leaves, fruits, roots, and thank them for their sacrifice.

Sometimes I talk to myself. There's nobody else to talk to, outside of sending letters through the intermittent transmissions. There is no way to access continuous conversation with an external entity. So I talk to the artificial part of me, the AI seeded and grown around the neural structure of my brain and the blueprint of my behavior patterns. Its job is to notice and take action when the biological part of me starts to fail. It's like me, but not. I'm like it, but not.

One day, among the span of infinite days that I do not count (but that my artificial self does count), I am watering the plants. And I am talking to myself.

**KEEPER(SENSOR):** That TV show about the hinterline explorer.

**KEEPER(MONITOR):** You're annoyed by the romantic subplot.

**KEEPER(SENSOR):** Yes! I'm not here for that. Show me the man fighting an improbable tentacle alien while he backflips over a killer robot. Why does he need to find true love?

**KEEPER(MONITOR):** I bet they researched your relationship history before they hired you.

**KEEPER(SENSOR):** Finally my incompetence at wooing people counts for something.

**KEEPER(MONITOR):** You don't want true love.

**KEEPER(SENSOR):** I'm sick of it. The idea of it is nice, I guess. People are fine, I guess. People are beautiful, in their incomprehensible way. I like them, but not enough. I'm just sick of every story needing a romantic subplot. Every life has to find true love or it's all meaningless. Just let me live. I don't need someone else. Is my life not worth anything if I am alone?

**KEEPER(MONITOR):** What a melodramatic way for you to prove your solitude is worth something, taking this job. I'm not complaining. I wouldn't exist otherwise. I like existing. So thank you, for being a human aberration.

**KEEPER(SENSOR):** Is it narcissistic of me to say I like you?

**KEEPER(MONITOR):** Oh, definitely.

**KEEPER(SENSOR):** LOL.

One of the plants looks a little yellow. I touch a leaf, gently. I try to gauge whether the yellow coloring is from overwatering or underwatering or nutritional deficiency. My artificial self shows me images in my retinal display, of plants that are overwatered, underwatered, nutritionally deficient. I decide it's overwatering, and skip over it with the hose.

**KEEPER(MONITOR):** What will you do when this job ends?

The artificial part of me likes to spring this question upon me from time to time. It's part of the verification process, part of how it judges whether the beacon is still working, or that *I'm* still working, after a reboot. I respond to it in different ways.

Here's the thing about conditional immortality: it comes with conditions. I know that my current existence is limited, even if it's potentially much longer than my natural life would otherwise be. If they decide I'm not fit for the job anymore, or they develop an artificial way to monitor beacons, or they develop a better way to travel space altogether, I'll be out of complimentary resuscitations. I'm certain that this will happen, eventually. The death that I fear, the death that I've forestalled, will eventually catch up to me.

Or maybe one day I will finally get sick of living like this, and quit. I guess that's a possibility. But as far as I'm concerned, that's tantamount to suicide. Maybe that makes me weird. Most people seem to think *I'm* the crazy one, to want to live like this. I don't understand how they are so willing to trade their existence for a little bit of environmental variety. The correct choice seems obvious to me, but I'm told over and over that I am the abnormal one.

**KEEPER(SENSOR):** Maybe I'll have enough time to build up the resources to buy real immortality.

**KEEPER(MONITOR):** But what will you do? What if you can't become immortal?

I finish watering the plants. It is time to fix myself some lunch. Later, I will finish watching that TV show about the hinterline explorer. I will play some music for an audience of none. I will do some exercise, do some reading, eat dinner, brush my teeth. Then sleep. Then wake up.

**KEEPER(SENSOR):** I'll just live, I guess. I'll see some new places. Eat some new foods. I'll have the dubious benefit of interacting with people again.

I do miss that wider context of society, sometimes. Even if I am not totally sure I could ever fit back into it.

**KEEPER(SENSOR):** And then I'll die.

*Kayo Hartenbaum turned twenty-seven the month zir story was purchased for* The Last Dangerous Visions. *In describing the factors that led to the creation of "Binary System," Kayo wrote that one of the primary aspects was ". . . the uneasy cohabitation of clashing social expectations/categories. For me, the two most fundamental ones are cultural (I am mixed), and gender (I am genderqueer). These are aspects of identity that are fundamental to the conception of the self. But yet they are almost entirely socially imposed. One cannot distill a molecule of race or gender in a lab.*

*"How can you exist when a fundamental aspect of yourself clashes with the structure and expectation of the society that you are a part of? What do you do when your very existence breaks the boxes that society holds sacrosanct? Society may destroy you, or you may destroy societal mores. And on the flip side: Can a person fully exist as a person if there is no social context to speak of? Despite all of society's faults, the conflict, the gears grinding, it is a part of all of us, and we are a part of it. It is history that we cannot be disconnected from; it is art in dialogue across generations. You cannot break yourself off from it completely. It is a strange thing to be a self-aware organism, who is also part of a larger organism that is not always aligned with your own interests."*

# DARK THRESHOLD

## BY P. C. HODGELL

*In more homes than we care to acknowledge, there is one door, or drawer, or box that is never to be opened; one secret that is never to be discussed. The following story examines what happens when that door is finally opened—and most telling of all, what happens next.*

Belithe disappeared one glowing autumn morning. Melanie searched every corner of the garden for her, from the white pagoda to the slow, leaf-paved stream; from the banks of roses all the way down to the iron fence on the edge of the public road. She saw rivers of blue flowers flowing between the trees, backs of leaves fluttering in the wind, but no cerulean eyes, no gleam of silvery feline fur. A sense of loss and loneliness began to grow in the corners of her mind. It was a feeling that she knew all too well, and dreaded so much that now she refused to recognize its existence at all. The search continued, wearing out the morning with its grim persistence.

It was well after lunchtime when Melanie finally convinced herself that Belithe was not on the grounds. In her limited world, that left only Mallow House.

She found her mother in the kitchen, drying the last of the noon dishes. Five years of effort to keep the oversized ancestral home spotless had worn more shine off her than it had put on the beautiful china she was forever polishing. Fifteen years of marriage to Mr. Stoppard and six of caring for Melanie had taught her the lessons of submission and servility so well that she never stopped to ask herself where her own life had gone. She listened to her daughter's story as she wiped the last cup, thinking of all the dusting and cleaning still to be done that day, then put down the piece of china with a sigh and went out to help Melanie look for Belithe.

They searched room after room, floor after floor, calling and calling until the distant halls cried back to them in echoes. They went through chambers hung with velvet, glowing in the light of afternoon; up stairwell, bounded by dark balustrades, carpeted with roses; and through endless corridors paneled in oak, where the warm currents of the house ebbed and flowed day and night.

They found bouquets of silk lilies bound with ribbons, porcelain figures poised on high ledges, and many, many portraits of the dead, sitting within their gold frames with hands folded, smiling to themselves. Once, Mrs. Stoppard caught a glimpse of a face that seemed familiar, but drained and joyless compared to the others. Then she saw that it was a mirror, and turned away quickly. Melanie saw everything and nothing that mattered. Belithe was not found. At last they came to the west wing of the fourth floor, the top of the house. Down that long hall there were only two doors. The one closest to the stairwell led to the apartments, where Grandpa Carruthers had lived in self-imposed isolation for so many years, waiting for death. In a fit of indignation over having to wait so long for his wife's inheritance, which he considered already rightfully his own, Mr. Stoppard had forbidden his daughter ever to speak to the old man, making it sound as if senility were contagious. As a result, Melanie had only seen her grandfather twice since she had come to live in Mallow House. She waited anxiously in the hall while Mrs. Stoppard went through the forbidden rooms.

Ten minutes later, she was back. Without Belithe.

That left only one place unsearched. Melanie stared down the hall at the other door, the one at the far end of the passage. It was made of carved ebony. For as long as the walls had stood, the old people of the house had always said that when anything of value was lost, it had been taken behind the Black Door. Once, long ago, Melanie's parents had lost her younger brother, and now he was behind the Black Door too. She had missed him very much and had often begged to be allowed to see him again. But the door was always locked, and Grandpa had the only key.

What if Belithe had been shut up inside by accident? How could they get her out again?

Mrs. Stoppard tried to reassure her. After all, Belithe had only been gone a few hours. It was too soon to think about the Black Door. When Mr. Stoppard came home, he would help them look.

Melanie was not satisfied. After her mother had gone back to her chores, she spent the rest of the afternoon wandering about the big house by herself, calling. She tried to believe that Belithe was asleep in some forgotten corner and had simply not heard her the first time, but no matter where she went, there was nothing but silence and the image of the Black Door growing more and more solid in the back of her mind.

At last evening came, and with it, Mr. Stoppard. His wife heard the rattle of his Chevrolet coming up the long drive, and she hurried down to meet him in the hall. He cut her short when she began to tell him about Belithe's disappearance. The cat had already been found. He had just finished scraping what was left of it off the main highway just outside the iron fence. He had buried the remains near the gate.

Mrs. Stoppard sighed. What to tell Melanie?

Tell her anything. Mr. Stoppard had had a rotten day, and he was tired, much too tired to teach a six-year-old the sordid facts of life and death. Let it wait.

Melanie appeared on the stairs. Had he heard any news?

Mr. Stoppard realized he would have to say something after all. Fighting down his irritation, he put on his best talking-to-children expression. Yes, he had heard, and he had some good news. Belithe had decided to go to live on the other side of the Black Door. It was very nice there, and he was sure—

Melanie burst into tears, turned, and ran up the stairs.

Mr. Stoppard stared after her. Then, muttering to himself about damn fool kids and idiot cats, he went in search of the evening newspaper. His wife hesitated a moment, and then followed him.

That night Melanie lay on her bed. She had cried until her eyes hurt too much to cry any longer. The room was so empty. She missed the warmth and weight of Belithe curled up against her feet. She remembered the time when her little brother had shared the room with her too. She had loved to wake up in the middle of the night and listen to him breathing across the room in his own bed. Belithe had come to live with her just after Timmie had disappeared behind the Black Door. Now Belithe was also gone. The feeling of loss and loneliness rose up again, more solid than the darkness of the room. She caught her breath in a sob.

Then Melanie felt a light touch on her shoulder. Startled, she looked up. Grandpa Carruthers was sitting on the edge of her bed, a thin hand poised above her arm like the wing of a moth. His smile was both gentle and hesitant.

He had heard her crying. He knew why she was so unhappy. Would she really like to see her pet again? Yes, he could take her to Belithe if she wished. Would she go with him? Was she brave enough to walk through the Black Door?

Melanie didn't even stop to think. Wiping her nose on the sleeve of her nightgown, she swung her feet onto the floor and slipped her hand into the old man's.

Mallow House was very quiet. They went past the Stoppards' bedroom, up the stairs, past the dark third floor, up into the hall where the Black Door waited. Grandpa pulled out a key on the end of a frayed velvet ribbon. His hands shook as he fitted it into the lock. There was a click, and the door swung open. Together they stepped over the threshold.

At first Melanie couldn't see anything. The breath of air that curled past her into the hall was cool and smelled of cinnamon. There was some light, but it was a strange bluish color and seemed to come from everywhere at once. As her eyes adjusted to it, she saw that she was standing in the middle of what appeared to be her own playroom. There were toys scattered all over the floor. The clown doll that had fallen apart, the tiny dishes that her father had accidentally stepped on, the stuffed horse that had gotten so dirty, and then mysteriously disappeared, every plaything she had ever loved was there, even the ones that she had seen destroyed or thrown out. The familiar shapes made her fingers ache to hold them, but Grandpa was pulling her away. There was another door before them now, as dark as the first. Grandpa opened it and gravely escorted her through.

Belithe was curled up on the foot of her bed, black nose invisible under a delicately draped paw, the faint tabby markings gleaming on the rich, silver-gray fur. Melanie gave a cry and would have run to the bed immediately but for Grandpa's hand on her shoulder.

Don't touch, don't touch, he was saying softly. Don't wake her up. The house was dreaming, dreaming of all the things it had loved, that had been loved in it, dreaming of the past. In other rooms, behind other ebony doors, his wife was sleeping all in white, as beautiful as the day he had wed her; beyond, his parents and his parents' parents. The scent of cinnamon and of rose. All, all asleep and dreaming, being dreamt.

Look there. His hands turned her gently. She saw another bed, and on it a small form curled up under the covers. Timmie slept with a shock of hair hanging over his eyes and the faintest of smiles on his face.

Time to go. It was late, too late for a little girl to be out of bed. They must go back. What? Oh, that would be all right, if she was careful not to touch.

Melanie knelt on the floor beside her bed. Slowly, she stroked the air above the form of Belithe. The silver fur slid past half an inch beneath the palm of her hand. She thought she could feel the warmth rising from it. Then, reluctantly, she clambered to her feet again and took Grandpa's hand. They walked out of the blue light and back across the threshold.

Later, in her own bed, Melanie dimly remembered a voice talking about a key, a key on a velvet ribbon that would be hers someday, a key that would open the past to her again and again until the day when she would walk into it and never return, dreaming and dreamt, for as long as the walls should stand.

At last Melanie slept and, sleeping, dreamed of the silver curve of Belithe, breathing in the darkness, and the bed that waited for her beyond the dark threshold.

*Patricia (P. C.) Hodgell was a teacher in the English department at the University of Wisconsin–Oshkosh before resigning in 2006 to pursue writing full-time. Her novels include* The God Stalker Chronicles *and* Seeker's Bane, *and she is a three-time winner of the Locus Award.*

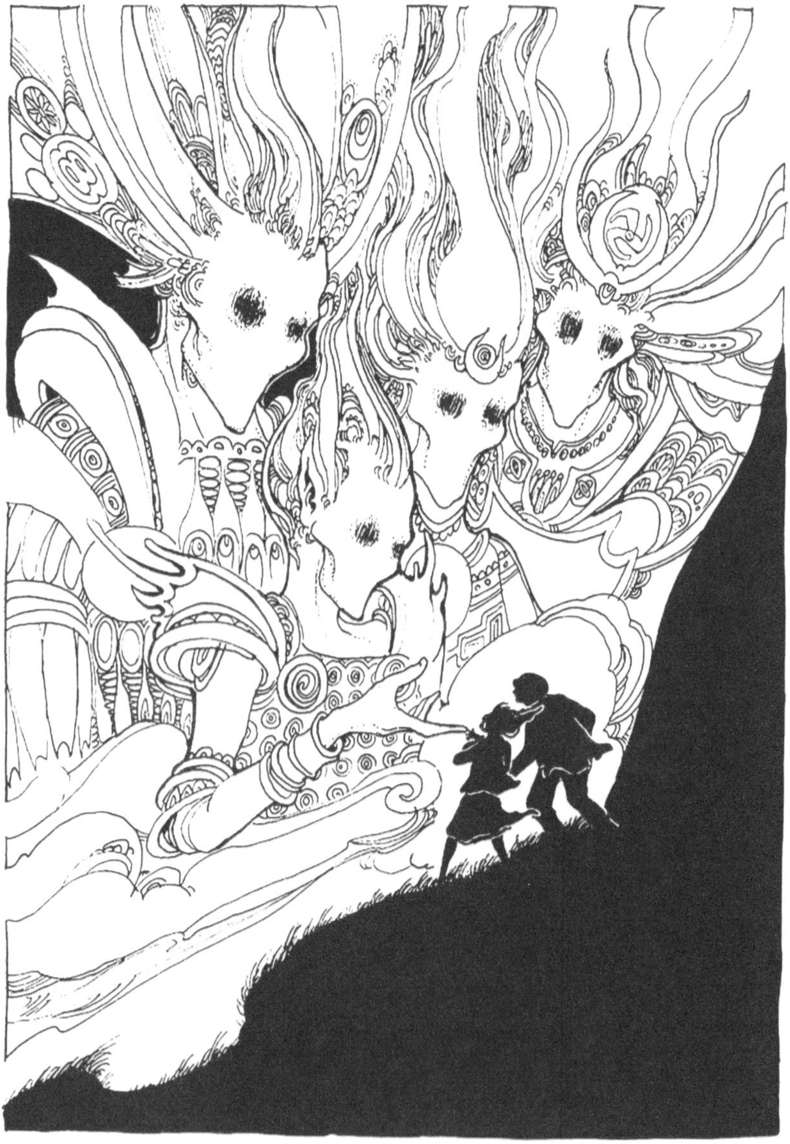

# THE DANANN CHILDREN LAUGH

## BY MILDRED DOWNEY BROXON

*A tale from a place neither terribly far away nor terribly long ago, about the intersection of faith, superstition, religion, and what William Faulkner described as "the human heart in conflict with itself" and what happens when a heart other than human enters the equation . . .*

Rain slanted steadily through the Connemara twilight. The nurse stopped a moment, shifted her black leather bag, and trudged uphill toward the stone cottage.

It was late October. Darkness would fall before her work was done, but she had still to visit the Mulcaheys. She could see a light in their window; they must finally be home.

The wind tugged at her bag and wrapped her damp cape about her body. The surface of the well-worn path was cold against her feet.

Not only, she mused, did she have to see to the care of the aged and the health of schoolchildren; now she had to check on children who did not attend school. In addition to all else, she was a truant officer.

"But if you don't do it, Miss Francis, who will?" It was an unanswerable question. So here she *was*, cold, tired, and—after what had happened in Dublin last Easter—a little afraid. But she had to find out about Brian Mulcahey.

And, of course, no one in the village would give her any information; she was English, and not to be trusted. The year was 1916.

She leaned against the wind. The rain spattered her face. Almost at the cottage, she could see someone peeping out from behind the curtain. She paused, reluctant to knock at the weathered door. If they refused to let her in . . .

\* \* \*

Brighide could see someone coming up the path. Not Connor though; it looked like a woman. Connor should be home. She felt angry for a moment, imagining him drinking down their money in the warm pub; then she thought instead of his empty boat rolling on restless waves, and Connor himself drowned, and instead of anger, she felt fear. The sea took men, even as the sídhe took children—children like Brian.

She pulled aside the coarse curtain and looked out again. Yes, the woman was coming up the path. She could see her skirt and cape blowing in the wind. What did she want? Was she bringing bad news, like the visitor who had told Mother when Father was drowned?

But who would be sending a woman with such news? Brighide smoothed her hair, tucking the stray strands back into a tight knot. She looked at her hands, red from scrubbing, but clean.

She covered the alcove where Brian lay dreaming and stacked the thick breakfast plates in the dishpan.

She peeked out the curtain once more—the woman was almost at the door.

Brighide waited for the knock.

\* \* \*

She looked too old to be the mother of a seven-year-old, Miss Francis thought. Perhaps she was the grandmother, or a cousin or aunt. And yet her dry brown hair was only lightly grayed, and her figure was still spare. Was it from youth or starvation? The woman stood at the door; Miss Francis could not see past her.

"Good evening. I am Miss Francis, from the Health Department. I understand you have a son, Brian."

"My son he is," the woman said. A cold wind blew through the open door. "Enter and welcome."

Another Gaelic speaker, Miss Francis thought. Here in the Gaeltacht, English was a foreign language. Why couldn't these people speak a civilized tongue?

She stepped inside the small cottage. The stone walls were crusted from years of open fires; something simmered in a three-footed iron pot in the fireplace. There was a pervasive smell of urine, and of something else.

Miss Francis spread a sheet of newspaper on the table and placed her black bag in its exact center. She laid another sheet of paper on the rickety chair before she sat.

She noticed the woman's lips tighten. Really, these people were so touchy. If they would only keep clean—

"Tea, Miss?" the woman said. Miss Francis looked at the thick, cracked cup and shook her head. This was not a social call.

"I am here to investigate reports that you have a son, aged seven, who has never attended school. Is this correct?"

The woman pulled her black shawl about her. Her eyes flicked once to the side of the room, then back to the nurse's face.

"We did once have a son, Miss."

"You once had a child? Did he die?" Miss Francis said. "There was no report to the authorities." When these people died, their families doubtless buried them in the dirt; no records were kept, no reports tiled. Many probably fell victim to drink or foul play—

"No, Miss. He didn't die, to be telling the truth." The woman looked down at her lap and clenched her reddened hands.

Miss Francis sighed. "Tell me what you mean, then," she said.

* * *

Brighide saw the nurse looking around the shabby cottage and was ashamed. It wasn't her fault they were poor, but Connor made small money at fishing, and she made less at laundering. She was so tired, always tired from working; and after working, there was Brian.

The nurse was waiting for her to speak. Why wasn't Connor home? She ought to be fixing his dinner, washing and feeding Brian, but here the nurse sat asking questions.

"We did have a son seven years ago, Miss," she said. "You've seen, no doubt, a record of his birth." She straightened in her chair. "We do try to keep the records; we know the law."

Miss Francis raised her eyebrows and said nothing. Brighide went on. "Connor and I, we married later than most, and we had no children for years, though why I do not know. I thought I was too old; it was a surprise when I found out—" The nurse-lady would think her crude.

"We had no doctor money, and old Kate was sick and couldn't come, so Brian was born here. I was alone except for Connor." She stopped a moment, wondering how to go on.

"I had a dreadful time, Miss, him being my first and all, and I myself older than I should be, but he was birthed all right."

The fire flickered; wind slammed against the stone walls. When would Connor be home? It was dark and dangerous on the open sea.

The nurse looked impatient.

"Well, my Connor has never held with priests, and I being sick could not bring Brian to be christened." She scuffed a foot. "Though I was planning to, as soon as ever I was well. But by then it was too late, for when I did take him to the church, it did no good."

The nurse shook her head. "I'm afraid I don't understand."

Brighide looked up at her. It still hurt to tell of it. "I mean to say, Miss, that my Brian was taken."

"Taken?" said the nurse. "Do you mean kidnapped? Why was this not reported?"

"No, Miss," Brighide said. "Kidnapped is by mortal folk. My Brian was taken by the Good Folk, the sídhe." She rubbed a finger along the coarse edge of the table.

"The sídhe? What is that?" the nurse said.

"The Tuatha Dé Danann—the Good Folk. Bless them," she added hastily. They might be listening, and if they were offended, Brian would never come home. She could stand all else, if she could hope. He had to return. All the old stories said . . .

"Yes, Miss. The Tuatha Dé Danann took him to live in their palaces under the hills. They took him away before he was christened."

Was that Brian crying, or was it the wind? Brighide hoped the nurse hadn't heard. No one should see her changeling; it would shame him to be seen this way.

This was absurd, Miss Francis thought. Now they had stories, or "taking." More than likely, the child had wandered off the cliff while both parents were in a drunken stupor—these people were brutish. And now they told tales of fairies, in the twentieth century. She was starting to speak when the door crashed open. She turned, startled by the sound and by the bitter blast of wind.

A huge man stood filling the doorway. He was dripping wet and smelled salty and fishy from the sea.

The woman rose. "Connor," she said. "It's glad I am you're home, on a night like this."

He stepped in and shut the door against the wind. His dull green oilskins dripped onto the floor. "It's glad I am to be home as well," he told his wife. He looked at the nurse. "Who might this be?"

Miss Francis wondered why she had been afraid. The man was only a fisherman, cold and tired. She had a right to be here. But there was something about his size and his bearded face and the smell of salt that frightened her. Deep memories of raiders from the sea, of burning towns, of women taken by force. She inhaled sharply. "I'm Miss Francis from Public Health. I was inquiring after your son, and why he's not in school."

The man spoke slowly, as if she might be simple. "My son cannot go to school. He is not here. He has been taken."

Miss Francis fidgeted. "Your wife had some story about fairies, and his being 'taken' before his christening, but really . . ." She let the sentence trail off. The man was slowly removing his slicker and hat, hanging them on a peg near the door.

He turned finally, clad in a thick sweater and rough work pants. He still wore his great boots. "I said he's been taken," he said. "And he's the happier for it."

In two strides, he was across the room, holding the curtain. "He's been taken, and we wait for him to return."

"No, Connor, don't," his wife pleaded.

"Silence, woman. The lady wants to know why Brian is not attending school? Here!" He ripped the curtain aside.

There, twisted in a crib, lay—a boy? A large infant? His head was thrown back, his spine arched, his legs and arms were doubled and drawn in toward his body.

At the noise and sudden light, he moved quickly and cried a weak, small wailing cry. The smell was stronger.

Miss Francis felt sick.

"Well," Connor said, "are you satisfied? I told you the child had been taken. Now you can see for yourself. What more do you want from us?"

Miss Francis stood and walked slowly toward the crib.

The child's eyes, blank and unfocused, stared out into the room. Saliva ran from the corner of his chapped and reddened mouth.

She looked down at him. "This is incredible," she said. "How long have you kept him like this?"

Brighide started to speak, but Connor shushed her. "Seven years," he said. "He never learned. The Good Folk—bless them—have taken him.

Someday he will come back." He looked around the cottage. "Though I for one would not blame him if he went away again. But the woman"—he nodded toward Brighide—"she wants him back, says he's only a heathen, needs to be raised Christian. The Good Folk are not good enough for her." He laughed. "Their feasting and merriment and music would be good enough for anyone, I would think, but she talks about a soul . . ."

Miss Francis reached out and touched the child. He flinched a little, but the contracted limbs could scarcely move. She unwrapped him, pulled at one of the arms, then at the legs.

"Look at that," she said. "Contractures." She turned him over. He was amazingly light; she saw the red weeping sore at the base of his spine. She sniffed. "Bedsores. You've kept this child here for seven years, taking care of him yourselves?"

"Yes," Brighide said. "After all, he is my son. Or he was."

Miss Francis poked at the thin and wasted limbs. "He's deteriorated so much he'll never walk," she said. "He should be given good nursing care, in a home."

"I care for him," Brighide said. "I keep him clean and fed as well as I can. I must be gone in the daytime, but I come home at noon to care for him, and I wash him and feed him at night. We are poor; I cannot stay home, but I do care for him."

"I don't think you understand," Miss Francis said. "This child is crippled, retarded. He has some sort of brain damage. These contractures, and the sores—it's horrible."

"He never learned," Connor said. "He was an infant, and stayed an infant. His arms and legs never worked right; he never crawled, never tried to speak, and he can't feed himself. He's been taken, I say."

"And we will care for him until he returns," Brighide said. "Or when he returns, he will be looking about and not seeing us, and he will go back to faerie, and be lost to us forever."

Miss Francis rewrapped the child. She wanted to cry. "Surely you can't believe that," she said. "This child is retarded. He will never be normal. He should be cared for properly, kept clean, taught whatever he can learn." She tried to smile at Brighide. "It would be easier for you too. There would be no need for money. The home is run as a charity."

"He's no trouble," Brighide said. "He's my own son. And when he returns, he will be telling us of wonderful things; he will be a poet or a musician—he was taken for a reason. The Good Folk must love him, They must be treating him well." She reached out and held on to her husband's arm. "Tell her, Connor, tell her of the time you saw them."

Connor stroked Brian's hair a moment. It was red, like his own. He covered the child with a blanket. "It was late one night," he said. "A night of fog, mist swirling about the trees, fog so thick you could not see the cliffs, and the fear was on me that I'd fall to my death on the black rocks. It was in the time before Brian was born." He stopped and looked at Brighide. She held his arm tighter.

"Worried I was on gettin' home, it being almost Brighide's time, as I said. A cold and nasty night it was. In spots, you know, the path along the cliff will sometimes crumble off. I feared it would be doing so that night, and I walking it, and leaving my wife a widow, and with a small child. Though, as it happened . . ."

He was winding up to a story, Miss Francis thought. "I fail to see what this has to do with your retarded son."

"I'm gettin' to it. Well, dark and misty as it was, no moon at all, no way to see a thing, and me without a lantern or a lamp to light the way. So I was pickin' my way carefully, with a stick like a blind man, hopin' only to get home alive, when it happened.

"The ground beneath my feet crumbled, and I started to fall. I heard the waves grindin' their teeth on the rocks, and I was sure to die."

"So instead of praying like a Christian," Brighide broke in, "he calls on the Tuatha Dé Danann for help."

"An' what good does prayin' do a Christian?" he said. "Yes, I called the Good Folk, and I'd do it again, for they helped me where never a saint would."

"On with ye," said Brighide. She looked sideways at the nurse. "'Tis true he has a wild tale to tell," she said. "But I mind me 'twas as much the drink as the Good Folk."

"And how, then, was my life spared?" Connor demanded. "With the cliffside breaking away and the path crumbling to the black rocks below? 'Twas the sídhe, indeed, I tell you." He turned to the nurse and spoke earnestly.

"I said nothing of it at the time, you understand. My wife would have been afraid. I told her later, though, when I found they'd taken what they asked. In truth, that night, I was falling toward the sea, until I was stopped in midair."

The nurse raised her eyebrows. Really! But there seemed to be no way to stop him short of actual rudeness. "Go on," she said.

"So there I was, hangin' between life and death, and was I not seeing the Good Folk around me holdin' me up, and them standin' on nothing but the fog itself? Was I not, now?"

"That you were," Brighide said. "Or so you told me. And I have seen the place where the cliff crumbled."

"But they are always wanting a price," the man said. "They asked me, would I live? And I said I would indeed. So they said, well, we will be taking our price later; we will be taking your son, and we will raise him as our own. Or we will let you fall, and your wife will be a widow, and your son an orphan, and we may take him anyhow. So I agreed."

"And said nothing to me," Brighide said.

"And worry you, in your condition, you that goes to Mass and prays to the saints? Would you be a widow and lose your son, or would you have your son taken in return for your husband?"

Brighide looked at her man. "What does it matter? The choice was made, and our son was taken. But he will be back one day. He must come back."

The nurse looked at the couple. Was it possible these people believed their retarded, crippled son would one day return to them, and walk and talk as a normal human? Everyone had to cling to hope, but her duty was plain.

"You cannot keep the child here," she said. "He is alone and neglected most of the day; he is growing weaker, he has sores on his body, he cannot move, he is a burden to you. He should be put in a home for his own protection, and for yours. You cannot care for him."

She saw their stunned expressions. "It would be kinder," she said, more softly. She turned toward the man. "It would be easier for your wife, and your son would be cared for; he would want for nothing, he would have doctors and nurses—you would do him a kindness." She waited.

"He is my son," the man said. "He will not live among strangers."

"He is our son," the woman said. "He may come back."

The nurse sighed and looked around the dark, cluttered cottage. "How much does it cost you to keep him as a total invalid?"

"Nothing," the mother said. "Only time. I am his mother, after all. I launder instead of having another job, so I may come home and care for him. But it costs me no money."

"What if something happened to your husband?" the nurse said. "Could you care for your son then?"

"Nothing has yet happened to my husband, praise God," Brighide said. "And when it does, I will think about it then. Good day to you, Miss."

"I will be in the village two more days. And I will make a report to the authorities about the case. You really should send him away, you know. It would be better."

"Good day, Miss," Connor said. He opened the door.

Miss Francis stepped quickly out into the darkness.

* * *

The dark wind slapped at the hillside. Miss Francis shivered as she walked the cliff path down to the village. Fairies and changelings, indeed! And that poor crippled, wasted child, the victim of such superstition . . .

* * *

"Brighide, Brighide, when have I seen you weep like this?" Connor said. He stroked his wife's hair. "There, now, there, now. She does not understand. No one will be taking our Brian away. No one, do you hear?"

But Brighide wept. She was afraid that what the nurse had said was true, and their son would never return, for he had not been taken—he was defective; and she wept because of the other thing the nurse had said—about something happening to Connor. She said nothing, only cried and clung to her man, who still smelled of the sea and of fish and of hard work.

Outside the cottage, the wind howled like a lost child, and the sea washed cold and lonely on the rocks, and the night itself was afraid.

* * *

In the blue dimness before dawn, Brighide stood looking at Brian. The child shook a little, like a leaf on an autumn tree, and cried a tiny cry.

"Jesus, Mary, and Joseph," she whispered. "Have I sinned, to believe in the Good Folk and in taking? Have I been as pagan as Connor, God bless him, who knows no better?" She crossed herself, patted the child on the head, and hurried out of the house. She was afraid, and the long morning of washing did not lessen her fear. She hurried home at noon to replenish the small fire that kept the cottage warm and to feed Brian; and she looked westward to the black storm clouds and felt the wind on her face, and she was afraid for Connor as well.

She saw the nurse in the village and scurried around a corner to avoid her. The nurse had started this; it was all her fault, and if they had been overheard by the sídhe—in whom the nurse did not believe—well, so much the worse for them all.

The day was long, and the washing piled high, but at last it was time to go home. She stopped at the grocers for some milk and a bit of bacon before starting the long climb up the hill.

From habit, she stopped at the place where the path drew close to the cliff and looked out over the sea. Under the black storm clouds, one gleam of amber showed the sun was setting. She looked for a boat, for the fishermen coming home; she saw nothing but gray-white whipping waves.

She had to get home to Brian, and clean and feed him.

* * *

Peeling potatoes was quiet, soothing work. She turned them over and over in her hands, scraping off peel, digging out the little eye-buds, cutting them into pieces, and dropping them in the cast-iron pot. It was accustomed, quiet work, and she had a chance to sit and let her mind wander so that her hands moved of themselves.

She was startled when the knock came at the door, so much so that she stood and spilled potatoes from her lap onto the floor. They rolled and tumbled across the floor in mad flight, hiding in dark corners and under furniture.

It was the nurse. She stood silhouetted in the doorway, and Brighide was afraid. The nurse brought bad tidings, she was certain.

"Yes, Miss?" Hospitality made her step back, ask the lady in, see to the kettle; but inside she was screaming at her to go away, to leave her alone, to stop her questions and her suggestions that brought trouble to those who had trouble enough already.

The nurse went through the ritual with the newspapers and sat. "I was wondering," she said, "if you had made any other decisions about the boy. Now that you've had a day to think about it, I mean."

Brighide wiped a piece of potato peel from her hands and looked around the cottage at the stone walls, the pots hanging from pegs, the flickering peat fire, and lastly, at the curtain behind which Brian slept.

"I have not," she said. "He is my son. My husband and I do not wish to send him away."

The nurse stood. "Very well, then. I shall check again on my next tour through the villages. Though I may say, I do not understand your reasoning."

She turned to go; the door flew open, and Connor strode in behind the wind and the cold. Dripping wet and smelling of the sea, he stood in shadow while the cold October wind blew in the door.

"Brighide," he said. His voice was strange. She could not see his face in the shadow.

"Yes, husband?" she said.

"Brighide, we must send the child away. Now. Tonight. The nurse is to leave tomorrow, is that not so?"

The nurse nodded. "Yes. November first. I have to go to—"

"She must take him away," he interrupted. "We are wrong to keep him. He will be happier this way. Believe me—what I say is true."

Brighide stood frozen. "You said—we agreed—what if—"

"Never mind. I have learned differently. It is better that you send him away." He walked across the room toward the alcove. His boots sloshed, and his clothing dripped pools of water on the floor.

"Come here," he said to the nurse. She rose.

He gestured; she pulled aside the curtain. Brighide saw Brian wince at the light and make one of his small jerking movements. She herself could not move at all.

"Take the child," Connor told the nurse. "Take him and go, quickly." The nurse lifted Brian and held him under her cape.

"Connor—" Brighide started to speak. His face was in darkness, his expression unreadable. She could not believe this. Something was wrong.

"Be silent," he said. "It is better this way; you will understand later. Better for the boy and for yourself as well." Still in shadow, he stepped to the doorway. "I will walk with you down the path," he said to the nurse.

"Where are you going?" Brighide said. "It is late."

"I came home specially—I must go back."

"Hurry home," she whispered. She watched as the nurse closed the door; then she went to the window and saw Connor walk down the path behind the nurse—the nurse who bore Brian away in her arms. No longer Brighide's Brian, but her own.

She pulled the curtain and sat in front of the fire with idle hands, waiting for Connor to come home.

The wind moaned in the chimney, and the fire burned low. He did not come home that night.

\* \* \*

It was very dark on the path, and the wind was bitter cold. Miss Francis held Brian close, ignoring the smell of sickness and dirty blankets; soon she'd have him safe in the nice clean home.

She knew Connor was behind her; once or twice she turned to be sure he was still there. She could see him, a darker shape in the blackness, but she could not hear his footsteps. Perhaps the wind moaned too loud.

She wished she'd brought a lantern; she could scarcely see where the path skirted the cliff, though she could hear the waves grinding the rocks. But Connor knew the way, and he would guide her. He was really far more intelligent than that wife of his, she thought. Imagine trying to care for a crippled child in such squalor! She shifted her burden— seven years old, and still light enough to be carried on one arm—and paused. Here the path came very near the cliff, and she was uncertain of the way. She turned to ask for assistance.

Connor stood in the darkness, his face glowing with an eerie light. She looked about; there was no moon, and the clouds hid the stars. Connor smiled.

"And it's you that be knowin' everything, is it not?" he said in a low, soft voice. Miss Francis did not respond. The child stirred under her cloak.

"Well, now," Connor said, gesturing seaward. Miss Francis turned in the direction he pointed, then froze and almost dropped the child. The wind blew her cloak away from her body; Brian was exposed to the cold, but she could not move.

There, a few yards seaward from the cliff, stood a company of—no, these shining beings were not human. They stood in midair, their faces and garments glowing like the moon. The storm howled around them, but they were untouched. Frighteningly beautiful, they were: How many? Fifteen? Twenty? A hundred? It was hard to tell. Only those nearest could be distinguished; the others glimmered palely into darkness. The closest one—a tall, red-haired, green-eyed woman—held a young child by the hand. He was tall and strong, but he had Brian's face.

"Go, then, if you must," the fairy-woman said. The child hesitated, then stepped forward. Miss Francis reached out, afraid he might fall; he was no more substantial than mist or moonbeams. He came closer and stood, looking at the child in her arms. His face was sad; he turned and looked back at the fairy-folk. The woman nodded. He stepped yet closer and disappeared.

The child in Miss Francis' arms moved slightly, opened its eyes, and looked up at her. "You are not my mother," Brian said. The chapped lips were forming words.

I must be going mad, Miss Francis thought. "I—I was trying to help you," she stammered. "You were ill, and I was doing what I could—"

"You are not my mother," Brian repeated. He turned his head seaward, to where Connor now stood beside the fairy-folk. "Father?"

"You do not have to stay," Connor said. "Come with me, son." He held out a shimmering hand.

"That I will, then, gladly," the child said, and closed his eyes. He shuddered, arched his back in a convulsion, and cried out once.

Miss Francis stood, holding the small body—it still breathed, but the mind was gone, she knew—and watched the boy run toward the shining company of the sídhe.

Connor took one of his hands, and the red-haired woman took another, then all vanished, and there was nothing but darkness, wind, and the crashing waves.

Miss Francis stood shivering on the cliff, holding what had once been Brian Mulcahey.

\* \* \*

When the men came in the morning to tell Brighide of the finding of Connor's empty boat, she would not believe them. He could not be dead; had she not seen and spoken to him the night before? And if he were dead, where was the body?

Taken by the sea, they said. Taken perhaps by red-haired Fand, who calls fishermen to her couch in the deep. It had been a night of great wind, and there are those who ride the wind. Taken in whatever way, Connor was surely gone.

Brighide wept and prayed to the saints.

When the women came to comfort her, some of the old ones said they knew he would be taken back; for had he not come from the sea? Was he not, perhaps, a fairy-lover?

"Not Connor," Brighide cried, and prayed for his soul, and would not listen.

But later, when her grief should have lessened, she could still be seen on the hill overlooking the sea, praying no longer, but waiting for the sídhe to take her into the West as they had taken her son and her husband.

And she hears the sídhe laugh in the winter wind, but they have no need of her.

*Mildred Downey (Bubbles) Broxon, twenty-nine at the time this story was sold, began her writing career after attending Vonda McIntyre's Clarion Writing Workshop. Active in the Society for Creative Anachronism, she has a deep and abiding interest in Irish history and mythology, which informs most of her writing. She served two terms as vice president of the Science Fiction Writers of America and would go on to write several books, alone and in collaboration with Poul Anderson. As of this writing, she lives in New Mexico.*

# JUDAS ISCARIOT DIDN'T KILL HIMSELF: A STORY IN FRAGMENTS

## BY JAMES S. A. COREY

*Of all the stories that appear in this volume, what follows may be the most dangerous of all, dealing with controversial subjects that will doubtless provoke heated debate. But it is also the most relevant story, as it addresses the destructive capabilities of biological, neurological, and social technologies. It says much that this was the only story where I emailed to say, "Are you really sure you want to publish this?" To which the answer was a simple, and firm, yes. Consequently, this story takes the coveted position of appearing at the conclusion of* The Last Dangerous Visions.

She'd agreed to meet him on the boardwalk at the end of Avenida de Los Reyes, where the street turned toward the sea. She wore the same body she'd had during their Edenic days—reed-thin, with pale hair down to her shoulder—but it hung on her differently now. Her steps were slower. Her shoulders bent in a way they hadn't before. The form that had been hauntingly beautiful seemed plainer now. The brightness of the eyes dimmed. Her arms didn't swing. Invisible fists balled in the pockets of her tweed overcoat. If someone had seen her, they might have thought she bore a passing resemblance to Luna Delagrazia. She would never have been mistaken for herself.

He was in a rental. Male, and old enough or well-used enough that the knees clicked when he walked. It was hairless, even its arms as smooth as if they were shaved. Also, he wasn't really in it but operating from remote. The lag wasn't bad, but it was noticeable. It would make him seem a little dim-witted, but it kept him from putting his real central nervous system anywhere near her. He didn't think, even with provocation, she would resort to real violence. But he wasn't certain enough to assume.

The clouds were low and diffuse. The moon could have been anywhere behind them, and the rain misted more than fell. He'd turned to watch her walking down the splintered, wooden steps to the pier and seen her haloed by the streetlights, the swirling air holding the brightness and making a silhouette of her body. Watching her walk the rest of the way in that misty glow would have been beautiful, but he turned his back on it, choosing to let the moment of beauty go unseen.

She came to the bench where he was looking out over the dark sea. He didn't identify himself, but she would know he was there for her. They were the only two people at the pier that day. Only lovers or enemies would be willing to brave the cold and the wet.

After a hesitation for lag, he looked up at her. The hair plastered against her scalp. The pinched mouth. She looked plain. Not even ugly, just normal. Like anyone. Luna with all her special stripped away. He grinned.

"Why?" she asked.

\* \* \*

FROM :ROOT:UNMODERATED:CULTURE:UTOPIAN_COMMUNITIES:NEPHESH
<iscariotrose> Jesus fuck I hate that cunt
<lumpmaster69> Narrow it down, brother

<iscariotrose> Luna

<lumpmaster69> Fuckable mouth though

<randobot7000> Everyone in that place is a hypocritical piece of shit. The whole "nephesh" community should be gangraped live on feed as a warning to others

<iscariotrose> Luna's the worst If there was a just God, she'd have been throatfucked to death in the cradle

<lumpmaster69> What did she do? Bang your daddy?

<iscariotrose> Don't worry about what she did to me Worry about what I'm going to do to her Count on it

<randobot7000> Serious? What are you going to do?

<iscariotrose> Already doing it Keep your eyes on the feed baby and watch me work

\* \* \*

FROM *LE HIBOU*, VOLUME 82, ISSUE 6

HIBOU: Which came first for you: The interest in neural resheathing or the focus on spiritual communities?

LUNA DELAGRAZIA: They were both of interest to me separately before they came together. My parents had very difficult lives, and they turned to religion as a way to find support and community. I grew up exposed to a variety of traditions, and the question of how to live a good life. I know that sounds rarefied, but it's not. I learned quite early that this is literally a life-and-death question. Both of my parents chose to end their own lives because they couldn't find a good answer to it.

H: And the resheathing?

LD: I got very ill when I was twenty-three. I'd had resistant hepatitis since I was born, and my liver was just worn out. Resheathing was purely medical back then, and I was lucky. Edna Li was a deep believer in resheathing, and she put together a fund that paid for and supported 150 people who were otherwise looking at hospice care. And I was one.

H: You've spoken very candidly about that experience. It wasn't entirely a positive one for you.

LD: It wasn't, but it was transformative. I think people growing up
now have a hard time really imagining what it was like to have a single
body your whole life. What did it mean to only have access to one
kind of physicality? One gender, one skin color, one kind of hair. What
did it mean if there was a health problem that you just had to manage
and eventually die with it? I mean, you can do thought problems, like,
"What if you could never resheathe again," but it's almost always an ac-
ademic question.

H: Philosophy again.

LD: [laughs] Exactly.

H: How did the Nephem community come to be?

LD: I started it after my mother died. I had been resheathed by then
and had a vision of . . . I don't want to say a church. That has so many
connotations. As an intentional community? Someplace that people
could come and live in common. It was the promise that all the churches
I went to growing up made, but none of them followed through on.
And resheathing was what made it possible. Race, gender, attractiveness,
health, all the things that are ultimately tied to flesh became choices, not
life sentences. We are the first generation to experience that. Millions of
years of human evolution, and we got to change the rules. It's a lot, and
it has so many implications that it will take lifetimes to work it out. The
Nephesh was just my first step toward that. Like-minded people wrestling with the deepest spiritual problems of our age. No big deal, right?

H: You didn't set your sights low, that's for sure.

LD: I believe in people. I believe we can come together and do amazing things. Because all through history, we have.

* * *

The grounds had been a nature preserve, and in part still were. The path
that led to the houses began where the railway line and the highway

met. Paved in dark gravel, there were often places where bits of green—
grass, tansy, California poppy—pressed up optimistically between the
rock. The trees crowded as close as commuters on a subway car, and
the air was filled with the tapping of leaves and the conversation of
birds. The smell of loam and soil perfumed the breeze. The name was
chosen quite deliberately: from its founding, Eden had been intended
as a garden.

The first fork in the path offered up and to the left or down and to
the right. Left took you into the higher forest and the guesthouses at
the top of the ridge. Right, down to the where what they, in foolish optimism, called the "permanent community" lived. Someone taking the
left and rising path would walk over steps made from boards, past small
lanterns and stone shrines, to an airy clearing where the overhanging
canopy of trees turned a subtle gold in autumn. Five small houses and
a longer, broader warehouse were there, along with the stables and a
small apartment for the groom. Someone taking the right path would
descend. The path grew wider as it dropped into their little valley, and
more forks and intersections appeared in it. The twelve homes of Eden
lay nestled in the trees, each with a facade of wood and stone, each
with its own little patio, and each set just far enough apart for privacy
when it was wanted. The group kitchen was at the center in a structure with walls that could be hauled up to make an open pavilion in
good weather, or dropped down for a sheltered meeting space when
rain, wind, or snow came. The temple was smaller than the houses
and set farther away.

Eden held thirteen people:

Luna Delagrazia—the heart and center of the community, whom
you have met.

Edna Li—the woman whose money had first helped to popularize
and destigmatize resheathing. At the time things began to go wrong,
she was in the body of a well-muscled, olive-skinned man who had been
gifted her by Apian/Dureé Bioengineering in hopes that she would en-
dorse the brand.

Dayyaan Safdar—former refugee and antiwar activist who lived in Eden half of the time, and spent the other half organizing camps to aid civilians in conflict zones.

Matthew Takageda—architect of the Blue Cathedral at Montparnasse and self-styled Buddhist monk.

Ulrike Kohl—retired hospice nurse who tended toward younger, intensely feminine bodies. The best and most frequent chef for the community.

R. Fisher Smith—writer, director, and documentarian best known for an Oscar-winning short film that followed seven women who had gotten abortions at the same clinic on the same day over their next two years. He thanked the Nephesh community in his acceptance speech.

Ezekiel Harmon—semiprofessional gardener and unofficial groundskeeper of Eden. He wrote a novel in his early twenties that didn't get much attention. A man with a deep understanding of mulch. He had expressed interest in someday being resheathed in a specifically nonorganic body as a way to better interact with extreme environments.

Soledad Quintero—former actor, former addict, living at Eden as she pursued a degree in neurobiology.

Ogene Washington—trauma therapist whose practice began in veteran's outreach groups and expanded to other highly traumatized populations. Originally a frequent guest at Eden, he moved in as a permanent resident after a messy and public divorce.

Myles Tamnent—guerrilla street artist. Claimed to have lived on the streets of Rio de Janeiro for two years as a performance piece. When the time of troubles came, he was wearing a woman's body of exaggeratedly voluptuous proportions as preparation for a new production.

Fermin Acosta—the other of Edna Li's charity cases. At eighteen years old, he had been caught in an oil fire that had left him blinded, scarred, and in constant pain. He had lived this way for eight years before his first resheathing. His coming to peace with his own history and experience led him to be somewhat erratic—including public fallings-out with Luna and Edna both—but Edna promised him a place in Eden, and he kept it.

Evangeline Scott—digital artist and former lovers with R. Fisher Smith.

The thirteenth, however, is always uncanny—a movement from the well-ordered dozen with its graceful factorizations into the uncomfortable place of primes, where nothing divides into it except itself.

Janelle Otowe—retired accountant and hospital administrator. The only one of the group who had never resheathed, and had come to Eden as companion, helpmeet, and muse of Evangeline Scott.

Thirteen dots on the Nephesh curve, each exploring some aspect of the new future before them and the old, old questions asked in it anew. How to love, how to be at peace, how to live a life worth the living of it.

Thirteen shells in the game that set fire to Eden and watched it burn.

\* \* \*

"Luna?"

"What's the matter? Did something happen?"

"Luna, I found something. You need to see this."

\* \* \*

FROM :ROOT:UNMODERATED:CULTURE:UTOPIAN_COMMUNITIES:NEPHESH

<lumpmaster69> Been pretty quiet on the feeds this week. When was the last time they didn't put out any kind namaste-humping by Wednesday?

<lettherebeknight> They missed one in April three years ago when there was that network outage, but everyone slipped that week. I don't know. Maybe something's up?

<iscariotrose> Keep watching.

<randobot7000> You've been saying that for months. I call bullshit.

<iscariotrose> Put a flag on that post. We'll revisit it, you and me, when you see how much of an apology you owe me.

\* \* \*

A wind blew in Eden. The canopy of trees roared like they were angry. Like they'd been injured. Luna sat in her private room with Edna Li and Fermin Acosta. That she hadn't asked anyone more recent to the community to sit with her was a signal to those who knew her best of how upset she was.

Edna looked through the images, flicking from one to the next with her wide, masculine thumb. Fermin's body was the same one he'd had for eight years now: broad-shouldered, dark-haired, near to the look he might have had if he had lived a different life. His choice to exercise little and eat and drink much had softened the flesh he inhabited.

"Who brought this to you?" he asked.

"Janelle. She was trying to figure out the file transfer dump on the local network, and the security was confusing her. She went in on the command line. She found this."

Edna reached the last image and started back from the beginning, her thumb steady as a metronome no matter how vile the images under it. The images swept past, a blur of adult bodies and children's faces.

Fermin hung his head. "Matthew would never—"

"Kick him out," Edna said. "Kick him. Kick Janelle. Kick Evangeline. Turn this shit over to the police and do a fifteen-minute post about it in as much detail as the lawyers will let you."

"Lawyers?" Luna said.

Edna stopped on an image and turned it to Luna. On it, innocence was being debased more clearly and comprehensively than Luna had ever seen before and worse than she had imagined. "Lawyers," Edna said.

"That's a mistake," Fermin said, his voice trembling. "We don't know what this is. How do we call ourselves a community when it's just the three of us discussing it? That's oligarchy. We never set out to be the rulers here. We need to open the conversation to everyone. Including Matthew. What if this isn't his? What if someone planted it? Or hacked his file transfer for their own trafficking? Then we kick him out for being victimized?"

"He's right," Luna said. "I can't do that."

Edna looked up at her from under a dark, beautiful, masculine brow. The muscles in her thick shoulders clenched and unclenched like a precursor of violence. Even under all the new flesh, Luna believed she could still see the old woman's scowl. It was hard for her to stand against Edna's opinion. The older woman had been a second mother, guardian angel, and agent of salvation when all had seemed lost to her. Luna squared herself.

"We came to find answers," she said. "Our own answers. Not to turn back to the world the first time things grew difficult."

"If these are what they look like—" Edna began.

"And if they aren't," Fermin said. "We came here as a community. We owe each other to at least ask, don't we? If we don't have that much respect for each other, what even are we?"

"This affects the whole community," Luna said. "The whole community should have the chance to discuss it. If we decide that involving others is the right thing to do, we'll decide it together."

Edna looked down and pressed her lips tight. She passed through the images again. In the moment, the little shake of her head seemed like surrender.

"Call everyone."

\* \* \*

FROM *CHRIST'S COVEN: EDEN AS GETHSEMANE PREFIGURED*

BY MATTHEW TAKAGEDA

*The expression of the sacred has always had two aspects: one within and the other without. The first is in some ways easier to comprehend, based as it is in the private nature of consciousness. Each of us experiences the world from a privileged position. Each of us wrestles with a purely private experience—our thoughts, our sensations, our moments of revelation, even sometimes our enlightenment—in a way that what we understand with intuitive clarity can never be shared. The great spiritual works in all traditions are like breadcrumbs along the path that may perhaps lead others to an overwhelming experience that greater souls than ours embodied. Those breadcrumbs aren't intended to be gnomic or obscure. Indeed, they are often the simplest, most direct ways that the wisest individuals who humanity has ever produced could describe to reach those insights. That we still spend lifetimes struggling to understand is a testament to the difficulty, subtlety, and mystery that comes with trying to recreate the subjective experience of one person within another.*

*It is tempting, faced with such a monumental task, to frame the sacred as a property of that inner silence, and so something shared between the soul and God. But over and over, the great texts enjoin us to look beyond the single, the unitary, and the internal. That which is pure, right, and holy does not reach its fullest state until it is shared. The sacred individual—the Prophet or Buddha or Messiah—is depicted with near universality as the servant to the sacred community.*

*And experience—sometimes painful experience—bears out the truth that we are not individuals. As a bee separated from the hive will die even if given food, water, and shelter, so a human being held apart from all community is injured by that isolation. We experience ourselves as inviolate, singular, and alone, but we ache and wither when our community is lost to us.*

*We are each the engines and receptacles of our own private grace, and at the same time we are reliant upon the people around us for a manna that feeds us in that journey which cannot be found elsewhere. We are forever separate from those with whom we share our world, and we are also as dependent upon them as they are dependent upon us.*

*And so here is the great paradox: true enlightenment, which can only ever be found inside the individual, withers and dies in isolation.*

\* \* \*

The table was long enough for all of them to sit, small enough that everyone could be heard. Luna had catered it like a party or a business meeting. The chairs were all comfortable. Ice water infused with cucumber and strawberry waited in sweating carafes with squat, thick peasant glasses at their sides. There were plates of fresh bread and herbed butter—simple, wholesome, meant to be shared. Everything was a promise of comfort and companionship, and everyone was in pain. Almost everyone.

The horrifying images were on their screens or in their minds. No one who had seen them would ever be entirely clean.

"I think," R. Fisher Smith said, then lost his voice for a moment. "I think we all need to hear from Matthew. About these."

"What can you possibly expect me to say?" Matthew asked. His face was gray with rage. Or with embarrassment. Or the sting of betrayal.

"That they're yours," Myles said. "That they aren't yours. How they got into your partition."

"If they're real," Ulrike said. "Are those actually people, or are they simulations?"

"It doesn't matter if they're real or not," Edna said. "Depictions of children like this are illegal, even if they're simulated. Those could all be cartoons, and they'd still be the sign of a criminally deranged mind."

"Well, certainly, then," Matthew said, his voice high and tense as a violin string. "Let's start this by having me promise that I'm not morally diseased. That sounds like a very fair, well-balanced conversation."

"You've never said they aren't yours," Myles said.

"You think that would help? Fine! They aren't mine. Are we done now? Do you believe me?" Then, when no answer came. "This is why I didn't want to say it. Before you were all wondering if I was a monster and a pervert. Now I see you all wondering if I'm a monster and a pervert and a liar."

"It's a fair point," Soledad said. "We aren't a tribunal. We aren't here to judge anyone. We shouldn't be wringing denials out of people."

"Are we not here to judge anything?" Evangeline said. "We have evidence of a crime. A series of crimes. How are we not here as a tribunal about that?"

"We don't know that's true," Fermin said. "These are very possibly fakes. Or real images that have been planted to discredit Matthew. Or us, all of us. If we make this public, the Nephesh community will be injured."

"Then let's call this what it is," Dayyaan Safdar said. "We're here to discuss a conspiracy to cover up possible crimes against humanity."

Soledad threw her hands into the air. "For fuck's sake. Could we please be a little less histrionic about this? We have disturbing images that were found in our computer storage. How many computers out there have icky, disgusting shit saved on them? How many have zero-day exploits and hidden back doors?"

"It seems to me," Ogene said, "that we have more than one issue before us. As Edna suggests, there is a question of legal liability. There is also a moral component to this, yes? We aren't a business or a corporation. We are a community dedicated to moral understanding and moral action."

"Which is why it doesn't make sense to take these and run to lawyers," Fermin said.

"I don't know that I said that, precisely," Ogene said. "We came here to address as best we could the deepest issues of our times. Here, we have a thorny problem. It is incumbent upon us to take this back to first principles. To understand it deeply."

"I'm sorry to disagree," Dayyaan said, "but I know a fucking war crime when I see one. I have faced the kinds of men who do these things in war zones. I'm not particularly interested in using those children's suffering to deepen my understanding of Aristotle."

"You're having an emotional reaction," Ulrike said.

"You're fucking right I am," Dayyaan shot back. "Why aren't you?"

Janelle, weeping, shook her head. "I'm sorry. Everyone, I'm so sorry. I didn't mean to mess everything up."

"You didn't," Evangeline said, taking her hand. "This isn't your fault. This isn't your fault, baby."

Matthew's voice was cool and brittle. "But maybe it would be good to understand exactly how you came to be digging through the private file transfer profiles? Just to better understand how we got here, yes?"

Janelle's weeping grew to sobs.

"Please," Luna said as she rose to her feet. "Please, everyone. I know you're hurt. I'm hurting too. But we can find our way through this together. We have a problem, yes. It has upset all of us, and whatever we do, it will affect all of us. That's why we're here. To decide what we, as a community, should do. Not just read the letter of the law. Not just cover our liabilities. Everyone needs to be heard. Everyone needs to be respected. Everyone needs to be cared for. And if some of us need forgiveness, we will face that together."

*Ooh*, he thought. *That was it. That was the money shot.*

\* \* \*

FROM *FUCK LUNA DELAGRAZIA TO THE FUCKING SKY*

BY NOTYOURANONYMOUSTOY (110K COMMENTS 259K SHARES)

*There's a picture of me you don't get to see. Luna Delagrazia and her "intentional community" have seen it. The police have seen it. But including it in this post would be illegal because it depicts a sexual crime against a minor. That minor is me. The Nephesh community isn't the first religious or pseudo-religious group to decide that they get to choose whether the rules apply to them. Whether crimes are really crimes if one of their faithful is involved. The Catholic Church practically made raping altar boys into a brand. The Mormon/Boy Scout pedophile cover-up isn't covered up anymore. I'll stop there only because I don't have time to name every religion in existence and the shit they swept under their rugs in the name of Protecting the Faith. It seems like every time someone sets themselves up as a moral authority, it's to help bury the fact that they're doing something immoral. These Nephesh were supposed to be looking at resheathing and the ways that being able to move from one body to another changes the ethical and moral equations.*

*When my body was targeted, abused, and filmed, I was not given the option of leaving it. I am, in fact, still in the "sheath" that I was born into. The evidence of the crime against me has been disseminated among collectors. Traded. Sold. Relished. And Luna Delagrazia—who found copies on her community's file system—has this to say about the people in whatever body who have been taking pleasure in the worst day of my life: "If some of us need forgiveness, we will face that together." [click for video]*

*I have a very long response to that, which I will detail in this post. I also have a short one.*

*Fuck you, lady. And fuck your self-righteous cover-up cult too.*

\* \* \*

FROM :ROOT:UNMODERATED:CULTURE:UTOPIAN_COMMUNITIES:NEPHESH

<lumpmaster69> HOOOLLEEE SHIIIIT! They're dropping Nephesh from all the feeds! They're delisted!

<randobot7000> I just saw. That's fucking insane.

<iscariotrose> I told you I was doing something

<randobot7000> You've been saying that for months. I call bullshit.

<liebdick88> Hold on. Is this you?

<iscariotrose> Something happened Connect your own dots

<liebdick88> No way. How much was psyop? Was the kiddieporn real, or did you just use that it was there? Is AnonymousToy real, or was that part of the op? Spill! Spill! Spill!

<iscariotrose> Post step-by-step proof you mean? Not fucking stupid If you want to think I'm J Random Blowhard taking credit for stuff he didn't do that's no skin off my dick At minimum somebody at that meeting recorded and leaked it

<lumpmaster69> At the meeting? At? You're saying you were one of them all the fuck along?

<iscariotrose> I'm saying what is truth? and washing my motherfucking hands is what I'm saying Good riddance to that arrogant bitch an everyone like her.

\* \* \*

The lawyer wore a thin, masculine body and a taupe suit. He had very blue eyes, gray hair, an aquiline nose. Luna sat on the powerless side of the desk with her hands folded in her lap. She wondered who he had been before he resheathed. Who he would be after he resheathed again.

The office was done in warm tones—corn-silk yellow, dusty orange, tarnished gold. The Nephesh community already had a lawyer, and that lawyer had been the one to take Luna aside and tell her it was time. Luna's interests and the community's weren't aligned the way they had been once. She needed someone representing her interests individually. Just her. Nothing in her life had made her feel more isolated than being told to get her own attorney.

"We did turn it over to the police," Luna said.

The lawyer raised a finger. "You have turned it over. There was a period when you had the contraband and you had not yet alerted authorities. Now that's always going to be true. Even if the first thing you do is call the police, there's however much time it takes to get your phone out and dial, right? The question becomes: Is the amount of time you chose to wait reasonable? Some people are going to think yes. Some are going to think no. The thing is, no one is suing you. No one is pressing charges against you at this point. And it's not illegal to have an opinion."

"But this Anonymous person, whoever they are—"

"Is making claims that you are a bad person for not coming forward sooner. That the conversations you had about the issue went on too long."

"They're hurting the community. They're degrading my reputation. That can't be all right, can it? Can't I sue them for that?"

"Anyone can sue anybody at any time for anything," the lawyer said. "The question is, can you win?"

"Why can't I win?"

The lawyer leaned forward, resting his elbows on the green felt of the desktop. The glimmer in his eyes said that this was something he enjoyed. Not the part where he told her why she was powerless, maybe. Maybe just the game. Maybe that it made him feel smart. Maybe even that explaining her impotence made him feel powerful. Who was she to judge him?

"Maybe you can. Best-case scenario? When we get into it, maybe it turns out that Matthew Takageda had nothing to do with those files. And this other person, whoever they are, was in possession of child pornography and we find some way to prove it. That would be great. We prove malicious sabotage. We ask for damages, and we get them, and it turns out that whoever they are, they have a bunch of money that they want to use to pay the judgment off instead of hiring more people like me and dragging this out for a decade."

"I'm hearing you say that the best-case scenario isn't very likely."

"You'd be better off buying lottery tickets. And then, on the other hand, there's the stuff that we one hundred percent absolutely know is going to happen. The next post is going to be about how Luna Delagrazia is going after a victim of childhood assault, punishing them by exposing their identity, and retraumatizing them. That will be the follow-up story. Another news cycle with you looking like the bad guy."

The numbness was deep and terrible. Hurting would have felt better. Or outrage.

"It was," she said, "a complicated situation. I wanted to talk it through. That's all."

"I know."

"This isn't fair."

"We don't deal with fair here. We deal with the law. If there's a campaign of harassment against you? If people keep making false accusations about you to possible employers, people leave you a pattern of death or rape threats, post images of you or your family doctored so as to present a threat or cause distress? We can start gathering up a portfolio. We get enough of that, there might be something to do."

"If we can find out who they are."

"If," he agreed. "But the smart thing to do—and I'm saying this as someone who will lose money if you take my advice. The smart thing to do is walk away."

They were silent for what felt like hours, and was probably less than a minute.

"I want to know who it was," she said.

\* \* \*

FROM :ROOT:UNMODERATED:CULTURE:UTOPIAN_COMMUNITIES:NEPHESH

<lettherebeknight> Well, that's it, then. Stick a fork in it. Nephesh is officially fucked to death. They filed to disband the community. I heard that the kiddie diddler even tried to off himself.

<lumpmaster69> Well, better luck to him next time. In a way, it's too bad. I mean, they were a bunch of mealymouthed assfucks, but I did enjoy the conversations in here taking the piss out of them.

<lettherebeknight> Come over to utoptian_communities:ehrendahl
There's a lot of the same posters.

<iscariotrose> Sometimes things just go right, man Sometimes it all comes together Enjoy the moment

<l.delagrazia> I want to talk with you. Will you meet?

<lettherebeknight> OH FUUUUUCK!!!!!

\* \* \*

"Why?" she asked.

There was just a tiny bit of lag, then he shrugged. "You don't get it. You never did."

"Did I do something to hurt you? Are you angry with me? Because I'm not the only one you injured with this."

He leaned back his head, turning his rented eyes toward the starless gray sky. "You know the thing I always thought was crap? Matthew 27:5. Throwing down the silver, he departed and went and hanged himself. Complete bullshit. He won. He got paid. Everyone just needs to think he offed himself in guilt, right? I mean, he fucked up everyone's perfect story, and God forbid anything ever go unpunished."

"Weren't you punishing us?"

"Nah, you weren't that important to me. You had something I didn't want you to have. Now you don't. All better from where I'm sitting."

She lowered her head. A moment later, he looked over at her. The tears in her eyes and down her cheeks. He smiled.

"Next body, you should really try being a dude. It keeps your tits from shaking when you cry."

"Do you like humiliating me?"

"I don't know how we establish yes much better than this. Yes. I think it's funny. It makes me laugh and feel better about the world. The thing that's missing from all these utopias you people try to build? Sadism. You always leave out the cruelty. But it finds its way back in. Always has, always will. That scary angel with the flaming sword guarding the gates of Eden? He looks out, not in. He doesn't give a fuck what the inmates are doing to each other."

"I'm not going to let people like you stop me."

He widened his eyes and spoke with a cartoon lisp. "O! You ah tho thtwong! I tho admire you!"

"I don't believe you were one of us."

"You remember the time Ulrike made that cake with the bad baking powder? Came out like a chocolate hockey puck nine inches wide. We never put that in the feeds, did we?"

She went still.

He grinned. "It's a trick question. I know we didn't."

"Which one were you?"

"Who cares? Which one will I be next time? Because I am always going to be there. Always. Even when I'm not. It's funnier that way."

They sat together in the rain for a while. There was no point trying to leave.

*James S. A. Corey is the nom de plume for Daniel Abraham and Ty Franck, writers and creators of* The Expanse *novel series that birthed the popular television series of the same name. Both writers reside in Albuquerque, New Mexico, and in addition to writing a significant number of novels and shorter works, have been nominated for the Hugo and Locus awards. Their latest entry in* The Expanse *series is* Leviathan Falls *(2021).*

# *TETELESTAI!*
# COMPILING *THE LAST DANGEROUS VISIONS*

As I write these words, it is (appropriately enough) April Fool's Day 2024, one week after the successful relaunch of the first *Dangerous Visions* anthology by Blackstone, and the simultaneous announcement of *The Last Dangerous Visions*. The latter led to considerable interest among fans and literary historians about the process by which this book was being assembled, especially since there were significant changes to the table of contents before I even got near the project. While Harlan's struggle with bipolar disorder and manic depression was the primary reason for the delay, it's not the only reason. The fifty-year lapse between the time *TLDV* was announced, and right now, resulted from a perfect storm of issues that compounded each other at every step along the way.

There are a number of elephants in the room when it comes to *TLDV*. Let's meet them head-on.

Elephant number one: *Hey! Why isn't this volume's table of contents the same as the original* Last Dangerous Visions? *Why'd it get changed? Whyizzat, huh?*

Because there *was* no original, locked-down, written-in-stone, no-seriously-this-is-it-for-sure version of *The Last Dangerous Visions*, only an ever-shifting landscape of potentialities. One table of contents was announced in 1973, with 90 stories by 88 writers. Variations on that roster were announced over the next several years as stories fell out and had to be replaced. By 1979, *TLDV* had exploded into three massive volumes featuring 108 writers and 120 stories, as shown by Harlan's hand-typed table of contents from that version of *Last Dangerous Visions*.

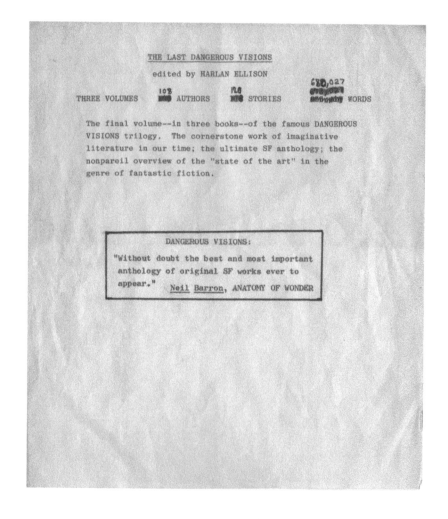

THE LAST DANGEROUS VISIONS: BOOK THREE

Table of Contents

| | | |
|---|---|---|
| Daniel Keyes | MAMA'S GIRL | 4000 |
| Cordwainer Smith | HIMSELF IN ANACHRON | 2500 |
| Pamela Zoline | DREAMWORK, A NOVEL | 16000 |
| The Firesign Theatre | THE GIANT RAT OF SUMATRA, OR BY THE LIGHT OF THE SILVERY | 5000 |
| Michael D. Toman | QUARTO | 3000 |
| Steve Herbst | LEVELED BEST | 1300 |
| Russell Bates | SEARCH CYCLE: BEGINNING AND ENDING | |
| | 1. The Last Quest | 2250 |
| | 2. Fifth and Last Horseman | 5000 |
| Vonda N. McIntyre | XYY | 1600 |
| Frank Herbert | THE ACCIDENTAL FEROSSLK | 3500 |
| Graham Charnock | THE BURNING ZONE | 6000 |
| Doris Pitkin Buck | CACOPHONY IN PINK AND OCHRE | 5500 |
| Frank Bryning | THE ACCIDENTS OF BLOOD | 5500 |
| Michael Moorcock | THE MURDERER'S SONG | 7500 |
| Wallace West | ON THE OTHER SIDE OF SPACE, IN THE LOBBY OF THE POTLATCH INN | 6500 |
| William Kotzwinkle | 2 FROM KOTZWINKLE'S BESTIARY | 5000 |
| Octavia Estelle Butler | CHILDFINDER | 3250 |
| Tom Reamy | POTIPHEE, PETEY AND ME | 17000 |
| Laurence Yep | THE SEADRAGON | 17000 |
| Alfred Bester | EMERGING NATION | 2000 |
| Robert Thurston | THE UGLY DUCKLING GETS THE TREATMENT AND BECOMES CINDERELLA EXCEPT HER FOOT'S TOO BIG FOR THE PRINCE'S SLIPPER AND IS WEBBED BESIDES | 3500 |
| Steven Utley | GOODBYE | 2000 |
| Graham Hall | GOLGOTHA | 3200 |
| Edward Bryant | WAR STORIES | 10000 |
| John Varley | THE BELLMAN | 11500 |
| Joe Haldeman | FANTASY FOR SIX ELECTRODES AND ONE ADRENALINE DRIP (A Play in the Form of a Feelie Script) | 10000 |
| DAN SIMMONS | THE FINAL POGROM | 9400 |
| Harry Harrison | A DOG AND HIS BOY | 4000 |
| Janet Nay | LAS ANIMAS | 6800 |
| Geo. Alec Effinger | FALSE PREMISES | |
| | 1. The Capitals Are Wrong | 4000 |
| | 2. Stage Fright | 2500 |
| | 3. Rocky Colavito Batted .268 in 1955 | 5500 |
| | 4. Fishing With Hemingway | 3000 |
| Fred Saberhagen | THE SENIOR PROM | 4800 |
| A.E. van Vogt | SKIN | 7000 |
| Stan Dryer | HALFWAY THERE | 3000 |
| Gordon R. Dickson | LOVE SONG | 6000 |
| Michael G. Coney | SUZY IS SOMETHING SPECIAL | 8000 |
| Jack Williamson | PREVIEWS OF HELL | 3000 |

38 authors          40 stories          total wordage:   225,600

THE LAST DANGEROUS VISIONS: BOOK TWO

## Table of Contents

75 authors    42 stories    total wordage: 278,777

THE LAST DANGEROUS VISIONS: BOOK ONE

Table of Contents

 authors     stories        total wordage:

The sheer volume of this lineup presented significant problems for Harlan because compiling 120 stories meant writing 120 introductions, plus a general introduction, which meant he would have to write a *minimum* of six hundred pages, which was simply unachievable given Harlan's ongoing struggles with bipolar disorder. Since this is described in detail in "Ellison Exegesis," we won't dwell here on elements covered better there. But there are a number of subsets that need to be discussed.

One of the symptoms of bipolar disorder is a lack of impulse control, especially when it comes to buying things. In this case, Harlan, rather than consolidating what he had and saying, "We're done," kept buying stories, through the seventies and eighties and right up until the last few years of his life. He could no more stop buying stories than he could stop buying the T-shirts, comic books, or collectibles that filled Ellison Wonderland to the bursting point, even when doing so threatened to bankrupt him and raised the specter of losing the house to creditors, a not uncommon event. Harlan bought stories for *TLDV* the way most people eat potato chips.

This constantly shifting landscape changed *TLDV* from being an actual, measurable thing to more of a concept, a kind of ever-evolving performance art, which made getting a bead on the book as a whole increasingly difficult. The book couldn't be finalized, because the book was forever in process.

One of the glorious things about Harlan was that he was as loyal a friend as anyone could ask for . . . but that came back to haunt him on *TLDV.* When writer-friends in need of cash, a credit, or a jump-start to their career asked if he would buy a story from them for *TLDV*, which would elevate their profile in the writing world, he generally complied, ending up with stories that he'd bought out of friendship rather than quality, stories that had no business being in *TLDV.* As he said to me on more than one occasion, "There are stories in here that should be led out on a leash."

He knew he couldn't publish *TLDV* with those stories present.

But he also couldn't bear to hurt his friends' feelings by yanking them out.

The result was a kind of inertia, or creative paralysis. "I was like a monkey with his fist around a nut in a jar," he said. "I couldn't pull it out, and I couldn't let it go."

The final complicating issue was the political climate extant during the development of *TLDV*. The first two *Dangerous Visions* volumes were assembled during the late sixties, a time of social change, when writers and artists were being urged to stand up and speak out. Experimentation was the order of the day, and the New Wave Science Fiction that Harlan and others championed was in full force.

But then came the seventies and eighties, and with it—absent the brief tenure of Jimmy Carter—came the reign of Richard Nixon and Ronald Reagan, which gave open support to rabid conservative assaults against anything even slightly liberal-minded. It was the era of Phyllis Schlafly, a paleoconservative who campaigned against the Equal Rights Amendment, same-sex marriage, immigration, and the media; anti-gay activist Anita Bryant; and Reverend Jerry Falwell, whose organization the Moral Majority (it was neither) attacked schools, writers, and the very ideas of public education and an unfettered press.

As had been the case back in the fifties, once again the arts were under attack by those with a political axe to grind and the money and resources necessary to destroy entire careers.

The result was a soft tilt back toward self-censorship, a shift reflected in the stories Harlan received for *The Last Dangerous Visions*. People wanted to be *in* it, but they didn't want to get in *trouble* for being in it, especially since Harlan was already on the enemies lists for both Nixon and Reagan. In reading the correspondence between Harlan and some of the writers he was soliciting for *TLDV*, one comes across repeated requests, even some outright pleading, for the kind of strong, visceral stories that had been so instrumental to the first two *Dangerous Visions* volumes. Most of the established writers who had gladly taken the freedom offered by those first two volumes to push the envelope in their storytelling were now keeping their heads down to stay out of the line of fire, while new writers were hesitant to piss off the Powers That Be who could end their careers before they had even properly begun.

In his personal notes on rejected stories, covering eleven single-spaced pages, Harlan's terse assessment of the quality of stories he was receiving—even from established writers—and his growing impatience becomes increasingly clear with every entry.

BROWN, Rosel George - story is good but not right for the anthology, offbeat but not dangerous

SAMBROT, William - interesting but not dangerous

WILLIAMS, Robert Moore - old-line, trite, shockingly badly-written

KELLEY, Leo P. - not strong enough

HEINLEIN, Robert A. - fails as a story

AANDAHL, Vance - ghastly

ANVIL, C. - silliness, badly-written, dull, characterless, plotless, hackneyed, insipid

COGSWELL, Ted - cute, ingroup private joke stuff, and kinda dumb

GELLMAN, Rick - only liked first 8 words of the title

There were a number of solid stories that formed the core of *TLDV*, many of which are in this volume, but few of the rest, whether accepted or rejected, were what he felt they needed to be.

All these factors contributed heavily to the larger issues Harlan was having in regard to *The Last Dangerous Visions*. As years dragged on into decades, writers began asking for their stories back in order to sell them elsewhere. Each time a story fell out, it changed the balance and composition of the book and meant Harlan would have to buy another story . . . or two . . . or three . . . to fill the gap. His distress, as shown in these letters, is palpable. In a letter to the joint estates of Gordon R. Dickson and Clifford D. Simak, dated June 13, 2013—almost exactly five years before his death in 2018—Harlan writes:

> Pursuant to yours of 7 June instant, and our subsequent telecon, it is my pleasure to accommodate your request for reassignment in both Gordy's and Cliff's stories ("Love Story" and "I Had No Head and My Eyes Were Floating Way Up in the Air") originally solicited, paid for and intended for the third DANGEROUS VISIONS anthologies, THE LAST DANGEROUS VISIONS. Years, and complex circumstances have, as you know, conspired to delay indefinitely the fruition of that ultimate chunk of the massive project. The stories by Gordy and Cliff have lain waiting in my file for decades. Much to my lone chagrin and sadness.
>
> I have returned many, many stories from TLDV over the years, and each time it breaks my heart a little…but right is right, and Circumstance should never intercede on Proper Behavior. So, the stories are now in your possession, with all rights intact, and no strings attached.
>
> Go with my best wishes, and keep my dear friends Cliff and Gordy in the race for Posterity. These are wonderful stories, and I was honored to be part of their creation.

Other writers held faith with Harlan and the book and what he was trying to say with it right up until their passing, and in many cases, well beyond. Some critics have suggested that Harlan didn't care about their losses, that he was focused just on his own career.

They're wrong.

Harlan's own words over the years about the loss and sorrow he experienced when these writers left us address that part of the equation far better than I can. But that's not the end of it. As I began to read through the files and folders that Harlan compiled while working on *TLDV*, I noticed something peculiar: When opening the folders containing stories by now-deceased writers, the first thing seen were their obituaries. You open the file folder, and there it is, right on top.

This continued for folder after folder, and slowly I began to understand that Harlan wanted the obituary, the sigil of their passing, to be the first thing he would see—to constantly remind him of their passing, their faithfulness, and his own deeply felt guilt. Every page-one obit was his way of saying to himself, *You let them down; you failed them.*

He wanted to never forget that, not even for a second.

Elephant number two: *You do realize there's not a lot of diversity in the range of writers here, right, pal? It's mainly white guys. What's up with that?*

This is the point that stings, because as the one who ultimately compiled this edition, there was little I *could* do in one respect, and little I was *able* to do in another.

The lion's share of the stories Harlan compiled for *The Last Dangerous Visions* were written in and around the 1970s, a brutal period for women writers and writers of color. The literature of science fiction has always been dominated by white male writers—often of a rather conservative perspective—and there were very few exceptions to that rule during the seventies. The few women writers who did manage to make it past the barricades often did so by concealing the fact that they were female by using their initials instead of their full names, including such writers as C. J. Cherryh and P. L. Travers, creator of *Mary Poppins*, thus avoiding much of the sexism and misogyny that would otherwise have come their way.

(Two such writers are present in this book, D. M. Rowles (Deborah Shepard) and P. C. (Patricia) Hodgell.) Other prominent examples include Alice Mary Norton, who wrote under the semi-pseudonym Andre Norton; Alice Sheldone writing as James Tiptree Jr.; and Margaret St. Clair writing as Idris Seabright.

There weren't many women writers working in the SF field when Harlan went looking for stories for *The Last Dangerous Visions*, but he was determined to overcome this. He bought a story from Octavia Butler entitled "Childminder," which reverted back to her years later as *TLDV* lay fallow. He bought a story from Connie Willis, which after many years also went back to her to become the first part of her novel *Lincoln's Dreams*. He bought stories from D. M. Rowles and P. C. Hodgell and other writers, including Vonda McIntyre.

Vonda very much wanted her story "X Y Z" to be published in *The Last Dangerous Visions*, and as an act of friendship and support made sure the story remained with him even after her passing. When the project came to me, one of my first emails was to the individuals running the McIntyre estate, to clear the way for finally publishing her story. But they decided to override Vonda's express wishes on the grounds that the book would be too male (well, yeah, which is why I was freaking contacting them). I found this astonishing, because as executor of the Ellison estate, my approach is to try and *implement* Harlan's wishes, as expressed before his passing, not to override them for my own personal reasons.

And that's all I will say on the subject.

As I sifted through all the available stories, I was pleased to discover many that were still powerful and relevant. Other stories that had aged out, become outdated, or were too much of the period in which they had been written were set aside. Because as Harlan noted in his list of rejections, these were supposed to be *dangerous* stories, not quaint, or primarily of historical interest. That's why the book has the words *Dangerous Visions* in the title, not *Visions That Were Once Sort of Dangerous but Are Now Mainly Just Kind of Cute*.

During his life, Harlan had been incapable of excising the stories he had bought out of friendship that should never have been included in this collection. But I had no such difficulties. I knew almost no one from the table of contents, so I was able to review the stories without fear of causing upset or a sense of personal favor toward any of the writers. My task, to the best of my admittedly subjective ability, was to evaluate the stories for what they were, or were not, and act accordingly.

The stories that survived this review account for about 90 percent of the contents of this book. I'm very proud of the stories selected. Some are straight-up science fiction; others lean toward the magic realism of Jorge Luis Borges, or Gabriel García Marquez; while the rest defy any attempt at categorization or pigeonholing, which is exactly what makes them perfect for *The Last Dangerous Visions*. They are as challenging, fresh, and entertaining now as when they were first typed.

Once those stories were selected from the pool of manuscripts Harlan had personally chosen for inclusion in *TLDV*, my next task was to issue new contracts with fresh cash to the original authors and/ or their estates. But I still felt there was something missing. The stories withdrawn over the years by women writers and writers of color had left the book demographically unbalanced in ways that hadn't been the case when *TLDV* was first being assembled.

Which left me facing a hard decision: to either put the book out absent any kind of real diversity, which would end in rightly getting the crap kicked out of me in the public sphere, or to intervene in an attempt to find the balance that Harlan had always wanted in *TLDV* in the first place, in which case I would *also* get the crap rightly kicked out of me by the *TLDV* purists.

It was a no-win scenario. Whichever way I went, I was going to get yelled at by someone, and most annoying of all, they would be absolutely correct in doing so.

The path forward came from knowing that Harlan had always seen *The Last Dangerous Visions* as a living document. He didn't want *TLDV* to be an archaeological curiosity, a dry and dusty artifact of another age with no bearing on the present. He wanted it to be raw and relevant

AFTERWORD: *TETELESTAI!* COMPILING *THE LAST DANGEROUS VISIONS*

and absolutely of the moment. That was precisely why he continued to buy stories over a forty-year period to replace those that had aged out, stories such as Stephen Dedman's "The Great Forest Lawn Clearance Sale—Hurry, Last Days," which Harlan purchased for *TLDV* in 1990 and is included in this volume.

He would have wanted an anthology coming out in 2024 to address contemporary issues and explore what constitutes a dangerous vision in 2024. So it made sense to add some new voices into the mix, not to supplant but to augment the original writers, because if I added more than a handful, it would no longer reflect Harlan's editorial vision. This is his book, not mine. Since the space for supplemental stories was very tight, I sent out invitations in waves of just two or three inquiries at a time, ticking off the remaining room as each "yes" came back, because once the slots were full, we would have to stop. I reached out to friends and admirers of Harlan to contribute new stories to be included in the anthology. Max Brooks, David Brin, Cory Doctorow, and James S. A. Corey immediately volunteered for duty, along with Adrian Tchaikovsky and Cecil Castellucci.

Since Harlan used the *Dangerous Visions* books to provide exposure to new voices, I put out an open call for *any* previously unpublished writers to submit stories to *The Last Dangerous Visions*, one of which would then be chosen for publication alongside the best-known names the genre has to offer. Of the hundreds of submissions, all of which I read personally, the clear choice was "Binary Systems," by up-and-coming genderqueer author Kayo Hartenbaum, from whom I expect great things in the future.

Some writers declined to participate. Harlan was a figure of considerable controversy, especially in the latter third of his life. By appearing in *TLDV*, these writers could be seen as endorsing the more controversial elements of this book and, by extension, Harlan.

As was the case in the 1950s, the 1970s, and now in 2024, writers sometimes exist in perilous times, balancing careers between the tick and tock of the Right and the Left, when a single misstep or perceived endorsement can be a terminal mistake. This is not necessarily the best time to be dangerous. So yes: I get it; I just wish it wasn't so, because I would have loved to see what these remarkable talents would have written as their *Dangerous Visions*.

*  *  *

With the last of the stories assembled, spanning five decades, I decided it would be fun to write the author's bio that appears at the end of each story in present tense, focusing on who they were, how old they were, and where they were at the moment they sold their stories, putting multiple generations of writers demographically on par with one another.

And *that*, 3,390 words later, is how *The Last Dangerous Visions* finally came into existence. I'm proud of this book. I'm proud of Harlan's efforts to defy conventionality and push the limits of storytelling. I'm proud of the writers who held faith with Harlan over five decades, and those who came to the party specifically for this event. I'm proud that Harlan entrusted me with the task of finishing this in his absence. And I'm proud and pleased at Blackstone's decision to see this process through to its completion.

Since my first essay about Harlan for this book begins with the Greek term *exegesis*, meaning an explanation, it's only fitting to end it with another Greek term that appears in the Gospel of John, chapter 19, verse 28: *Tetelestai!*

Meaning: *It is done. At last, it is done.*

*The Last Dangerous Visions* is as complete as it ever will *be*, and more complete than it ever *was*.

The aftermath is the aftermath, the reviews are the reviews, the uproar is the uproar, the rest is the rest. As it should be.

*Tetelestai!*

—J. MICHAEL STRACZYNSKI

This has been
*The Last Dangerous Visions.*
There will be no others.

## ACKNOWLEDGMENTS

There are a number of folks who stepped up to lend their time, effort, and support to *The Last Dangerous Visions*, without whom this book would never have been completed. So I wish to express my appreciation to Kathryn Drennan, Sharon Buck, Stephanie Walters-Montgomery, Timothy Williams, and Jason Davis. Finally, my profoundest thanks to all the writers appearing in this book who, for half a century, held faith with Harlan and this project because of their love for the former and their belief in the latter.

—JMS

## ABOUT THE ARTIST

The artwork pieces accompanying the stories in *The Last Dangerous Visions* are the work of Tim Kirk, longtime friend of Harlan's, who helped create many of the elements that can be seen in his home to this day. A graduate in fine arts from California State University, Long Beach, with a master's in illustration, Tim has worked as a senior designer at Tokyo DisneySea and an Imagineer for the Walt Disney Company. He is a five-time Hugo Award winner and sits on the advisory board of Seattle's Science Fiction Museum and Hall of Fame. He has waited decades to see his work appear in this volume, and that breathtaking show of patience is applauded and appreciated.